"RIGO, RIGO, KILL ME! LET ME DIE!"

"Can't do that right now, Jere. We need you too much. Then maybe later, we'll see." Glynn screamed a protest, but Rigo eyed Masady until she clapped a hand over the boy's mouth.

"See, we have to figure out who attacked you. Why." He scooted the stool back but leaned forward, intent on the opticam as if he could see within, into the depths of Jere's brain. "Left you with a brain to think with, at least. Why am I thinking it might *not* have been *you* the assassin was after?"

"BUT . . . BUT . . . WHY? NOT ME, THEN . . . ? GLYNN? GLYNN! NO, NOT POSSIBLE, NOT AFTER ALL THESE YEARS! DOESN'T KNOW, CAN'T KNOW!"

"You may think you know Rhuven, but I know better than anyone how Vitarosa's mind works! I should—I watched Rolando and her mother twisting it from the day she was born, turning her into a sanctified killing machine!" Rigo sat straighter, pounding his knee, "To her warped mind, Rhuven would view Glynn as a gift, the eldest male heir, elevate him above her, above their own children.

"So let's assume worst case—Vitarosa was after Glynn, not you. How do we buy time? Convince Rhuven there's nothing to fear, if it's him. Or convince Vitarosa she succeeded? Think, Jere, think!"

**Be sure to read all three novels in
GAYLE GREENO's
magnificent DAW fantasy series**

THE GHATTI'S TALE:
FINDERS-SEEKERS (Book One)
MINDSPEAKERS' CALL (Book Two)
EXILES' RETURN (Book Three)

MIND SNARE

Gayle Greeno

DAW BOOKS, INC.
DONALD A. WOLLHEIM, FOUNDER
375 Hudson Street, New York, NY 10014

ELIZABETH R. WOLLHEIM
SHEILA E. GILBERT
PUBLISHERS

First Printing, September, 1997
1 2 3 4 5 6 7 8 9

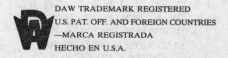

DAW TRADEMARK REGISTERED
U.S. PAT. OFF. AND FOREIGN COUNTRIES
—MARCA REGISTRADA
HECHO EN U.S.A.

PRINTED IN THE U.S.A.

I was singularly blessed by having caring teachers who encouraged my creativity during my years at Queensbury High School, and there are three I must especially thank:

Paul Cederstrom, 9th grade English
Joanne Perkins, 11th grade English
Betty Rooke, 10th and 12th grade English

What I learned from you gave me a solid foundation for the future. And I shall always remember that "a lot" is a parcel of land, not a descriptive modifier.

For Joanne Perkins Chambers —
My memories and the knowledge you instilled in me have lasted far longer than the amount of time you actually taught me.
With affection and respect,
Gayle Greeno
19 Sept. 1997

"What is Matter?—Never mind.
What is Mind?—No matter."
    —The British humor magazine,
    Punch, vol. xxix, 1855

ACT ONE

Date: 30 August 2158
Location: NetwArk, Texas Republic, Earth

Blue. It teased and tingled behind his sleep-closed lids, ebbing and flowing across the unseeing crescents of his eyes. Eye-blue skies, skies the color of his mother's eyes, except he'd never seen that shade of blue in nature, never seen these skies before yesterday—or had he, once so very long ago and far through space? He tossed, fitful, mind beginning to wake, though waking meant admitting what he faced today—the duel. And an admission of something more, something he'd refused to face for seven long, bitter months.

Glynn kicked back the sheet, forced himself to sit up, squinting at the alien, brightening blue of the sky through the window. Then, as he had each morning for so many months, he addressed the burled maple box centered on the bureau, the box with its dials, its sound-enhancing diaphragms, its lensed opticams on opposed sides, the Liquid Crystal Display strip that scrolled across its front. "Good morning, Mother."

"GLYNN, LOVE, TODAY'S THE DAY." The words printed themselves across the LCD strip, disappearing leftward to make space for more characters crowding from the right. "YOU'LL SUCCEED, GLYNN. YOU MUST AND YOU WILL. AND THEN WILL YOU HONOR LAST NIGHT'S PROMISE? WILL YOU LET ME DIE TODAY?"

**Date: Approx. seven months earlier,
29 January 2158 Location: Satellite Colony
PabNeruda, Waggoner's Ring**

Glynn sauntered along the crowded walkway that separated agricole plots from blandly smooth habitat tiers crowded together like mushrooms here on 4Echo/Mid, taking his time, relishing the "seen and be seen" looks that candidly followed his upright carriage, his every lithe move. No matter how long the inhabitants of the eight satellites comprising Waggoner's Ring had trained in Z-grav, indeed, even been born into it, none could match the fluid, kinetic grace of a Stanislaus Troupe member. Under the Earth-standard gravity conditions of most satellites along their equatorial bands, everyone else looked a whole 'nother species, clumsy and stolid, ill-tuned to their bodies.

Despite himself he preened, puffed with the innocent self-awareness of adolescence. He tossed the long, narrow braid of dark hair extending from browline to below his shoulders, ran his hands along the close-cropped sides, wondering if beta Masady should clip his scalp again before his ultimate performance. Short hair was cooler, easier under the heavy confines of the mask. Cooler here as well, blast the meteorologists and their computerized weather, the random programming that let each satellite level in for a different facsimile of "weather." Today's was humid-tropic, so much so that the rising moisture from the hydroponic crops faintly fogged the air. Sticky, ugh!

As he swaggered along, he resettled the thin, almost transparent tangerine robe on his shoulders, concerned that it flow, didn't snag on the formfitting flesh-colored knee britches, the only thing he wore underneath. Nor were his gestures or his vivid orange robe lost on the satrats huddled by an air vent's shadowy overhang, nearly lost in a cloud of condensation, and Glynn watched from the corner of his eye as three girls and a boy whispered, hissing behind their hands.

" 'Lo, Panny," he waved at the tallest girl, perhaps twelve, the least painfully thin and the cleanest of the four. Her skimpy dress was long outgrown, its purple faded to near-gray, but it was in good repair and scrupulously clean, as was the rest of her. He'd sensed that mattered to Panny right from the start when he'd met her four years ago. She'd appeared out of nowhere, black skin spectral in the ill-lit passageway, he already panicky, hopelessly lost exploring the subtunnels that ran between each satellite level, space for transporting waste materials and supplies, electrical cables and piping, ventilation ducts—all aesthetically hidden from sight.

Now he visited Panny each time they performed on PabNeruda—if he could locate her ever-changing doss, as mobile as the skittering, hectic life she led. Up or down several levels, nearer to the kernel or core, or closer to the satellite skin, switch from Alpha Sector to Bravo, from Bravo to Foxtrot, then Oscar, the rhyme and reason entirely hers, though she generally steered clear of the Caps with their Z-grav. It could take days of hunting, lurking in familiar and unfamiliar haunts to find her—if she so chose. And when he did, he shared what he had: food, toys, the odd piece of clothing and, most of all, stories of how he, how others lived openly on the satellites. "Everything spinning right for you, love?"

The boy with Panny, dark eyes narrowed and territorial, hissed at his familiarity, tossed an elaborate finger-gesture, the most extreme obscenity. Glynn ignored him, willed his eyes to meet and hold Panthat's just as he did with the audience each night onstage, only his eyes alive behind the formal, rigid mask that concealed his expression. "You know how to use your body, your voice," beta Masady had instructed time and again, "but you *must* make contact with your eyes, make sure each viewer is riveted on you, as if an umbilical cord connected your eyes to theirs. The soul resides in the eyes."

But that wouldn't suffice with this male satrat, so he concentrated on wooing Panthat and her two female friends, younger and shabbier, the pong of unwashed

bodies and clothing surrounding them like an aura.
"Ticky-ticks, Panthat, a lovely ticky-tick for you," he
crooned, praying his voice wouldn't break, swoop high
or low, "front and center for an old friend . . . and,"
his eyes casually encompassed them all, drew them
closer, "perhaps for your mates as well. Ultimate performance two nights from now. All sold out—'cept for
the few we've saved for friends."

"Ah, Panny'll be there, Glynnie." She quashed the
male satrat first with a look, then a neck pinch. "Seein'
play-pretty, then. Seein' you as pretty-playful as always, then no more. Them, too, do'm good, learn'm
manners." Glynn gave his right hand an outward roll,
each separate finger equally eloquent, and rested the
back of his fingers against his heart. The boy watched
avidly, a devouring look compounded of jealousy and
desire. Without actually acknowledging him, Glynn
raised fingertips to lips and blew a kiss in their general direction.

"I'll leave word at the box office for the hand-
stamp," he promised and moved on, the tangerine
robe aswirl. "Ha, little shite, I've trapped you right'n
proper," he gloated as he took the vactube to Level
1, then changed tubes to float up from the satellite's
equator to its Northern Cap. Holoverts of Stanislaus
Troupe had been posted at each vactube stop, disconcerting as he passed through a mini-mer sector, fish
swimming outside the clear tube. A montage of shots
of his mother, Jerelynn, the Great Lynn, costumed as
Tadanori, King Lear, and Oedipus, dominated, but in
the lower right glowed a holopic of Glynn, lounging
against a set, arms folded across his chest, eyes dancing. No elaborate costume or anonymous mask to hide
him from his public, here he stood vulnerable, his expression naked, real, the being behind the performer,
the person, not the persona. Type flashed above his
portrait, "Ultimate Performance!" and his visage
slowly dissolved into the artful masks of some of his
characters: Jocasta, Cordelia, Lysistrata. Bet Rigo-

berto had paid plenty for the holoverts, and the troupe had spent long hard hours and bribes posting them.

A magnetic hum and the vactube floor rose to meet his feet as he settled, waiting for the shield door to automatically slide open. He shivered, the hair on his arms rising as a tiny voice whispered, *"So who will you be after that? What happens after that final performance when you turn fifteen?"* Palms against temples, he strove to crush the voice in his skull. "Don't want to think about that—won't!" But the voice echoed on, relentless. *"Take orders from Staniar? Be like Staniar, miserable because he can't act anymore, miserable at being behind the scenes at the beck and call of every woman, and any rising male star under the age of fifteen?"*

"NO, no, no," he wailed as the voice took over. *"Your apotheosis, your final moment. And then no more? Nothing?"* For a long, frozen instant a memory pinned him in place and he struggled against it: a visit he and his mother Jerelynn had made to the butterfly farm on Satellite Amaterasu when he'd been eight. Ugly, complacent caterpillars chomping, chewing, then spinning themselves into chrysalises, breaking free as beautiful winged creatures. Except, except . . . he'd be transformed the other way round, turned into an ugly caterpillar, doomed to exist backstage forevermore, deprived of the sustaining laughter, the tears, the applause.

As the shield rose, he wiped his eyes, flicked tears away in case his public should see. With a swagger he stepped clear of the vactube, chin high. Two women oohed and aahed as he exited, giggling vivaciously, surreptitiously pointing at the holovert posted beside the vactube. Still upset, he wasn't sure he could muster the strength, the grace needed to smile, so he concentrated on his walk, let all the roles he'd ever played speak for him. A few more strides and he'd be clear of the artificial gravity platform, make the most of it.

The subtle hip sway, an invitation in a dipping shoulder, the delicate arch of a bare foot, everything that—had he been in costume—marked him as one of the premier female impersonators of the theater, just as his mother was the Great Lynn, capable of eliciting every nuance of manhood in her acting. He bent his head, eyes demure as the women drifted past, glancing over their shoulders, eyes wide with invitation. The automatic registering of another conquest, but right now he couldn't care less. Should they float too near, he'd spurn them, better trained in elusion and avoidance in Z-grav than they would be. Yes, superior training, the mark of a Stanislaus.

Jere, Mother, *wouldn't* let him be shunted aside, abandoned backstage with all the other overage males, would she? The Gemmies weren't near old enough to convincingly assume his roles. Couldn't they all pretend—beta Masady, bet Rigoberto, beta Majvor, bet Vijay—that his fifteenth birthday was far distant, or that it didn't matter? No tradition deserved to exist forever, did it? Rules were made to be broken—Jere could do that, must! The Stanislaus Troupe couldn't afford to lose her, and she could threaten to leave if Glynn weren't allowed to continue acting. None of the other troupes had that silly stricture about males not acting after fifteen, why waste those years of painstaking training? Why not build on it?

Courage and good humor partially restored, Glynn swarmed up the stairs to the Newcome Port Observation Deck, launched himself into the Zero-gravity environment. Dodging tourists, off-duty workers, tethered floating shrubs and undulating trees, trunks slowly bending and waving, he swam toward the curved, transparent wall, spiraling around floor-to-ceiling pylons. Star glow, satellite glow, and at the epicenter like an observant eye, Earth, the hub of their satellite universe, their connection to that other world. Peaceful here, PabNeruda's dredges churning back and forth from docking platforms toward Holm Port with loads of supplies from the sister-satellites.

He floated, robe billowing like a canopy, and rested a hand on a padded guide rail, briefly touched a burning cheek to the metallic ribs that supported the Observation Deck's glass walls. As a comfort he named the satellites, a familiar litany to calm and soothe, an anchor to an Earth he'd never known. Eight artificial satellites, each as large, as complex, and as populous as many cities on Earth. Each had begun as a tiny nub or kernel, the original space station, new segments formed at construction platforms from a moon-mined diatomaceous compound that, subjected to the proper voltage, extruded nacreous layers, almost as a pearl develops.

His favorite, first: PabNeruda, site of his ultimate performance and the most urbane of all the satellites; NelMandela hovering over the African continent below; YuriGagarin and SallyRide, the very first two lofted spaceward more than 125 years ago on opposite sides of Lagrange 5, that "sweet spot" equidistant from Earth and Moon where satellites took up permanent orbit. A vac-hound, air jets puffing gently from its silvery, cigar-shaped body, nosed him incuriously, odor detectors "sniffing," opticams spying out debris—ready to vacuum up a bead of sweat, a loose hair, a popped button, a floating leaf—anything free-floating that did not belong, Z-grav garbage. Nudging it toward a brochure of some sort, tourist litter, he continued his inventory.

CurieCousteau, honoring ancient explorers of very different sorts; Amaterasu, garden satellite and repository of biodiversity; Huang-ti for the founder of Taoism and current home base for brain research; and finally, Tane, the last satellite sent into orbit, propitiating the Pacific Island god of that name to continue separating heaven and Earth. A prayer that the satellites would remain literally and figuratively separated from the chaos on Earth, divisiveness fracturing it like a hard-boiled eggshell: haves and have-nots fighting each other, fighting other factions, splinter groups whittling other groups thin. Yes, so betas Masady and Majvor had taught him in the sparse intervals during his arduous training as a Stanislaus, the greatest troupe on Waggoner's Ring.

Floating, still moored by one hand, he let his legs drift, arching until his heels touched the back of his head. His braid floated, tickling his knee. Reaching back he clasped one ankle, considered releasing the rail to form a perfect circle, untethered, buoyant as a soap bubble. Attracting attention, he scolded himself belatedly, but attracting attention came as naturally as playing a role. Yes, why not show them? He started to let go, close the circle, but the voice was clamoring again. *"What will you do after your ultimate performance? Who will you be then? Who'll care, who'll notice? No longer the star, praised and petted. Just another anonymous mover and shifter, musician, costumer, set-builder, mask-tender. Ordered around and ordered around and ordered around. . . ."*

NO! He whipped out of his circle, his motions ragged, raw as a newcomer hesitantly testing Z-grav. *Don't think about it, don't think about*! So he didn't, and let the whispers and comments from the other Observation Deck visitors serve as balm for his body and spirits as he conquered his body's graceless momentum.

Time: Fifteen minutes later
Location: The Observation Deck
Aloft in Z-grav, hovering like a flying carpet, the pamphlet slowly began to unfold as an air vent blew on it, first one panel and then the next extending the piece, its bright holopics jeweling the air with their colors. As the creases opened, it moved, the panels acting like sails in the vent's breeze as it glided through the high-domed Observation Deck.

A vac-hound's sensors caught the movement, and its plump, cigar-shaped body turned and cruised toward it, soft, plosive puffs of compressed air jetting it forward. It reached the pamphlet just as its final fold unfurled; the paper wrapped itself cross the vac-hound's "eyes," the dogged little airborne waste disposal unit giving a mechanical chirp at the obstruction. "Tentacles" around its "mouth"—the opening to its disposal unit—delicately probed the slick paper to determine if it was suitable for collection. When input proved it correct, the vac-hound attempted its task of capturing and containing it. The problem was that the pamphlet did not wish to oblige in its demise, too stiff, too large to easily consume. A jet of air and the vac-hound maneuvered to the right, but the air also fluttered the outermost fold and the pamphlet spun away. The vac-hound dove after it, unable to read the lettering that announced:

A Beginner's Guide
to Satellite Construction on
WAGGONER'S RING
by Gene Padric Vlaserra,
M.S., NelMandela University,
Ph.D., MIT, Massachusetts Commonwealth

The Location of Waggoner's Ring: In real estate parlance, the three most important things are "location, location, location." While we all "know" that Waggoner's Ring is located at L5, few of us can explain what L5 stands for or accurately identify its exact site.

The "L" stands for *Lagrange*. Long before humankind could hope to travel or live in outer space, scientist-scholars studied and solved problems involving planets and their orbits. Scoffers deemed it a waste of time, but even without the prospect of space flight, such astronomic data were important in charting the heavens. In the 1760s the Frenchman Joseph Louis Lagrange was one such explorer of the unknown. He determined that certain points—five to be precise—existed where he believed a hypothetical space station could be stabilized—not trapped and pulled into the Earth's or the Moon's gravity fields. Such a station would revolve around the Earth just as the Moon does.

Lagrange said that the two best points, or locations, for such an undertaking exist at what we now call L4 and L5, with each positioned 60° to either side of the Moon. Measure the distance from L5 to the Moon or from L5 to Earth on Diagram #1, and you'll discover they're precisely equal—240,000 miles.

With that in mind what, then, is the distance from the Moon to Earth?

If you answered, "Exactly the same," you're correct, the three sides of the triangle are the same length. In other words, the Earth, Moon, and L5 form an equilateral triangle.

However, some two hundred years later, Dr. A. A. Kamel found that Lagrange Points 4 and 5 weren't as secure as science had posited. He calculated that regions *orbiting* L4 and L5 provided greater stability. And that is where the Waggoner's Ring satellites set up housekeeping, with L5 at the center of their orbit.

The Ring orbit is large, about 500,000 miles long; and it takes about eighty days to complete one cycle. The orbit doesn't form a perfect circle (See Diagram #2), but is actually a bit eliptical or oval, just as the Moon's orbit around the Earth is eliptical. By the way, that eighty-day orbit is not considered a "year" by satelliters. Instead, the Ring follows Earth's "standard" 365-day calendar year for simplicity's sake.

Another approach to thinking of that 500,000 mile orbit is to call it the *circumference*. You needn't be a Euclid to use basic geometry to figure that the *diameter* across an orbit is roughly 160,000 miles. Since the *radius* halves the diameter, its radius is about 80,000 miles.

Satellite Position and Distance: Waggoner's Ring consists of eight satellites, each one located about 12.5° beyond its neighbor along the arc of the circumference. The distance between one satellite and the next is a mere 62,500 miles, much closer than the 160,000 mile distance for satellites across from each other in the orbit pattern.

How far is 62,500 miles? (See Diagram #3—the

Mercator projection of Earth.) Well, it's close to the distance from the northmost tip of Ellesmere Island in the NordCan territories south to the old Panama Canal Zone (Line A). Or trace a line from Tokyo to Mecca (Line B). And (Line C) from old Borneo across the Java Sea to Wellington, New AustZealand. Give or take a few hundred miles—as the crow flies. Yes, that's how close your next-door satellite neighbor is in space.

Satellite Construction: No matter which satellite you visit, you'll find they all boast an almost identical construction. This is crucial to understand because it will help you orient yourselves, no matter which satellite you tour.

You may have heard the satellites described as a lollipop crossed with a pinwheel, or a bloated dragonfly (See Diagram #4). That's an oversimplification, but it gives you a visualization, a starting point. Now, add another pinwheel to the stick end of the lollipop, or another four wings to the dragonfly's tail tip (See Diagram #5).

As you've undoubtedly guessed, the pinwheels or wings are solar panels to generate power. The lollipop or dragonfly body is the station itself, while the stick or tail is an access tunnel from the landing docks at Newcome Port. Throughout the twentieth century scientists and engineers argued over the best configuration for a space habitat, with many proposing cylindrical or wheellike torus shapes. Fifty years apart, John Bernal and Gerard O'Neill opted for a spherical shape, highly similar to the construction here at Waggoner's Ring.

Why isn't there a shaft at the other end? Wouldn't it be more symmetrical, help balance things? That, however, doesn't take physics into account. That access shaft or tunnel is an extension, so to speak, of a satellite's axis. The *axis* is the straight line around which a body rotates. With or without a visible shaft at one or both ends, the axis exists.

The shaft's real purpose is more pragmatic: It

allows each satellite to hold visitors at "arm's length," to ensure they've been adequately screened for possible contaminants. Should it prove necessary, the shaft can be sealed off from the satellite proper. This is the Ring's final opportunity to ensure its future health and well-being.

As an Earth visitor, you'll land at Newcome Port—or more precisely at the shaft/tunnel connecting to it. All satellites have an arrival port bearing the same name and an identical location. Actually called New-comer's Port, the name's been truncated a bit through time. At the exact opposite side is Holm Port. Freighters and passenger ships traveling between satellites dock there, since there's no concern over quarantine procedures.

Now, in Diagram #6, you'll see a close-up of the satellite body proper—the lollipop itself or the dragonfly's body.

The Satellite as a "Miniature" Earth: Let's pretend each satellite is a miniature Earth and employ some of the same terms used to describe Earth. It will help you grasp satellite configuration.

Think what would happen if we "skinned" Earth and turned it inside out. There you'd be, standing on the inside, your head pointing to the Earth's core. And no, if you dug all the way to the other side, you wouldn't discover people standing on their heads! But you would be standing in a curve (concave), instead of on top of the curve, or the convexity of the Earth's surface.

Your new "sky"—the ceiling above you in any satellite—won't be a dome over your head, and your horizon will be different, curving up and away from you. Examine the figures positioned in the interior on Diagram #6. They move around, walk the inner circumference of the sphere. Yes, your ingrained habits and expectations, your "realities" of a lifetime have literally been turned inside out.

Your "North Pole" is Holm Port and the "South Pole" is Newcome Port; ships and transports dock at either end. Each "Polar Cap" contains an Observation Deck where you can scan the stars, the planets. Of course we Ring-citizens call them Observation Decks because we love to observe newcomers, tourists, discovering how to move in Z-gravity. You'll learn the tricks and techniques, if you haven't already.

After SallyRide and YuriGargarin expanded to three levels, scientists decided to create an artificial-gravity environment. No matter what biomedical specialists had previously believed about adjustment to long-term weightlessness, their theories and limited experimental data did not prove correct. Not just physiological problems, but psychological problems arose as well. That became especially clear in the first generation born and raised in Z-grav.

Each satellite revolves at about 1½ rpms (revolutions per minute) to create a simulated Earth gravity. At the "Equator" or midpoint of the sphere—halfway between the "Poles" of Newcome Port and Holm Port—you'll experience Earth gravity. However, travel toward either "Pole" and it gradually decreases to roughly 70% of Earth gravity at about 45° latitude north and south. (Think of these 45° latitude lines as the satellite equivalent of the Tropics of Cancer and Capricorn.) You're still firmly grounded, but movement is much easier. As you continue to either Pole or Observation Deck, gravity diminishes until Z-grav is reached.

Bear in mind that we've referred to the Observation Decks as "Polar Caps," because the term *Cap* will become important later, as will the abbreviated term *Mid* for the midpoint or Equator.

Inside a Satellite: For those ready to "jump" inside a satellite and view it three-dimensionally, examine Holograph #1. If you don't feel fully ready (and many don't), see Diagram #7 for a two-dimensional mockup showing the satellite as a nice, flat circle. Spatial abilities vary from person to person, so don't feel badly; some of it is difficult to grasp the first time around.

Note in Diagram #7 how we've drawn circles within

circles, labeled from One at the outermost circle to Seven at the next to innermost one. Inside, at the very center, is a small circle marked Kernel.

Each satellite was "birthed" from this Kernel, which consists of the original space station equipment launched from Earth—well over a century ago in the case of SallyRide and YuriGargarin. The station positioned itself in the orbit pattern with additional segments rocket-boostered from Earth to join it until it consisted of a 400-foot-long cylinder with various knobs or nodes attached to it. Think of these as additions to a house, adding on a porch or a new wing. These nodes attached to the main craft provided extra room for special experiments, astronaut living quarters, and so forth.

As manufacturing platforms were built and positioned around the "suburbs" of each satellite (75 to 150 miles away, a 10–20 minute commute), they refined and processed Moon-mined materials to enlarge each satellite, thus ending Earth dependency. New sphere segments surrounded the original Kernel, and atmosphere and pressure were pumped in once the newer, large sphere was sealed tight. Except for Amaterasu, each satellite has "grown" seven layers or levels. The outermost is always called Level 1 to remind us how near the outside atmosphere really is—only one layer of radiation-proof "skin" protects life inside from death outside. Amaterasu is the same overall size as its sisters, but consists of fewer and more widely-spaced layers, a necessity to more closely replicate real-world conditions for the zoological specimens it houses.

Consider these layers or levels, those circles within circles so like an onion. We've said the core or Kernel was 400 feet long, plus the length of the pylons or tube supports that extended to connect to our onion's first layer. This gives the overall core a 600-foot diameter. Each new layer rises 410 feet above the previous one; each becomes someone's "floor," while the people in the layer below view that floor as their "ceiling" or "horizon." Again, towers and tube supports connect and support each level. These 10-foot-thick layers are honeycombed with tunnels for cables and piping, walkways, and trash removal chutes.

As we began layering the satellites, obviously the diameter increased with each level. Interestingly, when you consider the space enclosed, a small increase in diameter means a large increase in volume. Each layer that was added increased the diameter by about another 820 feet, or 410 feet on each side.

All eight satellites have diameters of 1.2 miles, or about 6,340 feet. Mt. Washington in New Vermont rises 6,228 feet, not exactly notable heightwise, considering the Rockies or the Himalayas, but it does closely match a satellite. With a 1.2 mile diameter, its circumference is about 3 ¾ miles around. A distance you could walk in an hour without breaking into a sweat, you say? And so you could. But the surface area of Level One is 4.5+ square miles.

Counting all seven levels, the available surface area is just shy of 14 square miles for living and working, manufacturing and growing food. Anyone involved in farming or land development knows that one square mile is 640 acres. New York City's Central Park covered 800 acres before it was converted to high-rises. China's Hong Kong province takes up about 29 square miles, although it boasts a population density that would astound you. Manhattan Island in the heart of JerseyYork consists of 22 square miles.

Most satellite living quarters and agricole areas are situated in this "belt" or zone of standard to 70% gravity that we've discussed before. It's often called the Diamond Zone for fairly obvious reasons. Note the colored patterns on Diagram #8, rather like that of an argyle sock. Full diamonds and half diamonds, balanced like triangles tip to tip, green for agricole areas, red for habitat or residential areas. No matter what level you visit—from Level 1 to Level 7—the same pattern occurs. Beyond the Diamond Zone you'll find small manufactures where diminished gravity enhances production; also various lagoons and mini-mers where algae, shrimp, kelp, and fish are raised or farmed for the satellite's food supply. Each satellite is self-sustaining, producing adequate food-stuffs to support a population of 100,000 to 140,000. **Where Am I in a Satellite?** Now, to truly confuse you, let's take the onion image previously used in discussing levels or layers, and cross it with an orange. Divide it into segments exactly like an orange— wide in the middle (at the Equator) and tapering at the tips (the Poles). There'll be eight segments in all, and each segment has two names—top and bottom, so to speak.

The Holm Port or northern hemisphere segments are named Alpha, Bravo, Charlie, Delta, Echo, Foxtrot, Golf, and Hotel. The Newcome Port/southern hemisphere segments continue as India, Juliet, Kilo, Lima (say Lee-ma), Mike, November, Oscar, Papa. India is Alpha's "mate" or southern hemisphere counterpart, Bravo is Juliet's, and so on. These segments, in effect, provide our longitude. You'll notice a boldly marked red line on each level that serves as our demarcation line—our equivalent of your Greenwich Mean Time Line.

Hence, directions are given by saying 1Alpha/Cap or 2Kilo/Mid to indicate Level One/Alpha Sector/near Holm Port. (Because we said "Alpha," you know we're in the northern hemisphere.) Or Level Three/ Kilo Sector/near the equator or middle. The upper part of each hemisphere, from 45° to the port, is the *Cap*; the middle section is termed *Mid*. For precise locations, a full "address" includes latitude and longitude.

At last the vac-hound pinned the pamphlet against a stanchion and began to consume it, jaws inexorably working to compact the paper until internal pulping could begin. It gave a brief hiccup as it swallowed Gene Padric Vlaserra's name and degrees, as if struck with a sudden gas attack, but the vac-hound persevered, and the pamphlet disappeared with a final crackle.

With a burst of air the vac-hound jockeyed itself around and went in search of other debris to consume.

Date: Two days later, 31 January 2158
Location: Light Industry, 4Charlie/Cap, PabNeruda

Glynn jerked open the shop door, nearly leaped in startlement as an old-fashioned bell—obviously one of Chance's newest acquisitions—clanged warning from the doortop. For an unnerving moment Amaterasu's entire butterfly crop lodged in his belly, and all attempted flight at once. Jittery? Absolutely. Hadn't bet Rigoberto and Jere finally prevailed over beta Masady's hounding through dress rehearsal and ordered him off to calm himself? But somehow PabNeruda offered no hiding place, no spot simply to be himself—whoever or whatever that was . . . or would be after tonight. No place, except perhaps for Chance, Chance's shop on Level Four, on the cusp between Cap and Mid. He'd rushed for refuge, shame outpacing him, shame for his fears and an added shame that his panicky body had shed every hard-learned, perfect gesture, every ingrained, graceful movement it had ever absorbed.

If anyone could make it right, Chance could. Anything that needed fixing, Chance could fix. He hoped it applied to humans as well as machines. Panting, lungs on fire, he hovered just inside the door, waiting for Chance to answer the bell, face squinched in silent prayer.

"Yo, boy! That you, Glynn?" Dark movements against dim shadows in the shop's rear resolved themselves into a figure, crescent wrench gleaming in one hand as he moved into the light. Tinker II Evers II Chance stood behind the counter, massive brown shoulders and chest running with sweat, green eyes alarmingly light and bright against his dark complexion, not the aching blackness of Panny's coloration, but more a rich, warm cocoa. "Thought I wouldn't see you till tonight, Glynn." He scratched absently at close-cropped, tightly curled hair, rubbed at an absu-

rdly dainty ear with a thick marker pen, managed at
last to find a precariously balanced home for it behind
his ear.

A tight headshake of warning, palms raised to forestall any further conversation, Glynn took a shaky step
inside, inhaling, nose feasting on the scent of oil, the
faintly acrid smell of singed, burned-out computer
chips, the scent of solder. A chittering sound of delight, and a blur, gray-brown on top, white below,
sliced the air, sailing and tacking the way a piece of
paper drifts in the breeze. Sylvan landed on his shoulder, a pink-soled paw rummaging in his ear as if bur-
rowing for a nut. Prepared, Glynn reached into his
pocket for a real acorn—he'd squandered credits for
a half-dozen of Amaterasu's best—and held it up.
Rapid-fire chittering and the crunch of strong teeth as
the illicit flying squirrel gobbled the treat, shell frag-
ments littering Glynn's shoulder. Chance swore he'd
set up shop here for its 70% Earth gravity, a boon
when manhandling generators and other bulky, balky
equipment. Glynn suspected, though, it was because
Sylvan relished it, able to swoop higher, farther than
on Earth. If Chance were caught with Sylvan in direct
violation of Earth-species smuggling laws, who knew
what would happen?

"Pale as Sylvan's underbelly, you are." Chance
came round the counter, jamming his wrench into a
heavy tool belt that almost hid his abbreviated kilt.
"Spooked over tonight's performance?" An oil-
stained hand clutched Glynn's shoulder, and the flying
squirrel scooted along the bridging arm to perch on
its master. "Jere may not have admitted it to you,
but she confided to me a few days ago that you'd
be perfect."

Stomach yo-yoing, Glynn swallowed hard. "Don't
want to talk about tonight. Can't manage it." He swallowed again, gray eyes awash with misery. "It's tomorrow I can't bear to think about, Chance. Help me
forget."

Tinker II Evers II Chance nodded once, solemn.

"Let me show you the new things, then, Glynn. Made some good trades, some superlative repairs, and an absolute gem of a salvage this week. Come on, poke around, get grease under your nails."

And in a short while Glynn *did* feel better, hands sorting amongst the intricate pieces of a dismantled blunderbuss at least five centuries old, reordering the parts under Chance's watchful eye. What fascinated him more than its workings was the chasing on the gun's barrel, the intricate ivory inlay on the stock. The powder flask and molded bullets had their own beauty as well. That was what he loved about Chance's crowded, cluttered shop—it offered a feast for the senses, the human spirit's desire to catalog, collect, possess despite the rules—the antithesis of the pared-down lifestyle of the satellites. Except for the vivid, growing things that unfurled in the agricole sectors, always the same muted tones and hues for habitat areas—cypress green and olive, oyster, a blue-gray, a gray-rose—bland surface textures, recycled air and food, identical walkways and paths, segments and layers on each satellite. Predictably unpredictable "weather," artificially generated sunrises and sunsets keyed to Earth's seasons. A boring regularity—not a jot of Stanislaus Troupe's vibrant masks and costumes, so zealously preserved, or Chance's rummage of gadgets. For a moment this comfort would suffice, but not for long. Somehow he'd been hemmed in, trapped by everything.

"Chance, how did you feel when you realized, finally admitted to yourself, you couldn't ever take to space again? That everything you were, every way you identified yourself, had changed, altered in an eye blink?" He snapped his fingers.

Chance smiled wide, nudged a spring toward Glynn. "You mean what's it like to discover that a tinkerer, one of the great idiot savants of technology—able to fix anything with a twist of wire or a wad of chewgum, a plastispoon, whatever—couldn't fly the spacers anymore? Grounded with an inner ear problem neurologists swear is psychological, and psychiatrists insist is hardwired? A shame to both branches of my family, the Tinkers and the Evers?" A deep, rumbling belly laugh, but his green eyes hooded. "It hurt. Wasn't sure I was real anymore. That I existed outside of a job that identified me as who I was, what I did, even more than most people's jobs do."

A percussive clap of hands made Glynn start. "Always something new you can be, defy expectations. Whether those expectations are your own or others. Learning to manage Stanislaus Troupe might not be so bad, might provide more scope than acting. Ever think of that? Then again, might not." Abruptly walking away from the workbench, he signaled Glynn to follow into his private workspace. "Come on, see what I scavenged today before the sani-techs came along. Absolutely illegal under private ownership, and discarded as casually as if it were plain trash. A-mazing what people do these days. Top of the line model, bit out of date, that's all."

Roughly a cube of perhaps 25 centimeters on each side, the case was of burled maple, shining, satin-smooth; Glynn yearned to stroke it. Whatever it was, it had originated on Earth; the satellites offered only cellulose-based replicates, not real wood. Looking at Chance for permission, he did touch it, then picked it up, surprised at its lightness. Not solid, for sure, but what was it supposed to hold? Try as he might, he couldn't make sense of the dials embedded along its front, the curved lenses on opposite sides, the tightly latched lid and smaller sealed compartments along its top. "What was it?"

Retrieving it before Glynn could shake it, Chance set it in pride of place on his bench, voice as reverent as his touch. "A one hundred percent brand-new brain box. All parts pristine pure and accounted for, not to mention," Chance sketched an X across his heart, "a genuine instruction manual. The real one, the original."

Despite himself, Glynn whistled. "A Penrose, you mean?"

"Penfield, not Penrose," Chance corrected, "and no, it's not a Penfield. A Goldberg variation."

"Goldberg? It doesn't do the same thing as a Penfield?" Not that Glynn was sure how a Penfield actually worked. Still, life-support boxes for the human brain were few and far between at best, and all belonged to the top neuroscientists and the elite emergency med-squads who responded to major catastrophes.

Chance's green eyes turned distant as he groped for an explanation. "Penfield posited nearly two hundred yeas ago that a human brain could be kept alive and coherent in a vat, never realize its body was missing if the best computers in the world simulated an environment for it, provided input that mimicked human senses. But we haven't been able to do that yet—virtual reality isn't quite virtual enough for the human mind.

"Now Evelyn Goldberg was more visionary, yet more pragmatic than Penfield. What she created keeps the brain alive, offers it some sensory input, while a new body is regenerated to house the brain." He shook his head at the enormity of it. "Theoretically, that is. Imagine being able to regenerate a whole human body?"

"We can regrow fingers, toes, arms and legs even, if the patient's young enough," Glynn protested. "Sure we can regenerate bodies someday. Bet they're working on it on CurieCousteau. Safer and better life-support boxes on Huang-ti." Of course the rich and influential were eager to possess a brain box, the ultimate status symbol to assuage their fears of mortality. The body, the husk or shell might fail and be regenerated, but the brain would live on, immortal, until the new shell was ready to hold it. "But to just throw it out? Anyone'd be crazy to do that." Conspicuous waste to his way of thinking. "What're you going to do with it?"

Chance made a show of tapping the chrono on his

beefy wrist. "Stash your brain in it, boy. Because that's all that'll be left of you—if that—if you don't head back now. You be late for this evening's performance and Jere'll have my hide. Assuming beta Masady leaves any for Jere to work over. Now scoot! I'll be there watching, promise." A glance toward the front of the shop made him wince. "If you haven't jumbled those blunderbuss pieces so badly I can't reassemble it."

Date: Evening, 31 January 2158
Location: Gathering Rooms, 1Delta/Mid
(Please check at Admin. Office for rental fees
and availability), PabNeruda

Sweat-drenched, exhilarated, Glynn stood alone in front of the footlights, curtsied deep and low, arms sweeping back like a swan's mantling wings. With the help of Heike and Hassiba, still costumed as Spartan Ambassadors, he removed the oversized papier-mâché mask of Lysistrata that enveloped his head, obscured his identity, and bowed as his mother Jerelynn, the Great Lynn, entered stage left, still costumed and masked as Cinesias. She bowed back in homage. His love for her, her adoration for him at his zenith, *his* moment, almost broke his heart, aching with a fierce lust for a love he couldn't name, comprehend, except to sense that he needed and desired it above and beyond all things. Never could he put it aside, seek a replacement, he was sure.

He turned once again to the audience, and they rose in a surging wave, whistling, stamping, applauding, tossing ribbon bouquets and rosettes, expensive, exotic flowers cultivated on Amaterasu, heady with real scent, rich with startling color. He bowed, eyes closed, head high to grant them this singular look, let his features impress themselves on their memory as the greatest boy actress ever witnessed. His holovert likeness, unobscured by any mask, and this, this ultimate moment, were the only times his audience would ever see his true face. Few outsiders could identify any of the Stanislaus Troupe's actors and actresses, and that, too, was a part of their mystique. None of the other troupes, Tierney, Orvieto, not even the Magyar Players, boasted the intensely loyal, near-rabid following that Stanislaus commanded.

A single yellow rose with a salmon core, its petals just unfurling, landed at his feet and he scooped it up, pressed it to his heart. The man who'd thrown it edged closer to the stage, urbane, confident, temples graying but the rest of his short-cropped hair a deep gold. Dark blue eyes lifted to catch Glynn's, a summons, a promise in those blue eyes. Glynn fingered the scrolled note attached to the rose's stem. Notes were tied to the other ribbon bouquets and flowers that Hassiba and Heike busily gathered, filling his arms to overflowing. He bowed a final time, took a step back and, with perfect timing, bet Rigoberto and bet Vijay dropped the screen.

Rushing offstage, he piled the tributes at his feet, turned obediently to allow Staniar to unfasten the heavy costume, wincing at the unnecessarily rough fingers, the occasional pinch or prod that was no accident. "Bet Staniar, if you please," and let his words drip with scorn and warning.

From behind, Staniar's breath burned hot and angry on his neck as the older boy leaned closer. "Last time to play this game, Glynn. Tomorrow you're just like me, no more, no less. Backstage, anonymous, no applause. Oh, you'll love that, won't you, my little pet?" Despite himself Glynn stiffened, fingers splaying.

Bet Vijay cuffed Staniar as he swung by, reeling in the portable lighting cables. "Let him enjoy it, boy. You had your time in the limelight, don't begrudge him his." Staniar growled as he finished removing Glynn's heavy costume and took it to the tailoring area without looking back, already checking the seams, looking for stains.

Beta Masady and bet Rigoberto, the heads of Stanislaus, rushed to his side, Masady tiny and shrunken, leaning heavily on her cane, while Rigoberto flipped a towel around Glynn's neck, began to massage his shoulders, aching from the mask's weight. They were polar opposites, Rigoberto tall and thin, except for the protruding pot belly that made it appear he'd stashed one of the oversized masks under his robe for safe-keeping. Given his protective instincts toward the troupe, it was entirely possible. Dark, dark hair, too dark to be natural, for all that he was at least thirty years younger than his wife and partner, Masady. His hands were tender as he rubbed.

Masady fixed Glynn with a stare, head cocked bird-like as she looked up at him, eyebrows winged, her expression too subtle to reveal the workings of her mind. Twisted hands curled over the top of her cane, fondling it. Some swore Masady was beyond one hundred years old, granddaughter or even, perhaps, daughter of Siem Vy and Gennadi Stanislaus Rimsky-akoff, founders of the troupe who'd deserted Earth and its discontents to bring their art to the satellites. Masady still performed on occasion, the pains in back and legs and hands forgotten when she donned the costume and the mask, still able to convince an audience of her vitality and power, a man's man despite her diminutive stature. Once behind the mask, she lived the character more fully than any other actress alive. Only Jere's talent approached—many argued surpassed—hers.

"Very good, Glynn. Exquisite . . . almost." Crooked fingers grabbed his, bent his left wrist, flexed his fingers into the flying crane position. "Except for your third finger. Dammit, lad, your flying crane always flutters as if it had a broken wing." She folded his fingers together, touched them to her cheek, a brief smile flickering. "Other than that, exquisite." Masady was a hard taskmistress, and Glynn felt himself flushing at the criticism, most especially because it was justified.

He knelt, clasping her hands in his. "Beta Masady, I promise I'll master it next . . ." The words lodged in his throat, his mouth dropped open. There was no next time! This was the end, his ultimate performance. "I, I . . ." But beta Masady took pity on his unpardonable slip and pried one hand free to tap his shoulder, bring him to himself. "This is your night. Celebrate, don't mourn. Tomorrow comes when it comes."

Wrapped in a tatty robe, towel turbaning her head, Jere enveloped him in a hug. Loathe to break contact, he leaned away slightly to stare into her eyes, so blue that he always groped for words to describe them, as if a comparison existed somewhere beyond his ken, lodged deep in memory, if only he knew where to look. Eyes blue as . . . blue as . . . and every time he strove to capture the elusive comparative, the faintest memory, discomforting, disconcerting, threatened to catapult him to another time, another place.

"How was I, Jere? Truly?" He crushed himself against her as if nothing could separate them. Halves of a whole, a match both on and offstage, mother/ son; actor/actress. Nothing could sunder them—ever. Whatever he was, she was; whatever she'd felt portraying a man, he would someday experience or achieve, and whatever emotions he had tapped as an actress, she'd realized as well. The voice inside bemoaned its bereavement again. *"Lost, all lost, this night marks the end. The pairing gone."*

She toyed with his braid, her eyes half-merry, halfrueful, but blue, so blue. "I've shared a stage with seven final-night performers and none of them, not one, has ever embraced a role so convincingly. I say that not to a son, but to another performer—a peer. Although," she considered, "beta Masady *was* right about the flying crane. Even Little Gem mastered that years ago."

"I know." By the sun, moon, and satellites, would the flying crane haunt him to the end of his days?

"Still, it's not entirely your fault. That finger was broken when you were a toddler, and it never healed entirely straight."

"Broken?" The first he'd ever heard *that,* and he examined his left hand, perplexed.

"Yes, so there's some excuse, even if beta Masady says," and he chimed in, beginning to laugh, " 'Mind over matter, child. Training the body is difficult, but training the mind is even harder.' " Her cheek pressed his now, perspiration sealing them together. "So, have you decided whom you'll join tonight? In celebration?"

He began frantically pawing through the flowers piled at his feet. When he had relinquished it, that one perfect yellow rose, the blush of salmon at its petals' tips and at its heart? There, there it was. "I . . . I think so." He hadn't unscrolled the note, but it didn't matter. Somehow this was the right one, had to be. An ending, so unfair, and this token of a new beginning. Fingers working, he did unroll the note, glanced at it, not caring what it promised. Hadn't the promise been implicit in those eyes?

Jere glimpsed the signature and her expression stilled. "Are you sure, Glynn? Are you sure you understand, know what's expected? He's notoriously hard to please."

"Of course," he sought for an airy assurance to thrust his fears away, wondering about the note, wondering over his disloyalty to his mother, to the troupe. His inner voice rallied back. *It's their insistence on blindly following tradition that's betrayed you. You've one performance left—with an audience of one.* The celebrations could be held here, but it was *his* choice, wasn't it? "Bet Staniar explained it all to me. After all, he's nearest my age, remembers best. It's been a long time for bet Vijay, even longer for bet Rigoberto."

"Fine, then. It's your night." She hugged him again, then set him away from her, their smooth cheeks parting. Separation. How could she let them be separated like that?

Date: Early morning, 1 February 2158
Location: A hegira to the Holm Port Observation Deck, PabNeruda
He'd been quivering, huddled in a fetal crouch behind the elegant and oh-so-discreet Aventura Hotel tiers

when she'd found him, face streaked with tears that washed over a livid bruise on his cheekbone, a puffy lower lip. His gold-threaded robe was torn, the yellow rose woven into his narrow braid limp, its petals crushed. She could smell it, its bruised scent unappealing, already verging toward decay.

It had taken her a good half hour to uncurl the tight-wound limbs, cajole him upright; her stroking and murmuring, more than her words, had accomplished that. She'd patiently worked to soothe just as she had during his colicky babyhood, his body cramping, knees drawn high, tiny toes flaring as the pain gripped his gut. She spared a brief thought of gratitude for Chance, who'd commed a warning once he'd spotted Glynn's huddled form as he scavenged the rich pickings behind the hotel on his way home. He'd hovered at Glynn's side until she'd arrived. His stingingly silent rebuke as he left had been justified, she supposed. Only she could make it right with Glynn, undo as much damage to flesh and spirit as she could. Be nice to call Chance, assure him that Glynn would heal, but she didn't dare take the time. If she let him falter now, dwell on what had happened, he'd be immobilized again. His first failure. No, to be brutally honest, his second. He'd had no control over the first—the coming of his fifteenth birthday.

"Shh, love, shh. Let's go up to the Observation Deck, float free and easy, name the stars, the satellites." Her arm pinned his waist, his right arm draped around her neck. As she dragged him along, she realized he'd begun moving of his own volition, a good sign.

The few people still stirring, just ending or beginning a workshift, gave them a wide berth. Understandably so. Face and hands dirty, eyes sunken with exhaustion, she wore a threadbare pair of paint-spattered breeks—Vijay's, truth be told—and a baggy overshirt that looked as if someone had mopped the floor with it. A slight exaggeration, Staniar had only used it to dust the masks. She'd concentrated on menial, demanding tasks to avoid thinking about Glynn.

What Glynn resembled, she knew too well: he stumbled as if drunk or drugged, the loser in a lover's quarrel or in a loveless, impersonal interlude involving sex. Could she guide him to the Observation Deck without anyone interfering, calling security? "Tunnel Dweller Abducts Innocent Child," she could already hear the vidnews-caster, read the flimsy's headlines. Should she admit their relationship, it wouldn't be any better, "Careless Mother Puts Child in Jeopardy." Some things never altered, including the public's vicarious enjoyment of someone else's tragedy. Didn't matter where you went on Earth, where you fled to in the stars, the satellites, headlines like that titillated.

The drag on her neck and shoulder eased as Glynn walked more confidently, almost unaided, though his head still hung, eyes glazed and half-closed. Hand on his elbow now, she guided him with a push or pull toward the vactube. Jere sniffed once, finally identifying the urine stink mingling with that of the vomit and whiskey staining his robe. At least when they reached Z-grav, the smell would diminish, the scent molecules no longer volatile. His nose started to leak, and she absently swiped at it with her sleeve. Compassion struggled against disgust and dismay. Pretend it's a part you're playing, she advised herself, because you tolerated it when Glynn was a baby, a toddler, schooled yourself to accept these upsets, these upchucks. But now she felt immensely tired of such untidiness, such clinging need. Ah, fastidious, are we? A man in the red and tan of the recyclers stopped short, nose wrinkling as he edged away, determined not to share the approaching vactube with them.

Ah, wouldn't the headlines be even juicier if she were recognized? "Boy Child New Conquest of the Great Lynn?" Lucky so few knew her real face, even if they thought they knew her most intimate doings from the fanrags. Gossip gave greater scope for creativity than all the troupe's plays combined. Some gossip transmuted itself into legend, lore. She stiffened, shocked to realize that *Glynn* was recognizable after tonight's ultimate performance, and her mind recast the headline: "Boy Star in Clutches of Lecherous Fan." So much for ego.

At last the vactube arrived and lifted them up the curve to the Observation Deck, weightlessness embracing them as they mounted the top of the stairs. Glynn groaned, started to retch, stomach not floating in sync with his body. Desperate, she propelled him to one of the magneto-grav pads for the faint-of-heart, earthlubbers dizzied by the sensation of weightlessness. Hitting the "on" button produced gravity's familiar drag, and she flexed her knees, used all her strength to hoist Glynn slightly upward to compensate. Strange, not until tonight had she truly realized he'd grown half-a-head taller than she. How could she have been so oblivious to his body's changes, knowing his birthday approached?

A moan as his feet jarred the pad, his head lolling on her shoulder, face burrowed in her neck while she reflexively patted between his shoulder blades. "What is it, Glynn? What happened?" She had her suspicions, as had Chance, but he'd not noticed anyone nearby when he'd spotted Glynn. Trust the Aventura Hotel for that: discreet tourist trysts a specialty.

Another groan, indistinct mutters finally melding into sense. "The Spinmeister, he promised . . . prom . . . ised me dinner. With real meat, *real* meat," he wailed. Ah, that explained part of the smell she'd noticed, taken for a sense of rot before, not just the battered rose—he'd been carnivorous, eating meat. It took her aback how much she still craved it, just hearing the word. Near thirteen years since she'd tasted real meat, steaks, chops from cattle, sheep, goats. Even the thought of satellite-raised rodents, rabbit, cavy, the succulent flesh of fowl made her yearn for the taste. So much for a healthful diet of pressed algae and seaweed derivatives shaped to mimic—but not replace—your heart's desire, fish or shellfish, fruit and vegetables, varieties dependent on the satellite. Every-thing guaranteed one hundred percent nutritious, sus-taining, but with no savor or flavor. Flavor and savor cost credits, a perk of a legitimate career. Her mouth began to water, her vision blur with longing so that she nearly missed Glynn's next words.

"Know how much that *costs*?" he gave a spasmodic cough. "And all for *me,* he told me he'd ordered it all for *me.* How he'd been struck by my acting, my grace, my poise! And whiskey aged more years than I've lived! You know how much he *spent*?" Indigna-tion and pride. Oh, she knew all right. The cost of two prime Earth-grazed steaks up here was prohibi-tive; shuttle fare between Ring satellites was less exor-bitant in price.

"Yes, sweetheart, I know. He must have been very taken with you." No, the Spinmeister didn't lack for money, more than well-compensated for holding PabNeruda's most crucial post. The Spinmeister—a nickname for the CEO, Chief Engineering Officer—had the responsibility of maintaining PabNeruda's orbit and of monitoring artificial gravity spin. While the spin was programmed, a chance asteroid or meteor-ite crash could speed or slow it, as could a too-vigorous bump from a monster dredger or space cruiser. Regu-lating the magnetic fields that generated the satellite's radiation shielding also came under his purview.

The Spinmeister earned more than most, as did his sister-satellite counterparts, a munificent salary well in excess of the base indulgence wage an ordinary citizen drew to finance minor wants in a world where basic necessities were free—to a point—as long as job per-formance remained high. Only people such as herself and the troupe, or other entrepreneurs who coexisted within the Ring's self-contained society, knew the heady "thrill" of wondering if each day's earnings cov-ered survival expenses—their daily fee for "sustain-ables": shares of oxygen, water, food, habitat space, and more. Private contractors were rare—most worked for the satellites, received shares for Earth-trade, whether they grew crops to feed Ring citizens or worked in small shops or manufactory platforms producing export goods.

"But what he . . . wanted in return." He stood straight now, achingly separate; she longed to hold him again, but contented herself with tucking his narrow braid over his shoulder so it didn't dangle, fingered her own shorter braid as well. "Do you know what he wanted me . . . to do?" His sudden grip on her wrist made her wince, long to turn away, not face his reproach, his anguish. As well as to shield him from her anger, that *this* had set him off, that he *still* didn't realize, mayhap *never* would realize what survival *meant*. Not just his own survival, but the troupe's. Didn't he think they'd all participated, still did on occasion to pay their way? Let ticket sales slow, and the credits must somehow be earned to compensate. Bribes and barter existed in all shapes and sizes and values. How did Glynn think she'd met Chance in his literally "high-flying" days when he could name his fee to sign aboard as a tinkerer, the ultimate "fixer"? She'd charged a high price, but Chance had ultimately charged a higher one—friendship.

Sympathy or acerbity? Which would pull Glynn together more quickly? "I thought Staniar explained it to you." Start with that, see where it went. He slid his arm around her waist and she reciprocated, both swaying in place.

"I think Staniar enjoyed putting me on." A hiccup followed by a shaky laugh, "wasn't *quite* the way he described it." A pause as he considered. "Though mayhap that's the way he likes it. He's always been jealous."

"It isn't just jealousy, Staniar has the troupe's interests at heart, does what's needful when and as it's needed. He's mature enough to know that." She tensed, the whisper of distant bare feet near the vactube catching her ear, then silence as the person launched into the weightless atmosphere. Realized how deserted the Observation Deck was at this early-

morning hour, the sani-techs, the repair-techs else-
where. Even the vac-hound buzzed in aimless circles—
nothing to retrieve.

For no reason, she shivered, and Glynn, in a courtly
gesture, swept the stained, gold-embroidered robe
from his shoulders and slipped it around her, leaving
him clad in a discolored, torn shirt and equally messy
britches. "Not too stinky, I hope," though his nose
wrinkled as he settled it around her, "and I'm warm
enough. Don't worry about the noise, just some of the
satrats, probably Panthat and her gang prowling." He
started to turn and wave as the first shot rang out.

It slammed into her right shoulder, spinning her
toward Glynn, but the next shot angled high and wide,
spanged off a magnesium-alloy pylon looming above
them and sparked. Another wild shot, more sparks,
and the air was burning bright and hot, engulfing
them. Emergency sirens wailed, sensor strobes lanced
the smoke, faltered and failed as flames melted
circuitry.

Date: 6:00 P.M., 2 February 2158
Location: NetwArk, Texas Republic, Earth

Muting the volume, much as she'd dearly have loved
to hear the screams, Becca Connaught Alvarez hit a
control and zoomed for a close-up. Yes—a hit! Second
one wide, the third wider yet—bumbling fool!—but
those sparks! They floated, then sank, sucked downward by the force field generated by the artificial grav
pad. Sparks dusted the gold-embroidered robe like
fireflies, then burst into flames. ABSs, Able-Bodied
Savers, the worker bees of NetwArk as she conde-
scendingly tagged them, hurried by, but none noticed
the single monitor out of twenty-five not tuned to
Rhuven Fisher Weaver. Twenty-four repetitive Rhu-
vens, honey-brown eyes radiant with love, sweat dew-
ing his face, the yearning hands beckoning his
audience closer, gathering them into his embrace. Yes,
a beneficent touch, the blessed sensation of his hand
on a distant head and that person would be healed.

Monitors at the next workstation flicked from face to face at five-second intervals, images of his far-flung audience scanned and stored for future retrieval. Each faithful viewer part of the World Wide Web, each alone, each located somewhere across the planet yet near as near could be, all part of the whole, the congregants of NetwArk.

Her screen blanked, a snow blizzard of heaving particles obscuring her private viewing. Ah, well, too bad, but she'd seen enough—success. With a shrug she flicked channels, snapping the errant screen back to Rhuven, a tight, satisfied smile lurking at the corners of her mouth.

Let's see your therapeutic touch heal those wounds, Rhuven. If you hadn't strayed so long ago, this would never have happened. You chose the Great Lynn for your lover, your concubine. You chose to be unfaithful to Vitarosa, your wife. Yes, I've known for years but held my peace. I couldn't bring myself to hurt Vitarosa, my "little sister," our bonds closer than flesh and blood for longer than you've been wed. I remained true, never strayed, cherished her secrets as my own. How could I have suspected you knew our secret and kept it? I admit I didn't credit you enough for the compassion and courage that showed.

Well, there's nothing to heal, nothing to put together now, Rhuven, it's too late for all of us to pretend things are the same. Not since the blackmail notes began, and not since this. Who'd ever have expected you'd call me into your office like that, plead for my aid? "Please, Becca," you begged, "do what it takes, whatever it takes, to stop those blackmail notes!"

"Are you sure? The affair's long over, is it worth . . . ?" Actually, she knew to a penny how much it was worth. Not only had she stacked NetwArk's credits in her account, but she'd added a tidy sum—a handsome sum—by selling that information to Pope Jean-Chrétien I for "speculative" purposes. And speculate he would, in every sense of the word, once their contact freed him to exploit the information, not to mention the bonus clause they'd negotiated regarding the existence of a bastard son.

Rhuven sat beside her, head bowed, arms loosely dangled between his knees, the picture of dejection. "I can weather the storm, an indiscretion over fifteen years ago, but I can't stand what the notes are doing to Rosa, the way it tears her up inside." His sincerity lodged in her throat, made her cough to swallow it down. "Please, for God's sake, for Rosa's sake, find a way to stop the notes. I want no part of that past—wish I could erase it from Rosa's mind and mine as well."

A sense of release gripped her, the way a dog feels when he realizes he's slipped his collar. "You want me to erase the past?" Be sure, Becca, this isn't the time for mistakes.

"Oh, yes, yes," like an eager child, "erase it, so the notes will end!"

Unfair, perhaps, but she didn't care. Erase didn't mean to Rhuven what it did to her, but she had his orders now—and even better, his gratified approbation. Pleasant—but too late. To eradicate the past, you must destroy the roots to be completely rid of it. Yes, she'd started something, but Rhuven had given her leave to conclude it—for Rosa's sake. Always for Rosa's sake. . . .

So she had obeyed—and this was what had come of it. Becca sighed with an inward sorrow. Leave the past buried for too long and it doesn't heal—it festers. It's all been ashes, dust in my mouth lately—when did that begin? She jerked herself back to the present, almost smiled. The fire—truly a brilliant touch. Even you can't rebuild from those ashes, Rhuven.

An unobtrusive cough confirmed a hovering presence behind her, and Becca wheeled, sliding her headset around her neck. A swift adrenaline surge at the ghost faces mocking to her left. Ah, merely her multiple screen reflections. Dingy hair chopped no-nonsense short at ear-level, neck a bit stringy now, but the face

was still hard, determined, the body even more so—
like tempered steel. Hamish and Falid were satis-
fyingly real, striped sleeveless robes hanging open over
loose white trousers and collarless shirts as they
waited, hands clasped below their breastbones. Odd
how a chubby, florid blond and a wiry, inky-haired,
dark-complected man could appear so similar, so in-
terchangeable—but then tools often were. "So, you
are pleased?" Falid's lips barely moved. "You saw?"
Hamish quickly chimed in.

"Yea, verily." She hated those moments when she
echoed Rhuven, but NetwArk's language came easily
after so many years of lip service. "The fire was a
lovely touch. Planned or not?"

Falid inclined his head, humility plain. "Yes and no.
A matter of fate, some might say." His teeth flashed
predator-white, a very satisfied predator. "Others
might argue it was divine retribution."

"God's?" How far could she push him? Interesting—for future reference. Did his loyalties truly lie
with Rhuven, with NetwArk—or didn't her suspicions
matter? After all, a tool was nothing without someone
to ply it, and that she did very well. It felt good after
all these years of inaction, though not as good as serving as God's direct instrument of justice—a Little Sister of Mortality.

But Hamish answered, "Any hand, even the righteous hand of God, must wield a righteous weapon.
Thus we have been elevated in God's sight. We thank
you for the opportunity. For choosing us above all
other ABSs."

Rhuven Fisher Weaver's closing benediction came
through the speakers, "For I am the Weaver of the
Web of Faith that heals us all, for I am the Fisher
whose far-flung Net encompasses all right believers.
Remember, brothers and sisters, that God loves you
even more than I do. Until tomorrow, this is Rhuven
Fisher Weaver, Navigator of NetwArk, saying farewell
and Amen."

In dismissal she swung to study the screens, ostensibly to watch the credits roll. And let her glimpse Vitarosa Herrara Weaver, wife of Rhuven Fisher Weaver, clasping her husband's hand as he came offstage, exalted but weary, disconnecting the implant behind his left ear that let him commune directly through the Web with his congregation. No matter how often she'd experienced the Web-sharing herself, body almost convincing mind she inhabited the same space with Rhuven, it still shocked Becca how so many could prove so gullible.

But then she'd never quite merged with that charmed circle—the larger circle of faith, and the smaller, more intimate circle of Rhuven's and Vitarosa's need for each other. Well, they needed her now, but no matter how that charmed circle now embraced and encompassed her in their hour of need, she felt a lack, an emptiness. Theirs? Hers? It didn't pay to analyze too closely or the hurt would rise again.

No, she didn't like Rhuven Fisher Weaver, though she harbored a grudging respect for him and his healing skills. Why, how they worked she couldn't fathom, but work they did—and doctors agreed. Not just hypochondriacs experiencing "miraculous" cures, but the genuinely ill who rallied, tumors shrinking, blocked arteries flowing freely again. Still, something "indecorous" about such an intimate touch by a stranger, even at a distance, but then she was a Little Sister of Mortality, more comfortable with the truly intimate touch of death. Could Rhuven conquer the genetic "seeds" growing in her dear Rosa's breast every day? Rosa refused to consult a doctor, wouldn't ask for Rhuven's prayers. Becca was no longer sure it mattered. Too late, oh-so-late on many counts.

Once Vitarosa had confided in her about the lump, the blackmail notes, Becca'd been caught in a double bind. A relief to continue hiding behind the role she'd played for years, to help snip the threads of those rumors for Vitarosa's sake, grant her peace if she couldn't grant her health. If Rosa learned that the Great Lynn had borne Rhuven a child, the past would horribly recapitulate itself with even more ironic symmetry. A past she and Rosa had battled to contain, but as the cliché said, they'd won the battle but lost the war. The remembrance hurt more than she'd bargained for, had thought herself case-hardened steel. More than the "war" had been lost: a way of life, a home, a land, a position, only Rosa's love to sustain her. Love stretched too thin could snap and break, and woe to those the whiplike end brushed.

And of course, for NetwArk, for Rhuven and Vitarosa, she had done it, snipped one past thread even if its severing increased her risk. Again that whiplike end loomed near. But she'd had Rhuven's blessing on her task. Perhaps the blackmail demands *would* cease for a while. Yes, definitely. And if they began again, no doubt Luz Paiz was the author, Luz, who'd always suspected the truth of that long ago night in Vitarosa's father's study. Luz, so desperate now to rally supporters as she ran for Pope of the Nuevo Catolicos. Yes, mention that possibility to Rosa.

Woebegone at the exhaustion wilting Rhuven, Hamish rushed to his side, offering his own fresh handkerchief. It gave Becca time for a final whispered question to Falid, who'd lingered. "How long before the vidcasts pick it up? Before the headlines change on the flimsies as they pop out of the news-slots?"

"Soon, soon. I don't know why the satrat's microcam malfunctioned, but as soon as we retrieve it, we'll play back the ending. Again and again, if it gives you joy."

"Good. Anyone recognize the dissolute-looking fellow with her? Another of her conquests, I suppose. If he's dead as well, we should see about comping the family—through NetwArk's great love and compassion for all innocent victims, of course." Well, that was one of the problems with using tools, their blows rained on the innocent as well. A Little Sister could winnow one person in a crowd of hundreds and deliver her gift of death.

Time: Immediately after the attack
Location: Holm Port Observation Deck, PabNeruda

Swimming, crawl-stroking through the air, the smoke
and foam fire-retardant mists shrouding the atmosphere, Glynn fought Z-grav to reach his mother's side.
As the first shot had struck, Jere, with an almost su-
perhuman strength, had tumbled him clear of the grav
pad, momentum sending him somersaulting, pinwheel-
ing across the Observatory. The next shot had been
wide but had scraped a powdery residue of magnesium
from the pylon, while the final shot had sparked it,
causing it to explode and ignite. Jere'd been set alight
like a torch, the golden robe feeding the flames. Almost there, almost there, he groaned as a dwindling
flame licked at his foot. Kicking off against one of the
deck struts, he backstroked until he hovered over her.
It *was* Jere, wasn't it? Or was it a crumpled piece
of char?

A whining protest, a rumble, and the grav pad
failed, releasing Jere's body to drift up beside him like
a puppet whose strings had lofted it high. A vac-hound
blindly sniffed and butted at her side, its "mouth"
ceaselessly working to inhale errant ash and smoke
particles. He braced himself, gave it a vicious kick that
sent it tumbling away with a bleep and a whir.

A thump as the far doors burst open, flam-techs
and other support cadres propelling themselves inside,
wrestling canisters and hoses, more foam pellets
whooping from launch tubes, expanding and layering
everything with a thick, flame-retardant cloud. Trees
and shrubs now resembled giant cotton balls, obscuring his line of vision. The growing heaviness in his
lungs meant the flam-techs were slowly smothering the
oxygen content as well as cutting off the circulatory
fans.

He struggled to gather Jere—what remained of
Jere—in his embrace, first her arm, then a leg waving
free as he grappled. Got to get her out of here, get
her out, his mind screamed. A patch of red-black skin,
hard and crisp, sloughed off against his shirt as he

cradled her seared head against his shoulder. The vac-hound dove at it, a humming sound of pleasure as it port opened and engulfed the skin. Eyelids singed off, blue eyes exploded by heat, leaking fluids, mixing with the ashes, forming a little mud cloud.

"Shah! Shah! Glynnie, over here!" He whipped his head, unable to judge the sound's direction, muffled by the foam. "Shah!" and saw Panthat frog-kicking toward him, burned in spots, blood beading a cut on her forehead. Ahead of her she pushed an odd dish shape, a large, net-covered dish with a handle at one end and two wheels beneath it. At last he identified it as a "carry cart" that the sani-techs and garden-techs used to transport large debris. Its wheels retracted for Z-grav use, but Panthat had managed to engage them—why, he couldn't judge. Encumbered, he struggled toward Panthat as she battled the recalcitrant cart, both on wildly weaving courses that finally crossed. "She 'live?" More curiosity than compassion as she coughed once, spat, the globule a perfect, hovering sphere, marred by an ash.

He wasn't sure, let himself hang suspended, Jere's weight nothing at all in Z-grav, wondering how one decided. Pulse? Where, how to take a pulse on a body burned over almost every centimeter? Wrist bones, finger bones, tendons peeked through the skin on one bobbing hand. A fragile, squeaky whistle emanated from the holes of her mouth and nostrils, a desperate effort to draw air through singed nasal and throat passages, into seared lungs. The sound gave him hope. Breath meant life. He nodded once, all he was capable of doing.

Panthat the pragmatic shoved the cart beside him, yanked back the net. "Then'e better be lickity-quickity, be gone for help. Med-teckies find her, no health ticky, no record, she's mulch. No healing, just chop-chop!" A thought struck her, the notion appealing. "Fish pellets maybe, be nice, cycle round back to you."

"What?" he shook his head half-mesmerized by Panny's train of thought. "But how can I . . . ?"

"No buts. Run, Glynnie, run quickity-lickity. Mebbe Stanislaus got extra credits on demand, plenty favor-tabs to cash. Worth the try. Never know." She'd assessed the harsh reality far better than Glynn, but beneath her callused, twelve-year-old exterior Panthat was a romantic, though she'd have vehemently protested the label. With mother love in nonexistent supply, she'd not deny it to someone else. "Now git, 'fore the flam-techs cloud-shroud over here any more."

Laying the body in the cart as gently as he could, he fastened the net around it and grabbed the handle. "Come with me, Panny, please? Help me?"

Slow negation in her headshake as she scrubbed at a bloodshot eye, then spat again, watched it rise to join its twin. "Can't, pretty-Glynnie. Got a weasel sa-trat to cap-trap, take out best I kin. Weasel boy jist joined up, used me, he did, to git to you. Panny fix. Quick pick'n'pack." Out of nowhere a shimmer knife glinted in her hand, its blade vibrating.

Turning away with a shudder, Glynn manhandled the unwieldy cart ahead of him, no idea where he was going, what he was going to do, frantically mapping every back passage, dark tunnel he could remember from playing with Panthat. Think! He squared his shoulders, used the cart's handle as a rudder to ma-neuver it. When he reached the gravity belt, he'd work even harder. Think! Not much time! Dying, dying, dying. So little time!

Time: An hour later
Location: Chance's Workshop,
4 Charlie/Cap, PabNeruda

The fire squawkers' high, two-toned squeals jerked Chance out of a nightmare of faceless people manhan-dling him aboard a deep-space cruiser. The hairs on the back of his neck prickled at the sound all satellite dwellers dreaded, a warning their atmosphere might be breached, their satellite explode in a rush of burning gases like a new comet scoring the sky. Swinging his legs over the edge of the built-in sleep ledge, he sat, palms pressed over his eyes, heart pounding. At this possible danger or at the dream, he couldn't judge.

With an anxious chirp, Sylvan glided to his shoulder, nibbled his ear. Dropping his hands, Chance watched them shake, cursed himself, his fears, the cowardice chilling his body, the same sensations that now incapacitated him just thinking of boarding cruiser or a long-haul spacer. He punched unsteadily at buttons, flipped on the comm system. See if he'd hear the straight skinny or if he'd have to Web-link to learn what the alarm truly represented. No satellite wanted to frighten its populace—not since the mad stampede on CurieCousteau years back after the neurotoxin spill.

". . . reports of a small, self-contained fire on the Holm Port Observation Deck, Echo 2° slash 187°. So far no casualties have been reported," and then the smarmy voice faltered before urgently continuing, "Wait! A late-breaking bulletin from our reporter at the scene—a boy, perhaps ten, is dead, apparently not a victim of the fire. Before being ejected by security and flam-techs, Romaine McElderry observed what appeared to be knife wounds to the victim's chest and neck. From his clothing and undernourished appearance, she believes the child was a satrat, although we lack confirmation, I repeat, no confirmation of this." His voice rose with rich-bodied indignation, "And when, viewers, when will our government officials acknowledge the desperate straits in which these children live? What positive actions will they take to ensure their proper status in PabNeruda, in Waggoner's Ring as a whole? Can we afford to let any of our citizens, let alone the youngest, most vulnerable . . ."

Chance switched off the sound, relieved he hadn't keyed the screen. For one irrational moment he'd feared they'd found Glynn's body, that somehow he'd eluded Jere and fled to Holm Port to nurse his wounds. Sylvan chittered again, delicate toes almost as agile as fingers tugging at his hair, locked deep in the tight-wound nap. "No, silly, it's not Glynn, he's fine," he reassured the squirrel and himself as well. But the squirrel tugged harder as if to attract his attention, and Chance's ears strained at a faint, uncertain tattoo at the door, scraping sounds reminiscent of Sylvan's claws on plexiplast. At last his private eavesdroppers registered the vibrations, projecting a sound-wave frequency alarm designed to cross the threshold of pain.

Someone breaking in? Who else at four in the morning? Hardly the first time, or the last, that fools would attempt it. Given his unsanctioned repair projects and the often-illicit articles he collected, the security patrols refused to investigate when he was robbed; burglars knew that. Therefore he'd taken matters into his own hands, safeguarded his ship as best he could—and his best was very good, especially with the aid of some of his more unorthodox friends plus a liberal application of baksheesh to the proper authorities, both duly-elected and those who dominated behind the scenes.

Buckling his tool belt around his hips, robe forgotten, Chance stole through the cluttered shop, pipe wrench at the ready. The squirrel perched on his head now, ready to glide to safety. Muting the alarms to a level of mere tooth-grinding annoyance, he flipped on the scancams, adjusted the infrared, and checked the screens. False dawn at the upper edges, pitch-dark below. Strange, indistinct shapes. Cams off, out of focus? A large whitish bowl containing a black, contorted shape like a spider in the middle of its web? Too fanciful by far. Nothing he could identify. And nearly leaped with fright as a blurred face mashed against the right-angle cam, looming so large and awful that he expected it to jump through the screen at him. In case it spied him in return, Chance raised his wrench to threaten, ward it off. He squinted as the features coalesced into a fragment of a familiar face, soot-blackened with meandering white deltas of tear tracks sluicing through the dirt.

"Glynn?" he whispered, "Glynnie-boy, is that you?" Sylvan launched himself from Chance's head and pawed at the audio panel. Of course, no one outside could hear unless he wished to transmit, although every sound outside was relayed within. Cursing the alarm, he reached across Sylvan and shut it down, punched the comm button. He tried again, pitched his voice low, "Glynn?"

"Chance, please!" None of the polished intonations, the artful, balanced delivery that marked Glynn as a performer, just the sick pain and strident terror of a boy at the end of his resources. "Chance, it's Jere, she's hurt, bad! Help me!"

A trickle of sweat ran down Chance's spine. Of all the problems facing him, what now hammered at his consciousness was that he was stark naked—and shriveled with fear. Hardly the way Jere'd expect to see him. Unless—a giddy laugh—he could convince Sylvan to indulge in some concealing redeployment. Not exactly a wee, furry jockstrap, but close. But his laughter withered as quickly as the rest of him had as he swung the bars clear of the door—an old idea made of new, near-indestructible space alloys—and keyed the access code. It dawned on him that he hadn't responded to Glynn as he tapped the final numeric sequence. "Don't worry, Glynn-boy, old Chance can fix most anything."

A dull thud as Glynn rammed the carry cart at the door, the twisted blackened object on the cart almost shucking off; Chance at last made the connection, realized what it was. "Oh, sweet shit!" nearly gagging as he fought not to instinctively grab the beloved body, now more coal-black than his own, from the netted cart and clasp it to him. Still outside in the passageway, Glynn continued shoving at the cart, heaving blindly as if brute force could conquer all. "Wait, laddy-boy," Chance implored and counterthrust as hard as he could, Glynn's feet slipping, sliding back-

ward, a feral growl of anger and betrayal rumbling in
his throat.

"Easy, Glynn, easy." His massive hands, fingers so
delicate despite their size, grasped the sides of the
carry cart and crushed the rigid plexiplast inward, despite the pain. "Now push," he grunted, "we just need
a bit more ease," never wincing as his knuckles blood-
ied the door frame. His hands, his precious, clever
hands, but they were nothing as compared to the thing
in front of him, sheltered beneath his heaving chest,
that charred thing masquerading as a body, a cruel
parody of the lithe poise and grace that had been the
hallmark of the greatest performer Waggoner's
Ring—perhaps the world—had ever seen.

The cart grated clear, jarred hard against Chance's
thighs, Glynn stumbling, skidding beneath it. Finally
tearing his eyes away from the travesty of Jere's
scorched body, Chance flung himself at the door,
slammed it, whanging the bars in place. For a moment
he debated dousing the scancams and eavesdroppers,
but decided not. Best be aware of whatever, whoever
prowled these early-morning hours because something, someone had brought Glynn and Jere to this
pass. Even his own snug little shop promised no safe
haven.

Ghosted with smoke and soot, Glynn clambered up,
arms spread wide across the cart as if yearning to embrace the body he dared not touch. "Is she alive?"
incredulous, Chance stared at the figure, now desperately still and stiff once the jouncing had stopped. A
cautious finger traced the air above a filigreed pattern
imprinted on her body; the intricate gold embroidery
of an over-robe, Glynn's over-robe, melted into her
flesh.

"Barely." To Chance's consternation Glynn now
paced—no, darted would be more accurate—around
the shop as if in frantic search of something. No expression in his eyes, just an inward intentness that left
Chance doubting the boy's sanity.

"Glynn, let's get the med-techs here before it's too

late. I'll call . . ." and Chance stretched for the comm button by the door.

"No, I won't let you!" Amazed, Chance swung around in protest, found himself staring down the barrel of the blunderbuss. Damnation, why had he stayed up late after the performance to reassemble it? A smooth click as Glynn eased back the hammer and flint. "Don't know if I poured in too much powder or not," he noted in a flat, conversational tone. "Don't much care if it explodes and takes us all with it."

"Damn it, boy, you know anything that sparks is utterly forbidden, sure to be punished, get us exiled from the Ring, dumped back on Earth. Do you want that? Do you?" A roar burgeoned deep in his throat but subsided as the smooth, flaring muzzle made brief, cold contact with his chest. "Glynn, you're not making sense. We *have* to get help, we *have* to try!"

Glynn's finger tensed, testing the trigger's resistance. Chance winced, aware to an ounce how much pressure it required. Hadn't he carefully scraped the rust, cleaned and oiled it, polished it? One of his little vanities, collecting firearms from a long ago past, dazzled by their sizes, shapes, embellishments; their balance and heft; the daunting beauty of a utilitarian killing object raised to perfection in the proper hands. "Can't, Chance. No wellness-warranty, no repair fund. You've a pension, long-term spacer coverage. Blow you to bits and they'll patch you together again, mark it 'paid in full.' We don't have that luxury, you know that."

"But . . ." he protested, "Stanislaus Troupe isn't poor, they must have planned against contingencies— oh, nothing like this—but they're no fools. And they know who owes them favors—me, for a starter." Without Jere, he'd have lost his mind after his own accident, his grounding.

"That's why I'm here. We'll get the money somehow, transport her to CurieCousteau to the regeneration tanks. The shuttle costs, too, but again, that doesn't matter. What we *don't* have is time, Chance.

That's what I have to buy—*time*. And I'm wasting second upon precious second arguing with you. That's your first gift to Jere—time. Now get it!"

The dawning came slow to Chance, slower than he liked, but his brain had frozen, appalled. "There's no guarantee! Even if it works, there's no guarantee it'll do what it was designed for, not for any length of time. The regen specialists will need years!"

"Just get it."

Time: Perhaps ten minutes later
Location: Chance's Workshop

"Old Chance can fix most anything." The words hammered his brain at the ludicrousness of it all. His hubris for making such a promise. *"Yes, sir—old Chance can fix . . . can fix . . . almost anything,"* and he wanted to emend, *"that's mechanical."* This, this wasn't mechanical. Chance knelt with the burled maple brain box open beside him, revealing the stainless steel tank, countless packets of ultrafine gold wires and probes still neatly coiled in fresh-seal and laid in ordered ranks beside the box. Balancing the instruction booklet on his thighs, he skimmed it, concentrated on it exactly as he would a circuitry diagram. A sigh.

Knowledge, training was all well and good, but intuition guided him and his kin—always had, always would. Look at something broken and you just "knew" how to fix it. But another's brain was beyond his own intuiting. Didn't know how his worked, let alone someone else's. Sure as hell didn't want to find out. Risking a glance from beneath drooping lids, he stared into the round, unblinking eye of the blunderbuss barrel, still steadily pointed at him. Hoped that Sylvan wouldn't try to explore it.

"Glynn, don't make me do it." Hated his begging tone, heard it as genuine. "Don't know that I can—and even if I can—Jere'd abhor it. Haven't you any respect for her wishes, what she'd want? This is selfishness, lad, pure selfishness." Glynn rocked, humming between clenched teeth, ignoring Chance except for the fact that his knuckle bleached as it tightened on the trigger.

"It's my mother, my *mother*. Do it, Chance!"

Fingers trembling, Chance sought for a relatively unscathed piece of Jere's anatomy, a patch of skin near her left ankle, and felt for a pulse. Weak, very weak, there, then not as his fingers shifted, convinced he'd strayed from the pulse point. Sought and sought again, fingers probing, finally admitting the only thing he now felt was his own pounding blood. No pulse, and that tore it—because if he *could* make it work, it *had* to be done now.

"Clock-watch, Glynnie," he barked, "book says I've got three minutes before brain damage sets in. Oxygen deprivation. Shout when a minute's left." He cracked a vial of steri-seal in each hand, rubbed them together until the antiseptic fluid coated like a supple second skin, then cradled the laz-saw to his breast in a half-salute. With a sob he set to work, choosing the most delicate setting as he skimmed the circumference of Jere's skull, came back to bisect it front to back, working up from where the spinal cord exited, then making a V-cut toward each ear. Scalp wounds were bloody, he knew for a fact, two scars slicing across his close-cropped hair to prove it. But practically no blood oozed from his incisions, proof that her heart no longer pumped. That and that her scalp was so badly singed that most small vessels had been cauterized.

"Jere, I don't know, truly don't know what I'm doing, whether it will work, if you'd want it to work," he apologized. *"Only thing I can hope is that I'm too damned slow, incompetent enough to botch everything."* *"But no chance of that,"* another part of him crowed, *"after all, you're Tinker II Evers II Chance, able to fix anything. The human brain is very like a computer."* *"Liar, it is not!"*

He worked with a deft feverishness, one huge hand balancing Jere's brain and its stem as he severed the final connective fibers, brought it forth in both hands, those huge cocoa-brown hands with their paler palms dwarfing it. Two spheres so remarkably alike, akin to the halves of a walnut, strange fissures and corrugations and folds, Funny, you could cram more material into a tight space by crumpling it. No more than about three pounds. *"Do I hold Jere's essence, perhaps even her very soul in my hands?"* and a wash of awe enveloped him. Was it *this* that made Jere what she was, or something more—something different?

Shaking himself from his reverie, Chance began uncoiling gold wires, teeth sunk in lower lip as he eased each probe home, matching it against the diagram's lines. But unlike a piece of circuitry, no human brain was absolutely, perfectly identical to another. Miss by a width finer than the finest wire and he'd have nothing. Worst of all, Jere'd have nothing. More wires, left and right into the optic nerves. Got it?—maybe. Another cluster for the auricular nerves; a special probe with a Y-split to merge linguistic ability with verbal skills. And finally . . . "Thirty seconds, Chance!" the voice jarred him. "Damn! Told you to sing out when I had a minute left!"

Faster, faster now, sliding the brain into its stainless container, sinking home the master shunt that would carry glucose and chloride compounds, oxygen to nourish the brain. Prime the pump mechanism, program it—a tinny whir and buzz told him it had caught hold. Ah! Could breathe again. Him, that is, not just Jere's brain. Hadn't believed he could hold his breath for three minutes, but suspected he had. Time now, a little more time. Pour in the saline solution, bathing the brain, floating it. Slam the lid, so he never had to look at Jere again, see what he'd done to her. Began connecting wires to the computerized optical, aural, and speech simulator-chips. No, don't switch them on, not yet. Give Jere's brain time to settle down, settle in. No sense spooking himself, or Glynn—or Jere.

"Got it, I think." He rocked back on his heels, conscious again of his body's aches, the long, low shakes quivering through his muscles. Conscious as well of what remained of Jere, the violated skull, fractured, empty; the charred body stiffening. It brought him back to himself. The body. "What do we do with Jere's body, Glynn?" Despised himself for sounding so beseeching, so worried, a penitent on his knees before the boy with a blunderbuss.

The blunderbuss muzzle tilted floorward, Glynn following after it, collapsing bonelessly. A tortured inhalation so deep that Chance thought it swelled Glynn's toes, followed by an equally long, quaking exhalation that shuddered a tear free from the corner of Glynn's eye. Chance's own face was drenched, not just from sweat but from the free-flowing tears he'd ignored. "Just a body now, Chance. Isn't Jere anymore. *That's* Jere," and he pointed at the life-support box. The boy stretched across the floor, hesitantly reached toward the box, humming now, dials activated, readouts flowing across the mini-screens. "Mother, Jere, it's me, Glynn. I'm sorry, but you'll be fine like this, right enough until I get you somewhere, make you whole. I promise you, *promise* it!"

Slumping, he let his fingers caress the wood, stroke it, soothe it. A flooding bitterness in a voice so weary that Chance couldn't imagine how deeply he'd delved to find the strength for words. "No, mustn't let you get caught, Chance. Not with a body, not with practicing medicine without a license." He giggled, screeched the last word again in two high-pitched syllables, "LI-cense!"

Response beyond him, Chance scooped up Jere's body, wincing at the crusted flesh, nearly sickening himself when a giant blister peeled back to reveal red, moist muscles beneath it, oozing moisture. "Laser forge, then. We're halfway to ashes as it is. That should vaporize what's left." Take up the blunderbuss once he'd folded Jere's body inside the forge? Use the gun to blast the brain box to oblivion, then turn it on Glynn and finally upon himself? Reload twice. Debated it, but couldn't bring himself to do it. The instinct for self-preservation is sometimes called cowardice.

Time: No time and all time, rolled into one
Location: Inside Jere's brain

AAAAAAAH! AAAAAAH! NOOO! NO, NOOO!
Millions of neurons, millions upon millions, more
brain cells than there are stars in the universe are
firing, some randomly, some still in sync, struggling to
deduce what has happened. Electrical impulses hammer at the dendrites of each neuron's cell, not unlike
a human hand in shape, some "hands," some neurons
with more or fewer dendrite "fingers" than others.
New impulses shoot from each cell and race down the
long, thin axon which ultimately branches, each
branch transmitting its message to the neighboring
dendrite of anther neuron. And so the message impulses are passed along, like an old-fashioned tele-
phone party line. As the electrical message reaches
the synaptic cleft—the junction between axon and
dendrite—a chemical reaction bridges the gap. Some
dispatches excite, others inhibit the dendrite receiver;
others modulate.

Despite all this synaptic activity, the human brain
is both incredibly slow and incredibly fast. Even in
comparison to the archaic computers of the late twentieth century, its electrical impulses crawl at a snail's
pace. But the difference, the thing that compensates
for this "slowness"—a transmission rate of a mere five
feet per second, occasionally a racing three hundred
feet a second—is this: Computers transmit a single
electrical impulse at a time in a "linear" sequence,
sending it slaloming through each minute Y-junction
that directs the next segment of its passage, Yes/No
or the binary 0/1 choice. The human brain's axons
fire simultaneous synapses, hundreds upon thousands
upon millions at once, transmitting information back
and forth and round about in a way that would blow
the circuitry of any self-respecting computer.

And that is precisely what Jere's brain is doing: sur-
veying the extent of its damage, trying to "comprehend" what has happened, why so very, very many
parts are receiving no response from the body it once

communicated with—voluntary and involuntary muscle responses, senses, sensations. Bereft of so much input, Jere's brain is beginning to discover that a great loss has transpired, but it remains "hopeful," still attempting to map the damage, determine why response is so severely limited.

A question remains: How long before those neurons die, wither and fail, because they no longer have any use, any need for communication, their frantic electrical messages, chemical changes exploding in a void at the other end? How many will survive, how will they regroup themselves? The neurons do not experience hope or fear, do not experience pain, for the brain cannot "feel" its own pain, only the sensations of pain the body relays to it. Pain is information that helps the brain perceive the body's problems, and this information is sorely lacking.

AAAH! AAAH! NOOO! Jere's brain searches for alternative ways to complete its circuits, new combinations, new ensembles of cells. Within this, the essence that is Jere is tentatively returning to cautious self-consciousness, a dawning awareness that something is dreadfully wrong with its "selfhood," though the pieces have not yet meshed . . . and perhaps never will. And is what remains truly Jere or a simulacrum? Same or different? How much loss, how much paring down is necessary to create a new personality, a new identity out of the old? The brain does not know because it's not a question it has ever asked itself before. Indeed, it does not "ask" itself questions in the larger sense, merely questions each neighboring neuron for necessary topical information. For in this case the "whole" is far, far greater than the sum of its parts. But what is the sum, what are the parts?

AAAAH! NOOO! AHHHH! An electrical brainstorm whirls through the gray matter of Jere's brain. Reports from the "front" lines are dire: temporal lobes "hear" nothing, the somatosensory cortex receives no signals of a pounding heart, a churning gut, and so it goes throughout Jere's brain. AAAH! NOOO!

Time: About 5:00 A.M.
Location: Transient Lodging, 3Juliet/Mid, PabNeruda

Beta Masady paced with short, crisp steps, back totally straight, limp forgotten, though her cane maintained a nervous beat the way anxious fingers unconsciously drum a tabletop. Never did the path of her march bring her too near the table with its maple-wood box, or to Glynn and Chance, seated on stools about two meters to the table's left. "To think I'd live to see the day when Stanislaus Troupe . . ." each word pierced needle sharp, at least to Chance's oversensitive nerves, because Glynn half-slumped, oblivious to the turmoil surrounding them, ". . . would be involved in something like this. Beyond the law, beyond ethics, beyond common sense!" Her husband and partner, bet Rigoberto, trailed in her wake, wringing his hands as he towered over the tiny figure.

Pretty, buxom Majvor watched wide-eyed from the sidelines, the flowing partitions of multicolored drapes she strung at each stop to delineate rehearsal and living quarters. She clung against Vijay, one bronzed hand patting hers, the other still clutching the sitar he'd been restringing. They'd been slowly readying themselves for bed when Glynn and Chance had burst in.

Theater people were night owls, and after an ultimate performance, everyone was too keyed up to sleep. Tomorrow—no, today, there'd be no rehearsal. Nearby Staniar struggled to occupy the children—Hassiba and Heike, the Gemmies, Jasper and Jeremy— the children no longer actors, but spectators, an uncomprehending audience for this unfolding tragedy. Majvor felt queasy.

"Do you have *any* idea what you've done?" beta Masady railed at Glynn. "If word leaks out, we're doomed, disbanded, most likely expelled to Earth. They'll split us up, drop us wherever they choose— and the penalty could be worse than that! You had *no* right to do what you did. Chance had no permit to claim the box."

Painfully unfolding from his slump, Glynn picked absently at a burn-hole on his shirt. "I've saved Jere's life. Bought time to make her whole again." With stubborn effort he stood, staring down at Masady. "I saved Mother's life! I saved the life of the greatest actor our world has ever known. Don't you see?" he implored Masady, the rest. "Just as the first Stanislaus saved the young men in his troupe, insisting they hide backstage, dress as women once they turned fifteen to save them from being drafted. He fled to Waggoner's Ring—before it was whole, all the satellites in orbit—because even a new, dangerous world gave more scope for creativity than he'd had in the insanely fractured world he lived in!" He stood straighter, pouring every ounce of authority he could muster into his stance, his voice. "We *have* to get Jere to CurieCousteau now! Right away!"

Masady stubbornly shook her head, and from his new height he realized how thin her hair had become, scalp showing between strands at the crown. "Glynnie-lad, Glynnie-boy," balancing on her cane, she stretched to wipe a smutch of dried blood from his cheekbone, scraped it with a nail to flake it free. He refused to flinch at her touch. "As usual, half-right, half-wrong. Too young to plumb the depths yet, no matter how you try."

He strained away now, disavowing her touch, her words, his mind anxious to understand. "Well, what would *you* have done? What are *you* going to do? Let her die?" He launched each word as if to stone her with reproach.

"I don't know what I'd have done. Not for certain. Sometimes our wants and needs grow greater, more overwhelming than another person's needs. It's *her* fate, *not* yours, I'm concerned about right now." With the cane as a pivot, she swung on Chance. "What happened to Jere's body? Where is it?"

"Gone. Cremated it in the laser forge." Chance stared bleakly at his feet, a terrified apprehension unfolding under Masady's questioning.

"Then how can you regenerate her? There's no viable tissue to work from. Brain cells won't work. Too ultra-specialized." She circled Glynn, dark navy pantaloons, side-buttoned pale-gray overshirt swishing at her knees. "Her fate, not yours . . ." her words faraway, doom-distant, ". . . perhaps yours, perhaps Stanislaus' as well."

Rigoberto and Chance broke in together. "But it *may* be Glynn's fate we're discussing! We don't know—" "Glynn could have been the target, not Jere—" "Enough!" beta Masady yelled, cane thwacking stool for emphasis. The littler Gemmie, Jeremy, began to whimper.

"No, we don't know, do we?" and forced herself closer to the life-support box as if it both attracted and repulsed her.

"Why kill me? There's no reason . . ."

Masady overrode Glynn. "And no reason for it to be Jere, you think. Unless, unless . . ." Rigoberto threw her a sharp glance; Majvor and Vijay, even Staniar suddenly on the alert, poised for something. What? Glynn wondered, what? What did they know?

"It's part of a puzzle. We promised Jerelynn, we took solemn vows to never whisper Glynn's parentage to a living soul." With that she rounded so smoothly on Chance that he nearly toppled off his stool. "And how *you* learned of it—Mr. Fix-it, Mr. Tinker II Evers II Chance—I'd dearly love to know."

Chance didn't bother denying it. "You know *how* I know, and why I've been as bound by my vow as you." He rocked, stool legs stuttering against the floor, "I owe Jere my sanity, at least, if not my life."

"This is how you repay her? Prolong her life, but not her sanity? You mechanical marvel, techno-idiot of the first order!"

But Chance was nothing if not stubborn, a requisite trait for excelling at his long-lost job—there was *always* a way, *had* to be a way to fix things, even if not the normal, by-the-book method. "Don't you think it's time Glynn knew what we're talking about—the little

ones as well, since it'll involve them, like it or not."
He waved his hand at Glynn, then at the children.
"Jere swore you believed the well-being, the *life* of
Stanislaus Troupe, its *heritage,* rests in the children."

Masady glared at having her words tossed back at
her and, for the first time since meeting her, Chance
thought she looked her age—and more—her translu-
cent skin now the color of aged ivory, crazed with fine
wrinkles. Even Jere hadn't been entirely sure of her
age, but had readily admitted Masady was her grand-
mother, not her mother. Great-grandmother wouldn't
surprise him either.

"Then shouldn't we ask the one person with the best
reason for not revealing that secret?" Darting ta-
bleward as she spoke, so fast that no one could release
shock-frozen limbs to stop her, Masady laid her hand on
the box. "Well, let's see if it works, Chance," she
taunted, "let's see if our Jere's inside." Tears streamed
down her wizened face, opaquing the black, sparkling
eyes. "Let's hear what she thinks, because we don't
know if Jere was meant to die—or Glynn was!"

Twisting knobs, glaring at dials, unsure what to acti-
vate, Masady pushed and probed at every button in
sight. "And what if they *were* after Glynn? How did
they find out after all these years? What do we do?"

Why him? What was Masady talking about? Why
Jere, for that matter? Unless they'd mistaken Jere for
him? Mouth agape, brain cycling furiously over those
final moments on the grav platform, Glynn saw himself wrapping Jere in his gold-shot robe, how she'd
tucked his braid across his shoulder. From the rear it
would look no longer than her own. How she'd leaned
against his shoulder and he'd been so proud that he
now stood taller than she. With a muffled sob he threw
himself on the floor, holding his stomach and retching.

Date: 9:00 P.M. 2 February 2158
Location: NetwArk, Texas Republic, Earth
Vitarosa Herrara Weaver hummed as she scooped the
limp toddler from the braided rug where he'd fallen

asleep amidst his toys and tucked him into bed. A two-year-old terror, Algore in no way resembled his namesake, the capable but wooden-visaged forty-fourth President of the United States. Its final president, once the states voted for the demise of the federal government and reconvened as the Confederacy of States—the Untied States of America, as some jokingly called it. Why Rhuven had so admired the man she couldn't fathom, but he'd wanted to name the child for him, so she'd acquiesced. Just as she'd yielded on naming the eight-year-old Artur, an even older name, rich in myth and history. Artur slept, obediently in bed at her first call, as always. She rearranged Algore's covers, patted Artur's shoulder and kissed his brow, and then left their bedroom.

Hamish and Falid should have word by now, and her pulse thrummed with anticipation, left her as giddy as the carefree young woman she'd been when Rhuven had first begun courting her. Hard to think of a Little Sister of Mortality as carefree, but then they had all been younger, blessed with a self-confidence that bordered on arrogance that they, and they alone, knew what was right. Simpler, happier times before she'd assassinated her father and half brothers, before she'd fled to Rhuven for sanctuary.

Hurrying to the family room with its plastic molded chairs, a worn, wood-framed sofa with sagging, faded blue cushions, Vitarosa waltzed to a heady music only she could hear. Yes, revenge was a dish best eaten cold, and she'd savored the anticipation for so long. No, it wouldn't have done to have acted when she'd first heard the rumors, gone off half-cocked. She prided herself on that, always thinking things through, weighing pros against cons, so unlike Rhuven and his impetuous ways. But time was no longer on her side, so she'd subdue it by sheer willpower, just as she had so many things. Except . . . her right hand rose unbidden to touch the lump—a talisman of sorts?

Gathering her crocheting, she waited for the vidscreen to project Falid's and Hamish's features, audio muted so as not to disturb the children. Always tinny, always second-rate, secondhand. Rhuven never balked at spending beyond their means for the latest SenzAround technology to enhance his ability to touch his Web-flock. Was it always necessary to deny one's own for the greater good of others? A vicious stab and twist with the crochet hook.

The free-will donations from the flock had been dwindling; she saw their bottom line daily, did the bookkeeping. Peddling herbal pillows and scented oils and honeys brought in limited money, disappointing given her efforts supervising it all. Widen their market, their distribution? How? A niche market at best, unlikely to entice the megagloms. Loop and twist and hook. When would they, would *she* come first?

Off on a tangent. The moment to savor revenge awaiting her and she'd slipped into worry over money problems again. An upward glance showed her Falid and Hamish waiting patiently in the shabby tan family hall, and she buzzed them in, a finger to her lips cautioning them to speak low. A wondrously clandestine air to this meeting, the fact she'd adroitly cut Becca out, would hear their report firsthand, not filtered through Becca. A twinge of disloyalty—no, not that.

A final chance to stand on her own once again without Becca as her constant, well-intentioned buffer. True, the blackmail notes had shaken her—not their content, but the fact that some faceless being *knew*—had driven her in tears to Becca. Too much to bear as the lump expanded in her breast. She'd ensure the past would not, could not repeat itself, would not let it rob Anyssa of her due. Use Becca?—of course. Falid and Hamish as well. Rhuven, too. This time she'd reach her goal—NetwArk would be Anyssa's someday.

Falid clutched a wine-red velvet fez to his chest, its tassel swaying precariously, his fingers indenting its wool. "The boy's dead," he whispered, his lips tight with shame.

"What, you mean the young man Jerelynn was with when the . . ." she tested the euphemism, "unfortunate accident happened?" If so, she felt badly, but not seriously so. How many times had she viewed that grainy tape segment? The young man had been practically melded to that slut; if he'd died, it was hardly surprising. "Then we'll pray for his soul as well as hers." Yes, pray for the boy's, and pray Jerelynn's soul was condemned to the deepest reaches of hellfire.

Hamish reluctantly spoke when he'd determined Falid would offer nothing further. "I don't know what became of the person with her. Falid's referring to the satrat Becca hired, the boy with the microcam implant in his eye. Throat slit, body in custody before our people could reach him." Despite his usual puddinglike demeanor, he oozed a smarmy deference, eager. "Becca'd arranged to have him removed later, but someone jumped the gun. Not sure who. May simply have been another satrat he'd already crossed. Becca probably told you the microcam couldn't be retrieved."

"A shame. I'd have relished seeing better footage. We *can* confirm Jerelynn's unfortunate demise, can't we?"

"Oh, we'll have secondary confirmation shortly. The newscasts will jump all over it, gossip-flaks in their full, raving glory. From the transmission we saw—had to be. The wound might not have been fatal, but the fire would have been." Hamish placed his hand over hers, almost a little too proprietary, that, she decided. "We've no doubt Jerelynn's dead, just as we faithfully promised Becca. Tell Rhuven we accomplished what we were supposed to."

A faint hissing issued from between Falid's clenched teeth, Hamish's mention of Becca belatedly alerting him that something about this meeting felt false. "Becca's already told you all this, I know. Hamish and I can only confirm her—"

A sharp gesture silenced him as Vitarosa spied Anyssa standing in the darkened doorway from the den. It took her aback to see her daughter like that, the image of Rhuven when he'd been that age, sixteen.

And even at sixteen there had been something delicate, almost effeminate radiating from Rhuven's holopics, as if his love for God had unmanned him. She smiled at the thought; nothing would unman Rhuven. If it had, he'd never have had an affair with Jerelynn while she'd lingered in the depths of postpartum depression after Anyssa's birth. "Anyssa, excuse us. Business,' she commanded, and Falid and Hamish wheeled in shock. A long level look from those honey-gold eyes before she obediently departed, murmuring good night.

Fez dropping to the floor, Falid rung his hands. "How much did she hear? Does she know, suspect? Becca swore we had Rhuven's blessing on this.''

Rubbing a finger across her lips to erase her smile, Vitarosa let the silence lengthen, giving Anyssa time enough to reach her bedroom. "I shouldn't worry, you know. She's the spirit and image of Rhuven for looks, but she's *my* daughter through and through.''

And that was true. Just as coldly implacable, as capable of carrying a grudge as her mother, was Anyssa. Hadn't she trained her so? And if Rosa was tired of playing second fiddle to Rhuven's far-flung, Web-connected congregation, of course Anyssa was, too.

Time: Enjoy yourself, it's later that you think
Location: Inside Jere's brain

The neurons have slowed, steadied somewhat, almost as if clusters of them have set up a command team in the cerebral cortex, assessing the damage reports rolling in with each electrochemical surge, struggling to map the intricacies of survival. Much has *not* survived, clear from the appalling number of electrical messages gone unanswered, axons poised on the void's edge, desperate to communicate, writhing frantically when the message stops cold. Where are the transducers? Where have they gone?

The neuron clusters on the brain's left hemisphere are methodically seeking answers, and each nonresponse tells them that much more. The brain's right side toils as well, intuitively sensing something momentous is taking place, primitive feelings and emotions flooding it, equally potent and accurate at an instinctual level.

And the brain that made—and still makes—Jerelynn what she was, what she now is, continues to suppress Jere's consciousness until it can reconstruct and repair what it can, accept compromises, make itself as whole as possible. Any additional turmoil might dispatch more neurons into the void; the essence that is Jerelynn will abort itself if self-awareness returns too soon. Time is meaningless to the neurons, but time is what they desire, time to mend, heal as much as possible, reroute their circuitry. But time is running short. . . .

Shattering light floods the optic nerves—images race through different levels of brain identification, sorting and sifting to create a recognizable construct. A jumbling rumble of sounds invades the temporal lobes, echoing pops and crackles, high tinny shrieks of sound waves, long, undulating swells. Worst of all, the optical neurons can reach no agreement on the images they futilely piece together, two conflicting, disparate images that resist overlap into one overriding, identifiable shape. Lines and patterns of light refuse to cohere, baffled as they struggle to construct recognizable figures, not merely record them. Color is missing, perspective has vanished.

A jarring sensation. The brain notes it through vibrations that rock and toss the disparate images, further scatter them. The sound waves tell the same story. Battered by this barrage of conflicting external stimuli, Jere's brain begins to "awaken," neurons scrambling to present her with an intelligible world—and failing.

"Jay-ree, canoe ear auzze?" Warbling static warps the deep rhythms from low to piercingly high until they gradually begin to settle in a midrange. "Jay-ree, laav, weer rallear," and the neurons painstakingly filter not just the words ("Jere, can you hear us? Jere, love, we're all here."), but the voice, Chance's voice.

Or what Chance might sound like on a synthesizer. The aural neurons hum: a message to transmit, complete.

But optical neurons still battle each other, refusing to consolidate two disparate world views into one comprehensible pattern. Nothing that one side "sees" matches the information the other side is equally convinced is "right," or "true." Each side fights for dominance; neither is winning. Then, sudden, blessed relief as one side ceases transmitting data. "I blanked out the left opticam, should have thought of that sooner. Don't know why the hell they installed the opticams on opposite sides. We don't see like a bird with an eye on each side of our head. We have both eyes in the front of our faces."

The voice sounds as if it's speaking, explaining, just for the sake of saying something, but the words do give the vision centers a certain relief. This brings understanding: not binocular or stereoptic vision, but two monocular worlds, two separate sides—no wonder they cannot incorporate.

"Jere, can you speak? Think what you want to say, envision the letters' shapes. Form the words in your mind and project them. It takes time, practice, I'm told." The liquid crystal display strip on the front of the brain box continues to glow evenly; no words cross it.

"Ha! Sure you connected everything correctly?" Concentrating, the brain recognizes the high-pitched resonations as beta Masady's. Interesting. "Or that what's left of Jere there inside is truly Jere? Is able to communicate?"

Rapid shushing sounds implode from both sides, two different timbres. "She doesn't know yet, doesn't understand." "Later, we'll explain everything to her later."

But now an achingly familiar voice, despite its distortion, sound waves as familiar as her own heartbeat. For a moment a part of her registers the chill fact that the waves of swishing, thub-dubbing sound that have formed a constant in her life—whether or not she was consciously aware of them—have been silenced. But that half-thought—and its implications—is overridden by the voice. "Mother, Jere, please! I love you, I need you!" A pause, followed by a long, anguished wail, "Mommmmmy! Don't leave me!"

Vertical and horizontal bars begin to form recognizable shapes on the LCD, running from right to left as Jere struggles epochally to form her first coherent word.

"AAAH! AAAH! AAAH! NOOOOOOOOO!"

Date: Near midnight, 2 February 2158
Location: NetwArk, Texas Republic, Earth

Despite the late hour Falid and Hamish strolled the Tranquillity Gardens with its central water lily pond, banks of rigorously trimmed bougainvillea and oleander, spiked at regular intervals by tall palms like feather-duster-capped sentinels. Formal and rigid compared to the riotous acres of flowers and herbs cultivated for income. Though each strove to project the contemplative demeanor that went with the Gardens, neither was successful. Hamish's usually placid, smooth features had tightened and puckered, his lips rolled inward in a rictus meant to pass for a smile. Falid's hands, fingers interlocked and held at waist-level, quivered despite his efforts, nor would the outer corner of his left eye remain still, randomly fluttering as if a moth were trapped under the smooth brown skin.

The few others enjoying the Gardens now hurried in the opposite direction, Able-Bodied Savers and acolytes alike, eager for the evening's final prayers. Nodding greetings as necessary, Falid and Hamish kept their heads studiously downcast, eager to avoid prying eyes. Silence until they reached the artificial falls that backdropped the Gardens. Its water music, tinkles and splashes as the stream cascaded over different ledges, was deemed to soothe worries. "So, have we done rightly—righteously—my old enemy, my old friend?"

Falid's lean fingers unfolded, reclenched themselves in the once-crisp front of Hamish's white shirt.

Clearly the water music wasn't working. Hamish freed himself, trapped Falid's hands in his. "I pray we've done both, my almost-brother, sometime-enemy. We've done as instructed—by our superiors and by Rhuven's and Vitarosa's mouthpiece, Becca."

"Not quite as instructed by Becca, though." A giggle, pure nerves, not humor, exploded like a frightened dove from Falid's throat. "Strange and wondrous are the ways of Allah . . . your God as well." His eye twitched and he freed a hand to restrain the offending muscles, still the movement. "But what of the boy? The *other* boy?"

"The boy is our security for the time being." Hamish knew his partner did not refer to the satrat hired to kill Jerelynn, but to the boy who'd been with her, her son—and Rhuven's son. He should never have told Falid that. "We need some hold over NetwArk. Insurance—or we'll prove as expendable as the actress. We don't want to be expendable, do we, Falid?"

Time, long past time for the muezzins to sing out the evening prayers. Falid yearned to face east, prostrate himself, the old ways restored to their proper place, the charade done. *(In the Name of Allah the Merciful, the Compassionate . . . Guide us on the straight path . . . Not the path of those who have incurred Thy wrath and gone astray.)* Ah, so long since he'd had that luxury, not in the ten years that he'd been planted here as a "willing" convert by his Ayatollah. His "no" was little more than a yearning whisper, a hostage to the present. *(Gone astray . . . gone astray.)*

He knew Hamish's secret yearnings as well, a return to his past, to the beatitudes of his priesthood in Rome, but for Hamish even the old certitudes of faith had been cast down, broken. The election of Jean-Chrétien Aljuwani I—the first black, the first African Pope—elected four years ago made Hamish's position even more precarious. Sent to NetwArk by Aljuwani's predecessor, Hamish's return to serve a new Shepherd would leave him more than vulnerable.

Falid winced. Aljuwani had forced Old Catholicism in a groundbreaking direction, allowing women to be ordained to the priesthood in hopes of staunching the hemorrhage of believers to the upstart Nuevo Catolicos. To counter conservative criticism, he'd ensured that those guided by the holy vows of priesthood, male or female, would not fall prey to temptations of the flesh. Jean-Chrétien had revived his African heritage, decreeing that any ordained to serve the Lord be subject to genital mutilation—the women having their clitorises removed, their labias stitched shut; the men enduring a three-inch vertical slice through the tip of the penis.

Falid's own organs withdrew in sympathy. Allah, at least, was merciful, even if the Ayatollah wasn't, but this brutality went beyond the Ayatollah's Koranic reinterpretations. Hamish had loyally argued that Jean-Chrétien followed the Christian tradition of Origen, who wished to contemplate God without gender issues clouding his worship. Origen, said Hamish, had made a more radical move—self-castration. Either was too much to contemplate, and Falid saw the new fear in his friend's eyes when they talked of returning home—he to Alexandria, Hamish to Rome—someday.

"Better to keep the boy's identity shrouded, if we can, for as long as we need him." The water sounds had awoken a powerful urge to urinate; use his penis as Allah intended, without pain. He jerked his mind back to Hamish's argument. "That revelation could stop Rhuven and NetwArk in its tracks. It's guaranteed to set Vitarosa into a panic too." Hamish stared into Falid's anxious brown eyes, the twitching making him look so vulnerable. This knowledge of their shared bond of deceit formed a compact of trust in each other when distance, time, and politics caused them to doubt their beliefs, their leaders, their very faith.

Ah, who was he?—a man of God, a priest obedient to his Pope, infallible as the Lord? Not one of Rhuven's Web-woven—at least not in his heart of hearts, though he cherished the man's efforts. What was he now—coward? Afraid to suffer for his God when Christ had borne mankind's suffering.

"I think," he hesitated, "when my superior hears this news, he will suggest silence to protect Jerelynn's and Rhuven's son—hold his name secret in his heart, as we say. Protect the boy by leaving him anonymous. Reveal his existence only if NetwArk should ever truly threaten us. If word reached NetwArk's faithful of a woman murdered, that Rhuven had an illegitimate son by the Great—

"Day in the morning!" he exploded, clutching Falid's shoulder and spinning him to face the secluded path that wound down the side of the falls. "We'll be late for prayers if we don't hurry!" Falid's jaw dropped, his teeth flashing whitely against his skin and the gathering dark. Hamish shook him once for good measure, and the man snapped out of it.

"Becca, Anyssa! Forgive us for hurrying off." How Falid recovered his musical lilt so quickly, Hamish didn't know, but blessed his friend's sharp wits. "You'll be forgiven if you slip in late for prayers, but our heads will roll if we're late."

The image was too apt for Hamish's liking, but he saw no point in correcting it. Anyssa, her father's child in looks, yet so much her mother's child in personality—hard to believe that Anyssa could harbor danger behind that innocent façade—but she was danger . . . or could be. He'd been warned time and time again that Vitarosa was a trained Little Sister of Mortality— the assassin arm of the Nuevo Catolicos. Did Anyssa follow her mother's teachings?

Even worse, Becca stood beside her now, Vitarosa's confidante, closest friend, who'd fled Bogota with her when Vitarosa had sought out a younger Rhuven's sanctuary here at NetwArk. No one could fault Becca for lack of sanctity, indeed, she exuded it, but within it lurked a cool, foreboding danger. The previous Pope had warned him clear of her. At first he'd innocently surmised the Pope believed she had fallen from the ways of truth, just as Vitarosa had. True, of course, for neither Old Catholicism or the Nuevo Catolico faith said much good about the other, despite their common ancestry.

Only later had he learned about the Little Sisters, had shivered like a child hearing a horror story on a dark-stormed night. Perhaps it was all a complicated plot, and he'd suspected the Pope of setting Becca in place to watch his movements. Sheer paranoia—she'd lived at NetwArk far longer than he or Falid. And despite himself, day in and day out, he watched for signs, wondered if Becca were completely loyal to Vitarosa.

Watching their receding backs, Becca casually commented, "What did you hear, anything? Your ears are sharper than mine. You were ahead of me on the path."

"Nothing, really, Becca. Wrestling with personal demons, as we all do at times." But Anyssa hoarded the little she'd heard to her heart, the pain of betrayal stabbing her through and through. Father and another woman? A bastard child? Had he truly deceived Mother? Her as well? She examined it this way and that to see if it fit other bits and pieces she knew.

Wondered again who and what she really was in the bitter, blinding light of this new information—Father's child, Mother's child? Was that why she'd been trained as a Little Sister when the past was dead . . . gone? Why did it matter so to her mother, to Becca? Had they anticipated something like this happening? Still, Mother'd created a secret weapon in Anyssa, a secret weapon to save NetwArk, if need should arise. Save it from Father? No! It couldn't be true, why believe Falid and Hamish? Always she'd feared for Father, for NetwArk—the uncaring, outside world rolled over, crushed anyone and anything in its path. If NetwArk truly needed a savior, she'd save Father's reputation, NetwArk's as well. No one, no one to ask! She couldn't broach the subject to Father, to Mother.

Becca? No. Suspend belief, Hamish and Falid were fools!

Date: About 9:00 A.M., 1 February 2158
Location: Transient Lodging, 3Juliet/Mid, PabNeruda

It had been slow going—painful, laborious hours of constant subtle dial adjustments, recalibrations—to improve Jere's vision, hearing, her speech. Worse yet for Jere's nascent understanding, let alone true comprehension of *what* she now was, *where* she now was. Incredulity, disbelief, denial, anger, and more. Chance had talked himself hoarse, explaining in tiny, digestible doses, repeating himself, reinforcing and rewording his statements. From time to time Masady chimed in, reminding Jere of childish escapades, their unceasing love, all proof she still existed, was a part of them. Glynn had begged and pleaded, avowed his love, punctuated by agonizing bouts of crying until Rigoberto and Vijay had forcibly silenced him.

Jere's responses remained labored and limited. "BOX?" A long pause, "BRAIN BOX?" The scrolling letters lacked the subtleties of the human voice, the mutability of facial expressions, but they could imagine them all too clearly. "AAA . . . HAA . . . HAA . . . HA! NOOO!" The next pause stretched unbearably, until at last the letters poured by so fast they could scarcely scan them. "NOT DEAD? NOT? FOOLS, FOOLS, FOOLS! A HALF-LIFE IS NO LIFE! KILL ME, KILL . . . ME! LET ME DIE, PULL THE PLUG!" A shorter pause. "NOT HUMAN, THIS IS NOT HUMANE. I BEG YOU!"

Beta Masady and Glynn dissolved into each other's arms, their tears intermingling. Vijay and Majvor, Staniar sat in a half-circle, the children sprawled in their laps, Hassiba awake and alert, tugging on her lower lip, Heike teary and twitchy, Jasper and Jeremy sleep-glazed but struggling to stay awake.

After clearing his raw throat, Chance rasped yet another explanation of the dynamics, the technology of the life-support module in simple terms. A diminishing hope that repeating it often enough might convince Jere of its superiority over the alternative.

"No, let me." Bet Rigoberto eased Chance aside, thrust a beer stein into his hand. "Stop praising the mechanics. They won't convince her life is worth such a cost. She needs a reason to want to live." Dragging a padded stool in front of the one functioning opticam, he sat, wearily stretched his legs, folded his hands over his round, undershirted paunch. He needed sleep, a shave, longed for them. "Can you focus, Jere? Want me closer? Farther back?"

"BACK." He obediently scraped backward, pausing at intervals until "STOP!" flashed on the screen.

"Known me most of forever, haven't you, Jere? Who risked life and limb to stand between you and beta Masady, your blowups and squabbles? Who made you both see reason, admit to compromise? Though it meant a cold bed for me that night." A long, reminiscing chuckle. "Who argued with Masady for a day and a night that you were a born Stanislaus, not just by blood but by potential talent? Grandchild you might be, but Masady had set her heart on developing real prima donna potential. Remember that spindly redheaded child when she called open auditions?"

Chin tilted, he waited for an answer, but none came. "Sure you do! Girl had the length but no inherent grace. Tripped over her own feet, she did, and Masady swore she'd outgrow it, could be trained to be Stanislaus. Well, she's full-grown now and a fetching thing, but she's broken more props than the Magyar Players can count, not to mention several arms and legs of the fellow players she's accidentally tripped up."

"BET RIGO, LOVE . . . AL . . . WAYS THERE . . . FOR ME. RIGO, RIGO, KILL ME! LET ME DIE!"

"Can't do that right now, can't oblige." He tugged at the absurd little wisp of hair that sprouted beneath his lower lip, his "beard" as he so lovingly called it. "We need you too much. Then, maybe later, we'll see." Glynn screamed a protest, but Rigo eyed Masady until she clapped a hand over the boy's mouth.

"See, we have to figure out who attacked you. Why." He scooted the stool back out but leaned forward, intent on the opticam as if he could see within, into the depths of Jere's brain. "Left you with a brain to think with, at least. An obstinate, intelligent brain, same one that always caused such grief for thinking too hard, too deep. Creating burdens too heavy to carry, but you took them on. No wonder you fled for Earth's greener pastures when you were twenty. Returned finally with a wonderful little surprise package." He let that sink in. "Why am I thinking it might *not* have been *you* the assassin was after?"

"BUT . . . BUT . . . WHY? NOT ME, THEN . . . ? GLYNN? GLYNN! NO, NOT POSSIBLE, NOT AFTER ALL THESE YEARS! DOESN'T KNOW, CAN'T KNOW!"

With a shaky hand, Rigoberto stretched forward, the long sleeve of his nightrobe bunched between his fingers as he dabbed the opticam's nonexistent tears, stroked the wood as if the Jere inside could take comfort from his tender touch. It mattered, he dimly suspected, might make her feel more whole. Or drive home all she lacked. "You borrowed time, Jere, borrowed something else of Earth when you returned. Didn't ask permission, didn't even tell."

"NO, NOT POSSIBLE. OH, SHE MAY KNOW ABOUT THE AFFAIR, BUT EVEN HE DOESN'T KNOW ABOUT. . . . YOU, MAJ, VI, STANI, MASADY, AND CHANCE KNOW, BUT THAT'S ALL."

"Maybe, maybe not. Every contact I checked swore he was an honorable man—for all his religiosity. Never believed he'd name you partner in the affair, but it may have weighed heavy on him, led him to finally confess. A sore burden for a man of his kind."

"THEN SHE'D STRIKE AT ME—NOT GLYNN."

"And if she somehow learned Glynn was the fruit

of that affair? Information travels near-fast as the
speed of light these days. Any trail can be uncovered
with time and effort. What if *he* discovered, wanted
to raise Glynn as his own?"

Glynn broke free from Masady's restraining arms.
"What are you talking about? What?" He whirled,
glaring in turn at Vijay, Majvor, Staniar. "Explain!"
A half-spin and a shaking arm accused Chance,
"You?" swept on to Masady, "Or you? Tell me!
Now!"

"High time he heard the truth, Jere. Everyone else
learned on coming of age, Staniar most recently. Well,
Glynn's of age now."

"NO! YOU SWORE HE'D NEVER LEARN UN-
LESS I CHOSE TO TELL HIM!"

"You may think you know Rhuven, but I know better than anyone else how Vitarosa's mind works! I
should—I watched Rolando and her mother twisting
it from the day she was born, turning her into a sanctified killing machine! Heaven help me for not interfering! Cowardice!" His lower lip hung slack, trembling,
an upraised hand shielding his eyes. "A middle-aged
accountant—sickened by the marriage of religion and
politics—fleeing Earth, deserting his family, his coun-
try! And why?—because I didn't want to witness the
end result! Should have kidnapped little Vitarosa, her
half brothers, brought them all with me. It would have
saved lives."

He sat straighter now, pounding his knee, "Oh,
there was never a stitch of proof that Vitarosa killed
Rolando and Jorge and Leandro before she fled to
NetwArk, but I've never harbored any doubts, any
illusions. To her warped mind, Rhuven would view
Glynn as gift, the eldest male heir, elevate him above
her, above their own children. Just as Rolando did
with her half brothers."

"Who, dammit, who?" Nothing made sense; no one
would answer his questions. Like a fractious child,
Glynn beat at Rigoberto's chest, urgent for answers,
not a cataloging of some stranger's past. But bet Rigo

ignored him, although little breathy sounds of pain escaped his lips. "Who's Rhuven? Who's Vitarosa? Aren't you my father, aren't you?" He'd always assumed so—Rigo, possibly Vijay. Glynn lunged toward the box, fists upraised, wanting to threaten, to hurt in return for his hurt; Chance tripped him, sent him sprawling. Despite the pain from his burns and scrapes, he stayed kneeling, staring at the box. Who was he—*really*? Why was his world crumbling at his feet?

"So let's assume worst case—Vitarosa was after Glynn, not you." Rigoberto continued as if there'd been no interruption, no rain of blows, Masady beside him, rubbing his bruised chest. "How do we buy time? Convince Rhuven there's nothing to fear, if it's him. Or convince Vitarosa she succeeded? Think, Jere, think!" Rigo was not a betting man, but he did believe in a good bluff. "Still want to die now? Condemn Glynn as well?"

"AAAH! DAMNNNN! DAMN THEM ALL! EVEN HERE THERE'S NO ESCAPE FROM THEM!"

"Well? Railing at fate won't help, but a plan might." He clutched Masady's hand, didn't dare look at her. "How can we hide Glynn, protect him? Maybe we can sort this out, counteract any threat they pose."

Chance's brain churned, assembling facts, discarding surmises, desperate to divine Rigoberto's goal, where he was leading Jere. Surmises, though, ran in abundant supply. Funny, he'd never thought much of the old man, considered him slightly ineffectual, indecisive, despite his meticulous handling of the troupe: its scheduling, its travels, its productions, the million-and-one details demanded of a producer/director/accompanist/costumer, plus their most dispassionate critic. A shock to learn Rigo hadn't been a Stanislaus forever. Clearly he must have a plan, or he wouldn't press Jere so, forcing her to participate in its outcome. Strange therapy, but it might work.

"HIDE IN PLAIN SIGHT. SIMPLE! GLYNN'S

ACTING CAREER IS OVER, HE'S SUPPOSED
TO WORK BACKSTAGE NOW. THE GREAT
LYNN WILL NEVER ACT AGAIN, NOT LIKE
THIS. BUT THERE'S ALWAYS RESURREC-
TION—WOULDN'T RHUVEN BE PROUD OF
ME? GLYNN TRANSFIGURED AS THE GREAT
LYNN. A TWIST ON STANISLAUS TRADI-
TION—IS THAT WHAT YOU WANT ME TO
SAY?"

"Yes, darling. That's my Jere!"

Time: A half hour later
Location: Transient Lodging
Still tremulous with shock, her disciplined body dis-
obedient, jerkily clumsy, Majvor struggled to herd the
children to bed, mind stuttering in a thousand directions. No wonder her body didn't know what she
wanted of it. Taking advantage of that, the Gemmies
exploded with destructive energy, acutely aware something momentous had happened, though not entirely
sure what. Shrill giggles and nervous, rolling eyes, wavering grins that veered and cracked, Jasper and Jeremy egged each other on, daring the other to
approach the . . . the . . . She bit her lip, the soft,
inner flesh. Didn't want to think it, let alone say it.
The box. Jere.

"Leave it alone!" Vijay commanded Jeremy, making her wince at his reference to "it." Dragging both
boys toward the sleeping area, he caught her eye,
shrugged as best he could, winged brows drawing
down as his mistake registered.

"Is it really Jere, Mama?" Heike, her little blonde
treasure, slipped an arm around her waist, buried her
face in Majvor's side. No need to look, to *see* the box.
Majvor longed to do the same. "Really inside there?"

"Yes, now go to bed. I'll explain later, but things
will be all right, love. Jere'll be fine." Prying Heike
free, she boosted her along. "Help distract Jeremy,
sweetie, before Papa paddles him."

Hassiba's face, so like her father's, Vijay's, was sol-

emn; clearly momentous thoughts chased behind her
wide brow. "I'll take Jasper. He needs sitting on." A
sigh, exasperated, as if she were many years older.
"You know what children are like."

With effort and soothing words, they finally settled
the children with meaningless sounds of reassurance,
generalities.

Finally Majvor sank on their sleeping mat while
Vijay handed her a cup of jasmine tea, settled beside
her, blessedly near. Real flesh and blood—and hers.
"Carrot loaf?" he pushed the plate at her. "Eat, Maj.
No one had dinner . . . breakfast, whatever we were
supposed to have. Things are brighter when your
stomach's full."

They were accustomed to whispering around the
children. Few of their rented spaces boasted separate
rooms, so all made do with the demarcations of drapes
hung from pipes. Considerate, averted glances under-
scored private areas. Amazing how people could live
together so intimately, yet maintain a sense of
seclusion.

She picked at the carrot cake, broke a corner
smaller and smaller before reluctantly raising a bite to
her lips. An orangy-pink shred caught her eye—carrot?
Desiccated shrimp? Whichever, the scent revolted her
and she tossed it back, shook her head in tight negation. "Jere loved carrot cake." And started, at last, to
weep in silent anguish. "Jere, Jere, how can we manage without you, what are we going to do?" Bending
forward, she buried herself in her blonde hair, another
curtain of privacy. "Oh, Vijay, she was *so* wonderful,
everything I'm not! I worshiped her! Wanted to be
like her in every way!"

"You're more than enough," Vijay consoled as he
pulled her close to bury his face in her hair. "I married
you, not her. You're all I ever wanted, more than I
ever dreamed I deserved."

"I can't take over Jere's roles. Beta Masady can
handle some, but she's too old to act full-time now. I

can't do it, I don't have what Jere had, we're not the
same. We had the same father, but it wasn't enough!"

"What do you think about Glynn taking Jere's
roles?" Vijay projected neutral, polite curiosity. At a
fresh sob from Majvor he continued. "It's not a bad
idea. It just might work." He rushed ahead, "Keep
Stanislaus in business and Glynn safe."

Indignant, Majvor reared up, shoved damp hair from
her face. "And break tradition? How could you?"

"I don't know if we broke tradition, but we broke
something when Glynn rescued Jere and put her in
that life-support box. Like breaking a taboo, turning
things topsy-turvy, making us think the unthinkable.
Given that, breaking Stanislaus tradition by allowing
Glynn back onstage is minor."

"Do you think it was right . . . what he did? Do
you think . . . Jere can be content like that? Is she
still Jere?" Her hand ran down Vijay's lean, muscular
thigh, yet didn't seem to feel it. He sighed, she was
somewhere else again. "Unnatural to have both arms
and legs amputated . . . that would be unspeakable
horror to any Stanislaus, but this?"

Jeremy whimpered sleepily, and Vijay whispered
apologies, disengaged himself to move lithely to the
boy's sleep ledge where it extruded from the wall. He
tucked an errant arm back in, tugged the sheeting
close as he bent to kiss the moist cheek.

"We could leave, run away from it all. Go back to
Earth, even. Start our own troupe." He refolded himself beside her, face studiously averted, but she registered the wistful hope in his tone. No, perhaps he was
testing her, wanting her to reach deep inside and think
for herself. Not easy—or necessary—when she surrounded herself with strong-willed people ready daily
to make her decisions for her—Vijay, Masady . . .
even, Jere.

"How can you say that?" She rebuked without conscious thought, a rightness from her very soul as she
challenged Vijay. "Stanislaus stays together."

His low chuckle finally tapered off. "So, when things

are most unnatural, we have to act natural. If we learn to accept Jere for what she is, the children will accept her as well." He held up a restraining hand as he pondered that, began anew. "Maybe it's the other way round. If the children can accept her for what she is, perhaps we'll be able to."

But Majvor, truly engaged by thinking on her own, uncovered a new concern. "It's Glynn I'm worried about. Jere's his whole universe. He's always been everyone's pet, even more so when we admitted Staniar would never be top-notch Stanislaus material. But what he did was so selfish, like snaring a wild bird, caging it." Selfishness was a foreign concept to Majvor.

Vijay rocked her as he'd rocked their children through the years. "Think you could sleep now? You have to try. Things will look better tomorrow."

"I doubt it." A sudden, puckish pout as she stifled a giggle. "It's still going to look like a box, you know."

He grinned at her joke, gave her a quick kiss. "That's my girl!" Rising, he began to strip off his overshirt. "Staniar? Are you coming to bed?" Shirt dangling from his hand, he walked to the far wall where Staniar sat, unmoving, laid a hand on his head, fingering the narrow braid. Should have cut it off four years ago—no need now for short hair. Staniar would never wear a mask again, not even with the tradition broken.

Staniar shrugged off his hand, continued staring at the box from a safe distance, mesmerized by it. "Poor Jere!" Vijay muttered, simply to say something.

"Poor us!" Staniar moaned.

Time: A few minutes later
Location: The same

Glynn burrowed behind the hanging, trailing costumes, one impatient arm thrusting them aside, the other clutching the life-support box to his ribs, careful to hold it level. Chance swore it truly didn't matter; the internal tank gyroed automatically, but he didn't want to frighten her, turn her new world upside down.

Maybe it didn't matter and Jere thought she floated in Z-grav again. And maybe it did. Shouldering aside two trunks, he crouched between them, used his feet to further separate them until he'd shaped a little cavern—snug, dark, hidden—just as he'd done as a child when he needed a place to escape, be alone and think.

Safe from prying eyes, Staniar's and everyone else's. Eyes closed, he inhaled the scents, soaps and cleaning solutions, the faint residue of years of sweat, each intimately known, even those long gone. Color and texture surrounded him as well, equally evocative within his imagination: aquamarine, malachite, scarlet madder, copen blue and aubergine, saffron, ebony and ivory; satins, brocades, velvets and silks, faux fur, plush and down. No, no drowning in sensation, he was supposed to be thinking, thinking.

Besides—tonight, this morning, whatever it was— he no longer belonged with the children, Hassiba, the Gemmies, Heike, not since his ultimate performance. Nor was he ready to share the communal adult sleeping arrangements. Thinking was what he'd come for, and thinking was what he needed to do, *had* to do. He shifted the box from lap to thighs, the LCD's faint glow reflecting off his face, his chest within his cavern. Strange, it glowed blue as her eyes, that alien blue he recognized yet couldn't name. No characters scrolled across the LCD, Jere silent as well.

Never had he wasted much thought about his father—had presumed he knew who he was. Either Rigo or Vijay were suitable, had acted in that role. Acted? Had they been acting, pretending all these years? What mattered above and beyond parentage was being part of a loving whole, an extended family, Stanislaus. Jere was his mother, not Majvor, all soft-curved giggles—that he was sure of, he'd inherited Jere's coloring, her uncanny acting skills. Oh, sometimes children were contracted for from outside the troupe, like the Gemmies had been, three years apart, out-acquired at an early age to avoid inbreeding. Even older adults, usually male, were recruited to fill a gap in the backstage crew, but they usually possessed some theatrical talents, even if not the rigorous training Stanislaus demanded of its members. A jolt that bet Rigo hadn't always been Stanislaus.

That confessional conversation between Jere and bet Rigo? Confusing, oblique enough to make his head explode. What their hesitation steps, their circling dance had unveiled was that Rhuven Fisher Weaver was his father. A man with millions of faithful followers, a man most satellite-citizens found faintly absurd, if not downright amusing, for his "healing" touch. Oh, he'd read the flimsies, skimmed the Web for fun, was as skeptical as every other satelliter about religion in general. He ran a finger across the LCD strip.

What had Chance said later?—that at first he'd speculated, partly because of his full name, Glynn Webster Stanislaus, and partly because some of his gestures, expressions, seemed so foreign yet familiar on a face stamped with Jere's looks. But he hadn't known for sure until Jere had admitted it to him. Webster, Chance had explained, was an old word—meant the same as Weaver. Given Rhuven's Web-preaching, a subtle way for Jere to denote the kinship. Chance had flirted with Rhuven's Web-preachings when he'd first gone on the disabled list, listening for hope, a message, that he'd never quite found. His "cure," the message of his self-worth, his still-viable talents arose from his friendship with Jere, not the long-distance laying on of hands that Rhuven offered. No matter what had been implied, Glynn thought Rhuven Fisher Weaver sounded a good man, though misguided.

But what to make of Vitarosa, Rhuven's wife? Why could she possibly want him dead, want Jere dead? Why such hatred, such a desire to humiliate and crush, when they lived so far distant, powerless to hurt Vitarosa? Ice spread from the pit of his stomach, cramped him over the life-support box. *"Oh, Mother, oh, Jere! Did I do wrong, did I?"* The words warred in his head. *"I won't let her kill you, I won't! How could anyone*

want you dead? Is she that powerful, is he?" Refused
to say "Father." *"What's happening on Earth, at that
place called NetwArk? Maybe I'll understand later,
maybe it will mean something. Could Rhuven and his
NetwArk threaten the Pope and the Ayatollah? And
why should we care here on the satellites? Let them
squabble amongst themselves, just as always."* His head
ached, he wanted sleep so badly.

Yet a part of him bubbled with elation, yearning to
caper joyously despite every horrible, confusing,
frightening thing that had crushed his world this day.
He could still act! Not be relegated behind the scenes
with Staniar—bet Staniar, he corrected himself
wryly—and bet Vijay and bet Rigo. An awesome challenge—to assume his mother's roles! A man pretending to be a woman pretending to be a man
onstage. Think of the complexities, the subtleties he
must learn to evoke!

The box's weight on his thighs, its edges impressing
grooves in his bare legs, silently reproached his heedless pleasure, reminded him why he could still act.
Only because of *this,* and because Jere had promised
to live, remain sentient—at least until they could ensure his safety, determine the dangers. Choking now,
mucus flooding his throat, filling his nose, eyes swelling shut. He howled, mouth wide with anguish, just
the breath of a sound escaping, so much like Jere's
first words. "Aaah! Aaah! No!"

The LCD flickered to life, letters forming, not words
so much as nonsense syllables. AA-AAH—AA, AA-
AAH-UM, AA-AAH-AA—AA, AAH-UUM-UM,
UM, UM, UM, UM, AA-AAH, AA-AA-AH-AAH-
AH-UUUM. Curiously comforting, as if he remembered it from old. No rise or fall to the syllables, no
cadence, but he gradually recognized it and was lulled
to sleep at last.

ACT TWO

ACT TWO

Date: Afternoon, 3 February 2158
Location: NetwArk, Texas Republic, Earth

Sleek chromes, silvery ice-blues—from a super alloy she could never remember—stark whites and matte blacks made up NetwArk's "heart," its Comm Center, exactly as she'd envisioned it before the renovations had ever begun. They'd gathered around a round white table, at its center, an incongruous burst of scarlet—roses in a clear crystal vase. She'd complimented Leslie, only to be indignantly informed they were Walter's "pets."

Vitarosa didn't mind the semi-silence as Abel and Walter and Leslie, NetwArk's finest communications specialists, mumbled to themselves, each pointing and waving at diagrams on their personal computer screens. Leslie and Walter hunched in muted argument, backs half-turned to her. Muscular, tanned, handsome as a holovid star, Walter's mere presence overwhelmed Leslie, waiflike in oversized, hand-me-down clothes. Leslie's mind, however, easily outpaced Walter's.

Stretching, Vitarosa tousled her hair with both hands, shook it back, couldn't restrain an impish delight at Becca's stolid discomfort. The heated discussion had flown totally beyond her range of limited expertise, though Becca continued to direct it. If you desired an intelligible, intelligent answer—plainspoken in words of mostly one syllable—Becca would pry it out of them. And in the process make the specialists redesign, refine their ideas.

Yes, this was NetwArk's heart, responsible for sending Rhuven's Web-messages on the Internet, the Senz-Around synthesizer in pride of place, not much larger than a weekender suitcase. Connected to it, a variety of keyboards and monitors for input and "value" gauges to measure and track twenty different facets of Rhuven's transmitted image and message to his far-flung faithful. It convinced viewers that Rhuven spoke directly to each of them, reached out to heal each soul as if the invalid knelt before him. In turn, their images were beamed to NetwArk, identified and filed to create the tithing list they used. Not to mention the marketing lists. Increase the viewer base and the list increased—and so would the money. A start, but hardly the only way to raise funds. The blackmail notes had bled their reserves to nothing. Donations, pillow sales, were slow and effortful compared to the income generated; her one call to MabasutaGenDy had garnered a hundred times that from their petty cash fund.

Strange, she felt tired, almost "let down," just as it came time to forge ahead. Abel growled at Becca, hit his head with the heel of his hand, took a deep breath, and rephrased whatever he'd said. Somehow she'd thought the sense of elation, almost of repletion she'd felt last night on learning of Jere's death would be longer lasting. An anodyne to her soul's hurts, if not to the growth within her. Mostly she was angry at having made so much of the blackmail notes, of losing her control. Somehow, the notes had been a slap in the face, a reminder that yet again there were some things she couldn't control. Just when she'd been forced to confront how limited, finite, her life was, with so much to do still remaining undone. Yes, she'd leave her children, especially Anyssa, a legacy her parents had never bequeathed to her.

Somehow Waggoner's Ring—untouchable, distant—had come to symbolize the unattainable things of her life. When or how it had happened, she didn't bother to judge, simply knew. For once she'd attain what *she* truly wanted! Make Rhuven literally reach for the stars, bring the Ring under his sway, something no other megaglom or religion had ever accomplished. With that, the money would pour in and NetwArk would truly fulfill its (her, truth be known) dreams, a force to be reckoned with out of all the religious sects, all the megagloms tripping over each other to partner them. Let Rhuven guide the religious drivel, and she'd direct the rest! Control something worth controlling, something capable of making a major difference in the world, just as the Little Sisters made a difference through parts of the South Americas.

She heard Becca emphasize, "We want to beam stronger, farther, than we ever have before. We'll have to boost our signal. Is that simple enough for you?" Crusty old Abel—superfluous now with the modern equipment, but a genius at eking the most from obsolete models—snapped back, "With money, anything's possible."

"You mean faith isn't enough?" Becca let her sarcasm show.

"Let's not squabble," Vitarosa interjected. "Abel, I assure you we'll find the money for the fees. Don't let that be a stumbling block."

Just then Rhuven walked in, a blink of surprise at discovering some sort of meeting taking place. Hardly surprising, he was always abstracted, fidgety before broadcast time, his sermon building and shaping itself in his head. "No trouble, I hope?" Bending, he kissed Rosa on the forehead, turned to pat the SenzAround as one would an overbred pet. It *was* high-strung, so to speak, requiring painstaking calibrations and readjustments to remain in peak running order. For a few moments one memorable night, congregants had sworn Rhuven had been cloned, a shadow double beside him. One woman had sworn Rhuven'd accidentally blacked her eye when stretching out a healing hand, the first hand swatting her, the second identical hand halting just short as its knuckles lovingly brushed her temple.

Plucking a rose from the vase, she went to his side, tucked his arm in hers. With his free hand he took the rose from her and slipped it behind her ear. "Darling, we need a special message tonight, a very personal one. We must reach out to all those who are so far away and lost to God's word. Tonight I want you to embrace the satellites with your healing love."

"Is it really time, Rosa? We've talked, I know—but now?" He leaned toward her, his breath ruffling the rose. "But with the notes, is it wise?" She saw the anxious look he cast at Becca, wanting yet not wanting to know if she'd solved their problem. Well, if he preferred not to ask, that was his affair. A shiver at that; it had been his affair with Jerelynn so long ago that had remapped their journey to this place in time.

Fiddling with the cuff of his chambray work shirt, she rolled it, smoothed the long, golden hairs on his forearm. "We can't let it stop us. I was wrong to let that stand in the way. 'Behold, you shall call nations that you know not, and nations that you knew not shall run to you, because of the Lord your God, and of the Holy One of Israel, for he has glorified you.' He shivered, as she knew he would, always did when she touched him like that. "Your glory will make it up to me."

His mouth was serious now. "I've made it up to you in every way I could for years. To you and to the Lord." A smile now, "And I'll glory in making it up to you, forever and ever, world without end."

She turned from Rhuven now, still holding his arm. "So, can we do it? Abel? Leslie? Walter?"

Leslie, half hidden behind long, straight sandy hair that always curtained her face, tossed one wing back, and answered dubiously, "Yes, can do." Abel and Walter nodded.

"Well, then, do it," Becca said briskly. "You heard what the lady—and the gentleman—want. Let's do it."

Date: 2 February 2158
Location: Borealis Organic Grill and
Coffee Bar, 5 Lima/Mid, PabNeruda

Hands clasped around a mug of steaming sea foam, Rigoberto concentrated on the tiny table that extruded from the wall like a fungus. Its edges were scalloped and chipped with age, dirt embedded in its "growth" rings; its color the shade of a long dead cadaver—or would be if there were more light. The only thing that made the sea foam palatable was that he'd had the bartender add a tot of whiskey to it on the sly. Otherwise, stewed, brewed kelp wasn't his idea of a drink at any time, let alone six at night. Organic? Ha—wasn't everything they ate organic? Better be!

Head bent, apparently engrossed by the steam, he eyed the few patrons, nursing his privacy as well as his drink. At least this place was "themeless:" no leis and grass skirts, no balalaika music, or rootin'-tootin'-shootin' Wild West. The changing borealis lighting behind the coffee bar glowed unobtrusively, almost pleasantly. Just standard wood-grained plastic wainscoting, durable plaid cushions to soften extruded chairs. A horrid thought struck and he frantically scanned for places bagpipes might be hidden. Naturally he'd worn his charcoal-gray kilt—knee-length, of course, not like those young bucks sometimes wore. His was tasteful, just a touch of the bohemian.

Taking a sip he grimaced, both at the taste and at the fact his guest ran late—any later, the work shift'd change, the bar'd fill up. *Edgy, edgy,* he chided. *Get it out of your system now, you don't know her that well.* Damn Aloysius Tierney for handing the reins to his youngest daughter. He and Wishy went back years; dealing with Wishy-Washy he could handle. As for the daughter, not a clue. He stared, morose, into the sea foam. Why, why did things have to change? Well, changed they had, to something far beyond the ordinary. Even the Greek gods of ancient drama would weep at their plight!

The woman slipped across from him, startling Rigo

so badly he jarred his arm, the sea foam spreading like a tidal wave. He half rose, wiping with his sleeve as he extended his other hand to the woman in the umber skinny-suit. Unappealing color, but well-cut, business professional, not entertainer. "Clea Tierney, my dear, thank you for coming. Please, may I offer something to drink?"

A snub nose sprinkled with freckles twitched, sniffed. Blue eyes innocently forthright, honest, met his own. "Why, exactly what you're having, Rigoberto, but tell them easy on the sea foam." Without expressing surprise, he ordered two more drinks, but, with back safely turned, smiled despite himself; the girl didn't miss a trick. He'd seen Clea perform a few times when younger, hadn't thought much of her abilities, but he began to wonder now if there wasn't acting and *acting*. Managing a troupe required acting skills as well, could require even more subtlety than the stage. Maybe Wishy hadn't chosen foolishly, letting his youngest guide Tierney.

Back with the drinks, he slid into his seat, clinked mugs with Clea. They sipped while the silence lengthened. Not that he didn't know how to begin, but that he feared where the conversation might end. "Clea, I've been remiss. My thanks to you and the whole troupe for letting us stage Glynn's ultimate performance on Pab-Neruda. It's his favorite satellite, and we knew the populace would welcome his final appearance."

With four major theatrical troupes on the eight satellites of Waggoner's Ring, performance schedules were dickered over, worked out to avoid as much competition as possible. True, none of the troupes performed the same pieces, but wisdom dictated not to overwhelm any satellite with a surfeit of entertainment. Tierney Troupe tended toward music hall amusements, raucous singalongs, flirtatious, bawdily suggestive, even salacious lyrics. Orvieto specialized in the operatic repertoire, both Eastern and Western; while the Magyar Players veered between solemn and slapstick: impeccable productions of newly commissioned, often controversial plays alternating with high-spirited acrobatics and juggling acts. The Magyars always struck Rigo as a crew of bipolar personalities, but their matinees delighted children and indulgent parents, while the evening performances drew discerning adult theatergoers.

Graciously Clea nodded, red hair tumbling forward as she sipped her drink. "Well, PabNeruda *is* our site for the month, but anything we can do for Stanislaus, we're happy to—Da's been grateful for your aid many a time. The Ultimate's a bit of a silly custom by our standards, but we appreciate what it means to you." She set the mug down and those forthright blue eyes raked Rigoberto again. "I saw his farewell performance. A shame to lose the boy now that you've lost Jere as well."

The sea foam rushed down the wrong pipe, leaving him choking, wheezing, face red as Clea's hair. She'd risen, begun thumping his back, gradually changing to a rhythmic rubbing to override his spasms. A final gasp and whoop and Rigoberto straightened, eyes bleary, nose adrip. Back in her seat, arms crossed on the table, she regarded him, bright-eyed as only a Tierney could be. "We've some talking to do, Rigo," and for a moment she sounded exactly like her father, Aloysius. "I'll get us another sea foam, but even easier on the foam this time." A wink and she was gone; Rigoberto used the time to pull himself together, blot his chin whisker, wipe his nose, slick back his thinning hair.

"You know, then?" he quizzed her on her return. Did this make it more or less difficult? Clearly she was already aware who held the upper hand in this.

Not quite able to meet his gaze now, she spun her mug in circles on the table. "Some. Not all. Rumors about rumors. You should know—all troupers listen long and hard for anything that touches them, their livelihoods." A shrug.

"What do you know? What's your surmise?" At the least he could dole out information, control what she learned from him.

"Quite an accident, quite a fire the other night." She leaned back and exhaled, popped forward again, intimate. "Even more interesting what caused it— illicit handgun's one guess, real old model with metal-jacketed bullets. Most forget magnesium can spark." Her fingers snapped from her thumbs, miming the sparks. "Either Jere or Glynn's been wounded. Could be both, maybe not. Me, I think Jere was, though I'd not wish that on Stanislaus for anything in the world."

A way to save face? A way to tell the truth, yet obscure it? Haltingly, he began. "Well, Glynn's days of playing female leads are over and—"

"Of course. He's turned fifteen; that's why we abdicated for his farewell performance." Her freckles twitched as she screwed her mouth, clearly exasperated. "Tell me, Rigo, Tierney Troupe can't help if you don't. Wishy'd want me to help, and I will, but I refuse to commit half-blind. Our business is illusion onstage, not behind the scenes."

"Jere's alive—so to speak. If you call the confines of life-support box *living*." His words tumbled herky-jerky, as if he'd commenced the inevitable slide down a long, steep incline with no inkling what awaited at the bottom. "Glynn wasn't hurt—or at least not badly—but he refuses to let Jere go, let her die in peace."

A silent whistle, her face screwed in sympathetic pain. "You want credits, false papers, what? Take her to Huang-ti, CurieCousteau, and maybe she'll have a chance. Just ask. Tierney and the other troupes'll go in hock for it." Pulling their tattered schedule out of a pocket, she began to scribble. "Hold a competition—all the troupes together. Battle of the Thespians. Pull out the stops, put on our best shows—a benefit performance for Jere."

Battle of the Thespians? Beardlet quivering with suppressed laughter, Rigo desperately shook his head. "Bless you, but no one's to know about this. Glynn swears CurieCousteau could regenerate Jere's body, but it still wouldn't be her. The new body'd have to relearn all the movements for the stage. No matter how young, how elastic her new body would be, she's too old mentally for it to succeed."

"Wouldn't be bred in the bone any longer? The kinesthetic 'memory' trained into her body would be erased, I'd guess." The enormity of the loss hit Clea. "Having a new body that didn't react as it should, as she's used to . . . that . . . that would be another sort of death, wouldn't it?" Hard to imagine, even harder to comprehend, but that was Stanislaus Troupe for you, with their fetish of body training from infancy on. She backed off, unwilling to grapple with the enormity of Jere's loss, intent on finding the right question, the right offer. "Do you know who tried to kill her, why someone would want her dead?"

"I think so." The coffee bar was filling now with shift change workers, their table slowly hemmed in, but the sound of laughter and raucous talk provided a curtain of privacy. "I think so, but I can't prove it." He leaned closer, clutching Clea's wrist, leaning his head toward hers. "Can't be sure if they wanted Jere—or Glynn—dead."

"Not a crazed fan or some such thing?" A slim hope, but Clea found it more comforting than the alternatives. Discarded the idea before Rigoberto could contradict her. "No, silly. Sorry."

"What I'd ask is that you and Tierney keep your ears open, sift and winnow every piece of gossip, any rumor you hear. Ask Magyar and Orvieto the same favor, tell them as much as you feel necessary. Feed anything back on a regular basis; sooner, if it seems important." The next statement cost him his pride, but pride didn't equate with survival. "And I'd ask each troupe to assign us a player on a rotating basis for bodyguard duties."

Clea's eager nodding tapered off, replaced by round-eyed shock. "Bodyguard duties?"

A bleak smile was Rigo's only concession. "You see, Glynn's going on in Jere's place, acting her roles. We'll say Jere's had an accident but is fine, though very shaken by the experience. If people notice changes in her style, they'll put it down to that. Glynn, of course, is working backstage now, just as he should, staying close to his mother, lending her moral support."

"Can he pull it off?" Clea sparked with professional curiosity.

"I don't know, I hope so." An open-palmed toss as if to cast their fates to the winds. "There'll be some leeway, less criticism if people believe Jere's been injured, may not quite be herself."

May not *quite* be herself! The reality shivered down Clea's spine, the truth of the life-support box finally striking home. The sea foam gave off a noxious smell and her stomach churned, but she pulled herself together. "Fine. Busybodying and bodyguarding. Anything else?"

Rigoberto rose, took Clea's elbow and began working them both through the crowd. "Yes, ask yourself, all of you—especially ask Simoneta Orvieto—what anyone knows about Glynn's parentage? If what you know differs from what the public knows. Simoneta knows every troupe's lineage inside out."

But before Clea could ask why this mattered, he'd grabbed her hand and was dragging her toward the exit. Or rather, sometimes he dragged her, sometimes she bulled her way through a break in the forest of shoulders and legs, tugging him after her. Assign her tasks like that, and she decided he deserved to bob along uselessly behind her. *Oh, Wishy!* she cried, *he was a loyal friend to you, but I'm not sure what he's gotten us into. Well, hell, neither does the audience when a new play begins, but at least they can walk out, short only the credit for the admission.*

Date: Evening, 2 February 2158
Location: Rehearsal Studios, 1Delta/Mid
(Please check at Admin. Office for rental fees and schedule availability.)

Chance wasn't pleased the troupe had ventured from the relative safety of their lodgings, but knew their crucial need for rehearsal time. If they rehearsed, life must be "normal"—whether it truly was or not. He'd crammed his massive body into the right stage wing, the better to watch the rehearsal or—more accurately—who watched the rehearsal. An equally pressing task awaited him. Punching at the keyboard, he waited, jittery, as various signs and symbols appeared, then logged on before he lost his nerve. Despite the red bandanna he'd tied round his forehead—both as a sweatband and as an outward, physical control—a free-floating dread flooded both body and mind.

Before Rigo's meeting with Clea Tierney, Chance had hurried back to his fourth-level shop by the most tangled route he could map to collect what he needed in the way of clothes, equipment, and, of course, the flying squirrel, Sylvan. He'd beat an equally hasty and cautious retreat after setting the long-term alarms.

The only living soul who'd glimpsed him was a satrat pressed beneath the overhang of the trash tubes behind the shop. Scared him half to death, materializing out of nowhere, the sound of her hissed "Shah!" burning his ears before he fully identified who, what the shape was. "Shah!" Shah!" she'd implored, and he'd struggled at his belt for a few of the smaller tokens used for impulse purchases. Holding them out, waiting for her to snatch them from his hand, he'd been shocked at the insult of saliva splattering the top of his sandaled foot. "Nah, *nah,*" her emphasis deliberate, as if speaking to someone with limited brain capacity, "Nix! Shah *nah.*"

The nonsense syllables turned a key in his brain, released an old, forgotten song stored deep inside. Smiling at the memory, at her, he spread his arms, began to chant, "Shah-nah-nah-Nah, Shah-nah-nah-nah-NAH, de-Boom, Shah-nah-nah-Nah, Shah-nah-nah-nah-NAH."

A dubious step back as if he'd lost his mind, expression as darkly severe as her complexion, yet despite that, the satrat's shoulders and hips began to sway, her feet shifting in time as he continued. "Shah-nah-nah-NAH! Nah-nah-nah-nah-NAH," she mimicked, finally shook herself to dislodge the gibberish from her brain. "Not beggin' tokey-tokes, smokey-smokes, just beggin' the gift of an answer."

"To what?" Curiosity struggled with caution within him. No matter how small and pitiful a satrat looked, any and all of them could be lethally dangerous. No sense blaming them, any more than one would blame a wild animal for protecting itself. Some came as stowaways from Earth, either fleeing an untenable life or too damn curious for their own good. The stowaways were few and far between—most children didn't know to select a pressurized cargo hold. Others somehow fell between the cracks of satellite social services— born but unregistered, an automatic nonperson. Baby down the trash chute! Other reasons he didn't dare imagine. He'd only seen five or six in his time, rarely the same ones. But then, when had he ever made a point of looking for them?

On his shoulder Sylvan sat still, balancing on his haunches, obviously unalarmed. "What can I answer for you, Missy, or may I say Madame?" Surprising she was so clean and tidy; somehow he'd expected a feral stink to her. Or did the idea of stink go with slinking?"

She preened and twirled, casting a come-hither look at him over her shoulder. Had he erred, somehow indicated he wanted to seduce her? Nausea gripped him, and sadness that a child should know so much, too much, of sex and death. But her question jarred him back to reality. " 'Tother night, charcoal lady, Glynnie's mum." He kept his expression bland, appalled she should know. "Hopin' you tell me a-okay, alpha-okay—not omega, over-an-out?"

Despite himself, Chance didn't equivocate, offered a wary truth. The body was a child's, but her soul was far older, capable of seeing through deceit. "Not a-okay by a long shot, but not omega either."

A nod, slow and serious. "Better'n I'd 'spected, then. Not fish food, least." A furtive but fully self-satisfied grin played across her face. "Tell Glynnie Panny offed the satrat done it. Fishies got fed after all. Shah!" With that she edged away, finally turned and began skipping down the path like a child. No, more as the child she should have been, Chance told himself. . . .

Sylvan's tiny paws tugged his headband, claws pricking around it and under it, bringing Chance to the here and now, poised at his keyboard, the nearby rehearsal brisk but curiously flat. Who had emotions to spare for the tragic plot of a long-dead play? Lights flashed a familiar rhythm on his computer, Sylvan recognizing the code before he had. With a certain regret he wiped away his final vision of the satrat and concentrated. Tackle the problem a strand at a time, work it, tweak it from there. That's what's crucial now. Let the information, the answers, build, accrue.

Although his fame had faded, no longer celebrated for rocket repairs, a wizard fixing the unfixable, Chance still boasted connections, planned to parley them into whatever protection he could muster for Jere and Glynn. The question: How fast could he finagle his way to the top, to the governor of each satellite? Once they'd vied for his calls, outbid each other for his services on their spacers and shuttles; now it depended on how much they pitied him, or how well they remembered debts owed him. Well, he'd soon see. Flipped a mental coin: SallyRide or YuriGagarin first? His fingers hovered, indecisive.

Sylvan leaped straight down, no attempt to coast, and jammed the icon for Satellite SallyRide. Chance's call code traveled through the ranks of officialdom, and he grinned when the light took a sudden shortcut on the grid. The squirrel's claws scrabbled against the screen, chasing the light. Well, Sylvan had no doubt who owed them the most, as well as who cared for him best.

Ngina Natwalla had been second-in-command of the Shuttle *Lady Madonna* when a carbon monoxide leak had silently and lethally incapacitated half the crew and the captain, leaving Ngina in charge. Woozy, head exploding in pain, Chance had found and sealed the leak. Further, his pretrial testimony had helped Ngina expose the filtration system's shoddy manufacturing, leaving the head of Aris AirPure to hustle Earthside one hop ahead of an arrest warrant. Luckily for Aris AirPure, Earth had no planetary extradition treaty with Waggoner's Ring, although a few of the more reliable nation-states and megagloms did. When the next elections were called, Ngina Natwalla had been elected governor of SallyRide. Insight struck him—Ngina's election had grounded her just as effectively as his disability had grounded him.

"Hello, Chance?" The screen shield pulsed its scrambled image until the security sensors identified her voice pattern and the pattern cleared to reveal Ngina's long skull, the powerful jaw, the facial axis closer to horizontal than vertical. "Chance? That you, truly?" She looked pleased to see him, only a certain tension around her eyes revealed concern at the unexpected call. "Hit the brights, man. You holed up in a closet?" Meaning he was near-invisible, dark skin melding into navy stage curtains drawn in folds behind him. Her own skin was a lighter, almost a tawny shade, the muted gold of a lioness, glowing against the screen. So did the gold bars on her shoulders. He fiddled with the controls, leaned closer to the minicam, pressed his mike firmly against his voice box to transmit every whisper.

"Can't hit the brights, Ngina. Don't want to disturb people."

"Well, rig something, a screen shield. You can fix anything, Chance, can't you?" A flippant eyebrow twitch challenged him.

"Stop teasing. Don't have the time for it." When had he become so sensitive? He stretched at a costume rack, snagged a jade green robe barred with azure, tented it over his head and shoulders, jacked up the light filters. Jere's scent enveloped him. "You like being stuck on one satellite any better than I do? Watching those shuttles and spacers lift off without you? Tell me you don't miss it. Make me *believe* it, girl," goading her when he should be goading himself.

A swallow, her long, golden throat rippling, the thought of flight like sweet water. "Touché. But that's not why you called, Chance, is it—to compare notes on the mental stress of grounding? The Chance I knew never whined or sulked about fate. Just took it on the chin and kept scrambling to figure out a way to fix it."

Beta Masady's cane thumped and he jumped, a big man outlandish beneath his robe-tent. Eying the action on stage, he checked for intruders, shadows that didn't belong. It let him avoid answering Ngina, confessing that the new Chance *did* whine, impotently shake his fist at fate. As Masady's cane struck the cadence, Glynn moving in time to it, he turned again to the screen. "What do you know about Rhuven Fisher Weaver of NetwArk?"

"Ah, the Navigator of NetwArk? The Weaver of the Web? He of the heavenly, honeyed tongue? Senz-Around so all-encompassing, the touch so real that all true believers are healed?" She shrugged. "Thought you knew more than I—heard you tangled in his Web for a bit, poor little fly. No joy there, eh?"

Head high, green eyes level, he refused to shy at her mockery. She did it to everyone, took it equally well. "When you hurt that bad, you'll try anything until reason catches up with you. But that's not why I'm asking, Ngina. What's his position Earthside these days? Web-site hits growing or shrinking? Still innocent of megaglom support? Anyone worried about him there—or here?"

"Funny you should mention that. Why so curious?"

"Don't know if funny's the word I'd use, but I asked first. You plan to answer?"

Full lips pouched, compressing her thoughts, her dark eyes shone wary-bright through the screen. "I tell some of what I know, you'll share in kind?" Without waiting, their word between them too dependable to doubt, she continued. "SatGov meeting tomorrow to discuss this. Neither I nor the other governors or the Ring Council like what we're seeing below. He's gaining power, gaining adherents. Oliver-sudden like. Money beginning to roll in—more than tithing brings, or the sales of his herbal simples." A grimace from Chance—he had one of NetwArk's pillows at the shop. Sylvan hated its scent.

"Rumor, more than a rumor that he's finally sponsored, and it's driving the major megagloms wild, especially MitRock and McBS. Why the Ayatollah should care, I can't imagine, but I can imagine why MitRock might. Weaver still seems just as innocent, just as guilelessly honest and believable as ever, but there's something subtly different in his messages. Those who can translate the religious babbling think he might be getting ready to mount a crusade." She rested chin on hand, thought deeply. "No pragmatism to Weaver, just pure faith, Chance. You must have felt it, even if it didn't do any good. Some can't cope with that. Not sure we can, either."

His low, soundless whistle of amazement ruffled Sylvan's fur. "No, the Pope and the Ayatollah and the rest can't be thrilled by Weaver mounting a crusade. Nor us here on Waggoner's Ring either. A crusade means conquering, gaining converts. Anyone, anything becomes too powerful on Earth, controls all of it or a significant portion of it, they'll reach starward, try to control us. Last thing we need. Hard enough to keep the megagloms at bay."

"Elspeth Marsden Waggoner would be spinning in her grave."

"If they could ever find enough pieces of her," Chance reminded Ngina. "But can we get back to Rhuven—and his crusade? Ngina, did anyone, has anyone ever taken much notice of his wife?"

"Not sure. Wait." A curse followed by a new finger-tapping configuration. "Got it. Files don't have much. Latina blood, doesn't say where she was born. Some German and Italian as well? Devoted mother, bulwark of the faith and her Rhuven, sharp businesswoman with NetwArk's herb farm—blasted fanrags. That's about it. Funny how the old labels stick, isn't it? Just when you think we've progressed beyond the idea of saintly motherhood or ethnic peculiarities up here, those old thinking habits slap you in the face."

Close to losing patience, Chance snapped, "Ngina, a straight answer! Stop the static—buzz, buzz, buzz." A glance from under the draped robe to damper his frustration, check the happenings onstage.

Her chin rose—he recognized the pose—as she stared down her nose at him. "Gave you one—you asked what I knew and I told you." She held herself still and sure, a reminder of her command abilities. "Waiting to see what you're hinting at, love. Toss a card in, unless I'm playing solitaire."

"What would the reaction be if the SatGovernors, the Ring Council discovered Rhuven Fisher Weaver, or NetwArk, had begun assassinating satellite-citizens?"

"Depends, and you damn well know it, Chance. Wouldn't be tolerated under any circumstances, but governmental reaction—and response—would depend. Was it an individual vendetta or part of a more elaborate plot to damage, overthrow the Ring government? Who's the Navigator supposed to have assassinated?"

Ngina's cool rationality made Chance's heart sink. The situation was damn near hopeless. Marginal citizens at best, acting troupes didn't truly "belong" to any one satellite or another, didn't labor for the Ring's common welfare, even poked fun at the government at times. A step above satrats, definitely, but not by much. More fool he to think that Ngina, the other SatGovs, let along the Ring Council could help. A personal feud, hardly a threat to the Ring's autonomy or its economy. Best call it quits, say thanks.

But Ngina didn't appear in any hurry to conclude their conversation. "Chance, are you with Masady Stanislaus' Troupe? I can hear music in the background, not to mention the old diva's cane-thump when she pounds a beat. Sat in on rehearsal once, years ago. Does this have something to do with them?"

"Yes. Someone tried to kill Jerelynn Stanislaus, the Great Lynn, last night. Nearly succeeded—maybe should have. She's brain-boxed."

Ngina's complexion drained to a waxy green and Chance fiddled with the color focus before he recognized it as shock reaction. Not a spacer who didn't abhor the nightmare image of dependency on a life-support box—a bodiless, sensationless captive. "Deep space, I'm sorry! But what," she spoke through clenched teeth, "does that have to do with Rhuven Fisher Weaver?"

"Spacer's Seal?" He invoked the oath belatedly, hated his distrust, his caution. Waited until she flipped an esoteric finger signal. "Might have been after her son, Glynn, instead. Don't know for sure. If so, they can return, try again. Rhuven's Glynn's father, though it's not for public consumption. Given Rhuven's so-called 'purity,' the revelation that he'd fathered a son out of wedlock—indeed, while he was married—might undercut his message. Don't know—doesn't seem enough by our standards, our morals, but some religious folk are different. We're hunting for reasons ourselves."

"So what do you want me to do?"

Truth was, he didn't know. "I'll contact CurieCousteau and NelMandela, can still pull some strings there, I hope. You sound out the other Governors about Rhuven, about his proposed crusade. What it might mean for us. See what they know before you meet. Think about what it might mean for Waggoner's Ring. That's all I ask." Vain hope, that a personal vendetta might be but a prologue to something larger, more complex, something that might endanger the satellites. Problems enough without that. Except that with it, the Ring would support, protect Jere and Glynn.

"Worse comes to worst we could hold Glynn as surety against Weaver's intended crusade. Religious crusades, with or without soldiers, can cause as many casualties as political wars."

"There's that," he agreed heavily. "If it'd protect the boy, protect the Ring from meddling. But there must be a simpler way. Besides, you can't threaten to kill a boy to halt a crusade of words, of beliefs—that's insane!"

"Don't be so melodramatic, Chance. Not kill the boy, just threaten to reveal his parentage to the world at large—our world and Earth. Hate to say it, but it sounds simpler than all this skulduggery, cloaks and daggers. Still, if there's risk to him or the Great Lynn, I'll keep mum." She made a sharp ticking sound, tongue behind front teeth; Sylvan chittered an excited response. "Give him a nut for me, Chance. Maybe we're all being nuts over this, we'll see. Let you know if the meeting produces anything worthwhile." She held up a hand, forestalling him. "And yes, I'll be discreet—Spacer's Seal—won't say more than I have to, and I'll listen first."

Protocol demanded that as his superior, she should sign off first. A slight wave, a half-smile he remembered so well, and she was gone, the screen changing to a colorful kaleidoscopic pattern. He thought her smile remained, floating like the Cheshire cat's.

Time: Simultaneous to the above
Location: Inside Jere's brain

Neurons flicker, ceaselessly transmitting the same damage reports: no heartbeat to regulate, no lung compression or expansion, no circulation. No movement: fingers and toes, arms and legs, eyelids, lips, tongue not only do not respond, they seem to have vanished, as if a body could disappear, melt away like frost under an equatorial sun. But other neurons still refuse to accept the message, and at times Jere feels as if she's been torn in two, suffering a literal pain of loss. She veers between raging anger and total denial, snared by a claustrophobic, smothering sensation, trapped by a hallucination of monstrous proportions, proportions that no longer match her body.

How can her body be gone if she can feel things— a tingling, burning sensation at her right ankle? A heartfelt desire to sneeze? An arm she swears she could raise if she could only decipher the needed commands. But the commands are in a new, uncrackable code at both the conscious and autonomic level. Her vision works—after a fashion—but she still can't reconcile the two disparate images, can't bring them into focus as one. The reason for this she vaguely remembers, knows it's logical. She lets both images exist simultaneously, then concentrates on one, permits the other to float in the background, noticing it only if it scans some difference or danger that flags her attention. Even focusing on one image, her perspective is subtly skewed, distorted. Right now Masady looms larger than Glynn because she stands nearer. The mostly bare stage offers Jere little of comparative value.

Her hearing doesn't fare much better, squeaks and whistles, elongated slurs and blurs of sound, possible to translate by listening hard, reordering the sounds until they form cohesive words. "Dddoughaun swswishhhh yoe—or ipppsss sssoe-ah m-m-muttch!" Masady orders Glynn, and Jere wishes she could help. "Leee-yorisssa m-m-m-aaann. Yoe-er rack-ting-inginga m-m-maann naoaoaow, n-n-not a woem-m-maaaann."

At last, meaning: as if she's learned to decode an archaic yet hauntingly familiar language. "Don't swish your hips so much! Lear is a man. You're acting a man now, not a woman." Ah, they must be rehearsing *King Lear,* with Glynn playing—not Cordelia, his traditional role—Lear himself. Now Glynn must consciously mute the feminine movements he'd built his acting career on, yet not appear to be a man playing a male character. He lacks the utter conviction needed to act as a woman playing a male character, a double-role, a role within a role. Jere does not know who . . .

what . . . she is now. Glynn must be experiencing similar feelings.

Glynn and the others aren't masked, not wearing costumes today, simply rehearsing. The discordant plinks and hums, the sharp warbles, the low thrums that roll over her with the regularity of a pounding headache gradually resolve themselves into the background music that accompanies the scene. Out of the corner of her eye—no, that's not right—in the other image she holds in reserve, Vijay alternates between sitar and drums, Staniar's cheeks puffed as he plays the flute. Rigoberto should be playing the sitar, but Jere can't locate him. Where?

Having satisfactorily solved the mystery of the "music," she switches her attention to her dominant image: Glynn, tense and intent, face and chest bathed with sweat. Even in the abbreviated version of *King Lear* that they present—Stanislaus nowadays lacks the cast members to perform any major play in its entirety—it is a formidable, demanding drama. The regal, self-confident motions of a monarch must yield to the halting, tentative gestures of a blind man, king no more. A man stripped of everything, his kingship, his sight, his daughters—and nearly his sanity.

"Glynn, back on your mark!" Somehow Jere now "hears" Masady without the aching, conscious effort of "translation." Ah, practice *does* make perfect! "More shoulder, more confidence! Less hip swishing." Jere yearns to help, but is unsure. Tries to jump back more than twenty years to when she learned to play Lear. Good to concentrate, delve up memories of the past, not the "now." True, the mask, the padded costume, will help, give him the authority of bulk, alter his center of gravity ever-so-slightly. It struck her— chest, not bosom; chest, not breasts.

The life-support box gives a series of rapid, high-pitched beeps, the LCD blinking blue in the darkness. Everyone wheels in panic, desperate to see if she's all right. Now if she can make the words form; she isn't positive if what she thinks actually appears on the

screen because she can't see it herself. "CHEST,
GLYNN! THRUST IT OUT. NOT THE SUBTLE
FLAUNTING YOU USED TO SHOW YOU
ACTED A WOMAN'S ROLE. PROJECT A
CHEST, BROAD ENOUGH TO DISPLAY THE
MEDALS OF STATE. POWER, A BREADTH OF
AUTHORITY IN THAT CHEST."

Somehow she judges that her instructions—or whatever she may have said—have flayed Glynn's nerves,
his body rigid as stone, stone with rivulets of sweat
seeping down it, eroding it. He does strive to thrust
out his chest, make his still-narrow shoulders carry an
aura of mature power and authority, override Cordelia's delicate dips and subtle curves. Oh, Cordelia
evokes her own quiet power, but it does not resemble
her father's.

Better, yes, marginally better. Masady doesn't contradict Jere's instructions but continues running Glynn
through the acts, transforming him from assured,
prideful king to the wreck of a ruined man. Sometimes
the play's lines reach Jere's brain, sometimes not, but
it doesn't matter, because she knows it all, could recite
it in her sleep. Does she sleep now? She isn't sure.
Yes, if she sleeps, this is all dream. One line makes
her wince, neurons spiking at the irony of it all.

"Might I but live to see thee in my touch, I'd say I
had eyes again,' Glynn spoke, intent on remembering
what came next, the counter lines he'd always head
but had never recited. Masady pushing, pushing, literally and figuratively, manipulating his body this way
and that, poking, prodding, dragging emotions to the
surface, stressing anguish, disintegration, screaming
pain. Not just the intonations of the voice, but the
subtleties of the body, burdened almost beyond recognition by the fates.

Close to the end now, and Glynn's voice deepens,
roughens with an anguish that echoes from the soles
of his feet to the crown of his head.

"Howl, howl, howl, howl! O! You are men of
stones:

Had I your tongue and eyes, I'd use them so
That heaven's vaults should crack. She's gone for
ever!"

"For ever!' he shrieks again as he spins on his heel
and races from the stage. Masady starts after him,
limping, but Jere flashes at her and the older woman
stops short.

"NOT THE BEST CHOICE OF PLAYS."

"No, perhaps not," Masady agrees, uncomfortable,
leaning heavily on her cane. "But name me one where
he won't find some reminder of you, of him, of what's
gone wrong."

Date: Evening, 3 February 2158
Location: NetwArk, Texas Republic, Earth

Anyssa shifted, stylus digging the palette screen.
Sometimes her words bottlenecked, her mind so
flooded by contradictory emotions that she feared
mere words constrained, even deadened such highs
and lows. How could anyone bear such visionary exal-
tations, only to experience crashing despair within seconds? How could mere words represent, replicate such
feelings? She chewed the end of the stylus, stopped.
"Crack the casing and flood the chips with saliva,
young lady," she mimicked Becca, "and you'll short-
circuit yourself and the note-palette."

Instead she switched to rubbing the stylus along her
jawline, contemplated the shifting shadows at her bedroom's perimeter. Why were girls' rooms always
pink?—so childish now. Was it written in the Bible?
Heard in the distance the creak of an oil rig, its repetitious marching in moonlight shadows on her wall—
bending, folding, up-down, up-down. Parts of NetwArk were so old—back to her great-grandfather's
time—that they still ran on petro products, whatever
they could siphon from the near-empty well and refine. Still, its sounds, its distorted moving shape had
conjured up dinosaur nightmares for years. Until one
night her father'd rushed in at her screams, tamed her
fears. "It's not a raptor, Anyssa. Can't you tell by

its shape? Vegetarian, surely a plant-eater, grazing in NetwArk's fields." Yes, another of Father's flock.

Why should words be so hard-found tonight? If anything, it had been another impromptu—and boring— lesson. Ancient history. Ancient family history reassured, the jumble of old family photographs, antique black-and-white prints of Biblical scenes. Some more current and more cheerful—colorful as well—adorned her bedroom walls. Noah's Ark, the animals boarding two by two. But the tangled undercurrents of tonight's history lesson hadn't eased Anyssa's mind. A surreptitious lick on the end of the stylus and she began to write in her diary:

Mother's in one of her moods again. When she's that way, I think of her as Vitarosa, someone other, separate from me, our connection severed. Mother still, and yet no longer mother. Anger, a slow-simmering rage always just beneath the surface. Even more frightening to realize she can be frail, troubled, answers no longer clear. It's happened more and more lately. She always acts certain, so sure. With Father, that uncertainty's part of his charm—makes him so approachable. You feel he hurts and feels, yearns and seeks like every one of his congregation. But sometimes those same hesitations, his fears make me feel superior, turn me into his older sister, not his daughter. I've seen the same look in Mother's eyes—that she, too, is superior, vexed by his childish insecurities.

Anyway, Vitarosa was spinning that damned globe again, the antique one she inherited from her father, the only thing she claimed from his estate, she always insists. It's big, that globe—at least a meter in diameter—and dingy, the oceans' blues overlaid with dirty tan, the different countries' colors faded, almost blending, so you have to strain to trace the boundaries. (Mother swears the globe was old when her father bought it.) She maintains I should recognize *all* the names of the countries on it, or I'm not studying hard enough. Ancient history is right! Practically nothing now exists as the globe shows it, only the basic shapes of the continents, the seas, and oceans.

She spins the globe, jabs with a finger to stop it. If she pierces it, will the seas gush out? Will it deflate? She pierces so many things—hopes, dreams. Reality, she calls it. "Germany, West and East," she snipes. "A fluke, the last real unification before the world split. The Soviet Union, fragmented like a shattered crystal vase into smaller and smaller pieces. Are you listening, Anyssa? Africa—smaller and smaller segments, tribes at each other's throats. No, mind you, no recognition they were all African, a common continent and racial heritage. And what of the United States, Anyssa?" She spins the globe again, slaps it to a stop so the U.S. faces me.

A deep breath. I'm on firmer ground here (a joke), better than explaining China any day. (Three or four men to every woman—no wonder they were desperate for Formosa, as the globe calls it. That's what sticks in my mind about China.) When I was younger, it always frightened me that the globe didn't show NetwArk. As if we'd been scoured off the face of the Earth, because to me NetwArk had existed *forever.* I touch the curve in the Gulf Coast where Galveston's located—for luck—and begin:

"And it came to pass that the people of the United States of America grew concerned by encroaching federalism, feared for their freedoms, and determined to wrest them back—not allow their consolidation in the hands of an all-powerful government, heedless of its peoples' wants and needs. 'Self' became paramount to 'other,' and selfishness caused the divisiveness. At first the various states voted to return to the earlier Articles of Confederation, a loose alliance that was minimally binding." So far I knew I did well, reciting it word-perfect.

"The final disintegration began, though, when the Mashantucket Pequots joined forces with their ancient archenemy, the Mohegans, to purchase the state of Connecticut outright. Other Native American tribes followed suit, buying their home-lands—and more—with the gambling revenues they'd amassed. Emboldened yet frightened by this, militia groups in the Rocky Mountain regions declared their own independence, not with money but with force of arms. Major inner cities were riven by guerrilla warfare, revolutions in the streets, 'have nots' seizing what they declared rightfully theirs from the 'haves.' City and state boundaries collapsed, were constantly redrawn, enclaves growing in the middle of larger enclaves, crowding out others, each supported by people professing similar beliefs, concerns."

I began to falter, because the recitation always gives me nightmares (not that I'd forget it and be punished—and I would be, that was certain) but because of what it *meant*. Everything shattering, nothing secure, stability gone. And *what* would happen to NetwArk, *when* would it happen? *How* would it happen? Nightmares of explosions, of flames and destruction, submission, that wake me up screaming; the ones Papa can't calm. Net-wArk's the gentle, herbivorous dinosaur, ready to be devoured by the meat-eaters—some megaglom or religious faction. Look at the Israelites, the Arabs, their ancient enmity—vanished in a puff of smoke, massive nuclear implosions that smoothed the map, erased thousands of years of history, friend and foe impartially erased. Now the Twelve Tribes are truly doomed to wander, homeless—so many others, too.

The Canadas with its Francophiles, the Nord-Can Inuits, the Maritimes; its Pacific Provinces in alliance with the Eastern Russias. Or the grandfather I'd never known, Mother's father, struggling for peace, democracy, in the Latin Americas, dead so suddenly and so suspiciously that Mother fled for her life, fled here to NetwArk and married Father, bore me and Artur and Algore. Every time Mother speaks about the sundering of the Latin Americas, she begins to cry. That's history as well, though not ancient history.

I *care* about history—my history, mine and NetwArk's. We're so vulnerable; Father's never accepted megaglom money, corporate sponsorship. Religion's not a business, he says. Multinational conglomerates have no boundaries, encroaching over all the globe. Their spheres of influence spread wide, but would never show on a globe, not even a new one. Money taints, but if it would save NetwArk, give Father more scope for his healing, I'd consider the taint, I think. So would Mother, always tired of making ends meet. Even our house is for the greater glory of NetwArk—public rooms lavishly decorated, and our private living quarters shabby.

No wonder Father's grandfather, the televangelist, seized land on Galveston Island, in what had been Texas, called it his Ark, an ark to ride out humanity's storms and hatred. And with him, a handful of the faithful, the Able-Bodied Savers with their laptops, determined to reach out the olive branch of peace, of faith and healing over the Internet, the WorldWideWeb.

God knows, I'd do anything to protect NetwArk, save it from dying. But this I don't say to Mother as her combined history/geography lesson grinds to a close, my eyes red, my lip chewed raw. I know she wants me to say it, pledge it, but I'm stubborn sometimes. Like Mother, I don't enjoy revealing myself. There's so much she hasn't revealed to me. Let her think I've forgotten, chastise me, but the problem is that I remember all too clearly. Her ghosts haunt me as well.

So I asked Mama if she'd ordered a woman killed, anything to distract her, but I didn't ask any more than that. Nothing about the boy that Falid and Hamish whispered about. It is *not* true! I will not let it be so. I have two brothers—Algore and Artur. No more! It's my secret for now. Besides, always save something for later when you bargain with Mother. Papa taught me that. I used to believe he was teasing, but he wasn't.

At first I thought she'd look straight through me, her vision pinning me to the back of my chair. As if I'm a specimen she's examining, one that hasn't met her exacting standards—boring, useless. "So, word's gotten round already . . . interesting. Yes, Anyssa, I did. The person I ordered killed would have hurt your father, destroyed everything he believes in, everything he stands for—destroyed NetwArk as surely as if she ground it to dust beneath her feet. You must believe that. You wouldn't want your father hurt, would you? Or NetwArk?"

And when her eyes fix on me like that, I'd do anything, anything to make it right, change the world if I could. It's when her eyes go distant, faraway, that I'm not sure—like a moment ago. But what else have I trained for all these years? What else than to be my father's righteous sword? Just as Mother and Becca trained to be Little Sisters, instruments of justice. Maybe I'll understand it better tomorrow.

Sliding the stylus under her pillow, Anyssa hit the "save" button on her note-palette. Weeks of labor to devise a foolproof, unbreakable code so no one could tap in, read her thoughts. Or so she hoped. Becca couldn't crack it, but then, Becca's idea of forcing information would be to literally crack the note-palette open, crack it like an egg and spill my thoughts. With a smile at that image, she slipped toward sleep.

Time: After Chance's call.
Location: Rehearsal Studios, 1Delta/Mid

Still intent on the kaleidoscope pattern, as if he could will Ngina's return, know in advance what the Sat-Gov's meeting would reveal, Chance abruptly realized the stage stood silent, empty. Sylvan busily fiddled with the wires and cables connecting his computer to the power jack, his scrabbling overloud. The squirrel enjoyed gnawing at cables, twisting and disconnecting wires, even working his way inside the casing to nest, warm and sheltered.

"Don't you dare. Don't even think it," he warned, stroking the squirrel's underbelly fur as he swung around to see where everyone had gone. Too early for rehearsal to end, but undoubtedly he'd lost track of time while talking with Ngina. The only thing—the only *person,* he corrected himself—still onstage was Jere, the brain box atop a tall prompt stool. His critical look, intense and searching, assessed her vulnerability, alone and in the open until he spied Staniar seated against the far wall, mending costumes, glancing up every now and then, checking, keeping watch.

He walked behind the curtains to Staniar's side. "Best not leave her isolated like that, even though you're watching. Keep her beside you for safety's sake."

The crimson velvet cascaded over Staniar's lap like blood, his needle flashing as he tacked on additional gold braid. "Don't fancy having her that near." He bit the thread close to the fabric, reknotted the remainder, and continued stitching. "Makes me queasy-like. Something abnormal, unnatural 'bout it—her—like that. Damn freakish."

Chance bit off a rebuke, reining in his irritation at the callous response. No, not callous, as much as fearful. And weren't they all fearful of what Jere had become, what she now was? "Hush, she *can* hear, you know." He shifted to stand between Staniar and Jere, block her view, glad he did as Staniar made a face of disgust. "We've got to treat her as normally as we can, if she's going to adapt," he half-whispered, half-mouthed the words.

"Still freakish, downright repulsive." Staniar obstinately repeated. "Hell of a Stanislaus legacy to pass along. Wasn't meant to be like this. Guarding the brat, guarding that!" he jerked his fingers in a warding sign. Fear, yes, but overlaid by a whining, peevish spleen that set Chance's jaw tight.

Jerking Staniar to his feet, Chance shook him, heard a hissing intake of breath as the boy's eyes slitted with hatred. "You're supposed to be a full-grown man, not a child like the Gemmies. It's your legacy, too, Staniar. Next to beta Masady there's more knowledge of Stanislaus crammed in that box than all the rest of you could piece together. You want Stanislaus to stay in business, guard it well. You don't have to love the box, but you'd better be civil to Jere."

Staniar's face crumpled, eyes screwed shut, tears forming. "She was *so* beautiful, *so* talented! I . . . I . . . not like that . . . an . . . abom . . . in . . . ation!" An . . . and . . . Glynn . . . pran . . . cing around the stage . . . pretending to be her!" He pulled free from Chance's now lax grip, resettled his baggy dun work-shirt. "I . . . could . . . do it better! But always *he* gets what *he* wants whether he deserves it or not. *Her,*" he flung impassioned arm, "mewed, up like that! Not what *she'd* want. Or him onstage after his time has passed. Spoiled little brat!" His face flushed with the passion of lost dreams, nose runny and unlovely. The boy—the man, Chance corrected—wept openly now.

A melange of jealousy, envy, adoration, infatuation, panic at a safe, known little world turned upside down. Nothing they all didn't feel. "Go, now," Chance rubbed Staniar's neck, his shoulder, ashamed of his bullying. Staniar was what?—four years older than Glynn? All of nineteen. Still more boy than man. "I'll keep watch. It takes time. With time and perspective you can come to grips with anything." After all, hadn't he? As Staniar dashed toward the stage lockers, scarlet mending streaming behind him, Chance walked stage left where the box—no, Jere—sat in solitary splendor.

The LCD was blinking fast, then slow, pulsing a bright neon blue, then nearly fading dark, but no words scrolled across it. With a sigh he busied himself checking the system, the dials and indicators that monitored battery levels, the pump systems that circulated nutrients and oxygen. Its sophistication left him more awed the longer he studied it, its redundancies and backups designed for utter reliability, continual life-support. Goldberg had been a genius in her way, but an absolute innocent, bereft of the most elemental logic when it came to placing the opticals. Or had she had an eye on each side of her head herself? Probably over each ear, Chance shook his head, glad he stood to the front so that Jere couldn't view his dismay.

The LCD brightened, letters spilling across it. "CHANCE, IS THAT YOU? I CAN'T FEEL YOU, BUT I KNOW YOU'RE THERE . . . SOMEHOW."

"Yes, it's me, Jere." He took a deep breath, exhaled. Did it sound like a heavy wind to her enhanced auricular abilities, unable to filter out the unwanted? "How're you feeling?" He'd braced himself to ask, the one question no one else had dared, for fear of her answer.

"S T R A N G E." The letters came widely spaced as if she'd internally drawled the word. "WHY CAN'T I . . . FEEL . . . ANYTHING? WHY, CHANCE?" More words poured, rushed and cramped now. "CAN'TFEELMYARMS,MYLEGS,CAN'TMOVE-THEM,CAN'TMOVEANYTHING." A halt as she gained a modicum of self-control, though her litany continued. "CAN'T HEAR MY HEART, MY BREATHING, NOTHING! CAN'T SENSE THE BLOOD POUNDING IN MY VEINS! EVERY-THING'S SO EMPTY, GONE! WHY?"

"You know why, Jere. Think." Could he bear repeating the story, bear repeating his complicity?

"STAND WHERE I CAN SEE YOU!" she demanded. "DON'T MAKE ME BELIEVE I'M BLIND AS WELL!"

Shifting to her left, he stepped away three paces and squatted to bring his face level with her "eye." "I'm here, Jere. Not just a disembodied voice. I'm here. Can you see me all right?"

"YES." A pause. "DON'T LIE TO ME, CHANCE. I'M PARALYZED, AREN'T I? THAT MUST BE IT. DID I BREAK MY NECK? THAT'S WHY I CAN'T SENSE ANYTHING ABOUT MY BODY, ISN'T IT?"

He'd hoped, he'd prayed, that she'd absorbed it all, had understood. And perhaps she had at the time, but she'd either willed herself to forget or had embraced denial, rejecting that which was impossible to grasp, believe. "Jere, there was an accident, a fire. Someone wanted you dead, almost succeeded."

"I . . . ? GLYNN? GLYNN WAS THERE . . . BUT GLYNN'S FINE. HAS TO BE, JUST SAW HIM. HELPED HIM, ACTING MY ROLE, YES?"

"Yes." He could not, *could not* force himself to maintain eye contact with the round cold lens, the implacable optical camera more accusing than her eyes. Stared at the floor, twisted uncomfortably to scan the LCD, read what she said. "You're not paralyzed, Jere. You've no body left to be paralyzed. It's gone, burned beyond salvaging."

"GONE?" The intensity of her thought clear from the LCD's frenetic brightness, throbbing, snapping blue like lightning. "GONE? HOW GONE? CAN'T BE GONE! NOT AND ME BE HERE! YES? RIGHT? BODIES CAN'T VANISH, LEAVE YOU HERE TO THINK ABOUT THINGS."

"Jere, ever remember hearing about Goldberg and her life-support system? Her," he choked, squeaked an octave higher as if reliving adolescence, "brain box?"

If it were possible for the brain box to hum and vibrate, practically levitate from the force of Jere's thoughts, Chance suspected it would, but Goldberg had been too competent for that. "BRAIN BOX? BRAIN BOX! NO, NO, NO! PROVE IT, CHANCE, PROVE IT! YOU CAN'T PROVE IT! YOU TREACHEROUS, PERVERTED LIAR, DE-CEIVER! I THOUGHT YOU WERE MY FRIEND, TRUSTED YOU! LYING, LYING, LYING! MON-STROUS NIGHTMARE WORLDS BEYOND THE NIGHTMARE OF BEING PARALYZED! PROVE IT!"

On his knees now, hands clasped against his chest, head downcast, tongue too numb to mumble a prayer, any prayer regardless of belief or disbelief. No comfort from him—or for him. He reared back, eyes still closed, yearning for the stars somewhere above him, somewhere around him outside the layers that made up PabNeruda. Oh, to be flying free among those stars again! Flying through space as he was meant to fly. Tinker II Evers II Chance, the greatest fixer of them all. And look how he'd fixed Jere. No escape for him or for Jere, both snared by his skill.

The final "PROVE IT!" trembled, flashing accusa-tion at him, paling and brightening, brightening and paling.

As he rose, every muscle in his body ached as if he were ancient, older than beta Masady. And in a way, he was at this moment. Shoulders slumped, arms dan-gling, he twisted around, searching for what he needed, afraid he'd find it. Yes, over there beside the costume rack, as he knew it would be. A full-length mirror on a stand, the kind that can be tilted or angled to reflect high or low. Breath steaming the glass, he manhandled it into position in front of one optical. Scouted around, located another, smaller hand mirror propped against a trunk, took it and positioned him-self at right angles to the larger full-length mirror. Damn, wait. Readjust it so it cants slightly toward me but basically faces Jere.

"Can you see, Jere? What do you see?"

"A TALL STOOL. A . . . BOX . . . ON IT.

YOU'RE IN FRONT OF IT, HOLDING A HAND MIRROR."

Chance shifted the larger mirror, repositioned it, walked around the stool and the box until he stood on the opposite side. "Now what do you see?"

"YOU . . . DIRECT IN MY LINE OF VISION, NOT JUST REFLECTED IN THE MIRROR, THOUGH YOU'RE REFLECTED IN IT AS WELL."

"And what's between me and my mirrors?"

"TOLD YOU. THE STOOL, THE BOX."

"Then where are you, where are you looking from that you can see that? Where *are* you, Jere? *Where are you*?" He hammered it home, matched against the hammering in his heart.

"I . . . DON'T . . . DON'T KNOW . . . CAN'T UNDERSTAND. . . . SEEING, BUT CAN'T SEE . . . MYSELF. WHERE AM I? CHANCE, WHERE AM I?"

Balancing the smaller mirror against a jutted thigh, he stretched out an arm, covered her right opticam. "Now what do you see?"

"CAN'T SEE . . . YOU DIRECT. SEE YOU IN THE REFLECTION OF THE DRESSING GLASS. WHAT ARE YOU COVERING . . . ?"

He pulled his hand clear, let her refocus, then recovered her right opticam.

"NO BODY . . . ? NO . . . BODY . . . ? JUST ME . . . IN THE BOX . . . ? BOXED, BRAIN-BOXED? OH, GOD, OH, GOD. AAAAAH! NONONONONOOOOO!"

The LCD dimmed, blanked to opaque black, and nothing he said or did could rouse her again.

Date: 5 February 2158
Location: NetwArk, Texas Republic, Earth

Ah, sanctuary—of a sort. If a musty, shabby storeroom that had once served as the acolytes' change room— long before the Comm Center's expansion and modernization and, he almost hated to say it, decoration to meet Vitarosa's demanding requirements—could be considered a sanctuary. Boxes of papers, stacks of floppy disks (somehow accorded the same awe as printed material, worth saving, if not on hard disk); the remains of a dead plant, broken furniture and obsolete comm equipment crowded the room, relics of bygone days, happier times. Some months ago he'd located it, burrowed his way in, rescued an overstacked easy chair of its burdens of the past, ready to hold him and his burdens of the present.

No true escape, not even here. *Sanctuary,* from the Latin *sanctus,* or sacred. Even the word *relic* throbbed with religious mystery, signified an object of religious veneration. *Sanctuary, relic,* commonplace words to many who ignored or were ignorant of their religious underpinnings. Would that he could be so willfully blind.

A holopic hung crooked on the wall, a younger Rhuven Fisher Weaver, beardless, barely out of adolescence, eager to claim the mantle of responsibility for NetwArk. Banish his late father's fire and brimstone rants, his grandfather's isolationist paranoia, reach out to the world. Arms propped on dusty damask that crushed and tore from the pressure of his elbows, he sighed, buried his head in his hands. Had he truly been that young once, that supremely self-confident? So sure of the good he would bring to people, good works and good words? Turn the holopic to the wall? But the effort of stirring, committing himself, meant action.

Here, briefly, he could indulge himself, be himself, not what others wanted, needed him to be. No, be fair, he wanted it, too—power. Power and riches after years of hardscrabble struggle—within his reach at last. To preach the Word for new worlds to hear, to heal body and soul, cure the afflicted of the universe. "Plenteousness within thy palaces," he rolled the phrase on his tongue. "O pray for the peace of Jerusalem: they shall prosper that love thee. Peace be within thy walls; and plenteousness within thy palaces. For my brethren and companions' sakes: I will wish thee prosperity." (Prayer Book, 1662, 398:12) So his ancestors had prayed, hundreds of years ago on arriving in America.

Pleasant to bask in these dreams, just as he always basked in Rosa's approval, warmed himself on it. Except her warmth could not penetrate this sanctuary, and he felt cold, stripped bare. Wasn't that the whole point in retreating here, to expose himself to himself?

When had things changed? What had turned him so insecure? Doubts gnawing until he wondered if anything physical remained of him, or just an insubstantial spirit who meant to do right, do good? Nothing had been the same since the blackmail notes had begun—and halted, he hoped. But difference did *not* indicate wrongness. After all, the notes had brought Rosa and him closer. But the last few days of constant exhortation toward the satellites as well as his nightly Web-links with his believers, the necessary healings, had drained him. Sometimes he possessed faith in abundance—in himself, his goals—with Vitarosa by his side, adamant in her belief in him and in God's will. She was his rock.

Still, doubt, struggle, was *good,* laudable to wrestle with and conquer. It proved him still a *man,* tortured by doubts and demons, no more exalted than the least of his listeners. Human, fallible, weak. Let none dare say that Rhuven Fisher Weaver's grown arrogant, uncaring, or worse—that he'd elevated himself to God's right hand, all others beneath him, fit only to serve his needs. Humbleness, humility.

Staring blankly at the water-stained ceiling, fingers picking the chair's fraying fabric, he asked, "Am I doing right, O Lord? Do I carry out Your wishes? For years I've striven to bring the Gospel to those in need, to share what You've shared with me in permitting me to see Your light. But," his eyes closed, "is it right to batter them with Your message? To make Your Word not only a mission, but a battering ram to conquer unbelief? Aren't there other righteous creatures who tread a different path to You? Are equally precious in Thy sight? Even those who espouse no God at all? It's right to teach, to proselytize, to pray they'll at last glimpse Your Light in the midst of darkness, that I believe.

"But," up now, pacing the constrained path he'd carved through the debris to the easy chair. "I don't know if You've truly chosen me to save Waggoner's Ring, or if You tempt me. No, no, forgive me. You'd never tempt Your children to sin—within Your embrace I have free will. If I fail, sin, the fault is mine, and You will mourn my fall, forgive my weakness. We need money to spread Your Word—an end result that must surely, for once, justify the means." No, he'd not mention the blackmail or reveal Vitarosa's sin of parricide. God already knew, and Rosa had found peace, had clearly been forgiven.

"There was a woman once," he stared at the picture of his younger self, hands clasped as if to mimic his pose in the holopic, but his face was older, bleaker, devoid of the spiritual ecstasy that had enraptured his younger self. "Born and bred on Waggoner's Ring, though I met her here. As honorable and decent as anyone I've ever met, believer or not. But what I did was not honorable, not moral, and I dragged her down to my level of sinning. Betrayed her, myself, Vitarosa, betrayed You.

"I must believe, I *must*! Not sin again, drag thousands down with me this time!" He groaned, then lifted his voice. "Did Your son not say 'Come, O blessed of my father, inherit the kingdom prepared for you from the foundations of this world.'? Shouldn't Waggoner's Ring be a part of us, the blessed of this world? Yet I sense divisions, house set against house, brother against brother to achieve that goal, despite Rosa's urgings. And most of all, let me not cause division with my wife, my Vitarosa. Two souls as one. Am I obeying your will, O Lord?"

He listened long for an answer, accepting as always that no answer was an answer itself. So he must still struggle, persevere. No obstacles hindered his path; his chosen path was right but arduous. Must be right.

Dusting himself off, he prepared to return to Vitarosa and the children. He felt quietly revived, cautiously optimistic. Had confessed his frailties, his failures and sins, and not been struck down. God was always ready to share his darkest moments. And God's voice would speak to him during tonight's Web-healing. He did not doubt; he would be God's healing conduit. To doubt that gift would doom not just him but the thousands upon thousands who depended on him. No, God would not let him fail at that, would countenance him as His vessel.

Would Vitarosa plead again tonight to send Able-Bodied Savers to the satellites? Waggoner's Ring had canceled all tourist visas, a legitimate excuse to counsel patience. Besides, what if she wanted to send Anyssa, daughter of his heart, to those distant circling spheres? The thought of her absence left a void in his heart. Why did he love all his children so hopelessly, so helplessly? Perhaps because they mirrored his looks, but reflected Vitarosa's internal toughness, a moral certitude he could never match.

"Please don't make me send Anyssa," he prayed, unsure if he begged God or Vitarosa. The thought of the satellites, so far away, so far beyond imagining, a sealed existence between Earth and stars, made him feel as Abraham must have felt on being ordered to sacrifice Isaac. If God ordained that Anyssa must go, he'd accept it as a test of faith. Do what he had to do, what he *must* do—reluctantly, perhaps—to protect his wife, his children, his God. Now was not the time to turn the other cheek to those who might threaten NetwArk.

Time: 6:00 P.M., 5 February 2158 and, over halfway around the world, 9:00 A.M., 6 February, 2158
Location: Megaglom HQs, Tokyo and Paris
Taylor Barham slouched in her middle-manager chair (the exclusive, comfy-mold kind that conformed to her

body), stylus drumming the table's edge. As if the increased distance and staccato beat could hold the News Alert at bay—ha! Despite her propitiatory attempt it scrolled up inexorably from the bottom of her screen. The dull red strobe in the lower right corner flashed a constant reminder it was coded Ultra-Sensitive, meaning that only she and a dozen others (all far higher on the food chain than she) at McBoeingSony headquarters in Tokyo were privileged to receive this information.

The major news organizations worldwide doled out limited details, the usual propaganda supporting their megagloms. And why not?—infotainment was infotainment. ViacomDisneyBertlesmann was the biggest and best at gorging the masses, but what she had clearance to receive contained somewhat more accuracy— she hoped.

"Let's watch the world go by." PfizerRainForest-Glaxo set to market a new, patented antimalarial drug, outstripping its competitors yet again. Soccer-drug war paralyzes PacificoPanama Confederation and MedellinManazales Strip. And on it scrolled, each misfortune someone else's good fortune. Ah . . . Despite reports of a terrorist suicide squad prepared to detonate another nuclear device in the Sinai Wastelands, no bomb has been found. We repeat, there is no bomb in the Gilead region. Found she hummed an old hymn, belatedly realized what had caused it to surface.

So this was Privileged Information? Ha! She'd discover how much "privilege" she had any second now, her body clenched, waiting for the klaxon, the warning to alert her that the Ayatollah wished to communicate. ("Oh, where and oh, where has my Ayatollah gone? . . . He's gone to fight the foe, give all competing religions woe . . .") Oh, not with her precisely, but with McBoeingSony, current primary investor in the great faith of Islam—and whatever petroleum products it still controlled. She squirmed, half-aware her navy uniform jacket had slid off her chair-back.

She'd stripped it off as soon as the News Alert had begun its feed, her windowless, high-security office suddenly airless and hot. Even her sleeveless white body-shirt felt heavy, damp with sweat, so she undid a couple of buttons at the neck.

Years of study, a double masters in mathematics and music history (specialization: Western Music, eighteenth-twentieth centuries) and *this* was her career? What had the megaglom recruiters seen in her that she hadn't seen in herself? Whatever the answer was, she liked it less and less. Five years, five long years as a Surrogate, a handler, the liaison or human conduit between McBoeingSony and whichever religion it currently bankrolled. Because support of a religion—be it the Old Catholic Faith, Islam, Dry Baptists, or some other splinter group or sect—helped McBS (as she privately called it) ensure that no nation, new or old, or any special interest group, could wield more than a tentative power.

After all, religion boasted greater strength of numbers than most national armed forces. A very simple equation. (Oh, good! An equation—her math degree was useful after all.) Such continued destabilization, artfully enhanced by a handful of multinational conglomerates, McBS among them, ensured their power and productivity, their de facto world rule. Well, of Earth, anyway, Taylor scrupulously corrected herself, not Waggoner's Ring. That was their eternal "carrot"—wave it in front of any megaglom's nose and it would gallop after it.

At that moment the klaxon gave its rude blast, almost as if capable of puckering mechanical lips to blow a raspberry at her. Wincing, she spun her molded chair (such lumbar support!), wildly reaching to kill the News Alert, prepare herself for her audience with the Ayatollah. The wall screen began to brighten, its minaret and crescent moon pattern flowing faster, a countdown clicking in the top right corner.

Oh, damn! Her uniform jacket! Bloody damn! A grave insult to greet the Ayatollah with bare arms.

Bad enough she was a woman (well, excuse me!), she had had to be declared an honorary male to continue as Surrogate when McBS's support shifted from the OCF's Pope to the Ayatollah. At least she didn't have to cover her head, veil her face. Eight seconds until direct contact, the Ayatollah eyeing her, she eyeing him, assessing his wants and needs as the cool, collected official representative of McBS. Throwing herself clear of the chair, she grabbed for the jacket, stuffing arms into sleeves, forcing a hand past the snarl where one sleeve had half-turned itself inside out. Scrambling back, she took a breath, steadied her face as the Ayatollah appeared on-screen, hawk brown eyes darting, wheeling, going into a stooping dive to strike at a spot about thirty centimeters below her own eyes. Below?

Akbar Hasan al-Basri's nostrils flared once and his eyes hooded, an appreciative smile tickling the corner of his mouth for a brief second, followed by a tongue tip that barely parted his lips before vanishing. Whatever glacial demeanor she'd projected melted in a volcanic flood of shame as Taylor realized that while she'd modestly covered her arms, the neck of her shirt remained unbuttoned. Males, honorary or not, did not boast her cleavage. Damn, damn it for being female at a moment like this!

Lifting her chin interrogatively, she forced Hasan al-Basri's gaze upward to meet hers. "So, I gather the news has reached you? It surprises me that Your Excellence should find it worth smiling over, but subtle and perspicacious are the ways of Mohammed's most loyal follower." In full view of his offended glare she rebuttoned her shirt. *Little pervert. Someone ought to trim your sails. May your mast break!* That knowing sexuality, that assessing leer had never crossed the Pope's face. Nor was it likely to, given the OCF's new sacraments of service. Damn McBS for switch-hitting just when she'd figured out Jean-Chrétien.

"I shall file a formal protest." A vigorous head toss and she feared he'd dislodge his turban, curious how he'd react if he did. "I must know, has McBS funded that upstart Rhuven Fisher Weaver and his NetwArk? Will you play him off against me and my followers? Allow his crusade to continue or nip it in the bud?"

"McBoeingSony is equally shocked, Your Excellence. We don't yet know which megaglom is financing him, but we *have* received assurances that none of the major players are." An upstart out there? A minor meggie jockeying for power? Or one of the majors using Rhuven as a decoy, a distraction? Anything was possible, but once McBS fixed its sights on it (oh, blast, the man's ego still required currying). . . .

"Assurances are one thing, absolute proof another. Proof is what I wish, what I demand!" He strained forward, face enlarging, dominating and domineering, ready to erupt through the screen. "Rules, sacred honor demand I be treated *justly,* although perhaps that concept eludes a pack of infidels, jackals rolling in their own dung! Rhuven's paltry dreamer's crusade will be as nothing against a jihad by my people, a jihad aimed not at crushing him—and why bother to crush a noisy, irritating fly when one can simply flick him away?" His hand shot forward to spear her, then flicked dismissively. "But a jihad of righteousness against a more worthy enemy, a true infidel like McBoeingSony would reveal Allah's will—not that I harbor any doubt of it."

"May you truly perceive Allah's will, because jihads endanger both sides," Taylor kept her voice neutral, neither appeasing nor condemnatory. "I remind you that Abraham's Holy Land has already been irrevocably lost, turned into a wilderness both to you and the Jews. Are you prepared to sacrifice Mecca as well?"

"Perhaps Rome would suffice as a sacred home for a new, more enduring faith?" he shot back. Predictable, and now Taylor had him in balance again, ready to rage against his old foe, the Pope.

Raised eyebrows acknowledged his wit. "Still, let us compare notes; tell me what you know, what you've heard about Rhuven Fisher Weaver's plans. . . ." Satiate him with hints, innuendoes, and actual facts (she had enough in reserve), while efficiently stripping him and his sources clean. That was why McBS paid her, so now was the time to begin. . . .

More than halfway around the globe in Paris, and almost simultaneously, Owen Pollakowski sat in a similar secured office at MitsubishiRockwell staring at a similar screen, wondering how the dark face beneath the white skullcap could exude such benevolence and gentle restraint while recriminations exploded from its lips. "Most Holy Father," he tried to interrupt, stem the flood of abuse being heaped on his head. No, on the putative "head" of MitRock—if a megaglom could be assumed to have a head, though it boasted innumerable arms to do its bidding.

Nothing to do but to let Jean-Chrétien run down. At first he'd been delighted at MitRock's decision to back the Pope. After all, he'd been raised a Catholic— Old Faith, naturally, not Nuevo Catolico—and surely he shared more in common with the Pope than he had with the Ayatollah. Regardless of that, his first loyalty was to MitRock. But then, he hadn't counted on the old Pope dying, or Jean-Chrétien being elected, the white smoke floating up from the chimney an ironic emblem in retrospect. Even his sainted mother couldn't abide all the new Pope's decrees, not with his sister Marie hell-bent (and he truly meant that word) on the priesthood. Chastity was one thing, ritual mutilation another. He'd sooner put his mother in an early grave, ship Marie to the Nuevo Catolicos, than let her suffer that!

Jean-Chrétien's rapid-fire delivery was running down now, he recognized the signs, the man almost wilting. "Blessed Father, do you truly believe that the Navigator Rhuven Fisher Weaver and his NetwArk represent that pernicious a threat to the Holy See?"

The Shepherd's Crook smashed the floor. "And if he wins Waggoner's Ring to his faith?"

"But, Blessed Father, think." Owen oozed sincerity. "None of the megagloms have succeeded in annexing the Ring, not without destroying themselves through infighting. If there's one thing we've realized, it's that sometimes the status quo is best." As long as MitRock retained the highest status in the status quo.

"Those who dare little gain little. Those who dare greatly gain greatly. Did not Goliath fall against the sling of a David?"

Intrigued, Owen pressed, "Do you truly think, in all your wisdom, that Rhuven Fisher Weaver could be a David?"

"A misguided one to be sure, one who deserves to suffer in the deepest pits of hellfire. Any Protestant is close to being saved—more so than the misguided Jews. May they rest in peace," he added perfunctorily as he made the sign of the cross. "More so than Muslims, or Buddhists, or followers of the Confusions of Confucius. If all Protestants could only see the light— let alone the Nuevo Catolicos—acknowledge Old Catholicism as the sole path of wisdom, *true* salvation, our numbers would surpass those of that simpering, dangerous fool, Hasan al-Basri. Even Mohammed acknowledged a debt to the Son of God, but not Hasan al-Basri." He mopped his brow. "Ah, if Rhuven Fisher Weaver would but turn toward the absolute light, build his church upon the one true rock."

Except that Rhuven's choice of "rock" was a satellite system! Owen waited, patiently stifling his cynicism while he pried what he could from Jean-Chrétien—never would the man tell him anything directly, not if indirection, circumlocution, would do. He needed lessons in exegesis to discover his deeper meaning. And Owen would painstakingly unravel it for MitRock, because the Pope was no fool.

Did he dare call Taylor later, compare notes? Doubtful—in all honesty, he was too bashful, too bridled by MitRock's rules. All Surrogates craved the support of someone who'd also experienced the hellfires of being a Handler. A whip and a chair should be standard issue. Body armor to stop the piercing stabs of hypocritical cant that nearly bled him dry.

Indeed, the longer he worked at this job, the more convinced he was that religion, *nay* religion, brought out the demons in humankind. Still, he was dubious he could cope without believing in *some* Thing, some Greater Being. The megagloms were a secular substitute, but they weren't what he wanted either. They played the various religions like a set of musical water glasses, the level of the water—more accurately, the level of money, support—determined the tone or chime each gave off. Ah, If only he could create—not his own religion—but his own Godhead. The best of the best of all beliefs. One pure tone that all could hear and heed without intervention, intercession by another.

Date: Late evening, 4 February 2158
Location: Transient Lodging, 3Juliet/Mid

Panthat stood perfectly still, listening, slow-glancing the semidarkness. The key to survival as a satrat, a successful satrat—and successful meant alive—was prudence. Prudence and cleanliness, and she was prideful of that as well. In an antiseptic, controlled atmosphere, odors stood out, could reveal one as quickly as an unwary footstep, a revealing shadow. Ruby had taught her that long ago.

Avram benRuby had scavenged her from a trash can, newborn legs kicking fretfully against the trash sack. Another half-hour and she'd have been dead one way or another, the virtual weather turned cold with icy rain, and auto-dumpers ready to do their duty. Flip, suck, crunch, crush, and whoosh through the tubes. Ruby constantly cleaning her, daubing, wiping childish messes at either end—that was her first and strongest memory. That, and his constant "Shah!" Sometimes he crooned it, or laughed it, disparaged or corrected with it. Other times its exact meaning was self-evident: instant, obedient silence to avoid discovery. Skimper-scampering through the access tunnels that honeycombed the layer separating each satellite level, more spry than the occasional child he'd salvaged. Rough hugs, and the best examples of survival. Long gone now, so long she couldn't remember when—just that Ruby was, and then he wasn't anymore. Why you didn't get attached.

She stood in the shadows, winged an elbow to sniff beneath an armpit. That cleanliness and her complexion, almost blue-black, had allowed her to slip unregarded into Stanislaus Troupe's living quarters at Level 3. But first she'd prowled the agricole tiers, steppy-steps of veggies, grains, bush fruits. Satisfying late at night, the different scents of growing things, new textures to touch with no one to watch and yell, illicit tastes. A sample here, a sample there. No radishes, they made you burp.

Curious, oh, yes—but not stupid. Still, the idea of Glynn's mother brain-boxed boggled her; the only way to overcome it was to see for herself. Owed her that, Glynnie did. Payback for helping rescue Jere. Friendship?—nah! Payback she could accept. Deserved to see it, she did, see it true, that it really worked. Techno-marvel-aculous-zam! Zamdamn! Could anyone stop her? "Shah? Nah!" and gave a derisive snort at the scene before her. Not that oldy-moldy lady, slip-slumped in her chair, scrawny legs spindling out, cane atween them. Much good biddy-boo'd do if she was all the guard they'd set. Not with sleek-slick Panny on a trick. Old biddy-boo wasn't hardly big as she was.

Soundlessly humming "Shah-nah-nah-NAH, Shah-nah-nah-nah NAH," she glided nearer the table that held the box. That it? Faint disappointment, almost a sense of betrayal—that was *all*? Pause in the shadows again, waiting, watching to see if old biddy-boo would move, sense her presence. Ruby'd cautioned how some felt vibes, vibby-vibes beyond their senses, had trained her to feel them as well. Nah, not this one. Pie-easy, candy-grab, simon-simple. Shah-NAH!

With easy motions she began to circle the table, moving nearer with each rotation. Funny-boo box, dials and gauges, blue-pulse strip on front, or what she judged to be front. A further shift and she froze, lung-locked, staring at an opticam, momentarily convinced it glared back at her. Nah, not a vibby-vibe, just a fear-feather brushing her. Still no reaction, no sound, so she breathed again, soft and low, crouching until she was level with the opticam, staring at it, into it, wondering if she could see what was trapped inside.

Eyes half-hooded, mouth slightly ajar, head tossed back, Masady tightened her grip on her cane. Not asleep, but woolgathering, a prerogative of the old, but dangerous, still. Old she was, older than she should be, replacement hips constantly afire with pain, knees and ankles throbbing. Every plastic knuckle a hot coal. A purpose to it at last—pain to keep her awake, let her guard Jerelynn. Ah, Jere, granddaughter, reduced to this, this circumscribed half-life!

As she often did when wakeful—more hours of more nights than she'd bothered to count—she recited lines from the plays they'd performed for more than twelve decades. Tonight for consolation, for distraction, she methodically worked her way through *Oedipus at Colonus,* one of her greatest triumphs. She'd last performed it seven years ago on Tane, with Jere playing Theseus and Glynn, so young then, as Antigone, Staniar sullen at the lesser role of Ismene.

"Oh, Theseus, dear friend, only the gods can never age, the gods can never die. All else in the world almighty Time obliterates, crushes all to nothing." It looked as if Time, almighty Time, had finally prevailed, would crush Stanislaus after all. How ignominious to end thusly, Jere there but not there, Glynn attempting to fill her place onstage. Oh, Majvor had her talents, especially light comedy, made a strong second lead, but was it enough? And how Hassiba and Heike would develop over time remained to be seen; girls were given more leeway, more time to develop since their careers ran lifelong.

Oh, how the troupe had dwindled through the years, once twenty or more strong in front and behind the scenes. No one in training after the Gemmies—a fatal oversight. She should have insisted Majvor or Jere, indeed, both, become pregnant again. At least insisted on more out-adoptions to increase their ranks. Somehow she lacked the driving strength of the past, ignoring Rigo's pleas for more members. Now, given their size, the blow of losing Jere, she didn't know what to do. Give in, give up? Disband? Was this their final act?

No! Never! For if they did, the chance of exposure for Jere, for Glynn became far greater, threw them into danger's path, no one to protect them. The greater safety, slim though it was, lay in remaining in the troupe, depending on the other troupes as their eyes and ears. Danger in that as well if someone harbored a grudge, toppled Stanislaus from its pedestal as best acting troupe.

A flicker of movement, so easefully deceptive it seemed only air moved, a greater darkness surrounded by dimness. A slow, careful blink, but her eyes hadn't lied—something, someone. So, so, they'd try again, would they? She watched, wary, gauging her position as the figure circled. When it turned its back, crouching to investigate Jere's box, she rose with all the supple silence she could command, overriding the pain just as she had onstage these last years, conquering it for the triumph of bringing a role alive, living through it. Four rapid, sliding steps forward and she jabbed, cane aiming for a kidney and the spearing pain it would provoke.

With a screech of fury she threw herself atop the collapsed figure, her sinewy old fingers wrapped round the throat, thumbs jamming at carotid arteries, an ancient, aching knee slamming hard into the gut. One wrenching gasp beneath the throttling fingers, and the dark shape set itself in earnest to fight back. The intruder was younger, stronger, but not quite as savvy as Masady, and she willed that savviness to counteract the grappling twists, the fingers clawing at her eyes. The one question she refused to think was how long she could prevail without help. No energy to spare for a second shout; she poured what remained into her hands, clenching tighter, harder, thumbs driving deep into pulse points. Wouldn't Siem Vy be proud if she could see Masady now?

Shock exploded into desperate survival instinct inside Panthat as the hands gripped tighter, old biddy-boo steam-hissing against cheek, ear. She bucked, scrabbling for the discarded cane as darkness swam before her eyes. Brain old biddy-boo with it, she exhorted herself, box the old biddy-boo just like Jere! Not win over Panthat, nah! A flailing elbow and the cane rolled, grab! Fingers slippy-sweaty—pick it up, grab it! Panthat the survivor, super satrat! Not go down like this! Shah? Nah! Too dark, too hard to breathe, so hard to hold it tight. Must! Do it! Now! Slam under old biddy-boo's chin, thrust, thrust her back and away, break her neck. . . .

Lights flared, Vijay's mellow voice high-pitched in panic as he wrestled the cane away, clutched at the figure while Chance struggled to pry Masady's fingers from its throat. More roaring voices, angry, confused, flooded over Panthat as she faded into the dark, began to meld with it, heard Glynn shout, "It's Panny! Panthat! Don't hurt her."

Maybe it would be all right, the crushing pain in her throat would ease, the air would flow again. Shah, yes, yes. Ss . . . ss . . . sweet air, so sweet, so rawly harsh. And much to Panthat's eternal shame she smelled herself, the rank stink of fear, raw sweat. Damn, damned waste, would need more tokey-tokes, chitty-chits for another bath. Waste, that. Heaving herself onto hands and knees, shaking, head hung low, she rasped for breath. The constricting hands on her body began to loosen. Feel bad?—act worse, lull them, Ruby had drummed into her. Covertly she watched to see which hands would grab again, readied herself to run.

The center of all eyes and, because she was at the center, beside the table and the box, Panthat was the first to notice the box come to life—proof it wasn't an inanimate, wooden object, might truly contain Jere.

Blue flickered, letters began to scroll, and she gasped, pointing, squinting to make them out, wishing she could read better.

"LET THE CHILD BE. LET HER SEE THE FREAK. ONLY NATURAL TO BE CURIOUS."

Relief and anguish swamped Chance. Jere's first words in two days, ever since he'd revealed to her the enormity of her change. "Are you sure, Jere?" Satrats could be dangerous, that was a given—especially one cornered like this. Yet there had been something about this urchin from their earlier meeting that made him suspect she harbored her own code of honor. No danger to Jere, to Glynn, though he'd not bet on anyone else's safety.

"COME, CHILD, COME CLOSER. LOOK ALL YOU WANT, LET ME LOOK AT YOU." Not quite daring to rise, giving a warning snarl as she brushed Masady's knees, Panthat crawled toward the box. She plunked on her bottom, rubbed at her throat.

"Does keep you living live, heh? Shah! Wowsome wondrous, that. Better'n being fishy-food." She rose, stared into one opticam, circled to stare into the other, striving for impartiality. "Odds-bods funny way to live."

"IF YOU CALL IT LIVING, CHILD."

Date: Evening, 7 February 2158
Location: NetwArk, Texas Republic, Earth
Rhuven Fisher Weaver stretched, arms contentedly reaching heavenward, back arching in the overstuffed old easy chair. Algore slipped from his lap, toddler bottom wedged between his father and the chair's arm; Rhuven hastily scooped him back, but the child never wakened, simply made a grumbling sound as his thumb slipped from his mouth, tiny, damp fist wadding his father's shirt. At his feet, Anyssa and Artur played a board game, Artur draped across his father's shins, Anyssa's back to the chair, her head and shoulder bumping his thighs as she gauged her position on the board.

He could assess her edge as well as she, and he
stretched a hand to her head in restraint. A resem-
blance almost unnerving, yet reassuring as she turned
to face him, his paternity unmistakable. He rubbed,
rueful, at his receding hairline, dark honey hair graying, and Anyssa reached lightning fast, tugged at his
beard. "We could trim it, glue it on top?" His mock-
scowl scarcely deterred her. Only now was she developing into womanhood, curves remolding the slim
body that so mirrored his adolescent self. Except lately
he couldn't remember being so young, so carefree, so
sure. Had Becca done as he'd asked? Had the notes
truly stopped? If he asked Rosa, all it would achieve
would be to upset her again.

Her eyebrows rose, dramatically wriggled at the
board, demanding he acknowledge how she'd trapped
Artur. Folding his arms around Algore, he bent forward to whisper, "Would it be so terrible if you let
him win?"

Raising a hand to shield her mouth she whispered
back, "Yes. You know how Mother feels about that.
Artur's not a child any longer." The words, the tone
a carbon copy of Vitarosa's, naught of his. The dice
scattered from Artur's hand and the boy began methodically counting out his options. "He *does* have a
chance, not much, but a chance if he makes the right
choice. If . . ." and rubbed her hands together in
anticipation.

He slumped back, bundling Algore higher, not especially wanting to view the kill, looking to Vitarosa for
support. Strange how she could inhabit the room with
him, with them all, and yet make it feel empty, as if
she were physically absent. Despite that, Rhuven relished these evenings with his family, the conclusion
of a day of faith, the message of grace delivered, the
redemptive, curative powers of the mind-body connection. Now for his own private moment of thanks with
his children, his wife. Sinful to savor it so much? These
moments of quiet communality, the connection to his
loved ones, body and soul. No use pondering how Vi-

tarosa could be "here" yet simultaneously "else-where." He'd experience a similar sensation when he preached.

An indignant howl as Anyssa swept her brother's final playing piece off the board. Face red with rage, Artur lifted the board, ready to thwack it over his sister's head. "You tricked me!" he screamed. "Damn you, Anyssa!" The board sank to shield his face as he realized what he'd said.

"We don't damn anyone here, Artur. Let's not usurp the Lord's power and prerogative. Even He doesn't damn so much as allow us to damn ourselves through our words, thoughts, and deeds." Rising, the sleepy Algore like an unwieldy sack of grain, he stretched a hand to his elder son, raised him to his feet and pressed his fearful eyes against his waist. "Remember, blessed are the meek, for they shall inherit the earth."

'Who'd want to inherit it?—not these days," Anyssa sniped. "NetwArk, yes."

"Bed, all of you." Vitarosa laid aside her note-palette, mind still immersed by their discovery that the satellites had blocked Rhuven's Web-message the last two nights. Intentionally blocked—not some accidental mechanical failure, not sun spot disturbance, as they'd first assumed. "Anyssa, tuck them in for the night, please. Then come back and clean up the toys."

She looked ready to protest, but Vitarosa forestalled her. "Winners have responsibilities, too—especially to the losers." The slanting look Anyssa cast her way while scooping Algore from her father's arms didn't sit well with Vitarosa. Not surly—that she would have expected, sat on it—but something else, something deeper, as if the child-woman hoarded a secret that she, Vitarosa, didn't know. Almost an assessing look, the sort she herself had measured her father and half brothers with, found them wanting so long ago. Even Artur subconsciously sensed the mood change as he trailed after his sister, clutching her hand, pressing close as if she represented a surer safety than the room's adults offered. Hmm? Ask Becca tomorrow if she'd noticed anything different about Anyssa recently. Still, emotions weren't Becca's strongest suit.

As the door closed behind them, Vitarosa breathed a silent sigh of relief. She loved her children, yet despised them when their demands, their very physical presence separated her from Rhuven with the finality of an ever-widening canyon. Without her on the same side of the divide, he could be so weak, so fallibly human . . . thy prop and thy staff, Rhuven, though you sometimes forget. . . .

"Becca and Abel have been at it nonstop," she informed him. "The blockage is deliberate. They're denying the satellites your message of redemption." He frowned, not with anger but with genuine puzzlement, astonished anyone would do such a thing, purposefully deny God's word to others. "Becca thinks we've figured out how to avoid their blockade, beam our signal off an independent comsat orbiting beyond them, let it ricochet back through their home world comm system. Once it's Web-linked there, it'll be impossible to clamp down on it. Not unless they want their whole Ring communications system down. That should hold us until we find a more secure method."

He ran his hands through his hair, disheveling it until he looked like a young Aslan, the lion she'd thought so brave, so true, so honorable and strong in his righteous faith in those long-ago children's tales. And she his lioness; lionesses killed for their mates, made sure they were fed. "But if they don't want my message, don't choose to seek redemption, that's their choice, you know that, Rosa." He shared a rueful glance, "It's rather dog in the mangerish of them."

"It isn't the people's choice, it's the Ring Council's choice. Some don't believe—fine. But to deny others what you don't choose to cherish? When you preach you aren't specifically attempting to convert Hindus, Muslims, Old Catholics, Nuevo Catolicos, Baptists Wet or Dry." She smiled, "But if any have hearts and souls yearning to bask in the light of truth, of faith, your words will shine on them. Just as they shone on me once."

"I remember." He'd wrapped his arms around her from behind now, and she leaned against him, relieved that he couldn't see her face. His left forearm pressed warm and true against the lump on the lower half of her left breast. Nothing happened; she could still feel it, sense it growing, rooting deeper. Nothing, nothing left over for her. No healing grace.

"Just think, Rhuven. Think of it," she implored, tilting her head until it brushed his beard. At least he'd kept the beard; smooth-shaven, it was all too clear how malleable he was. "Waggoner's Ring ranges so much nearer the heavens than we and yet so much farther distant from God's love—if you don't help them. We must reach out, not merely concern ourselves with sharing God's message here on Earth. Maybe you were right before without knowing it: The meek shall inherit the earth, but those with vision can reach for the stars. Think about it, Rhuven, think of it," she urged, her arms clasped over his.

"This is your crusade—to bring faith to Waggoner's Ring. No one else has dared challenge their godless state. None of the other faiths. And do you know why?" Why wait for him to fumble an answer? "Because they're afraid of offending their megaglom sponsors."

"I don't know . . ."

"Do you remember the old hymn? 'We are climbing Jacob's ladder, we are climbing Jacob's ladder,'" she parted from his arms, striding to the words as she tossed her dark hair back, " 'Oh, we are climbing Jacob's ladder, Soldiers of the Cross. Every round goes higher, higher . . .' "

His eyes glowed a warm brown-gold—the color they took on when he became as one with his congregation, his God—but he still looked infinitely exhausted, as if the thought of shepherding yet more devotees who needed his strength, his belief was beyond him. "Can we, should we, do you think?" He flung his shoulders back, stood tall, proud, staring starward through the ceiling. "Not can, but must!" he exulted. "Not as soldiers on a crusade, but missionaries spreading the Word, the message of God's healing love. Even if but one soul on one satellite wants to be saved, I have to try! Yes, reach for the satellites!"

Ha!—that one soul was now dead. Let him cope with that when the time came! If they could control Waggoner's Ring, they could control the Earth! Yes, it was all about control! Never to be saddled with starry-eyed dreamers again!

With a start she realized Anyssa had knocked, slipped into the room to gather the toys. On her knees, industriously scooping up game pieces, wooden blocks, stuffed animals, she tilted her head up at first one, then the other. "I want to visit Waggoner's Ring someday, see what it's like."

"And maybe you shall, sweetheart," Rhuven answered her, still half in the sway of the old hymn, "higher, higher . . . !"

That narrowed, knowing look again. "I could do a great deal of good there, don't you think, Mother? Don't you?" That final question was more than a question, more a command. Yes, perhaps it was time to remove the hood and jesses, set the fledgling free, judge if her training had been true. But if so, there must be bait, a lure for her to strike. Think about it later. Right now she had to decide how to pay for renting MabasutaGenDy's satellite—Rhuven'd never think of that!—or whether it should be the megaglom's first "gift" to NetwArk. Free-will offering, if you liked, and she knew what she'd offer in return.

Time: Morning, 6 February 2158
Location: Transient Lodging, 3Juliet/Mid

Chaos—or so it appeared to an outsider like Chance—as the troupe began readying itself to move, continue its tour on another satellite. In short, to marshal a semblance of normality intended to sow confusion in any enemy stalking them, intent on determining whether Jere—or Glynn—was alive or dead. Barely controlled chaos as people darted around, packing costumes and masks in sturdy crates, props collapsing, telescoping into themselves for compact transshipment.

Dressed in a sweaty gray singlet and sagging trousers, Rigo orchestrated, gesticulating, pointing, waving each member toward new tasks while Vijay checked against the manifest. Heike, Hassiba, and the Gemmies, now joined by Panthat—neat and tidy in her actions, as if she'd performed these tasks forever—scampered like squirrels, small hands deftly packing things into the smallest spaces. Squirrels? Spinning, Chance checked desperately for Sylvan, momentarily afraid they'd packed him as well. Strained to hear the irate chitters, the scolding sounds that would reveal his whereabouts. With relief he found the flying squirrel clinging upside down to a cable, bright eyes dancing. Chance whistled and the squirrel let loose from his perch, gliding to his shoulder.

He thought again about Ngina's message. With the SatGovs' recommendation, the Ring Council had voted to cancel all tourist visas to Waggoner's Ring for an indefinite period. The loss of income had brought howls from many. Whether the move might protect Jere and Glynn, he couldn't judge. The assassin had been native-born, but no one knew where or who his instructions had come from. Further, the Council strongly suggested the troupe continue its usual tour. As to official security, impossible—too obvious, and Chance grudgingly had to agree. Better to make do with whomever they could borrow short-term from the other troupes. Safer to trust your own, not outsiders. Startling to admit he thought of himself as one of them now.

Besides, the Ring Council had more pressing worries, including NetwArk's escalating transmissions, its signals pingponging from comsat to comsat in a random pattern almost impossible to block. So far, Ring Intelligence couldn't determine precisely which megaglom backed Weaver's sudden incursion, making it impossible to invoke trade sanctions. The decision to cancel tourist visas meant that none of Rhuven's followers could visit, proselytize directly. And every Ring inhabitant's vital stats file now spun through the Ring's megacomputer, ready to flag any sort of deviant behavior, most especially strong religious belief. Private belief, fine; public profession of it, not.

How had Ngina put it? That Waggoner's Ring espoused freedom *from* religion, rather than freedom *of* religion. The satellite settlers' belief in themselves, their talents, had created the Ring while the rest of the world jeered, called it an impossible vision. Believe in yourself and your fellow satelliters—not an impossibly distant deity. Perhaps some Godhead *had* created the universe, but men and women had labored for far longer than six days to build Waggoner's Ring. Safer and saner not to speculate whether some supreme "intelligence" existed beyond the universe. Sometimes the idea comforted, and sometimes it terrified Chance. Give him proof, the way the satelliters had proved what they could accomplish.

Something whacked his leg, lightly but insistently enough to seize his attention. Looking down, annoyed by the distraction, he realized he should have known. Masady stood to one side, cane tattooing his shin. "Have you decided yet?" Normally he reveled in her voice, the way she played it like an instrument, rich, inviting, compelling . . . but now, striking fear in him. Sweat clamminess sheathed his body like a second skin, his stomach tight, ears ringing, balance starting to fail, the pressure in his head building just as it did, just as it would if . . . if he . . . if. . . .

Panthat scooted by, halted and reversed herself, sniffing. "Fear stink," she announced, face impassive except for her flared nostrils. "Beta Lady Masady scare big man like you?" Masady shooed the satrat away.

"You don't *have* to come with us." Masady surveyed him up and down, assessing his condition. Once

Jere had told her how space travel now affected Chance, why he'd mewed himself on PabNeruda, though he'd been the greatest space tinkerer of them all. A pity, that, but the troupe's need was larger than his fears. Whatever she had to do, she would to ensure this man stayed with them, this man called Chance. There was always Fate, but the one thing that might ameliorate Fate was Chance. His mechanical aptitude would guarantee Jere's survival if something went wrong with the box.

"Is it your body or your head—physical or psychological—that overreacts when you fly?" A grown man, cringing in terror at the mere thought of a minor shuttle leap between satellites—pitiful.

"I'm not sure," he managed a sickly smile, licked dry lips. "Doctors aren't either, said they'd never encountered a case quite like mine." Squaring his body, he tried not to sway at the vision of his body hurtling through space, the void around it; a tiny body encapsuled in a shuttle, equally frail against the galaxies of danger outside. "I want to come . . . I truly *want* to. . . ." His breath fast and harsh as if he'd run a race, he concentrated on slowing it, light-headed. "They've tried it all, from hypnotic suggestion to inner ear surgery. I've been scanned and imaged from top to bottom, inside and out. Enough to fill an album."

"Will you try one more thing, see if it might help you board the shuttle? If it doesn't work, you don't have to go." With a twist of both wrists Masady unscrewed her cane, upended the bottom half over her palm. A paper-wrapped tube about the size and length of Chance's little finger fell out. He could smell its pungency. "Ganja. Sometimes the old ways still work. We'll see if it separates Chance from Chance so the body doesn't mind traveling. Or the mind. Think of it as a cane, a crutch, just like mine." Rejoining the two cane pieces, she gave his shin one final, stinging tap, "Let it be 'a stick tapping before you step by step,' (*Oed.King*-should be him/not you. 1. 519) to guide you beyond your blind fears."

Time: Sum-time Location: Inside Jere's brain

The sense of stasis was terrifying. Absolute motionlessness, no way to judge up from down, side from side. The body informs the brain that the commanded movement is taking place, voluntarily or involuntarily: a limb flexation, an eyelid flicker, a heart contraction, or some nearby object's successful transposition. Her brain box securely enclosed in a leather tote, bereft of the pseudo-vision and hearing granted by analog, Jere cannot judge where she is. Even her "voice" is stilled, her frantic LCD queries obscured from anyone who might read them, respond.

Nothing to fall back on except her brain, fleeting sensations of electrical connections, and a constant, grinding effort to determine who and what she is, what makes Jere uniquely Jere. Who was it so long ago who'd said, "I think, therefore, I am."? Am what? He'd forgotten to ask that corollary question, so obvious to her now. Am me? Am human? What? Who? Which electrochemical impulses, which series of connections, relays, form the unique pattern of Me? Can I consciously identify them? If I can, could someone else, some "thing" else replicate them—and hence replicate Me? Do those unconscious workings make me consciously Me?

Terror, a rising terror that threatens to unhinge her. Funny, I have no mouth but I must scream, I have no mouth but I must giggle. Unhinge? If I become "unhinged," will I fall out of my box, my shell, my replacement skull? What would I fall into—nothingness? An end to it all? The whole sensation a cross between claustrophobia and its opposite, agoraphobia. Am I completely enclosed in my brain, my box? Or am I spinning in an emptiness of incredible, indefinable dimensions? Am I Me if I am alone, denied contact with any other being or thing? Am I Me only in relation to some One, some Thing other than Me?

Clamping down on her spinning thoughts, she forces them under control. Whose control? Hers? Not easy. Distraction, find a distraction, make a distraction.

Neurons, at-TEN-SHUN! Hup, two, three, four, Hup, two, three, four. The animals came two by two, one more river to cross. The little one stopped to tie his shoe, one more river to cross. One more river, and that wide river is Jordan. Mastiff, greyhound, mongrel grim, hound or spaniel, brach or lym; or bobtail tike, or trundle-tail; Tom will make them weep and wail. Rich man, poor man, beggarman, thief, egg man, walrus, Indian chief. Cabbages and kings, candlesticks and . . . what, what had the Walrus said?

Enough, enough. To prove her sanity she quotes insanity. Not exactly comforting. No way to be sure, but she assumes they ride the shuttle. But time is a commodity she cannot buy, so she has no idea. On the shuttle? Waiting for liftoff? Underway? Landing?

It strikes her then. Chance. How could she forget him? Has he stayed behind or has Masady contrived some plan to bring him along? If she courts insanity, what was the shuttle flight doing to Chance? Too good a man to destroy himself over her. And so compassionate he might well do so. Ironic to be bound to the supposed security, stability of a satellite when that satellite itself constantly moves, gyres through space in stately circuits. No different from being on Earth, although how easy to forget that the Earth moves, revolutions within the confines of a larger orbit. For every thing, turn, turn, turn, turn; for every season, turn, turn, turn. . . .

It does no good, means nothing because there is no one to "hear" her oath, read her bluely-flickering vow. But saying it affirms it, binds her to an oath she'll honor. 'GLYNN, CHANCE, I WILL TRY TO REMAIN . . . WHAT REMAINS OF ME . . . TRY TO REMAIN AS SANE AS POSSIBLE. SOMEONE HAS TO BE. I WILL LET NO ONE HARM MY SON, AS RHUVEN'S GOD IS MY WITNESS. SOMEDAY, SOMEHOW, SOMEWHERE, WE WILL MEET. I WILL SNARE AND SMITE MY ENEMY DEAD. FOR ONCE THE DANGER IS VANQUISHED, I CAN ASK FOR MY RELEASE.

UNTIL THEN I WILL REMAIN AS SANE AS IS HUMANLY POSSIBLE! FORGIVE ME, IF I FALTER ALONG THE WAY. FORGIVE ME AND DENY ME, IF I BEG FOR RELEASE. FOR WHATEVER I AM, WHATEVER IS LEFT, I AM ONLY HUMAN."

A time to seek, and a time to lose; a time to keep, and a time to cast away; A time to rend, and a time to sew; a time to keep silence, and a time to speak; a time to love, and a time to hate; a time for war, and a time for peace. Yes, recite it in memory of Rhuven, once loved, once trusted so long, long ago.

ACT THREE

ACT THREE

Date: 1 May 2158 Location: Medical Center, Houston, Texas Republic, Earth

"Ms. Herrara, I wish you hadn't waited so long to see me." Vitarosa stared back across the desk at Dr. Chun, comfortingly wide, implacably professional with fine-fingered, flittering hands that revealed emotions that never appeared on her face. "We see so few breast cancer cases these days, and those we do," her fingers splayed, then curled up to gather all the cases into a compact ball, "almost invariably show the same genetic signature yours exhibits, those markers like red flags. . . ."

[Her mother at the end, body wasting, her mind still febrile and bright, fingers weaving over the keyboard, reorganizing files, explaining to Rosa the intricate system of checks and cross-checks that moderated and protected the Little Sisters of Mortality from overzealousness. "Vaccine didn't do any good, Rosa. Lucky me to pick up an aberant gene somewhere along the way, good old BCRA-10. May've mutated on its own or been passed down to me. Family medical history isn't always that clear—too many records destroyed in the wars." From her attitude and the medications' pain-muting abilities, Rosa found it almost impossible to believe her mother was dying. "Rosa, have yourself genetically checked, take the full series of vaccinations. Above all, don't ignore anything, don't get so involved in your work that you ignore too many things. I did—too busy to bother. Always thought, "Not me."

"Now, never forget that all these files are *only* potentials. Just because a person's name is listed, it doesn't mean he or she will inevitably become a 'target.' " A throaty chuckle too rich to emanate from her thin body, bones scything through flesh. "If they all did, we'd wipe out half our population, most likely some of the wrong ones as well."

An intent nod. Vitarosa knew this, had known it for years, but there was no sense halting her mother's enjoyment in lecturing. As an only child, she loved her parents with an overriding passion, thrived between the polarities of their personalities. Now, at eighteen, she knew with cold certainty that should she lose one of her poles, she, in turn, could easily lose her direction. The knowledge she'd inherit her mother's job of running the Little Sisters gave her some stability to cling to. Even Father refused to hear, still lost in pretending nothing would ever happen, could change. "And we update monthly with any new information, correct?" she added for something to say. "Each person's personal habits, their likes and dislikes, weaknesses and strengths, most of all any habitual routines, be it every third Tuesday of the month at the barber's, or a consistent route someone walks or drives."

Simply stated, let anyone even attempt to oppress the Nuevo Catolico faith or its followers, and the Little Sisters of Mortality stepped in—silently, thoroughly, and definitively. Any major infraction: any injustice to the faith; any major denial of justice or liberty; socioeconomic or racial discrimination—all served as grist for the mill. Politicians and officials thought deeply before taking any action that might hurt too many people. Minor and temporary hurts could be accommodated—the closing of a plant or medical center recompensed by something else granted.

Thus, life ran in an amazingly cohesive and "democratic" fashion in RoraimAndes, that new-minted republic above the Amazon and below the mountains' rims, a swath of what had once been Venezuela, Colombia, a pinch of Ecuador, and the top of Peru. The process improved by leaps and bounds when politicians discovered that death was the ultimate accountability, not simply being voted out of office in the next election.]

Dr. Chun droned on about ". . . excellent success rates in the more traditional cases, though those are rare nowadays. Even with your genetic background, the cure rate can be good, except," her fingers flicked just above the desk surface as if whisking dirt away from her, "that yours is so far advanced. The test results show it's spread into the lungs, into the bone. I'm sorry. Still," again no expression, but a positive handclasp, "with a lung replacement, some work on bone eradication and regrowth, and—of course—ultrachemotherapy." Two fists lightly tapped for emphasis, "We can try to chase down every cancer cell wherever it may be. . . ."

[Mother's funeral mass had been held at the cathedral at high noon. Father in full mourning, wearing a severely handsome black tailcoat, anachronistic but now in style again. Herself in a smoke-gray silk dress with a side slit that showed her black, stocking-clad leg, her dark hair a veil unto itself to shroud her tears. Becca at her side, gauche in dress clothes, nothing quite fitting or attractive—other than Vitarosa's secret knowledge that locked within Becca's body was the lithe economy and grace of a natural killer, like having an attack dog at her side. Play with it, ruffle its ears, feed it snacks, but on command it would still rip its victim's heart out. As would Becca, if need arose—that was what they'd been trained to do. A small but honored cadre of killers of which Vitarosa and Becca were proud members.

Back at the mansion now, and Vitarosa sat at her mother's computer terminal, ran the codes, checking updates, any other indications that assignments hadn't been properly carried out. "Rosa, love." Her father stood behind her, hands on her shoulders. "I know what your mother wanted for you, what you wanted, expected as well. Taking over, running things in your mother's place would help you heal your pain, conquer the grief, but I can't allow it."

"What? What do you mean?" Thrusting back her chair, she nearly ran its casters over her father's patent-leather-clad feet. "If I don't take over, who will? You're the Prime Minister's chief adviser. You don't have the time, the patience to run this!" A covert look at Becca, uncomfortably sunk in a too deep, too soft sofa, to see if she understood? But no, equal perplexity there, and a new and assessing look at Rolando, as if truly measuring Vitarosa's father for the first time. "But why, Father?" and hated the little girl wail bursting through her question. But he was her father, all-powerful, all-encompassing, all-protective.

The dampness of his fingers struck through the gray silk at her shoulders. "Because I love you too much to lose you like your mother. I'm convinced stress played a major role in making her cancer come on so quickly. That if she hadn't worked so hard . . ." he bent, half-helpless with grief, and laid his cheek on her hair. "I won't let it happen to you. You're going to the best clinic in Switzerland, be thoroughly checked and tested. Anything they suggest to prevent you from meeting your mother's fate will be done. It may be old-fashioned, but if they recommend preventive radiation therapy, a double-mastectomy, so be it. Anything to reduce the odds of losing you. I love you, you're the only girl I have left now."

Too much, too much to take in all at once. Was her health truly in immediate jeopardy? She shook her head, felt her father's cheek slide away and reached to pat it, smelled his aftershave. "But who'll run things while I'm gone? How long does this take?"

"Armando's sister went five years ago. They kept her eighteen months for diagnostic analysis and DNA scans, cell culture monitoring, setting up a baseline for future comparison." A year and a half? She'd go mad away that long, nothing to do except wonder what might be growing inside her—if not today, tomorrow or the next. "As for who'll run things in your absence . . ." he'd stepped clear, almost purposely distancing himself. Stood beside the antique globe he adored, spinning it a fraction this way and that. "There are two people I'd like you to meet, though I'm so sorry it has to be now, at a time like this."

Reluctantly he walked to the carved double doors that opened on his private study, that so-masculine enclave of dark mahogany and heavy velvet drapings, homage to another age and scrupulously recreated, and threw them open. Behind them, two young men, one perhaps twenty, the other a year or two younger than she. Both wore correct mourning attire, and both exhibited the same unbroken brow-stroke across their foreheads that her father displayed without careful plucking. Too much else matched her father as well. "I'd like you to meet your half brothers, Jorge and Leandro. Believe me, darling, they've been working incredible hours to master the system since your mother was diagnosed."

Half brothers? Father had kept a mistress? Did he still keep her or had he moved on to someone else, someone younger, fresher—still alive! Had Mother known? A numbness, cold and immobilizing. When water freezes to ice, it expands, cracking any restraints around it. Exploding free. That was what she would do, explode, if only she could move. Becca's eyes on her, sorrowful and frustrated, wanting to help, not knowing how. Everything snatched from her—her mother dead, her father stolen from her as well, unfaithful to her mother and her, daring to give her heritage, her legacy to others! It was her raison d'être, her one goal in life, to run the Little Sisters. Move bastards into her rightful place, would he?]

"How long do the treatments take?" Vitarosa asked Dr. Chun. "And what are the odds of success?"

"Well, success is a relative term. True success means

that you've been completely cured, and that takes years to verify, to determine no roaming cancer cells have tucked themselves beyond the ultra-chemo's reach. For others, success means gaining an extra year or two, sometimes more. It sounds little enough, but it's better than the four to six months you have. Buying time for some of the unfinished business of life we all worry over—seeing a child or grandchild born, a wedding, a major life-work completed."

"Ah," Vitarosa made a polite, noncommittal sound. "Yes, a major life-work completed, grandchildren . . ."

"The timeline depends on precisely what course of action you take." Predictably, Dr. Chun's fingers stretched an invisible line between them. "Aggressive treatment requires removing your breast and surrounding lymph nodes, replacing and rebuilding the rib cage, and as much of the spinal column as we dare, plus the lung replacement. Then an immediate course of ultra-chemo. About two months. Then another two rounds of ultra-chemo at three-month intervals, more after that if it proves necessary."

For a wonder of wonders, Dr. Chun's face actually smiled. "I'm seriously recommending you consider an ancillary or complementary therapy along with what I've outlined. Being so close here in Houston," she skimmed through her note-screen for Rosa's cover file to check the address, the false address she'd given, "Local, so I assume you've heard of NetwArk?"

"The preacher, what? Weaver, Webster, some such thing?" The cold, the ice invaded again, her explosion frozen.

But Dr. Chun trundled right along, pleased to offer hope, however fragile it might be. "Yes, Rhuven Fisher Weaver does healing. Now mind you, I'm not suggesting this in lieu of more conventional medical therapies, but working in tandem, we've found we accomplish excellent results. If the mind feels it has some control over the disease or illness—the invader in the body, so to speak—it can positively affect the outcome, further mobilize and release the body's natural forces, its immune system, its brain powers. It's not a miracle cure, but it does help. It doesn't matter whether you or I believe in a—imaginary quotes sketched the air—"Higher Power. It's more a question of reaching deep within and letting your mind and body coexist, positively employing their combined energies to battle the disease, not each other. Now, let me give you the Navigator's direct number. He's always happy to work individually with patients, as well as having you join his evening Web sessions. I'd recommend both at first."

Her thanks burned like acid on her tongue. "I'd never considered it before, but I'd be grateful. . . ." Just play it out. Weigh everything in the balance, decide what most needed to be accomplished.

Up until a week ago, her life's work had been laid out so neatly and clearly. But now Waggoner's Ring meant nothing, less than the dirt under her feet. A girlish whim—believing Rhuven could finally be a conquering white knight, even as she constantly propped him on his horse! What was important now was NetwArk, to save it for Anyssa—her child, her daughter, just as Vitarosa had been her mother's daughter. Cheated, oh, so cheated!

A colossal joke, at first she was sure, it had to be! The Pope contacting her? Disbelief, then shock as every security check verified his clearance. Pope Jean-Chrétien I contacting her, Nuevo Catolico bred, now NetwArk faithful? Ah, she'd thought, he wants to deal, is willing to sacrifice his pride to be first. That should stick in MitRock's eye! But no, no . . .

"I've a message for your husband that I hope you'll pass on for me. Tell him that he who offers salvation should be pure. While the Lord forgives our past sins, purifies us anew, He expects those sins to be acknowledged, confessed to so we may truly repent." They'd stared at each other through the screen, and she'd sworn his sincerity was unfeigned. "Ask your Rhuven why he's never acknowledged his bastard son." Rosa's world went dark, spinning dark fractured by bolts of lightning anger. "His son by that Ring actress Jerelynn Stanislaus, the Great Lynn, I believe she's called professionally. The boy turned fifteen a few months back."

She'd escaped, throttled the conversation as quickly as humanly possible. A son? A child by Jere? No, no, no! She'd not see it happen all over again before her very eyes!

Yes, that was why she'd gone to the doctor's after waiting so long. To see what time she had left. Now she knew. Prioritize, and if her life turned out to be short, fine—if she managed to complete her life's work. . . . Becca would help. Becca would *always* help.

[Becca would *always* help, you could count on that. Bless her for her unquestioning, uncomplaining loyalty. The action would be simple, the planning minimal. First, make sure it appeared that the mansion had been broken into, just a trace clue here, a minor clumsiness there. Little Sisters never left clues, and the Little Sisters must be above suspicion, beyond reproach for this incident. Just one of those unlucky fates that happen to people now and then.

She'd not sully her hands by killing her new half brothers—she'd leave that to Becca. Becca relished what she called "twofers," a quaint term. A lovely economy of motion as Becca slipped the stiletto behind Jorge's left ear, the widening panic on Leandro's face as Becca hefted Jorge's body upright, dangling feet limply dancing—a distraction while her ultrasound gun pulverized Leandro's brains.

All that with Father watching, gagged, bound to a straight chair. Oh, gently, of course, the softest ropes, no chafing or burning. The gag his own fine, lawn handkerchief with his initials in the corner. Interesting the strain involved, tiny red veins in his eyes like scarlet threads, the way the veins on his neck and up his temples snaked and bulged.

So nice to have time, the leisure to do more, but that would be selfish, greedy. A muffled roar of anguish from him, almost distinguishable, " 'Ove ooo!"

"What, dear?"

A desperate straining at the gag, a paramount effort to push the words through, beyond it. Teeth bared by twisting lips. "Wanned oo ave ooo! oove ooo! Beh for ooo!"

"Yes, Father, all I want is what's best for me, too. Thank you for letting me see that." A single shot to the heart with a bullet that mushroomed on impact. Now, where should she and Becca go from here? Away, somewhere far away. That nice young man she'd met last year—Rhuven something? She was beyond all this now, didn't need it any more.]

"Yes, Doctor, I understand. I'll call and set up the appointments once I'm home and can check my schedule." But Rosa didn't, still didn't understand. Didn't wish to understand, because understanding might call for compassion. For people dead and gone, for those in the process of dying—herself included. That was a weakness she didn't need, not then, not now. Not if she wanted to save NetwArk for Anyssa.

Date: 8 May 2158 Location: Houston Shuttle Transit, Texas Republic

Kicking the carry-on duffel ahead as the line inched forward, Anyssa strove to mimic Becca's boredom, a seasoned traveler's ennui in the face of inexplicable bureaucratic delay. What she longed to do was dance, grab hands with Becca, Falid and Hamish just behind them, and spin them in dizzying circles. Easier said than done, even if Becca's protocol permitted it. The loader tube stretched ahead and behind, about four meters in diameter; a lightweight, over-flexible flooring had been laid along it to give boarders a flat surface. Someone, in a misguided attempt at cheer, had lined the windowless tube in dark rose carpeting. Too subliminal for words, but appropriate—wasn't she being reborn?

Off-planet! Traveling off-planet! And she, Anyssa, had been chosen to accompany them. Finally—her first true test, proof she wasn't just a trainee, but an initiate, nearly a full-fledged Little Sister of Mortality. Like Becca, like Mother. Her fine-honed skills part of a longstanding tradition, yet flexible enough to change, hold NetwArk dear in its defensive heart.

Fingering the shoulder patch of her olive jumpsuit, left sleeve navy to identify her Apprentice status, she concentrated on how a crystallographer might act. Hours of study to gain a rudimental fluency, the jargon to ensure she didn't "blow" her cover. Pull out her comp-slate, indulge in some muttering—adroitly re-configure a complex diagrammed formation? No, don't show off, don't expose yourself to questions you can't answer. Still, the disguise had to hold only long enough to reach Satellite Colony Tane. Some discreet favors, a few bribes, and Becca'd obtained IDs vouching they were CrystaCropCorp hires for the new crystal seeding project. Once there, they'd discard the olive jumpsuits and false ID for another identity and another. Attract too much notice and they'd go underground. It struck her, could you go "underground" on a satellite? Well, it didn't matter, because underground meant hidden.

And if there *were* an underground—how exciting, catacomb preaching, hiding like ancient Christians. Eyes wide, excited, she risked a glance at Falid and Hamish. Hamish turned the color of the surrounding carpeting, eyes sweeping upward in studious examination of the ceiling. Had he been ogling the curves of Becca's bottom in her skintight jumpsuit? Let Becca catch him and he'd be shark bait; she stifled a giggle. An extravagant eyebrow wriggle from Falid, white flash of a smile imprinted against his brown skin. With a finger-flick he indicated she'd best turn around; she obeyed just as Becca's hand clamped her wrist, reminding her of the stakes involved in this mission. Staring dutifully ahead, she feigned boredom as the line began to flow more rapidly, Becca urgently shoving her duffel at her.

The gesture, so seemingly innocent yet holding a hidden power to hurt, brought her to herself, who she was, why she was going. Father'd trusted her for this, had agreed. It signified as well that she'd earned her mother's respect, not to mention Becca's grudging consent. Don't screw up now. Yes, sow the seeds, bring the Word direct to those in need, exhort people to join Rhuven Fisher Weaver on the Web, add celestial members to the skein of believers. All in direct contravention of the Waggoner's Ring statute banning religious proselytizers. Hamish and Falid could preach, and preach well, would gather new members to the fold. And she and Becca, too, except . . . except. Anyssa bit her lip, suddenly unsure. The other task awaiting them burned in her brain.

Mind aswirl with speculation, she didn't notice the entry hatch to the shuttle cruiser had a raised lip, perhaps ten centimeters above corridor level. She tripped at the threshold, duffel flying inside, Becca's iron grip jerking her upright, despite the pain in her toe. Humiliation at her clumsiness, shame at drawing attention to herself. A Little Sister of Mortality was *not* clumsy or awkward or anything other than perfectly, silently, unobtrusively lethal. She knew their mission's goal, at least in part. What more she needed to know she'd learn when the time was ripe. Why would Mother, why would Vitarosa send two assassins—one a consummate expert, the other untested—to Waggoner's Ring? Unlikely Father required it, but then, Father couldn't know about Vitarosa's past, could he? Or what she'd trained Anyssa to become? It was one of their secret sharings, the secret bonds of womanhood, her coming of age, that she'd been privileged to take part in with Vitarosa and Becca.

Trying not to stare at the cruiser's seize as she limped deeper inside, Anyssa wondered whether Mother had found out about the boy yet? That might explain it. What was it like to have a brother near her own age, not the childish wants of Artur or Algore, but someone with whom to discuss serious things, like life and love and religion. And death. Could she kill? Kill a stranger? Yes. And what was he to her but a stranger? Keep that in mind and she'd be fine. Stranger or not, declare him the enemy, the "target," and she'd search him out like a heat-seeking missile. As Becca went to plant her in a seat, Anyssa moved as she'd been taught—tight and lightning-fast—and broke the grip. Becca's eyes widened, then narrowed as she flexed wrenched fingers but said nothing. "I think I'm able to seat myself, thank you," she commented and waved Hamish and Falid along to the empty seats behind them.

Date: 12 May 2158
Location: Aboard the luxury cruiser *Martin Frobisher*

A muted chime bonged twice over the PA system, and Anyssa's head snapped up, her whole body alert and ready. An abrupt end to her private fantasies—rehearsing her prowess as a Little Sister, her heroic bravery in protecting her parents, ensuring NetwArk's continued existence. Glowing daydreams of powerful adulthood, hers at last. If Becca could read her mind, she'd trample such musings. But then, perhaps Becca occasionally indulged in reliving past glories, anticipated future triumphs. Not that it ever showed. Apparently engrossed in her read-screen, Becca brushed Anyssa's leg and Anyssa obeyed her signal: Relax, act normal. So, Becca's "radar" *had* caught her abrupt tautness. Well, she *was* acting normal by most people's standards; her reaction to the chime gave her away only to those trained to read the subtle language of the body.

Now a mellifluous tenor echoed over the system. "Hello, I'm Diego Hwang, Information Officer aboard the *Martin Frobisher*. Some of you are old hands, have visited the Ring before, or hold satellite citizenship. But my passenger list shows many First Timers, and I thought you might enjoy hearing a brief history of Waggoner's Ring's founding. Don't know about you, but those school lessons didn't always stick once exams were over. I'll bet most First Timers can't name all eight satellites in proper order."

Someone in Tourist Class shouted, "Amaterasu, Curie-Cousteau, Huang-ti—"

Diego interrupted. "Location order, not alphabetical order." A theatrical hiss greeted his comment. "After all, we'll be landing shortly, and you'll be too busy peering out portholes to listen. If you're interested, move up to the lounge area and I'll refresh your memories about the Ring's beginnings and what each Satellite is noted for."

People shifted, made way for seatmates to go forward. Though the *Martin Frobisher* was a luxury liner, complete with artificial gravity, Anyssa'd been bored by nearly four days in space. What she wanted was to arrive; barring that, any diversion was welcome. Letting her wistfulness show, Anyssa glanced Becca's way. "Oh, go. Go ahead," a mock growl. "Take Falid and Hamish, too. Just don't," and the barest emphasis on "don't" drew Anyssa's full attention, "don't make yourselves obvious, draw any notice."

Despite herself Anyssa seethed; of course she knew better! Squelching a retort, she scrambled from her body-contoured lounge seat and up the aisle, gesturing for Hamish and Falid to follow. It dawned on her then, had Becca been off Earth before? She didn't think so, but then Becca rarely volunteered personal information, despite their years together. Hamish beamed as she turned for a final look at Becca, the large man even more transparently delighted than she, while Falid expressed his usual quirky, guarded interest.

Heedful of the caution, Anyssa stayed toward the rear, squeezing past people's knees to find three seats together, perhaps thirty people fanned ahead of her as a shield. A sniff at the heavy perfume wafting from a woman in front. Her fellow history buffs appeared to be mostly moneyed tourists—the Ring's tourist ban had finally been lifted, much to the relief of travel agents—a few business or technical types like herself, and a scattering of children.

Diego Hwang leaned against a carpeted wall panel beside the holoscreen, arms folded across the waist-length red jacket that topped his navy skinny-suit. Even at this distance his long lashes, the dimple in his left cheek showed. No clue as to age, his smooth complexion and youthful appearance at odds with his gold-braid rank.

"So," his hands flashed, "school all over again, another lecture, right? At least it's not mandatory, like the one the first day on satellite configuration. Quick, explain where 5Golf/Cap is!" Laughter, a heartfelt groan from a boy of twelve. "I'll make this as painless as I can. There's always something to learn from the past and the story of Waggoner's Ring is a history worth knowing. Ready?" The screen flashed on.

"The dawn of the twenty-first century could easily have been a new 'Dark Ages,' if it hadn't been for a few courageous individuals determined to make mankind's dream of living among the stars a reality. While most of Earth viewed such ongoing problems as hunger, poverty, overpopulation, pollution, refugee migrations, and war with the blinkered gaze of generations of failure, some—a very few—looked higher and farther. Refused to accept the same tired, bankrupt 'solutions' that, at best, slapped a Band-Aid on the world's newest laceration."

Anyssa squirmed as the screen flashed scenes of starving people marching on endless, dusty roads; houses destroyed by mortar rounds; malformed children and animals, all accompanied by somber music. The holoscreen almost bodily tossed her into the midst of each tragedy, Hamish's uneasy sighs echoing her own. As the screen faded, even Diego's crisp posture had bowed.

"They weren't easy problems to solve. Genocide in central Africa, refugees clogging the roads—what do they need first, most? Food, temporary shelter, proper sanitation to avoid disease, a safe place to live? Poverty-stricken countries so desperate for money that they begged to take in toxic and nuclear waste from other nations. Short-term gain, long-term environmental damage, right?" A half-smile, rueful, "*You* decide—what minimal level of health care is acceptable for everyone? No easy answers, are there?

"In hindsight it's easy to say too much was spent on short-term solutions for society's ills. At the same time NASA, the Soviet Space Agency, the European and Japanese Space Agencies, and others deteriorated or ground to a halt, their budgets plundered to salve more immediate problems. Few politicians or planners could see beyond their own national boundaries, discern new solutions to society's woes, but that's precisely what Dr. Elspeth Marsden Waggoner did."

A professionally posed portrait hovered in front of them with the dates 1980–2036 beneath it; others, candid shots from childhood to maturity, followed. "Despite PhDs in aeronautical engineering and management, Dr. Waggoner saw her job with NASA reduced to paper-pushing, her plans for a permanent space station scuttled. Galled by such shortsightedness, Dr. Waggoner set out make her dream a reality. Her dream: not just one permanent space station, but a series of space habitats capable of sustaining life and growth, a refuge from the factionalism splintering states and nations. Think of it—virgin space to be populated, new enterprises, abundant natural resources, greater productivity—and the potential to alleviate, even halt Earth's decline!"

Despite Diego's passion, someone behind her snored, made her quiver with embarrassed laughter. Falid, bless him, stretched back casually, jerked the man's foot. All Diego knew was that the snoring ceased.

"With her plan firm in mind and heart, Dr. Waggoner began contacting others who possessed a similar visionary spirit. They all shared the same zest for adventure that's always spurred mankind in quest of the unknown. Enough rebels, nonconformists still remained—engineers, physicists, biologists, computer experts, and a host of others—willing to place this new goal ahead of their national, ethnic, or religious identities.

"Given the ludicrous state of computer security, it was child's play to electronically shift funds from banks and investment houses, to de-access needed parts and materials from government and industry. In short, to hide things in plain sight until they took their first major step in 2027. Now, some historians have likened Dr. Waggoner and her supporters, including Kim Jin-Hwa, Ernst Grolsh, and Omara Suleiman, to latter-day pirates, guilty of everything except flying the skull and crossbones as they cheerfully plundered from everyone in their path." The boy yelped with delight as an old-fashioned pirates appeared on-screen, fiercely battling to claim a merchant ship. Diego smoothly overrode his cheers.

"It's a misguided comparison; if anything, compare the exploits of Dr. Waggoner and her followers with the wonderful old tales of Robin Hood and his Merry Band, stealing from the rich to give to the poor. Helping the world was their goal, not personal profit.

"Thanks to Juan Rogiers, last Secretary General of the United Nations before it disbanded in 2019, Dr. Waggoner knew diplomacy and bargaining could insure that more powerful governments didn't hinder them. What good would it do to build satellite colonies, only to have some grasping Earth government annex them? Her solution, suggested by Rogiers, bore his elegantly simple signature, yet harked back to the days of America's early colonies. 'Don't Tread on Me!' " Hamish shrank away; the coiled serpent dominating the screen a little too realistic for his liking.

"A series of Low Earth Orbit surveillance satellites were secretly launched—capable of tracking troop movements, missile sites, weather fronts, crop growth, and more. The fine-imaging capability of some let them read vehicle license plates, note a Prime Minister whose hurried departure from his mistress hadn't left

him time to shave." Chuckles at that, but Anyssa saw
no humor in it; it reminded her of a part of her mother's past.

"On 15 May 2027, Waggoner's cadre of loyal friends
spread out to visit every major government. Each message varied, but the overall essence boiled down to
'We know who you are, and we saw what you did.'
Aerial recon photos and videos, tracking maps, vividly
drove home their point. 'Of course you wouldn't want
us to tell your Western ally about certain clandestine
troop buildups in that vicinity, would you?' Let a
major power bluster about destroying these satellites,
and they politely responded, "Don't you think we
might have our own defenses aloft? Have already tar-
geted your capital, your major industrial and agricul-
tural areas?' It was a bluff on a global scale, but it
worked. After all, who dared find out for certain?

"As nation after nation, some reluctantly, many
willingly—especially smaller nations eager to reap potential future benefits—fell into line, Dr. Waggoner
sighed with relief and readied the next phase: a mass
driver on the Moon. Two years of grueling, urgent,
brute labor to build and ready it to slingshot the
Moon's resources to waiting dredges that hauled materials to the first two satellite kernels launched in 2029.
And oh, what bounty they harvested: silicon, calcium,
titanium, potassium, and more—plus ice that could be
split into both oxygen and hydrogen and fuel! From
then on, the satellites grew in size and increased in
number, thanks to the resources of the Moon and
nearby asteroids."

Alternately inspired and terrified by Diego's tale,
the rise or fall of each syllable emphasizing the flowering of Waggoner's Ring, Anyssa sat spellbound,
drinking in the scenes that flashed before her eyes.
Adventure on a grand scale, success against amazing
odds; somehow her lessons had never made it so real.

Oh, Lord, what had she missed? "It was on Nel-
Mandela in 2036 that Dr. Elspeth Marsden Waggoner
and more than fifty highly skilled workers met their

untimely end. A pressure seal leaked as they tested the third and newest expansion layer of the satellite. Part of the shield wall blew out, and all were killed instantly." A glowing, platinum sphere rotated slowly as Anyssa read the Ring's final homage to Dr. Waggoner and the brave souls lost with her.

The lights gradually brightened and Diego clapped his hands to bring them out of their reverie. "She and her coworkers died achieving their goals. Always remember that. How many of us can say as much?" He paused, let it sink in. "Now, let's visit the satellites in clockwise order, starting with SallyRide. Think of SallyRide at twelve o'clock high, which means that YuriGagarin is at 6:00. Of course, the satellites orbit, but let's momentarily still them." Anyssa listened hard as Diego succinctly outlined each satellite's unique features, committing them to memory as the holo-images spun their magic.

SallyRide: Launched with its twin, YuriGagarin in ("What year was it launched?" Diego needled. "Who's been listening?") 2029, it's home for SolaRing Power Corp, the Ring's major income producer, "exporting" solar energy to Earth in the form of micro-waves. (So much for Earth's old petrochemical dependence, except that NetwArk still obtained some crude oil from its ancient rigs. But solar energy is cheap and never-ending—as long as God's Sun shall shine.) Other major industries on nearby platform factories included extensive metallurgy and composite material production. ("These new alloys will knock your socks off!" Diego assured a businessman.)

Tane: At 1:30 on the clock, the "baby" of Waggoner's Ring, not exactly an afterthought, but a late arrival in 2039. Boasts of its crystal growth industry and semiconductor manufacturing, as well as its colony of crystal artists. (Gasps as the holograms revealed sparkling, breathtaking shapes.)

NelMandela: With its twin, PabNeruda, sent aloft in 2031 at the 3:00 position. Noted for its weather-watch satellites covering Mars, the Moon, the Ring, and

Earth. School of atmospheric physics. Major repair port for Ring satellites and occasional Earth-nation satellites.

Amaterasu: Launched in 2033 at the 4:30 marker. A living gift to the world's ecologists and conservationists. A cornucopia of diversity, preserving everything from single-celled creatures to the largest of species. Its genetic files contain DNA samples of many extinct and endangered species. Amaterasu has fewer layers than her sister satellites—only three, to allow its many creatures as close to a natural environment as possible. (The Ark painting on her bedroom wall. Hawks and eagles soaring high, whales cavorting deep in their seas. Wonderful!)

YuriGagarin: At the 6:00 position. Introduced in 2029 as SallyRide's twin, YuriGagarin traditionally serves as Command Headquarters for the Ring, with both defensive and offensive capabilities, should the need arise. (Luckily someone else voiced Anyssa's question. "You can't have just one defense station— what if it's far out in orbit and attackers hit the near side?" "Don't worry," Diego pacified, "all the satellites are defense-ready and also have outlying protection. But a command center does need a permanent site.")

CurieCousteau: Hmm, Tane's opposite number, at 7:30, but joined the Ring ahead of Tane in 2035. Preeminent in pharmaceutical research and actual manufacturing. Also hailed for medical studies, originally to monitor human adaptation to weightlessness, as well as for broader physiological inquiries.

PabNeruda: Namesake of the twentieth century Chilean politician-poet. (Mother'd appreciate that.) Opposite NelMandela at 9:00, founded in 2031 as well. A fitting name, given its cosmopolitan nature, rather like Paris, New York, and Vienna in their heydays. The arts, music, and museums . . . no wonder this is the satellite most tourists visit.

Huang-ti: 2033 and we've reached 10:30, almost done! Famous for its research into how the human brain works and its attempts to replicate it in computers. Other strong points are its glass fiber and optical lens industries.

Brain stuffed almost to overloading, Anyssa leaned to whisper to Hamish, saw him staring gamely ahead, a polite smile firmly pasted in place. She knew how he felt. Falid, however, tapped her hand, brought her back, still clearly absorbed by what he heard. Almost like a sponge soaking up information.

"At the beginning, many called it Waggoner's Folly, but they were proved wrong. Even today some complain that we've never quite lived up to her dreams of curing Earth's ills." Standing almost at attention, Diego refused to squarely meet his audience's eyes, uncomfortable with this part of his story. "Without Dr. Waggoner's vision, we did, perhaps, become insular. It's humbling to realize humankind can't play God, rain down new bounty on Earth. We believe over a century of efforts have stabilized, even improved the world. Our presence, our trade, ensures that no one megaglom becomes too powerful. We attempt to deal equitably with all our trade partners, rather than striking profitable but exclusive contracts with one or two.

"But as I conclude," Diego's mood abruptly lightened, an anticipatory grin narrowing his eyes, his dimple flashing, "another reason for insularity is because of infection. Remember, on landing we must ensure you've been adequately cleansed of any and all little Earth flora and fauna that we may not be immune to. I know you've been scoped and scanned, dosed and decontaminated before you left, but we require one final check before we actually let you aboard the satellite proper. One stray virus or bacterium could wreak havoc with us or with our food crops. Same applies for anything from Earth that's shipped up here—provisions, raw materials, whatever."

A groaning curse from a portly, balding man in the front row. "Does this mean we'll be dosed again? I've

never been scrubbed so clean inside and out in my
entire life!"

"No, it won't be nearly as bad, I promise. It's just
a final check. Better safe than sorry."

Beside her Hamish let out a deep sigh of relief.
Like the balding man, he hadn't taken kindly to the
antibiotics flushing his system.

"Thanks for your attention." A round of clapping
greeted Diego, some enthusiastic, some not. His final
comments had reminded everyone all too clearly that
they were venturing to a new world. Not the same
and yet similar. Something to bear in mind. Assumptions could be overturned in a familiarly unfamiliar
place.

Date: Evening, 14 May, and noon, 15 May 2158
Location: Megaglom HQ's, Tokyo and Paris

A wave of ebullience swept over Taylor Barham as
she waited for the "safe" line to chirp its readiness.
No holovid connection, just a nestling earpiece, warm
and intimate, confidential and confiding. Almost like
a lover's tryst in a moonless wood. Intimate? Her
Great Aunt Fanny! Even in the absence of a holovid-
tie Taylor glanced at the silver-framed mirror over
her workstation and primped, pushing flyaway, dark-
curled hair into place.

Intimate? On any unsecured comm line, the potential of sharing with a multitude was there—some simply audio voyeurs, others connoisseurs of collecting
tidbits of information for fun or profit. What made
this call seem "private" was that she knew the people
who would be listening in. Oh, not by name, of course,
or function—but what she was assured of time and
again was that *they* (nameless and faceless) had
McBoeingSony's best interest at heart. As, of course,
did she, they constantly reminded her. How comforting! "But my heart belongs to McBS . . . BS . . .
BS . . . BE-EE S!"

"Chweep-chweep, chweep-chweep," and she

punched the incoming-call button. "Hello," heaven save her, she was breathless, "Owen?"

"Ah, ah, Ms. Barham? A felicitous day for sharing the sweet sorbet of converse, is it not?" No! No, it couldn't be? The same clipped, faintly over-precise syllables overlaid with a subtly suggestive, caressing tone. How had the Ayatollah gotten through to this line? Trouble?

"M . . . m . . . most esteemed sir, shining crescent of the faith, Mohammed's chosen one . . ." Hasan al-Basri had just recently bestowed upon himself the most ridiculous farrago of honorifics anyone could devise. But ridiculous or not, something must be awry for him to make this surprise call. "Most Honored One, how can McBoeingSony serve you? Has something gone wrong? An unforeseen contingency?" And found herself surreptitiously pawing at the top buttons of her blouse, praying they were securely fastened. No more provocations of that sort—ever! She refused to give either McBS or MitRock any reason to think she'd failed them, was incapable of her task. Not after four fanny-puckering months of the most delicate negotiations to attain even this stage!

A garbled sound—coughing? Choking? What?—finally resolved itself into a chortle, followed by a final, moaning giggle. "Oh, Taylor! It's Owen. I'm *so* sorry." *Like hell you are,* she thought. "I knew I did a pretty fair imitation of the Ayatollah, but I never thought I'd fool your ear for an instant. My briefing noted you have a music background."

A stylus, a scratch pad, and a paperweight ("Greetings from Beautiful Bei-jing") sailed across her office. The paperweight—real marble—was especially satisfying. "Ours is not to reason why," she snapped, but before she could finish, he'd capped her.

"Ours is but to jump so high? How high? As high as you wish, noble sirs." A momentary snuffle indicated a discreet nose-blow, followed by total contrition. "Playing the fool a bit is part of my nature recently. Stress," he mocked himself with the sibilance. "MitRock politely doesn't notice. Rather like keeping a court jester around, as long as I don't ring my bells, caper too crazily around the Pope. And I don't, I assure you. But I'd never do anything to purposely make you look foolish. For that I'm sincerely sorry." He spoke louder and with a more impersonal tone. "Please note for the record, including my personnel file, that this frivolity was entirely my doing. Ms. Barham had no reason to suspect I'd pull a prank like that."

Taylor knew his intent: Recorders at both megagloms were busily filing reports, backups to reports, analyses of said reports, and more. Owen had set the record straight. "Thank you. Now, can we get down to business? It's not every day that Surrogates are accorded the honor of arranging an historic meeting between two such religious powers." Why not go for it? "Or between two such prestigious megaconglomerates. . . ."

Checking the second-flash on his chrono, Owen Pollakowski chewed his cheek lining as Taylor's platitudes rolled on. Good girl to make up for his folly. True, he'd turned manic in the weeks since his sister's ordination, but now it was time to curb it. He bit down on his tongue, the pinch bringing him back to reality. Damn all, why would MitRock and McBS entrust such a sensitive task to two Surrogates? Because of their superlative training, their ability to counsel and cajole, empathize and exhort, turn neutral or partisan in the wink of an eye? Of course. And their ability to be subservient, obedient to written and unwritten corporate rules, and never, *never* expect to make any final decision or any decision at all along the way. And accept how tenuous their positions were. With a rush of shame he realized he'd bent a finger to tick off each point, ignoring Taylor's speech Luckily she'd now started to conclude the platitude section, those laudatory introductory remarks that burnished each megaglom's self-interest. Er, self-image.

"Now, regarding possible locations . . ." he began listing the sites reconnoitered for the meeting, offering a cool assessment of the pros and cons of each, including any political or megaglomic repercussions. Throughout his inventory Taylor made occasional encouraging sounds, a phrase here or there. With a flourish he named his three best sites and detailed preliminary meeting plans. Truth be told, he relished the nuance, the protocol, the detail required. It took his mind off his sister's folly.

Now Taylor took over. "Owen, I agree about the Latin Americas. No point in making the Nuevo Catolicos nervous—not with their Papal Elections coming up. There isn't a megaglom that hasn't made recent overtures. [Translation: Not only offered but freely supplied financial aid with no strings attached in hopes of wooing them. No dice.] Someday some lucky megaglom will crack that nut. [And it had better be McBS.] Sending the Pope and the Ayatollah there would be needlessly provocative." Left unsaid but clearly understood was that PfizerRainforestGlaxo would go ballistic; they prayed their geographic proximity would someday give them an edge.

Taylor's assignment, Owen knew, had been to conduct a "power snoop," an informal canvas of major megagloms to analyze their probable reactions—overt or covert. Not that MitRock wasn't doing the exact same analysis as a countercheck.

An odd, almost *sotto voce* tune prefaced Taylor's next remark. To Owen's untutored ears, it sounded as if she sang "I heard it through the Net-line, oh yeah" and, even as musically inept as he was, the driving beat made him roll his shoulders. "Possible regarding Vancouver, since the PacRim Alliance's *so* diverse. RalPurCokenPepsi had no major objections."

Exactly as he'd suspected! Thank you, Taylor! But she continued, "Still, Angkor Wat has a certain cachet. Religious, but not overly religious, if you follow me." He uh-hummed. As if their debate on the merits and flaws of each site would make a difference—oh, they might—but the final choice wouldn't ever be theirs.

"Not too close to ViacomDisneyBertelsmann's

backyard for their liking?" In a strange twist of fate, China had become perhaps the world's most avid consumer and producer of "entertainment," from virtual reality amusement parks to SenzAround vids and more. Mickey Mao was revered.

Again he heard Taylor's background accompaniment, something mournfully romantic, what he'd classify as from the Southern Americas. "Via con Disnos, my Bertel, via con Disnos, my love . . ." Was she attempting insubordination as well? A gesture of solidarity? For a moment a heady sense of longing swept over him—either music *did* possess strange emotional powers, or he was truly falling in love.

"No, no problem there that I can judge. And to head off your next question, UniCarbBASF has its hands full with the Hindus." How polite of her not to mention the Muslim splinter groups on the Indian Peninsula who totally ignored the Ayatollah's edicts, much to his chagrin.

"Well, I'm sure the Ayatollah will be thrilled not to visit Calcutta. Its nearness flaunts it in his face, just as the Latin Americas would insult the Pope." Why had the Pope looked so self-satisfied recently? It had nothing to do with these plans, he was sure. But Jean-Chrétien looked as if he'd set a move into play on a chessboard, a seemingly-innocent move no one had yet taken into account. And all Owen's encouragements and cajolery hadn't been able to pry it out of him. Religion . . . !

Funny, early in the twenty-first century, roughly a third of the world's population were Christians, and of that, not quite 20% were Catholic, 7% were mainstream Protestants, and the remainder various smaller sects. Islam claimed somewhat more than one worshiper in six, around 18%. But with the split between the Nuevo Catolicos and the OCF, traditional Catholicism was left a dwindling faith—perhaps 5%, while the NCs had swelled to perhaps 18%, thanks to significant Episcopalian and Anglican consolidation. A weighty 14% of the world's faithful espoused Hinduism, but any power they might gain was eternally squandered in perpetual internal strife over the caste system.

God, what had the world come to? Continuing to argue with Taylor, attempting to save face for the Pope, Owen had a premonition they'd be visiting Angkor Wat. Well, make her work for it, then. He continued debating—or baiting Taylor—while another part of his mind ticked off Predominant Protestantism, Fundamentalists (sometimes called Dunkers), MormonOneWorld (good growth prospect now that it'd conquered racism and gender inequality in heaven and on Earth), New Religionists (quasi-Christian sects in Asia and Africa, leavened with a dose of homeland religions), and who knew who else? They shifted, realigned with the same easy virtue as the megagloms, buying and selling souls instead of shares. Enough to make one become a Buddhist—hence Taylor's preference for Angkor Wat, no doubt.

Back into the loop, Owen, he ordered himself. *Be part of the herd, be a good OCF, be pleased your sister has been accepted for the priesthood!* Before he could stop himself, he blurted into the line, "Taylor, my sister Marie was just ordained an OCF priest!"

His anguish pounded her eardrum, raw with regret and pent anger at such a travesty of religious faith. At first she feared he faulted her in some way, that she'd become a surrogate for his anger. "I'm so sorry, Owen. But it must be something she deeply wants, believes in." Wants? To be mutilated like that? And now she could feel an equal fury building within her, the injustice of it all that God—that any godhead of any faith—could demand so much of its followers. Where did a godhead draw the line—death, torture, mutilation? That made the battered soul a better follower? Or simply a more docile one? Sacrilege, blasphemy! *Confiteor deo.* He was Your son.

"I suppose," Owen sounded miserable and weary. "I wish I had her abiding faith."

As they wound up the details, Taylor raised a mental cheer for Rhuven Fisher Weaver—or at least the

Rhuven of yore—his own person, beholden to no one
but God. Now he was a man of dependence, not independence, a follower, licking at a megaglom's heels
like all the rest. What could she do about it? Nothing.
What could she do about Owen's sister? Nothing. But
she could do *something*—not much, perhaps—but
something uniquely hers to make the meeting between
the Ayatollah and the Pope truly memorable. Brighten
Owen's spirits, make them both briefly believe they
were creatures of free will, not a cog in a grinding,
soul-destroying megaglom.

Date: Late afternoon, 29 May 2158
Location: Transient Lodging, 2Golf/Mid,
Satellite Colony Amaterasu

A sneeze built, tickled his sinuses but refused to explode; Glynn touched an inner wrist to his forehead,
convinced he felt feverish. Also tired and utterly
grumpy—most especially at the meteorologist who'd
randomly programmed rain, cold, pounding rain that
had flooded the pathways and his shoes, dripped on
him even beneath the shelter of overhanging habitat
tiers. "Whaa . . ." he experimented, but the "choo!"
remained locked inside. A horrid feeling.

A thousand-and-one errands today—time-consuming
and tedious. Negotiate their "sustainable" payment
for their stay on Amaterasu. Since all the official records showed Jere as "living," a full share had to be
paid for her. Made him want to drink more, breathe
faster, put her shares of water, oxygen, everything else
to use. Actually, they were put to good use; Panny
traveled under Jere's name. Then the shoe repair
shop—almost an anachronism in a world of dispos-
ables—one of the few they trusted to work new life
and suppleness into old, leather performance slippers.
Candy for the children—not just the Gemmies, Heike,
and Hassiba, but himself. Well, Staniar, too. Plus the
extra trip over three sectors and down to the kernel
to buy the fiche Staniar'd casually mentioned the other
night—a peace offering. For Glynn's peace of mind;

perhaps Staniar'd stop glowering. Three shops lacking
the stitchstik Maj needed for everyday clothing repairs. They used it sparingly on the costumes because
it bonded for life; needle and thread were safer for
those—restitch, resize. Those were the "highlights";
didn't even touch on the other 996 soggy errands run.

Oh, he *could* have had Heike or Jeremy do it, but
he'd needed to get clear of the stifling lodgings, their
rehearsal space. Dumping his packages, he grabbed a
towel and scrubbed his head, squeezed the long braid
hanging like wet string down his back. No performance tonight—a small blessing. Somehow, performing Jere's roles wasn't as wonderful as he'd
anticipated. He hung the towel on its hook, grimaced;
cypress-colored towel invisible against cypress wall.
Mold attack! Yes, hilarious if he were Jeremy's age.
What had gone wrong? He hadn't believed he could
live without acting, without the thrill of going onstage,
the power he drew from the laughter, the tears, the
applause of the audience. Symbiotic—some word like
that? Needing each other?

But performing Jere's roles was grueling. The rush
of learning an entirely new character—oh, not entirely
new, and that was part of the problem. He knew, but
he didn't *know*. First he had to divorce himself from
the thirteen years of training he'd absorbed for *his*
roles—utterly forget each one, become the obverse
side of the coin, so to speak. Speak male, not female
roles. Didn't know if he'd land heads or tails some
shows. Some nights everything flowed, he and the new
character as one, and he soared on that old, familiar
surge of ecstasy. But most nights, *most* nights, an aching consciousness of being an inexperienced man (boy,
really, the candy didn't lie) playing a woman who was
playing a man. Even without his character's mask he
felt constantly disguised, one layer or another
shielding him from what he truly was. Claustrophobic!

Grabbing a dry towel and his exercise clothes, he
jammed them into a bag. A little more time by himself
to wallow in self-pity. Exercise, sweat, drive the cold

from his body. Despite the satellites' worries about infectious Earth-borne diseases, the common cold still reigned as king—the most resistant, resilient virus the Earth or the Ring had ever experienced. He sniffled, rubbed his itching nose.

"Miserable out there today, Jere," he commented as he hefted his bag over his shoulder. Complete Z-grav workout or not? No, the sweat would pool, not run, he'd be a floating puddle. Already did that today. "Rain, rain, rain," he whined. "And then *more* rain." A little sympathy would be nice, go a long way to improving his mood. So would a cup of Maj's tea. Maybe later. "I'm going to exercise."

Waiting for Jere to respond, he rubbed his hands together, confident she was searching for a clever response, a pun to cheer him. "Rain supreme," perhaps.

"GLYNN, PLEASE. LET ME DIE! HELP ME! I CAN'T GO ON, I'VE TRIED, BUT IT CAN'T! PLEASE, GIVE ME PEACE!" For a heart-stopping moment he thought tears flowed from her opticams, realized he was so wet, the lodging so warm, that condensation had occurred.

"Don't do that anymore!" He slammed his bag against the wall, stamped his foot, pettish, didn't care who saw, who heard him act this way. "I've had *enough*. Had it up to *here*!" His hand sliced the air above his head. Then he simply stood, mouth-breathing, wracked by the sickening unfairness of the whole situation—of what she'd done to him, what he'd done back at her. He sighed. She tried so hard, so rarely asked the impossible—as she had now—that it was easy at times to forget what she was. Turn his back and he could pretend the old Jere, the mother he knew and loved, had never changed.

Chance padded over in stockinged feet, hitching his kilt into place. A rough hug, half-strangling Glynn, before he turned to Jere. "Bad day, love? Want to talk to Chance about it?"

"SCREW YOU AND EVERY FIX-IT JOB YOU'VE EVER DONE! IF YOU'D ONLY LEFT

A SCREW LOOSE IN THIS MONSTROSITY, I MIGHT HAVE A CHANCE OF DYING! CHANCE OF DYING. A GOOD ONE, HUH?"

"Mother, don't!" Glynn scolded and Chance's face crumpled. Tucking the box under one arm, he gathered his bag and towel with his free hand. "Come on, let's go." Common sense said not to leave Jere near the children while this mood gripped her. She'd never lashed out at them before, but then she'd never attacked Chance either—until today.

Giovanna, their bodyguard from Orvieto, looked up from where she sat slicing water chestnuts with economical motions. An older woman with sunken, all-knowing eyes, she burst into an aria, the words meaningless, except for the bitter "ha, ha, ha!" at the end. Nothing fazed her, but her weary sarcasm at everyone younger than she grated on their nerves. "Shall I come, too?" Never shirked her duty, though. Sarcastic but dependable. Not a hint of an attack in months, but every troupe member still started at a strange sound, a wrong gesture from an outsider, a peculiar, anticipatory dread that left them all constantly wound tighter than Vijay's sitar strings. A constant siege state, siege mentality. Hardly a wonder something—someone—had to explode sometime, somewhere. Left you always with an ear cocked for the next bomb to drop.

He shook his head, managed to smile a thanks. "Was going to Z-grav it, but guess I'll pass. Just go over to the far side there and exercise." He caught her eye. "Some privacy'd be nice."

Catching his drift, Giovanna went back to slicing but kept her eyes open, daring anyone to cross the invisible boundary she'd set. If others couldn't see it, they'd sense it soon enough when her siren voice went off.

Isometric routines, push-ups and situps, jump rope, he whipped through them all, pushing himself harder and harder. *Don't think! Forget it!* But his racing heart couldn't drown out his thoughts. Ran the whole sequence again for good measure. As necessary as their disciplined training routines for movement. After all, the body needs all kinds of exercises. The brain, too— if only he could control the relentless memories. He flopped down beside Jere, all winded, body sweat-drenched and radiating heat as he leaned back and exclaimed "Phew!" to no one in particular. Whether Jere had watched, he couldn't say; sometimes she withdrew completely inside herself.

"YES, A PHEW TOO MANY WHINES AROUND HERE TODAY."

"Guess it's to be expected sometimes." He rubbed an aching calf muscle, strove for nonchalance. Except he couldn't manage it. "Why do you ask me? Why? You promised!" he swallowed unshed tears. "You promised to live to help save *me* from being killed. *You* don't want to be killed either, do you?"

"AH . . . I KNOW WHY. TO TEST MY RE-SOLVE? TEST YOURS? NO, SORRY. BUT GLYNN, THERE'S A BIG DIFFERENCE BE-TWEEN CHOOSING TO DIE AND BEING KILLED. REMEMBER THAT."

He did know the difference, would remember. But his resolve would never waver. If she died, something precious within him would die as well.

Date: 15 June 2158 Location: 2Papa/Mid, Satellite Colony Huang-ti

Gimlet-sharp stare camouflaged by the pretense of half-lidded, sleepy eyes, her shoulders slumped, walk draggy as if she'd just finished a long shift, Becca halted at a kiosk for a stim-drink. "Guaranteed All-Natural," the label proclaimed, though she didn't dare read the fine print too closely; the main ingredient was always some crustacean broth with exotic herbs and spices, supposed stimulants. Popping the spout she willed herself not to wince at her first sip, sprawled on a nearby plastic-pine bench and stretched, her signal that it was safe, clear. Falid and Hamish moved out from cover, diffident but not sneaky. Had pounded that into their heads often enough.

The late-afternoon "sun" baked her shoulders, an errant breeze tossing her hair. Damn! Enough to convince you it was real weather, real wind. Twist of a dial, and hello, sunshine! Too bad the horizons were high, the noon zenith so low. If they'd only do something about these colors—mashed pea green, gruel white, bleh blue. . . . Other than that, it beat NetwArk, especially in the hurricane season. Stationed at the far corner of the herringbone brick path, Anyssa threaded a star-loop through her viewer, apparently engrossed in her task, but equally, deceptively alert.

Although her self-appointed task was to watch for and divert potential trouble, suspicious natives, security patrols who'd roust them, Becca cursed silently as her eyes gravitated yet again to Anyssa. Always studying the girl too closely, as if the danger level rose in her presence. Lips puckered, as much by the stim-bev as her thoughts, she dragged her eyes away. *Do your job, woman.* Why distrust the child so? Or womanchild, more accurately. Not that much younger than she and Vitarosa had been that fateful night in Bogota. Vitarosa's own—her own as well—if not of her flesh then by the rigorous training they'd all absorbed until it was a part of them, motor-muscular memory and mind-set. Yes, Little Sisters of Mortality.

If you couldn't trust a Little Sister, could you trust yourself? The answer to that question, she hurriedly thrust from her mind. Never did a Little Sister experience guilt. Guilt incapacitated. How much was Anyssa Rhuven's child, how much Rosa's? So what? Competing genes, conflicting heredity, could be overridden by training. How many centuries had scientists tried to find answers—a gene for thrill seeking, a gene for placidity, a gene for the follower instinct? Which dominated? Genes or training? How genes meshed, what inhibited or heightened them, no one completely knew. And always expect a rogue gene or two, like the one romping through Vitarosa's breast, her vaccination useless.

With a bound into the mini-square, Falid momentarily blocked foot traffic, the shift-change crowd slowing, flowing around him like a diverted current. Dressed in a motley of colorful castoffs—painstakingly reconstructed by Hamish to reveal bands and diamonds in all color codes of the various manufactories—he reached into his waist-sack and pulled out three star-balls, glow lights flashing inside. Spinning slowly, white-chalked face intent, Falid raised his arms, two glowing star-balls in his left hand, one in the other. A wrist twist and the star-ball rotated around his hand, rolling over his knuckles and home into his palm. A backhanded toss and it hovered above him, precipitously joined by its mates, deft hands creating a continuous halo of light, tiny internal gyro-lamps steadying the star inside each sphere as they circled above.

His practiced hand sought the waist-sack again and additional spheres joined the halo; despite herself Becca was impressed. As physically skilled, as highly trained as she was, juggling was beyond her. Unless, a bare trace of amusement crossed her face, it required keeping weapons in midair, then success was guaranteed. Yes, a flashing climax of throwing knives, lethal mini-laser guns. But the best thing to master was one's body, muscles relaxed yet alert to move in any direction, a lethal killing machine that she "juggled" with as much offhand confidence as Falid did his star-balls. The homeward-bound crowds began to slow, milling around Falid, tired faces lightening, smiling. Whispers of awe and pleasure at the impromptu entertainment.

Street entertainment was rare on the Ring. Not because of regulation, but because self-regulation went far beyond Earth's norm. Hardly like her childhood streets and plazas in Bogota. She and Anyssa had charted its infrequent manifestations here, its hows and whys: sometimes the simple pleasure of sharing an exceptional talent; occasionally for tokens, a way to raise extra, unreported cash. That the guards frowned upon. She continued glancing at the crowd's fringes, noting who stopped to watch in delight, who stayed but glowered. Despite herself, she watched Anyssa watching, looking from her screen to the juggler. No signal, no sign to beware. The girl rubbed her upper lip, the "all-clear" indicating no danger lurked behind Becca. She returned the gesture.

Now Hamish jiggle-jittered into view, a mortified beet-red, gauzy pastel scarves suspended from arms and shoulders, stitched along pant-leg seams. One floated free, veiled itself across a viewer's face. Molting again. Revolving and dipping, scarves flaring, he worked the crowd's perimeter, thrusting a tray as if collecting chits. Although not near enough to see, she knew he'd reject any donations, return each with an eco-kind, printed card. Drop the card on the ground, it automatically decomposed to avoid litter. Indeed, stow it in a pocket or wallet, or tuck it inside a news-flimsy, it politely self-destructed in about two days.

The card read: "Blessed are those with open hearts and minds to hear the Word. Salvation/Healing—http:///www.network.tex/weaver 9:00 p.m. NACST" on one side; "Believe, be blessed, thy hurts and troubles healed." on the other. Sap, pap, pablum for the masses. Anger kindled within Becca at being here, promoting Rhuven's faith, but for the moment that was her assignment. That and guarding Anyssa.

The rest, the best would come later. Time enough for her task, once she was sure, once she'd gauged their reaction. Yes, easy to obey Rhuven's fervent instructions. Years of obedience to Rosa's needs, even her whims, years . . . a few more weeks or months could be spared. Especially since a new blackmail demand would reach NetwArk soon—with an extra, added surprise. That should turn the heat up under Vitarosa and Rhuven; there was no way either could know about the boy . . . unless the Pope had broken his contract. If so, she'd invoke the penalty clause—gutting and filleting.

As she watched, a girl, lanky thin and strikingly coal black, wormed through the crowd until she crouched front and center, careful not to obstruct anyone's view. Odd, yet not that odd; a few other youngsters dotted the audience, though most attended learning centers at this time of day. Now the child temporarily vanished, shielded by a shifting audience, though she tracked her again when Hamish's tray, hovering waist-high, dipped low.

Security cams on pylons and habitat tier-peaks revved, one squeaking as it pivoted, lenses retracting for a panoramic view. So, security had finally scanned this sector level, discovered the bottleneck in foot traffic, the impromptu performance. Guards would arrive soon, move everyone along, restore the tidy, orderly satellite environment. Becca gave a whistle the whole crowd heeded: a "heads up" signal that meant "move on," revert to anonymous business and busyness ahead of the patrol.

The crowd began to peel away, Falid and Hamish using them to cloak their peacock gaudery, fading away along with them. As if to provoke her, Anyssa waited with impeccable timing to move. Becca busied herself, returning to the kiosk, rechecking its selections before moving along, still mimicking the tired gait of a worker well-pleased the shift was done. Not until she briefly slowed to check the now free-flowing traffic did she realize the dark child had slipped into the dimness, frozen there. Ha, learning center truant— no doubt now! Well, they'd scoop her up soon enough. Anyssa now ranged ahead, quick-cutting through the walkways as if the paths were imprinted on her mind, timing her steps until Becca caught up. Something about the dark child, her look of utter self-control and wariness, made her wish she'd had the training of her at an earlier age. Too late now, of course. . . .

Satisfied, Panthat nodded. Almost missed it. Two hawks guarding multicolor birds of paradise. Paradise? Shah nah! Ticky-tacky, flashy-clashy—not fine like Stanislaus. Other hawk she'd not seen that well, but she'd look for her again.

Date: 19 June 2158
Location: 2Oscar/Mid, Huang-ti

Beta Masady stalked the walkways and ramps of Oscar Sector's blue-gray and gray-rose habitant tiers, cane swinging left, right, here, there with metronomic precision. At each gesture toward a convenient flat surface, either Staniar or Chance piled his load in the other's arms and approached the wall, unrolling a holovert poster as he went. Panthat trotted a pace behind, silent, solemn, glue pot in hand. Again and again she fingered the official seal on the side that authorized its use and noted the surcharge for seven-day adhesive, guaranteed to last for one week before causing the poster to biodegrade. Tomorrow Masady would pay another slightly lesser fee, be issued a pot of six-day glue, the countdown continuing until their performance date arrived. So it went on each satellite. Courteous bribery to obtain the adhesive, conscientious adherence to the rules. She pouched her lower lip, thinking. Yes, Masady *was* like glue, the everlasting kind.

With fierce concentration she ran the roller along the poster back at the top as Chance held it steady, then waited while he positioned it on the wall, raised its loose end while she rolled two quick verticals, one horizontal stripe at the bottom. Staniar wasn't above rushing her, jiggling her arm, always impatient. Made her mad-bad impatient with him. Shah! Cool, Panny, be cool. Mad-bad too dangerous. Every satrat learned early the importance of patience; those who didn't rarely lived. A huffing, exasperated sigh and she forced Staniar out of her mind, tested her previous revelation on Chance, whispering, "Masady kinda like glue, too, huh? Once she catch you, you stick-stuck to her, wanna or not."

Chance's broad face froze, then grimaced with suppressed laughter, his shoulders shaking. "Hush, love, or she'll glue us to the wall. Make us announce the show times when anyone passes by." His big hand downstroked the poster, removing air bubbles, smoothing wrinkles.

Despite the fact she'd now seen it and similar ones hundreds of times, awe flooded Panthat. "The Stanislaus Troupe presents the Great Lynn in *Joan of Arc*." Except the Great Lynn wasn't Lynn anymore, but Glynn; Jere's brain locked tight in a box. Any worse being box-locked than being on a satellite, in a satellite? Take out Jere, take out Panthat . . . whoosh! boom and damn-bam-dead! 'Cept Jere still wanted out, wanted dead, no matter what creeping glow-worm words said. Had secret-sneaked her begging words to Glynn sometimes. Panthat shivered, hands running up and down her thin arms, taking shelter inside the lapis sleeves of the kimono jacket Masady had given her. Old costume—made her a proper Stanislaus.

"Shah! Nah!" she mouthed. Not going to happen to Panthat, no way! Not, not! If she dodged on Stanislaus, satrat burrowed again, the odds in favor of her living would improve. Satrat dangers she knew inside out; Stanislaus dangers she didn't. 'Cepting . . . what 'bout Glynn . . . and Jere . . . ? Chance, even Masady? All the others she now cared for . . . 'cept for Staniar . . . sticky old Staniar. A vulgar gesture behind her back in Staniar's direction. Let'm try'n stick-pick her again. Shah! Fix'm, fix him good'n prop, old ball-fall trick. Fix'm good'n he'd act again, boy-voice, man-short, by ding-dong!

The cane's commanding thump and Panthat startled, dashed where the cane pointed as Staniar held the next poster ready, the rest in a sloppy heap at his feet. Glue roller across, wait as he sets the poster, then quick-flick vertical, verti—what? With a sidelong look of gratified malice Staniar didn't wait for her to finish, slammed poster down, swept a forearm over it, pinning her hand and roller between paper and wall. Wouldn't, couldn't dry so fast? Shah? Nah! Heart fluttery, she tried to jerk her hand free, not caring if the poster ripped, the potential of being trapped near-suffocating. Shah! Nooo! Her hand stuck in place!

Again she struggled to free herself, her hand still immobilized, Staniar laughing, half-doubled over.

Damn trusting, damn Staniar, damnall, damnall!
Leave her snared for seven days, hanging-dangling for
everyone to see? Utterly silent, contorted with rage,
she twisted, aimed a vicious kick between Staniar's
spread legs. As he screeched and bent, clutching himself, she grabbed his hair with her free hand, slammed
his head toward her rapidly rising knee. But Chance
intervened, tumbling Staniar backward, cradling his fall.
"He'll remember this. No need to bloody, him, too."

Damnall! Even Chance foe, not friend? Saving Staniar stupid-boy? Betrayal hurt. Dumb Panny, dumb little satrat to trust. Breathing shallow now, eyes slitted.
No hope now. Shim knife deep-burrowed in right
pocket-hidey, can't draw left-handed. No hope of
blading Staniar, sawing her hand free at wrist. The
only escape she could envision. All a trick, everyone
so so nice, so so foul! Laughing-daffy behind hands,
trick'n trap. Catch a satrat, glue it to the wall, nail it
there, watch it kick and scream and die. She'd seen it
happen once in a factory-tier, had slipped in and
bladed the child, no older than she, spoiled their fun
before he could suffer more. Never trust, no never. . . .

A cane prodding her back, that too-familiar spot
right over a kidney, and Panthat tensed to strike,
maim as best she could, goad them into a quick, killing
blow. Killing-kindness. "You're not Joan of Arc at the
stake, that role's been filled," Masady flattened her
against the wall. "Hold still, I have to lean so I can
spray high enough." A high-pressured spraying hissed
in Panthat's ears, the scent nose-burning strong, tear-
inducing. "Heavens, I've better things to do with you
than leave you hanging out to dry for seven days,
child." Panthat could feel her wrist and hand slip
slightly, easing down toward the poster's bottom edge.
" 'Besides, you could free yourself once it thoroughly
dried, but it's inconvenient, uncomfortable waiting.
Can you hang on to the roller for me so we don't
have to buy a new one?"

Mistake? Maybe wrong? No, no mistake with Staniar, maybe others . . . yes. Masady not leaving her. Mistake? What did Masady say? Joan of Arc? Steak? Considering it, Panthat decided she could live with being glued to a prime cut of meat, real meat. Ruby's stories, mouthwatering, about meat. But that didn't sound like what Masady meant. "Steak?" she asked, faintly, as more and more of her dark arm and hand, coated with a white powdering of spray and glue, slid free.

"Yes, you know, Joan of Arc tied to the stake, burned at the stake." Beta Masady sprayed again, was swept up in a flurry of explosive sneezes against Panthat's back, the child bracing herself to support the suddenly shuddering body.

"Make more sense to burn steak stead of Joan of Arc? Cook it, not her?" Free, she was free! Stood there cautious, unsure whether to trust again, whether to flee, but most of all wanting an answer, curiosity aroused as she peeled a thin coat of glue from her skin.

Staniar groaned, rolled over to glare at them. "Stupid satrat, brain-dead, assuming you started out with one. Probably didn't, why else'd you be thrown out to be a satrat?"

"On the contrary, Staniar. I sometimes think she has the makings of a better Stanislaus than you do." A cane prod at his thigh, a wave at the disordered pile of posters, then at Chance. "Let's be along, now. I paid for seven-day adhesive and I plan to use it." Still-dark brows winged toward white hair. "Don't blame Chance for rescuing Staniar. He knows I won't tolerate bloodshed within the troupe."

Vibrating with muttered curses and snarls, Panthat and Staniar maintained a calculated distance from each other, and the rest of the postings went without incident as they traveled from sector to sector and "south" until they reached Newcome Port Observation Deck. With a satisfied but tired sigh Masady sank onto one of the grav benches at the perimeter, short legs, tiny feet aswing. Chance sat behind her on the bench, his wide back a bolster for Masady. Swaggering as much as possible while still semi-stooped, Staniar brought drinks from the refreshment kiosk, presenting them with a flourish to Masady and Chance, taunting Panthat by holding hers as far away as possible, daring her to grab. Her least favorite flavor, a sickly-sweet concoction that set her teeth on edge, chosen on purpose.

"Staniar," Chance warned, and her drink edged closer. But Chance bridged the distance, hand engulfing the beverage pouch as he passed her his own drink. "I like this better—if you're willing to trade?"

In the distance the Earth, all swirls of blue and white, greens and browns, drew their eyes like a magnet. Unknown yet so known, a lodestone with seductive attraction. Always a subtle yearning toward it, no matter that life was better here than there. A remembrance of things past.

Shah! Nah! Panthat shook herself, broke the pull. Thanky but no thanky, happy here, who cares, who needs? Chance said that preacher man, that Weaver with his NetwArk promised a heaven of perfection up above, farther'n the satellites, farther'n Mars, Juppy-loopy-ter even. Silly. Silly, she groped for the word, nasti-algae, people felt for an Earth, a heaven they'd never see. Nasti-algae was right. Good ol' Ringy-Ding heaven and hell and Earth combined, best and worst of all places, righto-right. Ruby in rant'n-rave with stories of the past, hairy fairy tales to teach satrats. Today counted, now, tomorrow maybe. Past was past; either you survived it or you didn't. Same with the future. So far she had; Staniar a small thorn in her side compared to what she'd survived before. She took a deep sip of her drink, flashed Staniar a smile as sweetly cloying as the beverage he'd chosen for her.

Beta Masady's wrinkled face wore the same yearning look Panny'd seen on so many others, even BenRuby's at times. But his had been mixed—yearning with fury, a breast-beating, garment-rending display once a year, the sobbed "Next *century* in Jeru-

salem? So long, abba, too long!" What was it like to
have not only a past, but a heritage? A tentative pat
at beta Masady's thigh to distract her, just as she'd
done with Ruby. "Why did Stanislaus rocketa-socketa
to the SatRing?" Maybe it mattered to learn the hows
and whys of it all, the yesterdays past and gone.

What had snared Jere, boxed her tight, was her past,
Masady had sworn. 'Sides, she was furious-curious.
Shah, curiosity could kill—or help you survive if you
conned some new trick. Like why that distant blue
marble attracted, why lineage mattered? No baggage
on *her* back, nah, Panny all fresh and new.

Staniar grimaced and clapped hands over his ears,
subsiding at a dagger look from Masady. "You've
heard it before, boy, and you'll hear it again till you
appreciate its value."

Shifting his arms along the bench to support himself,
support Masady's fragile weight, Chance leaned back,
his head resting on her shoulder. "I've heard bits and
pieces from Jere. Never heard the whole story,
though."

Panthat slid her hands up her arms, clutched her
elbows in anticipation beneath the wide blue sleeves.
What made Jere tick-tock, not just the box, but what
gave her life, meaning, a being beyond the life-support
system? If she could snare a shadow of that, perhaps
she'd ken Glynn better, too. . . .

Date: 1 March 2032
Location: Zlanst, Lower Chechnya, Earth

Gennadi Stanislaus Rimskyakoff stretched his bad leg,
propped it along the length of his cane, and tentatively
shifted his bottom against the rotten olive-drab canvas
of his camp stool. A shiver at the cold, the dampness,
and he rubbed chapped hands together. The air hung
moist and humid, overpowering with chlorine, almost
enough to override the sour smells of perspiration and
dirty towels, mold and mildew. Another shiver; the
pool, at least, was marginally warmer than the air.
"Start again, ladies," he shouted and rubber-capped

heads turned, not in unison, but haphazardly, bodies
a distracting underwater blur. "If you can't manage
a unison turn, pretend your mismatched moves were
intentionally choreographed." Choreographed? Ha!
How to make them understand? "A chord of music
does NOT consist of random notes, but a concordant,
harmonic relationship of pitches." At least one head
nodded, too vigorously, and vanished underwater,
snorting bubbles of surprise breaking the surface, followed by thrashing waves. "Someone pull Katarina
clear, please."

How in the name of the Holy Ghost had he sunk so
low as to coach a synchronized (Synchronized? Only if
hell froze over and saved these girls from themselves
and the water?) swim team from the upstart republic
of Lower Chechnya? An embittered scrap of land renowned only for its poverty and the internal and external warfare that had reduced the male population
by almost half. The same rough-hewn pride and com-
bativeness he'd been instructed to refine and reshape
into competitiveness—-capture the gold in one or two
events in the forthcoming Olympics.

Ha! What did *he,* Gennadi Stanislaus Rimskyakoff,
know about swimming? He who could barely dog-pad-
dle! A gingerly punch at the button on the ancient
tape deck's "play" button, a prayer the grainy, worn
tape wouldn't break again. He'd already truncated
Handel's *Water Music* (the irony had not escaped him)
of nearly half the notes the composer had penned.
"Now remember," he shouted hopelessly, "grace,
buoyancy, fluidity! If you can't move in unison, think
of a domino effect, your gesture a beat after your
teammate's, in sequence down the line. Make it look
as if each one chose the other. Fluidity, fluidity! Remember, you're practically weightless, buoyant, you
float. Each action, each gesture must reflect that ease
of movement, almost like floating in space—you defy
gravity for the moment."

Defy gravity? Yes! An excited bounce on his stool
but Gennadi Stanislaus scarcely registered the canvas

giving another rip beneath him. Yes! And why not? He'd been born in time to remember the glories of the Union of Soviet Socialist Republics before its dissolution, the ensuing chaos, chaos he'd barely survived. So close! He'd been so close to making the final Soviet Olympic gymnastics team, but for a freak accident that sent him soaring off the rings as a strap broke, shattering his right leg and pelvis. The gold, the glory, once so tantalizingly close, now forever beyond reach, and at twenty-two he'd begun coaching. But the ability to "do" and to "explain" are two different talents. Mediocre as a coach, he'd bounced from republic to republic, his near-Olympic status his passport to coaching youngsters. Many new republics remained wary of anyone not of their religious or ethnic group but were willing to overlook it if he could train champions for them. As even his minor successes became rarer, the job offers dwindled, ever fewer and farther between.

He'd not coached in twelve years when this job had come along. Instead, he and his young wife, Siem Vy, granddaughter of Cambodian temple dancers—among the thousands upon thousands of artists and intellectuals slaughtered or driven from their land by Pol Pot— had formed an acting troupe. Its members: Gennadi Stanislaus and his wife, their four children, relatives from both sides of their families, and—as always—the luckless, ill-fated orphans cast up by whatever war was being fought in whichever lands they traveled through. Innocents, the flotsam and jetsam of a destructive world that smashed them with the same numbing regularity as the rolling waves themselves. At fifty-seven, Gennadi Stanislaus wasn't too old to fight, but his badly healed leg and pelvis exempted him from active duty—an escape that few other males from fifteen to sixty-five managed.

A way to protect his children, blood relatives or not, had been strikingly simple, once Siem Vy put her mind to the problem. Men in the troupe were relegated to backstage activities, did not appear in public to avoid being drafted. Their repertoire already consisted of snippets of classical works from around the world, and Siem Vy's uncle Saung had molded marvelously concealing masks that immediately identified each character. With masks, the audience couldn't tell who was behind them—young or old, male or female, native or nonnative. Siem Vy's final stroke of genius had been to advertise the troupe's "authenticity," its roots in the Yüan plays, Elizabethean theater, Cambodian temple dances, and more. Women acted all male roles, while the female characters were played by young boys who, on reaching the military service age of fifteen, would be patriotically released to serve whichever army now battled to liberate or defend their land. In truth, the teenage boys hid backstage. It was a tenuous plan, hardly perfect, but "out of sight, out of mind" did do wonders. So did the mystique, the legend in which they cloaked themselves. A troupe of boys, women, and a few old men.

Gennadi Stanislaus could scarcely wait for the water torture to finish, forcing himself to count all eight heads as they clambered out of the pool, struggling like beached whales. (Unfair—whales exhibited more grace.) Bidding them good night, he limped back to the square where Stanislaus Troupe was setting up that night's performance. On his journey home, streetlights shot out, the occasional tracer burning a red trail through the air, he ignored the crumpled buildings, the dark, shell-pocked streets, the hazardous footing, and peered into the night sky to spot the wheeling orbit of the first four satellites of Waggoner's Ring.

It all fit together—the incredibly subtle, graceful movements of Siem Vy's temple dancer relatives, rigorously trained from an early age; his gymnastics training; the water's buoyancy! Yes! Like Zero gravity! God, yes, train his people in Z-grav and he'd have a troupe like no other. And Z-grav meant Waggoner's Ring, a place of hope and harmony. Danger as well, but no more than here or any other land he knew.

Possible? Not possible? The satellites were still

growing, expanding in size, more to be launched if rumor could be believed. Given the notorious unreliability of the news, rumor was as credible as anything else he could measure by. Suddenly anything seemed possible—except the words—his bravura vision flaming and crashing as he haltingly explained it to Siem Vy. Reality struck: Little was possible, much was impossible, the story of his life. "And there's no reason they'd want us, let us in," he'd concluded miserably, wanting to kick himself for that animating moment of hope, the potential to fly, dream without the flaming crash. "They're only taking scientists, engineers, skilled technicians, people they can utilize. No need for us, a fifth-rate theatrical troupe."

Siem Vy, barely half his age, half his size, her long, dark hair like a river down her back, had stood on tiptoes and kissed him. "Stanislaus, you are a *genius,* a genius grounded by despair." Her arm floated above her head, curved, each finger a delicate petal-curve. A blink of shock as she broke the pose, brought her arm down in a savage slashing motion. "And the problem with geniuses is that they aren't practical, pragmatic. That's where I come in." Her exquisite fingers touched, thumb meeting first and second fingers in a circle, then she began to rub them together in an age-old gesture. "It's how my relatives escaped from Cambodia, how you, how we have survived here often enough."

She made the gesture again, fingers under his nose. "Bribes, Gennadi Stanislaus, baksheesh, payoffs, kick-backs, suitable and subtle remuneration to the proper authorities to make them more . . . amenable, shall we say? Able to turn a blind eye toward what they don't wish to see? We'll bribe our way onto the shuttles, offer payoffs to stay on the satellites. Don't you see, Gennadi Stanislaus, those people up there must be starved for decent entertainment, for *any* entertainment. They need pleasure, too. And that's what we'll provide!"

The rest was history, Stanislaus Troupe's history.

Date: 19 June 2158
Location: Newcome Port Observation Deck, Huang-ti

"And the rest is history," Masady echoed as she cuffed Staniar for staring at a loitering woman wearing a jumpsuit with the red-and-gray sleeve of a bioengineering tech. Panthat beamed, both at the story and at Staniar's comeuppance. Shah! Beta Masady's people had started life here much as she had, underground, wary of authority, eking out a living, or at least a life, in a world unfriendly to those who didn't fit in, who lacked technical skills. Canny Stanny Troupe! Canny Panny! Warmed by the thought, her gaze drifted toward the figure who'd captured Staniar's attention, brought him trouble. No secret face for Staniar, everything readable in each frown or scowl. Good thing he'd been safely masked during his performance days. Mask him again, not have to see old scowl-puss.

A vigorous head-scratch to clear her mind. Odd, odd, she'd seen that woman before. Impassive, she stared beyond the figure, running her tongue along her teeth. Where? This satellite or 'nother? Wait, wait . . . brain-pop coming! Same face, different uniform. Ah, the watcher woman that day the juggler'd stopped traffic, his clownish partner handing out little cards. 'Nother woman watcher, too, younger, though she'd never managed to squint her over. "Wonderthunderful story, beta Masady. Thanking you for sharing, make me part of you a small while." Her eyes still scanning, aching to crane her neck, check if the other woman loitered as well. First one too moldy-old for Staniar, too strong, too. Chew Staniar up'n spit him out. Ha! Maybe Staniar liking pain-play! Shah! Borrow beta Masady's cane, threaten, threaten, but never hit. Drive Staniar crazy!

She didn't realize everyone had risen until Chance plucked her up by the elbows. "Can't resist checking for danger, can you?"

"Danger? Shah? Nah!" Careless Panny, she scolded, careless beamy-dreaming and danger creep too close. Hide the shock that Chance had slipped inside her guard, caught her unaware. "I'm danger-ranger to anyone crossing me. Ask Staniar!"

"Well, danger's something we'd best watch for, child. Never forget it," Masady reminded.

"Shah!" Just then she glimpsed the other woman, but still not clearly enough to identify. Say hey? Or shah? Just be coiled and waiting, not get caught in beamy-dreaming or paranoid-void like the others. Shah, that best.

Date: 6 July 2158
Location: Angkor Wat, SoChinaSeas Territories, Earth

A hurried heel catching in the straw mat, Taylor Barham pitched forward, found herself in the arms of a tall, thin man with worried gray eyes and a receding hairline. "Owen?" She broke free, clutching for her battered dignity, angry at her lack of judgment. What if he *wasn't* Owen? Was a spy, an assassin, a danger to the Ayatollah or the Pope, due in minutes? An enigmatic Buddha figure loomed behind her, the granite-faced smile that had struck her as so gentle, guileless, now appeared to smirk at her negligence. As if to set her mind at ease, Owen Pollakowski handed over his MitRock ID, kept his hand outstretched while she played her mini-scan over his wrist chip and ID. And if he spoke, she'd know for sure, her musical training never let her forget the cadence and tone of a voice—especially after his previous prank.

Neutral territory, a neutral religion, a perfect place to hold a summit of such magnitude, she hoped. Yet no matter how many corporate raiders MitRock and McBS had stationed outside for protection, backed by enough firepower to demolish the rebuilt temple and the surrounding land for miles, all it would take to destroy this fragile entente was one assassin from a rival megaglom. The balance of power altered with one tug of a laser-gun trigger, or the precise overhand toss of a grenade. She shivered. A fear chill, not cold, and she wordlessly refused Owen's offer of the jacket he'd slipped from his shoulders.

A saffron-draped temple priest bowed tremulously at the pair, scurried close on whispering bare feet. "It is all arranged, Mr. Pollakowski, Ms. Barham." He folded his hands in front of him, the overlapping thumb anxiously fluttering. "Remember, this is a holy place, even if not of your religion, your beliefs. Treat it with respect, just as I would so treat your house of worship, should I ever have the humble honor to visit Mecca or Rome."

Inclining his head, eyes respectfully lowered, Owen reassured the priest. "It shall be as you asked, our word on it. We thank you, both of us," his glance included Taylor, and she smiled, "for making this holy sanctuary available. May Buddha's compassionate wisdom guide our discussions." Not bloody likely, he told himself morosely, not when devil meets devil. Could the world hold more than one Satan? God, how he hated his job! The monk slipped away, leaving him with Taylor once more. "Are we ready?"

Yes, definitely his voice. She'd regained her confidence, or at least enough to carry her through. A curt nod of acknowledgment as she placed the player on the floor, popped in a button-sized disk. "You remember how I've set it up? Two minutes dead-air before the music starts, time enough for us to reach the waiting rooms, ready to escort our charges. If we march to the music, use it as our guide, we should all arrive at the same time, thus," she made a face, "avoiding soul-searing questions of precedence."

A hint of near-malicious merriment flared in Owen's pale gray eyes. "Yes, the quandary of whether to salaam or prostrate one's self and kiss the ring could cause no end of confusion." His index finger tapped his lower lip thoughtfully. "What did you finally select? Something totally outrageous, I hope. Muezzin chants overlaid with Gregorian, backed by a throbbing hint of drums?"

She paused, hand poised over the "play" button.

"No, I decided on a truly celebratory piece. The joys of being a music history major. *The 1812 Overture.* Know it?"

Brow furrowed, Owen scrubbed meditatively, searching his mind for the little he knew about antique music. His slow, dawning smile widened. "That bombastic pealing of bells, the cannonades at the end? You *did* warn our corporate raiders outside, didn't you?"

"Yes. Played it through for them several times. Gave a disk to your security chief as well as with the same instructions."

"Be-ump, be-ump, be-ump, be-ump, ump, BOOM! Inspired! I salute you." Matching action to words, he kissed her on both cheeks, stepped back a pace, clicked his heels. "Ready." With that she depressed the button and turned, both of them briskly exiting in opposite directions, counting the seconds under their breaths. . . .

The meeting, a few minutes later, began with a greater bang that Owen had anticipated. "Pig of an infidel!" His turban partially unwound, looking as if someone had dumped a load of laundry on his head, the Ayatollah's dark eyes peered between streamers of material. "Antichrist! I spit on Mohammed's grave," the Pope screamed from his refuge behind a chair, face sweat-beaded, skin ashy with fear. "To attack so at a time of truce—" "Allah is merciful, misguiding your minions' shots—"

Jaw dropping, Owen worked to soothe, coax Jean-Chrétien into his chair, then whirled, whispering, "You didn't tell *them* what music you selected? *Either* of them?" An ear-splitting grin threatened his composure, not to mention his job. But discipline and endurance, not to mention self-abnegation had carried him this far in his career, and he wasn't about to jeopardize it.

"Well, it *did* ensure they met an equal footing," she hissed back, then spoke rapidly, quickly explaining as she chivied the Ayatollah from behind his redoubt of an overturned table. She scrupulously left his turban untouched, let the Ayatollah deal with its intricacies.

After their shaking and the joint recriminations finally dissipated, the meeting gained a semblance of order, Jean-Chrétien and Akbar Hasan al-Basri united in their contempt of their Surrogates, their corporate backers, and more than willing to reach an historic agreement: to work together, Catholic and Muslim alike, to crush the upstart Rhuven Fisher Weaver. Both Taylor and Owen were thick-skinned, used to the invective. What mattered was precisely what MitsubishiRockwell and McBoeingSony had planned, temporary religious and corporate unity to halt Weaver and that *arriviste* megaglom, MabasutaGenDy. Yes, MitRock and McBS had engineered events with implacable thoroughness. One could crush an upstart fire ant barefoot—or while wearing shoes. Better to wear shoes, although it didn't matter much to the ant, equally dead either way. So it would be with MabasutaGenDy, Owen knew.

Relaxed, suffused with pleasure over this genuine accord, Pope Jean-Chrétien lounged at ease now, sandals with fat toes peeping mouselike from under his robe, teacup balanced on his paunch. "We need an internal wedge, a way to drive Weaver and his wife apart. Her influence is greater than most realize; she initiated the contact with MabasutaGenDy. Always before they've spurned megaglom aid." Envy momentarily burned in his gut, but pragmatism conquered it. He leaned forward, intimately confidential, "Do you know any background?"

Toying with a macaroon, Hasan al-Basri's hand finally swooped, the sweet disappearing beneath his mustache. A loud smacking of lips. "No, but my heart and soul thirst for your words, the sweet waters of your vast knowledge. I, too, have warmed my heart all these years with some secret knowledge of these people." He placed his fist over his heart, then cast his hand open, "I stand ready to share with you, pool our respective wisdom." His eyes, however, kept straying to Taylor.

With a disapproving "ahem" to reclaim his attention, the Pope spoke. "The time for selfish hoarding has passed. My brother, I beg you, speak first in honor of our friendship." A snap of his fingers. "More tea?"

Owen reacted ahead of Taylor, stepping forward to pour. The way the Ayatollah ogled Taylor made him fume, and he refused to give Hasan al-Basri the opportunity to do it again at close range. Surrogates put up with too much, the price paid for working for a megaglom. Meeting in person was exhausting; the vidscreen salved dignity, professionalism with the balm of distance.

The Ayatollah dipped his mustache near his cup, blew at the rising steam, gaze again drifting toward Taylor's rump as she bent to reorganize the tea tray. "Admirable, admirable," and actually had the nerve to wink at Owen. "My secret is one I believe Rhuven Fisher Weaver himself knows not. That his wife, the lovely Vitarosa, is a beauteous but poisonous fruit on the vine. She is a trained assassin, one of the Little Sisters of Mortality, a cult that grew out of the outrageous political actions of your archenemies, renegade priests and nuns, Nuevo Catolicos in the Latin Americas." Jean-Chrétien gave a terse nod, made the sign of the cross, and clenched his hands tight on the arms of his chair at the mention of the Nuevo Catolicos.

The Ayatollah leaned forward confidingly, "Her final mission, totally unauthorized, shocked even her heretic order: She murdered her father and two half brothers. After that she fled, embraced Rhuven and his beliefs at NetwArk. He, foolish soul that he is, believed her virtuous, an innocent, traumatized by her mother's death, her father's sudden murder, and in fear for her own life when she fled RoraimAndes. Richly amusing, is it not? Such irony."

Another sip and he delicately wiped his lips, clearly pleased with himself. "Now, I know your heart rejoices at my news, just as mine will jubilate over yours," and paused, expectant.

Settling back in the chair, hands tucked inside his sleeves, Jean-Chrétien took his time getting comfortable, allowed Owen to hover with a neck pillow, only to refuse it. Stale news, very stale. Was this the best the Ayatollah could do?

"In my secret we may have the wedge we need to sow discord between the Navigator of NetwArk and his wife." The Ayatollah's eyebrows sailed like a hawk's wings catching an updraft, and the Pope continued, clearly gratified, "Unbeknownst to Vitarosa, indeed, unbeknownst to the holy Rhuven himself, we believe, a bastard son exists. This love child was conceived shortly after the birth of their daughter, when Vitarosa had sunk into a deep depression. He dallied with none other than the actress hailed as the Great Lynn, of Stanislaus Troupe on Waggoner's Ring while she visited Earth. Or so we've been led to believe." And so he would lead the Ayatollah to believe.

The Ayatollah stared into the distance, or so Owen thought until he realized he was admiring the carvings of sinuous, curvaceous temple dancers on the far wall. "Was there not some sort of murder attempt on the Great Lynn about . . . about a year ago? Perhaps less? Though it came to naught, so I later heard."

The Pope paused before answering, longer than he liked at his own internal debate. Tell Hasan al-Basri who'd ordered the Great Lynn's death? Tell him that, in truth, he'd already tapped the wedge firm. A mumbled prayer to disguise his dilemma. Finally he added, "Exactly. Her death would have deprived the world of a superlative actress, regardless of her morals." No, not all secrets should be revealed, some should be saved, savored, misered. There were sins of omission, and sins of commission, he consoled himself. The wedge still remained to be driven home, but Vitarosa would accomplish that herself; they need not further sully their hands.

Toying with his turban, Hasan al-Basri seemed

equally wrapped in thought. Why anyone would want to watch a woman pretending to be a man eluded him. Thoughts of Taylor in a diaphanous costume . . . as the Prophet's blessed wife, of course . . . not some houri. Very . . . edifying. With a jolt he returned to more immediate concerns. "If the actress lived, then clearly Vitarosa wasn't involved. According to what we know of the Little Sisters of Mortality, they *never* miss their target. Though I believe her injuries were worse than we've been led to believe." A stroke of the mustache, so wonderful for veiling expressions.

What was the value in telling that fat fool everything? How could one respect a man who believed in near-gelding his followers? And wondered for the thousandth time whether Jean-Chrétien had practiced his preachments, or whether the Pope, yes, their infallible Pope, was beyond sharing such suffering. Never trust those who enjoy mortifying their flesh for their god. Falid would remain his secret, still had a role to play, even though marooned in space, unable to report on Vitarosa's daily activities, Rhuven's expanding empire of the faithful.

Date: 27 July 2158
Location: Transient Lodging, 6India/Mid, Satellite Colony NelMandela

Dinner made palatable by indulging in her fantasy of Vitarosa receiving the blackmail note—ah, soon, so soon—Becca methodically shoveled the wretched food into her mouth. What she could truly savor was Rosa's shock, dismay, her wrath at discovering that Jere's son was Rhuven's son as well. Ah, a sweet recipe for revenge! Revenge? No, a mere balancing of accounts, of finally receiving her due. Hamish's leg flailed under the table, connected with her shin, brought her back to herself and the realities of the moment. Reality enough to set her teeth on edge.

Fastidiously pushing aside her plate, she brushed at the leftovers strewing the table, stared with veiled distaste at Hamish and Falid; Falid, fidgety, pickily precise; Hamish semisomnolent as usual after his gorging. She despised such physical weakness, Hamish's gluttony a barometer of his fears, rising and falling to indicate the pressures he felt. Falid's fussiness manifested his desperate need for order and control. Petty, weak men, both, but the best Able-Bodied Savers NetwArk offered for her needs. How like Rhuven to attract the weak, the malleable, trusting in a power beyond them instead of their own strength and determination. Depend on them in a pinch—hardly. Not as she would a Little Sister of Mortality.

Anyssa sat calm and watchful, earning her discreet approval. Well, her training wasn't complete, but the hard core of discipline showed in the girl, though still untested. Always the tendency to ask too many questions or, at least, think them. Command was a burden, especially if one lacked full faith in one's squad. Command without action—weeks of watchful waiting stretching behind her—no activity, wore at her, made her wonder if her edge were dulled. Drove her to stupid daydreams, the sort of thing she'd expect Anyssa to indulge in. Better to be the lithe leopardess stalking and striking her prey, not the cat watching the mouse hole, waiting for movement.

Banging the table—it was action, at least—she watched Hamish and Falid start guiltily, though Anyssa never flinched. "Word from Rosa today." Transmitted by MabasutaGenDy's aging comsats, the message had been heavily scrambled in their old childhood code. Shock—*weak, Becca, weak to let emotion betray you,* she chided—at the wave of longing that had engulfed her, a longing for those simpler, uncomplicated days of Little Sisterhood before Rosa's impulsive actions had severed them forever. No sense telling them the full message. No sense testing how much Falid or Hamish knew about NetwArk's MabaGD funding, no need for them to hear how MabaGD was beginning to run scared from the combined power of McBS and MitRock. Cowardice, always cravens around her.

Feverishly scanning the table for further sustenance,

Hamish finally contented himself with cramming a hoarded energy bar into his mouth, its wrapper crackling annoyingly. "What news, then? I know we haven't converted many yet, but we *have* increased the listening base. That's a start. Isn't it, Falid?" he appealed, the energy bar pouched in his cheek.

Falid stilled him with a warning hand, flicking away the wrapper before Hamish could crumple it again. "Is that Vitarosa's current concern?"

At least Falid possessed a functioning brain. A small blessing. "She's heard rumors, some displeasing rumors. We need hard evidence to dispel those rumors or accept them as gospel fact." She caught Anyssa's fleeting amusement at the phrase "gospel fact." Fine, be amused—just don't show it. If I can read you, so can someone else. Oh, there was Rhuven's gospel, but the gospel according to Vitarosa carried greater weight.

"Her question is this: 'Did you or did you not kill Jerelynn?' I've wondered that as well. In case you haven't noticed, every surface of each satellite we've visited is plastered with holoverts announcing her next performance in this or that. Well?" She rested her forearms comfortably on the table's edge, hands folded, lounging at ease. From that position she could move deadly fast, lunge for a throat. The pleasurable thought, the pleasurable feel of a windpipe being crushed was comforting.

Falid ran his tongue over his upper teeth, dark eyes calculating, while the last crumbs from Hamish's energy bar lodged in his throat. "It's not entirely clear, although we strongly believe we did. We think the posters are a ruse."

Wonderful! At least they "thought!" All she could do not to charge off the bench, thigh muscles tensing. "*Not* clear? How can it be *not* clear? What makes you think the posters are a ruse? Where's your evidence? Either she's dead, or she's alive—the two are polar opposites. I doubt there's an in-between." If there were, she'd dearly love to introduce Hamish and Falid to it. "The posters advertise their star, the Great Lynn.

True or not true? If she's dead, who's performing her roles? Are they pulling the wool over the eyes of their public, over *our* eyes? Have you even attended one show to determine the truth—with or without my permission? Or have you merely *assumed . . .* ?" she drew out the word with a hiss.

Hamish's voice trembled like a flute, crumbs spewing from his mouth. "We think the boy—"

"What boy?" How could they know? *Her* secret. Out of the corner of her eye Becca caught Anyssa's suppressed chin rise of agreement. Did *she* know? How had they stolen a march on her?

"Jere's son. We think he's performing his mother's roles." Falid answered with utter evenness, every betraying twitch mastered. "Or we inadvertently killed him instead of Jere. We didn't realize . . . they were on-deck together that night. He's near full-grown now. From the back they looked almost identical . . ." he trailed off.

For the first time Anyssa spoke. "You know who the boy's father is, don't you, Becca?" But before Becca could find a way to skirt the truth, Anyssa answered for her, coolly as if she'd solved an impersonal mathematics problem. "Rhuven's his father as well as mine." A calculated pause. "Or so I suspect . . . but that's not *proof,* as you and Mother always say."

God have mercy, first Falid and Hamish and now Anyssa? Do not allow the mind to reel, you control it. Calmness, rationality, think it through, Becca! Don't rip out someone's throat before you know. Analyze it. Hamish and Falid knew of Jere's son, but said nothing about paternity. Fine, any fanrag could tell them Jerelynn had a son.

But how could Anyssa know? Did Rosa know as well? The new blackmail note wasn't due for another week. Suddenly everything was moving too fast, sliding out of her control if she weren't careful. "How did you learn this?" she shot back at Anyssa, and realized with a sinking feeling she'd just helped confirm Anyssa's hunch simply by her choice of an answer.

"Your reaction," Anyssa muttered at her plate. "Your eyes bulged, not with shock at hearing me say something so stupid, but in surprise, astonishment that I could know." Clearly anxious now, she emphasized, "It wasn't meant as a trick. The pieces just fit together."

"Taught you well, too well." Becca rubbed her chin, her mind spinning, straightening out new kinks in her plan. Get out of this ahead, snatch back control—here and down below at NetwArk. Either way she'd best jump ship as soon as possible, but not until this was finished. She'd written the ending, refused to see it altered. *Her* choice this time, no one else's. Final payment for her love for Vitarosa, and then Becca's payment was due. Rosa'd never double-cross her, not her anchor, her beloved Becca, after all these years. Oh, Rosa was heedless often enough because she always believed Becca'd forgive her, had always forgiven the hurts large and small that friends, Little Sisters, inflicted on each other. "So what about Rosa's message? Is Jere alive or not?"

"There are a few pieces missing, but I think we can find out."

"Find out what? Be precise," she barked.

Eyebrows rocketed over innocent gold-brown eyes. "About Jere. And the boy, if we want more proof of his paternity." The cropped hairs on Becca's neck rose as if she'd been challenged. Would Anyssa wrest control from her? Or was the child merely striving to be useful? In those short seconds Becca decided she'd make a point of never turning her back on Anyssa again, the blend of Rhuven and Vitarosa more potentially volatile than she'd anticipated. She would *not* allow everything to be snatched from her grasp—not now! It was *her* turn now!

"How do you plan to do that?" Find out what Anyssa knows, use it, build on it. You have greater experience, a more logical mind, superior skills.

"Everything is recorded *somewhere,* easy to find if you know how and where to search." Anyssa almost faltered as she realized how dangerously close she'd come to lecturing Becca. "I keyed in the codes for roughly the last year of passenger lists for intra-Ring transit; the debit lists for 'sustainables' charges. Put them together, and you'll see that for about the last six months each troupe has been short a member for a month at a time. If they travel with twenty-five people, it's twenty-four that one month. Regular as clockwork, first Tierney, then Orvieto, then Magyar." She paused, considered.

"Interestingly enough, on those months, that missing member is listed under Stanislaus. The name shows up in their cast and crew listings—checked the Drama Library files for that. So what are these bit players, crew members doing with Stanislaus?" A deep breath. "I think they're protecting something, someone—Jerelynn or Glynn—I can't be sure. It makes sense."

Despite herself, Becca had to credit the girl for her thoroughness. It *did* make sense—in a way. Better yet, she had them back on track. "Then I just might slip into their quarters some night, do a little checking. Visual verification's next." And perhaps a little killing. Except, except, not the boy. Not yet, not until Vitarosa's heard the news, learned of his existence.

"Ah, yes, verification . . . but . . ." Becca knew that tone, waited with suppressed impatience to hear the rest. Oh, Anyssa'd make it sound—of course—as if Becca'd planned it. She'd done the same to superiors herself when she'd been Anyssa's age. "But don't you think a slower, more subtle approach might gain more, better information than a quick scan? Things can be hidden, people too, or simply absent for some logical reason the one night you choose." She held up a hand to forestall Becca. "Given the timing, Stanislaus is due to have a new member join them. From Tierney, no less, and they're performing here. That new member could easily be me."

"Absolutely not!" For the first time Becca looked to Falid, Hamish, praying for support, knowing they were too cowardly to give it. "If anything happens to you, Rosa'd never forgive me! It's *my* responsibility, my call as to who handles the job." God in heaven, she was slipping, slipping badly to allow Anyssa to manipulate her like that, maneuver her into agreeing with the plan, if not the person involved.

"Nothing will happen to me," Anyssa radiated calm reason. "And there's a logical reason why you can't. Why Falid and Hamish can't, either. The other troupe members who joined Stanislaus are either young, not full-fledged members of their troupe, or very old, useful but expendable. You, Becca, land right in the middle, neither young nor old, too obviously vital— someone who'd clearly be a major troupe member, someone they'd miss. Stanislaus'd catch that right away. Besides, they all at least casually know each other, would recognize major players. It's easy to forget the young or the old—they change."

Damn, how she hated to be cozened, flattered, because flattery meant someone wanted something of you—something you weren't initially prepared to cede. Double damn that beneath the flattery the child made sense. "And if we do it your way?"

"Then we have a real chance to determine if Jere's alive, perhaps find proof of the boy's heritage. Once we know, then we can deal with those problems—as Mother would want them dealt with. After all, that's what we've really been sent here for, isn't it?" At Becca's grudging nod she continued, "And training, preparation is what it's all about. I've studied everything I could find on the history of the troupes, viewed their performance disks. Absolutely immersed myself in them."

"Which explains that damn think-screen with you every second, during surveillance, during missionary sessions." The yielding didn't come naturally, comfortably, the abdication of control, command. And one question answered: Anyssa was more Rosa's child after all—the only one capable of making her yield. "There's one thing you must understand, and understand it well: We don't have final instructions yet. Until your mother sends them, all you must do is observe. Is that clear?"

"Fine. If he's there, alive. If he's who we believe he is. But if Jere's survived, she's mine once Mother gives the command." Yes, erase all stain, all taint of the woman who'd lured her father into an affair, for clearly she'd tempted him, lured him beyond all rational refusal. Yes, erase the stain of the woman who'd scarred Rhuven Fisher Weaver. Could she do it? Yes. The depths of her anger surprised her. Equally, a sense of betrayal for dragging her father, her perfect father into the mud and mire of real life. Fathers never failed, never disappointed their daughters. She would not fail, was not endearingly weak like her father, but strong, diamond-hard like her mother. But the sensation of being molded in Vitarosa's image gave birth to different angers, different fears as well.

Time: 31 July 2158
Location: Holm Port Observation Deck,
Satellite Colony CurieCousteau

Perched on one of the grav benches rimming the Deck, loosely cradling drawn-up knees, Glynn tracked the contrail of vapor etching the sky as Liam's shuttle departed for Tane. "Shuttle from NelMandela'll be in shortly," he reported, seemingly to no one, since he sat alone except for a case sitting half-under the bench.

"Staniar never gets the creases right," he complained at the case. Together, Panny and Chance had devised a discreet carry case for Jere's box; canvas and mesh screening made it appear outwardly normal but allowed muffled hearing and periscope vision. Another small set of mirrors reflected the LCD, making her speech visible through a flap at the top. He picked at the creases pressed into the old-fashioned canvas gardening overalls he wore. All the rage now as leisure wear for men and women, courtesy of Jere, of him, in the newly refurbished *Candide*.

"WHO'S MY SITTER THIS TIME?" Jere flashed at him, ignoring his complaint. "I HOPE HE DOESN'T BOUNCE OFF WALLS LIKE LIAM. MADE ME UNDERSTAND HOW QUEASY CHANCE FEELS IN SPACE."

Glynn smiled hugely, enjoying her disgruntlement, and a woman passerby slowed, captivated by his youthful handsomeness and merriment. For a moment his face froze, but he forced a superficial smile. Was she looking because he'd grown, matured over the last months, almost to full manhood? Easy to forget how well-muscled he was compared to the many Satelliters who made minimal efforts at exercise, especially those working month-long shifts in Z-grav environments. Movement with minimal physical effort meant the muscles became lazy, flaccid.

He'd marked the passage of time more by the plays they'd performed—*King Lear, Candide,* excerpts from *Ramayana*—than by the days or weeks or the satellites visited. Whichever the satellite, whatever the play, someone from Orvieto or Magyar or Tierney Troupes always chaperoned as bodyguard and danger-sniffer. That and by the fact that Jere hadn't begged him to set her free, let her die, since Amaterasu. Her request, the testing of his resolve, came less frequently, more an old habit than a true plea for a merciful release. So he thought, so he hoped.

Still, no danger had threatened since the initial attack on Jere and him in February—except for the freakish incident of the air duct inspector plummeting through the ceiling, almost landing atop Jere. That had been in—what?—late April? Amusing in retrospect, but it had nearly precipitated a crisis—the inspector's ID expired, authorization slow coming from Central. Tense hours holding him prisoner, on alert against possible further attack until SatGov Security politely retrieved the man. Somehow he didn't think the free tickets had mollified a man so close to dying.

No doubt the other troupes were rapidly tiring of their pledge. Safe to thank them, have done with it? How long could they keep looking over their shoulders? Look ahead and you might glimpse a future; look behind and you saw and feared the past, relived it. But if they looked ahead, what would he see—not just for himself, but for Jere? He stretched to touch the box for solace, his not hers since she couldn't feel a thing. To be bereft of the sense of touch was beyond his imagination . . . exactly as if you were encapsulated in a . . . and slammed the thought shut.

A soft, almost interrogatory sound. Preternaturally attuned to all the minor noises the brain box generated—its hums and buzzes, the faint ripple that indicated speech—it cued him to check Jere's LCD. All these sounds he knew as intimately as the musk of her perspiration and perfume, the texture of her hair, the blue of her eyes. "What, love?"

"IS LIAM'S SHUTTLE BOUNCING LIKE A BILLIARD BALL BANKING OFF THE CUSHIONS?"

"Nope, contrail's not wavering," he teased back. "Warned them to strap him down tight. Still, I learned something from him, and I think Majvor did, too." An acrobat on loan from Magyar, Liam boasted a mouth as elastic and inexhaustible as his body. Constant mindless chatter that wore on nerves; funny, in a macabre way, to speak of mindless chatter, as if Liam had a body and no brain, while Jere was the exact opposite. But despite Liam's garrulity, the lad was fast building a repertoire of sophisticated yet outrageous, outsized movements crucial for delineating the broad strokes of comedy. Blessedly, when he moved, Liam kept utterly silent, letting his body speak for him, narrate his surprise, happiness, sadness, yearnings. Perhaps Magyar was afraid he'd peak too soon if given major roles at his tender age. Still, Glynn suspected Liam'd soon be too valuable to loan as a bodyguard.

Yet the more Liam had capered and pranced and

pratfallen, turning backstage life into a comedic danger zone, the more control and precision Majvor had exhibited onstage, a new seriousness of purpose she'd previously lacked. Although she'd always excelled at comic roles and proved herself a solid second male lead, she now possessed the potential to assume a major tragic lead. If so, it would lift some of Glynn's burden.

"Shuttle's docking," he announced and balanced on his bottom, elevating his legs, stretching his arms overhead to form a V, despite the uncomfortable tug of canvas overalls. He held for the count to fifty, perfectly in control, then lowered his legs and stood beside the bench.

"GLYNN, STOP SHOWING OFF IN PUBLIC LIKE THAT." Her criticism stung, though she was right. Don't draw attention to himself, reveal himself as an actor. But such movements came as naturally as breathing—and she capable of neither now. Before he could apologize, she reminded him, "SO, WHO'S OUR NEW RECRUIT? YOU STILL HAVEN'T TOLD ME."

"I know, I know," he placated as he struggled with the pocket flap on his overalls, one strap slipping down his bare shoulder. "Can't remember her name. Tierney's turn anyway."

"HER? CUTEY OR CRONE? ANY BETS?" Any troupe lending support to Stanislaus would never send one of their leading players. It would detract from their box office receipts.

Unfolding the scribble-pulp, he shook it to flatten it. "Annie, Annie Marie Doulan from Tierney. That's all I know."

"TIERNEY'S WIFE'S FAMILY. HOW CLOSELY RELATED I DON'T KNOW."

A whoosh-clang as the shuttle locked on the landing pad, the tube-walk shooting out to meet it. Lights blinked, cycling from red to amber to "go" green by the hatchway as pressure and atmosphere seals ran their auto-check.

She floated down the tube as if born to Z-grav, economical of movement, yet gliding quick and smooth around the hoverers, the anxious ones eagerly searching for family waiting inside. One comprehensive glance swept the waiting area, and she zeroed in on Glynn, drifted across the Deck toward him with hand outstretched.

He took a step forward to meet her, pull her into the grav zone where she settled light and easy. "Annie? Annie Marie Doulan? A pleasure to meet you. I'm Glynn Webster Stanislaus."

"Yes, of course. Pleasure, I'm sure." One brief assaying look at the carrier in Glynn's left hand and her eyes met Glynn's. Damn! The thinnest crescent of dried blood showed under the nail of her little finger. Near bloodless the murder'd been, but she'd apparently gotten just a touch on her when she'd disposed of the body. Despite herself she shivered at the memory, the sudden limpness, the amazing weight and clumsiness of the inert body—dead weight. She shivered again, wishing she could wrap her arms around herself. "I always feel chilly when I land. Darn shuttles are always warm and stuffy." Anyssa Herrara Weaver, wearing Annie Marie Doulan's identity now and for the next month, formally shook hands with her half brother. Now she knew she could kill; now she knew for sure he existed. Panic and pleasure in that knowledge.

Time: A few minutes later
Location: A walk from the Observation Deck
to Transient Lodgings, 6November/Mid,
CurieCousteau
How to play it on the stroll to Stanislaus' quarters with Glynn? Mindless, chattering excitement at joining a new troupe? Calm but wary acceptance of this temporary assignment? A touch of pique? Be Annie Marie, but analyze as Anyssa. Clearly Jere's son existed, lived, so that meant Jere *had* died. Simple process of elimination, and grinned at her turn of phrase.

Becca would approve. Elimination of Jere: done, check, cross it off the "to do" list.

If only she could casually chat with Glynn, but she'd never mastered that art, except perhaps the baby talk, the silliness that went with having two much younger brothers. During her rounds at NetwArk, inspecting or working the herb plots, the drying facilities, the packing rooms, she was too, too conscious of her position, her status, uncomfortably self-aware because the ABSs never let her forget it. Someday NetwArk would be hers, inheritor of her father's mantle of leadership and prayerful guidance. Don't dwell on it—don't! It was too much to handle. Not a genuine prayer in her heart or soul, everything tangled, muddled.

Though pleasant, clearly glad she'd arrived, Glynn kept mostly silent, a few terse comments about her trip, a query about a new act Tierney was rehearsing. She'd murmured back about "working the stiffness out," gave a shrug, pulled a face. Some comments baffled her, as if directed not to her but to someone else, except no one else stood near. Limited luggage—indeed, she wondered what Annie Marie Doulan had packed, what she'd be forced to wear—a small knapsack of personal necessities slung over her shoulder while Glynn carried her larger tote left-handed, banging between them, counterbalanced by some sort of canvas and mesh carrier in his right hand. It didn't appear terribly heavy, but he carried it with instinctive care, never banging or brushing it against passersby or stationary objects.

At length, desperate for something to say, wanting to hear a voice, any voice—even her own—she ventured, "Remind me to comm Tierney once I'm settled, let them knew I've arrived safe and sound." And so she would, or a frantic search for Annie Marie Doulan would start too soon.

She'd never ventured this deep inside a satellite, up along stairs, through levels she hadn't fully comprehended before. The 3-D and flat-plate schematics made her feel "mazed," lost, no matter how hard she studied them. First they wound around, sometimes they zigzagged through habitat and agricole tiers, the levels growing older, shabbier, as if they traveled toward the beginning of time. And that they did, she knew from the mandatory lecture aboard ship, heading toward the beginning of the satellite station, its kernel or core. Some shortcuts made her panicky at their low ceilings, snaked cables and flexible pipings winding overhead and beneath her feet—a hidden world within a world—emergency ducts, pumps, and filters, and she didn't know what else. Rather like dissecting the guts of a strange mechanical alien. Satellite plumbing hadn't been part of her self-study course. Becca'd probably gut it bare-handed to clear a path.

Spinning the wheel on a sealed door, Glynn popped it open. "We're quartered here," and motioned inside as he propped the door with his shoulder, politely waiting for her to enter. "Nicer here, a bit more private than usual. Tierney usually stays on third level, Delta or Mike, don't they?"

She momentarily goggled, managed a nod. "I like Delta better, don't know why, just do." A response, and a safe one, she hoped.

"We've almost got the Rehearsal Room on 4Delta/Mid up to snuff. Orvieto did a good share of the repairs their last time through, and we've done more. Ought to mean a bit of a rent reduction when we're done. You'll be surprised at the progress. Blasted water damage shouldn't have happened to begin with." He thumped the door with his fist, his disapproval clear. "Avoidable accidents like that jeopardize structural integrity if they go unreported, unrepaired long enough."

God above! Don't forget you're Annie, not Anyssa, more than a little familiar with the satellites' infrastructure problems. The daily minutia of life could trip her up, expose her. At least she hadn't indulged in idiot-babble, gawping at everything as if encountering it for the first time. A dead giveaway, one that Becca'd never forgive her for making. A nervous sweat rose on her body, its sticky discomfort a practical reminder of her new role. "So true," she came down on "true" harder than she'd wanted. "Satellites aren't vulnerable only on their outer surfaces but internally as well." Like Earth? The equivalent of a precipitous earthquake, a sinkhole enlarging, swallowing more and more, a throbbing volcanic explosion? Because Earth still was plagued by natural vulnerabilities, not just the man-made ones of war, famine, plague, pollution on its surface skin. Or the sky-high dangers of weapons satellites and missiles. For the first time in her stay on Waggoner's Ring, she truly comprehended that each satellite *was* a miniature Earth with its own miniature ecosystem.

Before she could examine her insight any further— or tremble at how nearly she'd exposed herself as an outsider—a swarm of people gathered round. Glynn handed the canvas-mesh tote to an elderly man who hurried away with it. Another man—how young or old, she wasn't sure—with glistening dark hair and snapping eyes slipped her knapsack from her shoulder and retrieved her other bag from Glynn, only to pass both to a teenager clearly unenthusiastic at being chosen beast of burden. "That's bet Rigoberto, our manager and beta Masady's husband; Vijay's the dark, sleekly handsome one." Vijay's teasing glance vanished as a buxom blonde skimmed past and elbowed him, "and Staniar with your bags. He'll leave them in your sleep space."

Almost manageable now, only the blonde and the elderly woman to concentrate on, leave the children for later. "Majvor plays second male leads and, of course, our leader, beta Masady." At that introduction Anyssa bowed. Overdone, perhaps? She'd gauged the degree from watching videos; a Magyar troupe member would have been far more florid. With the children lined up, Glynn bounced his hand from head to head like descending chimes, "'Heike and Hassiba. And the Gemmies, Jasper and Jeremy."

Smile, smile. Nothing big, don't force it, but look, act friendly. The first girl dark, the second blonde; first boy dark, the second pale. "Why Gemmies?" she asked the dark boy.

"Cause I'm Jasper." Seeing that didn't help, he amended, "Jasper's a semiprecious stone." But the blond boy couldn't contain himself, chimed in, "And I'm Jeremy *Diamond* Stanislaus, and diamonds are more precious than jasper." They were shoving now, trying to unbalance each other. "Precious all right! Precious pest is more like it!" For a moment it felt like home.

As the children bickered, she found herself drawn away from the door, herded—no, escorted, she corrected himself—toward what she suspected was a temporary rehearsal space from its sparse decor. So far, six adults, four children—were some missing? "Not as many, I know, as Tierney Troupe. I'd like to expand, add a few more, but you know how it is, at least for Stanislaus," a toss of hands, as if that explained everything, his palms exposed, fingers unfolding, spreading. A commonplace motion with the grace of an unfurling cloud—and utterly natural. "We start training early because it's so long and intensive. Not always easy to think years ahead and add new members."

"And look what it produces." Safer not to lay it on too thick. "May Lady Luck travel your road, grant you new members." As if her words had conjured them, two figures suddenly loomed in the draped area to her right, shrouded with shadow, darkness reluctant to relinquish them as they came closer. One large, very large figure, and one small. Almost gasping in shock, Anyssa twisted the strangled sound into a harsh, throat-clearing cough as the figures assumed firm shapes, features, though still dark as Satan's sins.

The tall, broad man stuck out his hand—warm brown on the back, palm rosy pink—and as it grasped hers a tiny creature skittered down his arm and up Anyssa's until it reached her shoulder. Despite herself she shrieked as little, clawed feet tickled her skin, scrabbled through her hair until whatever it was perched on her head. "Steady, Annie, steady," the man urged, not releasing her, his handclasp stabilizing her. "It won't hurt you. I'm sorry. Forgot Sylvan came along for the ride. He's a flying squirrel—silly name because he can't, but he can glide. Harmless, friendly, curious." He pressed something into her free hand and she clutched it, its smooth, hard oval contour familiar. A pecan? "If you can—if there aren't any hard feelings—hold the nut up for him. He'll take it and scoot off to find someplace to stash it."

Delicate paws wrapped around her thumb as she coaxed him off her head with the nut. Onto her shoulder now, its poking nose inquisitive and moist, a large, liquid eye peering at her. "Th-tchk-tchkk," it happily announced as it seized the nut and sprang away. Despite herself she began to giggle, more in shock and relief than amusement, but she admitted the humor of it. Yes, drop that little rascal down Becca's skinny-suit sometime and watch the dance begin. "I think I'll like him once I see him better. No harm done, just a surprise."

"Good." He finally released her hand. "I'm Chance. Sort of an honorary member of the troupe, I guess you'd say. Jack of all trades and master of none, but if it's repairs you want, I can cobble anything together."

"Such humility," Anyssa teased, because even she, Earth-born and bred, had heard tales of the legendary Tinker II Evers II Chance. If Earth applauded his skills, then Satelliters must revere him. How'd he gotten to CurieCousteau from PabNeruda when he'd been officially declared disabled, even the mere thought of flight reducing him to jelly? "And the young lady with you is?" Odd, odd, the child looked vaguely familiar. Let it go, the connection would resurface later; wrestle with it and it'd vanish. Why were Chance and the child with Stanislaus? It changed the equation, altered the balance once more.

"This is Panthat, another honorary troupe member." As Anyssa held out her hand, the child shied away with a low, hissing "Shah!" Arms tight-crossed over her nonexistent chest, clearly sulky, she sidled behind Chance and then marched off, thin, straight back registering her disdain. "Bit skittish with strangers sometimes."

As the troupe members drifted back to their tasks, chatting, tossing stray comments at her, she turned toward Glynn, patiently waiting, body canted against the wall while he performed some sort of complicated leg workout. Limber she might be, supremely capable of flexing and twisting offensively or defensively, but compared to him, she realized how crudely trained she truly was—a revelation of sorts. "Don't try it," he advised cheerfully. "Unless you've mastered the moves leading up to this, you'll cramp so badly that you'll beg for six shots of muscle relaxant and three masseuses to realign you."

"Deal, if you'll show me how someday," and seriously meant it. Now, how to shift their conversation where she wanted it? Nothing to do but utter the name. "I . . . I mean I'm here, but what about . . . Jere? Is there . . . should I?" Her awkwardness was both intentional and not; leave the question openended, see how he responded.

"Yes, well," Glynn dipped, straightened with a spring that should have left him airborne. "If you think you're ready to meet her?" Meet her? Then she *was* alive? Impossible that *both* Glynn and Jere had survived the assassination attempt. "I mean, you understand, don't you? Been told what to expect?"

"Yes, but it's hard to . . . accept, hard to . . ." she waved a hand vaguely, let the words, her hesitancy work for her.

Taking her elbow, he escorted her across the rehearsal floor and into an empty cubicle—an illusion of privacy with its pipe and curtain walls. Devoid of everything except for a pillow on the floor and a table at its center, it looked barren, uninhabited. On the center of the table rested a box studded with dials and gauges. Glynn brought her about a meter and a half from the table, halted, and left her positioned by the pillow. "It's easier for her from this distance," he explained.

They stood for what seemed an eternity, waiting, waiting; increasingly anxious, Anyssa wondered when Jere would enter, part the draperies and reveal herself. Obviously enough of the prima donna—maimed or whole—remained to savor a grand entrance. Glynn joggled her arm. "Say something to her. She usually waits, lets the visitor break the ice, indicate the person's prepared."

"Good afternoon, Jerelynn. I'm Annie Marie Doulan, and I'm pleased to be here. Tierney is always happy to assist you and Stanislaus Troupe."

A soft susurration, barely there, like a distant, whirring motor. Without clear intent, Anyssa quick-skimmed the box, glimpsed bright blue bars, vertical and horizontal, crawling right to left across an LCD strip like stick insects. The same feeling of creepy-crawliness she'd experienced when Sylvan first darted up her arm swept over her, began to magnify, knotting her gut.

The blue stick insects began to coalesce, form letters, words. "HELLO, ANNIE. I'M PLEASED TO MEET YOU AS WELL. WELCOME TO OUR TROUPE, WELCOME TO OUR TROUBLES, AND WE THANK YOU FOR YOUR HELP. I REALIZE IT'S ALWAYS HARD TO LEAVE YOUR OWN TROUPE, YOUR TRAINING, ESPECIALLY FOR A TASK LIKE THIS."

"I . . ." a fist shoved hard against her mouth, muffling the words, damming the bile ready to rise, burst from her mouth, "I . . . didn't . . . brain . . . box. Oh, God, oh, God, I'm sorry . . . so sorry! Couldn't imagine anything like . . ." Retreat, turn and flee, escape, but her feet wouldn't obey her mind's furious commands. The rebellion in her stomach a straining riot now. Her eyes and nose ran, while the rest of her could not. She squinted through tears, purposely distorting the box, as if it would diminish its impact or,

best of all, make it disappear. Oh, God, oh, God, not
dead! Not dead. Worse than dead!

"IT'S ALL RIGHT, CHILD. IT'S NOT EASY
FACING ME THE FIRST TIME, OR EVEN THE
SECOND OR THIRD. YOUR REACTION'S NOR-
MAL. GLYNN, TAKE HER OUT NOW. IT'S NO
DISGRACE, ANNIE."

Before Glynn could react, Anyssa spun away, bolt-
ing, not caring where, as long as she found a waste
disposal unit nearby. Not the ultimate disgrace, please!
Fighting the drapery maze, she stumbled free. A
young man—Staniar, part of her brain informed her—
grabbed her, propelled her toward a hygiene closet.
Stood supporting her head while she vomited, vomited
again and again until nothing remained except a final
explosion of dry heaves. When she managed to rock
back on her heels, bleary-eyed, weeping from shock,
from the extremity of her internal explosions, she saw
his savage, commiserating smile as if he respected her
revulsion. "Perversions like that shouldn't be allowed
to live," and wiped her face with a damp towel.

His solicitude poured balmlike over her wretched
body, her wrenching thoughts, yet his comment caught
her offguard. A Stanislaus member voicing such
thoughts to a stranger? "Thank you." She took the
damp cloth and wiped her face again. "Thank you
very much. Is there a comm set I can use? Best let
my troupe know I'm on duty." A short, innocuous
whiz-gram, tippy-tap transmission, cheaper than voice
comm, ten words or less, to let Tierney know "Annie"
had arrived. And no word to Becca yet—because what
would she say, how could she phrase it?

Time: I got a right to sing the blues
Location: Inside Jere's brain

"Ah, Glynn," she thought as the girl dashed clear.
The play of naked emotion across his face, compassion, shame, pain . . . all so achingly distant to her
now. Not ashamed of her, no, but shamed he'd caused
the girl, Annie, to break down; shame that he'd ex-

posed her, his mother, to such an unseemly but hardly inexplicable reaction. A hopeless smile of expiation, and he'd started out as well, announcing, "Time to rehearse. No rest between you and beta Masady." He'd slipped his head between the curtains, popped back to advise her, "Staniar's with her, she's probably too embarrassed to see me right now."

"GIVE HER TIME," she'd replied. "IT'S ALWAYS A SHOCK."

In all honesty a shock to Jere as well, a crashing reality check that crumpled any self-deceptions, any delusions she might maintain about her wholeness. Not that she consciously harbored them . . . but, but . . . so much easier, simpler to pretend this was her role in some lingering, expanding nightmare. And when she finally awoke, she'd be whole again, body and mind as one. Just pretend.

No, never to be. And so much else lost as well, emotions flattened and with good reason: a dire lack of sensory input. Never to smell the heady scent as her fingers peeled an orange, or savor the little sacs bursting with juicy flavor against her tongue—well, so be it. Pretend she suffered a dire head cold. What she missed most, craved, was touch. So isolated, only pure reason left. Pure reason, eh? What a joke! Can one reason with most of the necessary physical input absent? What vision, what hearing she possessed was barely enough, an analog simulacrum of real eyes, real ears, to make her doubly mourn the lack. Sometimes she thought she sensed her brain mourning its lost connections, lost synapses, endlessly checking and rechecking to make sure they hadn't been misdirected, rerouted. Lately, even that sensation had diminished.

Was her brain atrophying? Parts of it shrinking, dying from lack of stimulation? Parts moribund, as isolated as she so often felt? Except . . . did it matter? Should she care? Easy to become habituated to anything, any lack—or was it? Well, one fallback position, one ace in the hole remained. An actor's ego could never be amputated, killed. An incredibly strong sense of self, yes, self-centered at times. I am the center of my own universe. Yes, the Me who I was, who I am—not what I've become. The brain is ego, not the body.

A simple question (don't shy away from it, Jere): How long can I go on like this? How long can they all go on? Like the half-life of some radioactive isotope, decaying by half and by half and by half, but still a measure, a trace after thousands of years. An atavistic desire to shiver, to feel the hairs rise on the back of her neck, her forearms, but nothing, nothing, though she felt her fear signal try to raise an alarm. Eee-Oo! Eee-Oo! Fear, foe, flee! Sorry, no one home today or tomorrow or tomorrow, for that matter. Legs, arms, heart, everything gone on extended leave of absence, absent without permission. So much for cranking up the sirens.

Back to the question, its answer: How long? As long as it takes to ensure Glynn's safety, that was how long she'd struggle on, half-life by half-life by half-life. Funny, never had thought of herself as a zealous mother, ready to rend and claw to save her young. So much energy spent on acting, communicating with hundreds upon hundreds of people, inhabiting, epitomizing some of the greatest roles of all time. Characters who'd survived centuries, who'd captured a universality of feelings, emotions. Now she played her greatest role of all. Ur-Mother. Playing it straight as well, mother as Mother, not mother as Father on stage.

How long? "UNTIL THE HEAVENS FALL. UNTIL THE GALAXIES EXPAND TO THEIR FARTHEST REACHES. I WILL NOT SACRIFICE MY SON. I AM NOT ABRAHAM, NO ONE CAN TEST MY FAITH, MAKE ME KILL ISAAC. I COULD NOT KILL OUR SON, RHUVEN, COULD YOU? ARE YOU BEHIND THIS? VI-TAROSA?" Limited emotions, eh? Flattened, faded, deadened? Not this love, not my love for Glynn.

A rising memory, unbidden, a recollection long forgotten, buried. Earth, the Can-Montan Territories, where she'd borne Glynn, where she'd fled after bidding Rhuven farewell at the retreat, never saying she carried his child. Yes, tall mountains still peaked with snow formed a half-ring behind a broad meadow with tall grasses and a riot of wildflowers, cricket chirps, hums and whines of flying insects, and overarching everything—a sky so perfectly blue it looked unreal. Hardly an unexpected response from one satellite-born, familiar with high horizons, digitalized sunrise and sunset, computer-generated weather. Glynn, just eighteen months, raced and wallowed through the grass, bits of leaf and straw clinging to baby-fine hair, slowly ripening from Rhuven's tawny gold to her own darker brunette. She'd finally decided to return to the troupe, to the satellites; if she didn't, it would soon be too late to begin Glynn's training. (Be honest, she missed acting—craved it the way an alcoholic craves a drink—the heady tributes of the crowds.) Beta Masady's grumbling complaints, their arguments echoed in her head as clearly as if the old woman stood behind her. Indeed, she almost cast a guilty look back, except Glynn chose that moment to charge at her, arms outspread.

Scooping him up, she held him tight while he wriggled and squealed. Ah, to keep him close and safe like this forever. With reluctance she set him free and he wheeled in a circle, arms waving at the sky. "Ba-loo!" he exclaimed, "ba-loo!"

"Blue," she repeated, emphasizing that the word consisted of one syllable, not two. Kneeling, she cupped his face, directed his gaze toward her lips as she articulated, "Blue. Blue sky, the sky is blue."

A tiny finger darted toward her eyes. "Ba," he paused, started again, "blue." He regarded her, mouth pursed to subdue an exuberant grin. "Blue. Skies. Blue skies," a shriek.

"No, you know the word. Sounds like 'skies' but it's not." She touched her eyes, touched his as well, gently closing the lids. "Well?"

"Eyes! E-ee-eyes."

"That's right. Mama has eyes like the sky, blue eyes, blue sky, sky blue eyes." Rhuven had whispered that to her one night.

"Eye blue skies!" His whole body rippled with mirth as he toyed with the words, and then abruptly froze, lower lip pouting, one arm rigidly pointing to a wavelike motion in the grass. Snake! With mounting horror she snatched the child tight, fled back to the settlement for safety. Yes, time to return to Waggoner's Ring. There were no snakes in the grass up there. Though she herself, perhaps, was one, the seductive snake who'd lured Rhuven from his Eden, snared a Godly man.

Date: 8 August 2158
Location: Rehearsal Studio,
4Delta/Mid, CurieCousteau

Sitting tailor-style on an embroidered cushion as far from Jere as possible while still being considered polite, Anyssa stared hard at the scriptodex, concentrating on that rather than the people surrounding her. One week and she'd progressed this far: able to remain near the box, ostensibly on guard, insinuating herself into the troupe's daily life, their banter, the minor theatrical crises that flared with a dramatic pacing natural as breathing to them. Heike and Hassiba, Jeremy and Jasper dashed around the table, scooted beneath it, engrossed in a game of tag. A jarring blow to a table leg and Jasper sang out, "Sorry, beta Jere! Germ-worm pushed me." Did the children truly *not* comprehend what the box contained? A brain, a live brain shorn of its body. Didn't they care? Or did they simply accept, a child's world-view where fantasy and reality casually mingled? How many times had she seen her brother Artur do it? Had done it herself, still did at times.

Damn it, Jere was *not* capable of jumping out of her box, biting her. Or worse yet, denouncing her. As who? For what? Jere's existence as pure brain did *not* endow her with superior mind powers. When had she become so susceptible, so vulnerable to nerves? Jittery, panicky, jumpy. Let Becca find out, she'd be finished before she'd truly begun. Once or twice she'd managed a cursory conversation with Jere, astonished at how clear and logical their talk had been. Yes, it was a brain inside, not some computerized model of Jere. Jere alive, not dead, but she would be soon. Unless . . . she mentally rotated the thought, scrutinizing it from all angles for flaws. Unless, unless . . . killing was a kindness, death a release. If so, let her live . . . suffer.

A sharp whistle distracted her—somehow Jere'd managed to crosswire one of the box's internal warning systems to call attention to the fact that she spoke, words flowing across the LCD. Except "crosswire" wasn't exactly right since she'd accomplished it through her brain waves, brain electricity. Chance had been proud, saying he couldn't have "Jere-rigged" it better himself. A veiled glance at the moving letters. "ENOUGH, CHILDREN! HASSIBA AND HEIKE—GO FIND BET GLYNN, TELL HIM WE NEED TO RUN LINES WITH THE GEMMIES. AND YOU'D BETTER KNOW YOUR LINES, NO PROMPTING."

"What are we playing today? How'll we know?" Hassiba frowned, chewed at a lock of dark hair, draped it beneath her nose to create a mustache. Heike sputtered, slapped a hand over her mouth.

"LISTEN EXTRA HARD AND IT WON'T BE A SURPRISE—WILL IT?" Wary at her sister's unexpected silliness, Heike dragged her away to find Glynn.

"What *are* we rehearsing today?" Anyssa called up the directory on her scriptodex, waited, finger poised to tag a selection. Acting as prompter gave her something needful to do, and kept her near Jere's side for protection. The troupe had undergone a major shifting of roles now that Glynn played Jere's parts; Jasper had inherited Glynn's old roles, while Jeremy assumed Jasper's.

'*HAMLET.* JASPER STILL AUTOMATICALLY RECITES JEREMY'S LINES. FORGETS HE HAS NEW ONES. HARDLY SURPRISING SINCE HE COULD RECITE THEM IN HIS SLEEP. AND GLYNN NEEDS A BIT MORE WORK, TOO— NOT THE MANNERISMS AS MUCH AS THE WORDS, THE INFLECTIONS."

"Oh." Say something else, prolong the conversation. Annie Marie Doulan would know what to say. "Glynn must be confused at times, playing a woman who's playing a male role. Thank the stars Tierney's more straightforward. If a man plays a woman, there's no question he's a man—and striving for the preposterous."

The LCD brightened and dimmed, Jere's version of laughter. "WITH WISHY TIERNEY'S 'WALTZING MATILDA' YOU CERTAINLY KNEW. BUT GLYNN'S A STANISLAUS BORN AND BRED, EVEN IF I DID UPSET BETA MASADY BY BEARING HIM ON EARTH INSTEAD OF HERE." Anyssa rotated her shoulders to release the tension Jere's unexpected confidence had generated, while Jere continued, clearly in a meditative mood. "BESIDES, WE ALL ASSUME MANY ROLES IN LIFE, ON AND OFF THE STAGE. DON'T YOU AGREE, ANNIE?"

Found out! Discovered—but how? How had she slipped? When? But why was Jere showing her hand? Quick—spring up and smash the box to the floor, pound it, kick it, demolish it! Sick dread flooded her mind—no way to succeed and escape alive, it was suicidal. *Don't jump the gun,* she counseled. *Think, think before you act, don't just react.* Mouth ajar, her exclamation of fear unvoiced, she blinked, refocused herself. "Oh, yes. Yes, certainly." A few chance words had goaded her into guilt. Thank God she didn't sport sensor gauges to reveal changes in breathing, pulse, respiration, all dead giveaways of her heightened anxiety and readiness to act. "Not only roles, but masks as well."

"WHICH STANISLAUS IS JUSTLY FAMED FOR."

Glynn slipped through the curtains with the smooth flexation of a silvered minnow in the stream, and Anyssa envied him yet again. Not massive but supple, hard-muscled through the chest and shoulders—as was all the troupe—from years of balancing the oversized masks that fitted over their shoulders. Handsome, yes—very. So very different from the ABSs at Net-wArk, a sensual exoticism they lacked. A strange longing—*if he were not my half brother*. Her heart was pounding again.

Concentrate on something else, now! The masks, yes, the masks. For the smaller youngsters, they posed a real burden; each mask molded to a scaffolding or frame that was harnessed on, raising the mask to "adult" height while the child peered through a slit in the mask's "throat." Despite this top-heaviness they always maintained an effortless poise conjoined with breathtakingly deceptive, simple movements that added an emotional resonance and realism to their characters.

"More rehearsal, *more*?" Glynn struck a histrionic pose, hand pressed against his forehead, head tossed back until she could trace a perfect crescent from his crown down through his arched left foot, positioned behind him, toes scarcely grazing the floor. "I shall be worn to the merest shadow of a player!"

The Gemmies giggled, punching at each other to desist before Jere could scold. But Glynn's pose unexpectedly collapsed as Panthat barged into the cubicle, hands slamming into the small of his back. "Do what boss-lady want, Glynnie. Panny here to see you no lazy-daisy through it. Lazy-daisy and beta Masady blaming me for not selling enough ticky-ticks. I tell her it bad acting, not my scowl in ticky stand, but she not believing. Shah!"

Panthat might not be a troupe member—Anyssa had yet to fully understand the child's position—but she harbored an equal dramatic gift. Beta Masady and the odd, dark child had a certain rapport despite their pretend barks and snarls at each other. And at almost any hour of the day or night, she'd observed Panthat's soft-footed prowling, checking the watcher entrusted with Jere's safety. Red-flag that, keep it at the front of her mind: to act against Jere or Glynn, she'd undoubtedly have to take out Panthat as well. Not that it would hurt her feelings; the child had an uncanny knack of looking through her, into her, reading some internal message she didn't realize she projected. Whether all satrats did the same she didn't know, but if they did, it undoubtedly explained how they survived.

"ANNIE, CUE US IN WHERE HAMLET ADDRESSES HIS MOTHER, THE QUEEN, AND HIS UNCLE, HER NEW CONSORT, AFTER THE PERFORMANCE. ACT III, SCENE II, ABOUT LINE 235."

Obediently Annie punched in the data, found her place and recited the Player Queen's lines. "Sleep rock thy brain. And never come mischance between us twain!"

As Hamlet, Glynn began, "Madam, how like you this play?"

"The lady doth protest too much, methinks," Jasper spoke the Queen's lines, and the studied maturity of his diction, his voice, belied his childish years.

With Majvor enduring a private tutelage under beta Masady, Jere filled in as the uncle/king: "HAVE YOU HEARD THE ARGUMENT? IS THERE NO OFFENSE IN'T?" And they were off, spinning the lines like gossamer webbing reinforced by steel-sharp wit and cunning, double-meanings and passion, first Jere, then Anyssa subbing in minor roles. Swift through scene iii and then into scene iv, in the Queen's closet, which Polonius has just ostensibly exited to conceal himself behind the draperies, eavesdrop when Hamlet enters his mother's chamber.

"Now, Mother, what's the matter?" Glynn asked,

and Jasper responded, "Hamlet, thou hast thy father much offended."

"Mother, you have my father much offended."

As the words of spite and distrust and reproach pounded home, Anyssa kept losing her place. Harder and harder to remember who was who, what was what, that Glynn pretended to be Jere playing Hamlet, that Jasper was Gertrude, that Heike played Rosencrantz as well as Polonius. Head pounding, faintly dizzy, everything turned amorphous, variable, her reasoning equally so. Males as females, females as males. It doesn't matter, she instructed herself, rubbing her temples. But it *did* matter, a message here she should decipher if it weren't obscured by the roles. Females and males, males as females as males. Masks that hid, disguised, so many, many semblances. On and off the stage.

Fine, then, direct, recast the roles: herself as Hamlet reproaching his mother Gertrude (really her father, Rhuven) for an affair with Hamlet's uncle, the new king (Jere). But Jere hadn't killed Vitarosa (Hamlet's father), but hadn't she turned Rosa into a ghost of sorts? Oh, to scream, vent her anger at Jere for seducing Rhuven, making him untrue, unfaithful to her mother! For so it *must* have happened, *had* to have happened. Yes? No? Rhuven would never . . . could never have. . . . She . . . and Glynn . . . would never . . . could never. . . .

She mind-spun on, random words—camel, weasel, whale—caught and lodged in the coils of her dream-web. "Good night, Mother." Shivering, thoughts muddled, Anyssa watched as Glynn began to drag Heike—supposedly Polonius' lifeless form, but acting surprisingly lively, giggling, hissing complaints that Glynn was tickling her feet—from the stage. Heike grabbed at Anyssa to delay her exit and, rudely returned to reality, Anyssa dropped her scriptodex, saw and heard the screen crack. With chill fingers she unwound Heike's grasp on her knee and ankle, rose stiffly from her cushion, and left without any apology.

"What's the matter with her?" Heike worried, propped on her elbows, raised feet still clutched between Glynn's arms and his waist. He absentmindedly tickled her arch, and she writhed but said nothing more, both of them still listening as Anyssa's rapid footsteps diminished in the distance.

"Don't know, love. Just moody, I guess." He watched to see if Jere'd comment, but the LCD remained infuriatingly blank. What to make of Annie? A subtle tension radiating from her, almost sexual, luring him on until her walls slammed in place and shut him out. Occasional moments of quiet sharing when they nearly connected, both lonely, both yearning to share—and that guard sprang between them. A bodyguard as zealous of guarding her thoughts as she was of protecting Jere. Odd for another player to so shield herself from a fellow actor, even if they came from competing troupes. Intermarriage wasn't unheard of. Troupe members, and troupe members alone, understood bone-deep what it meant to be a minority, dependent on each other for survival, not the satellites' beneficence.

Well, troupe members and satrats, too, he emended as Panny grabbed Heike under her armpits and helped lug her "offstage."

"Don't like Annie," Panthat announced. "Like to make her fishy food."

Wonderful. Now Panthat was jealous of Annie.

Outside Anyssa pressed her throbbing temple against the wall, molded herself against it as if to listen for something, anything, a clue, an answer, some meaning. Truth had a slippery quality. And beliefs could be more compelling than truth. Beliefs were compulsions of a sort. Beliefs could be true, or they could strangle truth. So many—how many?—fooled themselves with beliefs each and every day. Oh, I believe . . .

NetwArk—she believed in it because she'd never known, experienced anything else, her whole life wrapped up in it, unquestioningly, unthinkingly. So hard to see Rhuven, Vitarosa as separate entities, not parents but individuals hobbled by their own longings and fears, their beliefs. Beings independent of her, but she so dependent upon them. The days with Stanislaus were altering her focus, her vision halting at first. Jere's and Glynn's relationship— similar yet dissimilar from her own with her parents. Would she struggle to save her mother or father with the same unswerving devotion Glynn had shown—wrongheaded as it might be? A hissing inhalation, a wince at her choice of words. Wasn't that why she was here? To save her parents, save NetwArk from . . . from what? What?

She respected Vitarosa, was loyal to her. But . . . she didn't love her, doubted that Rosa unselfishly loved her. At least not as Jere loved Glynn. Armed with that insight, she asked, did Rosa love Rhuven? Did Rhuven love Rosa? What Mother loved was control, the manipulation of power, the puppeteer pulling the strings behind the scenes at NetwArk. Yet Father loved Mother—of that she somehow was sure—purposely blind to preserve some semblance of love's illusions. And within that daily struggle, she could dimly envision why Rhuven had once faltered and fallen, a heady time of freedom to love Jere.

A final acknowledgment made her eyes flood with unshed tears. *I am beginning to love Glynn. No, I love him.* And stepped away from the wall, began walking fast, anywhere to elude the next question she didn't yet dare contemplate. How do I love him? As a brother? As a friend? As a . . . possible lover? A worse wrong than Jere and Rhuven. What do I know about love? I won't love him, I can't love him! I am wrong to doubt, my life is NetwArk. I have a mission to accomplish, and I will!

Date: 18 August 2158
Location: Exercise Room, 3Bravo/Cap,
CurieCousteau
Dropping onto the floor beside Jere's box, Anyssa felt literally light—and well she should. After all, this seg-

ment of Bravo Three just beyond the Observation Deck's boundaries pulled only a sixth of Earth-gravity. Oh, she sat well enough: as long as she didn't reach for something, then bounce back on her fanny . . . or hiccup. A near giggle. Would a burp make her bounce, too? And if she . . . oh, dear Lord, no . . . don't even think it! Would she be jet-propelled if she broke wind?

"CARE TO SHARE? THE SOURCE OF YOUR AMUSEMENT, THAT IS," Jere flashed. "YOUR FACE IS AN ABSOLUTE STUDY IN SUPPRESSED LAUGHTER."

Despite herself Anyssa giggled. "It's so vulgar." Then squared her shoulders, "But that's never stopped a Tierney before, has it? Don't know what made me think of it. What happens if you . . . if you . . ." and sputtered, clasping her arms around herself to hold the laughter inside.

Jere took her time. "WELL, WE'VE FOUND IT DEPENDS ON THE RATIO OF . . . GARBANZOS TO BEAN SPROUTS IN ANY GIVEN MEAL, FACTORED BY THE FERMENTATION LEVEL OF SAUCES USED."

"You're teasing, aren't you? You know what we eat for breakfast, especially when Staniar's in charge."

"HOW COULD I FORGET? BELIEVE ME, I'D RELISH TASTING IT AGAIN. TASTING ANYTHING. BUT YES, I'M TEASING."

Wishing she could swallow her tongue, Anyssa fixed her eyes on the training session, concentrating on Jeremy, light and utterly limber in Glynn's hands. Checking his pose, Glynn eased back the boy's right leg, reangled the foot position. He turned to Jasper, arching the dark-haired boy, balancing him on his fingertips and murmuring about arm position as Jasper flexed deeper. Masady briskly put Heike and Hassiba through their paces, one routine gliding seamlessly into the next. First a still pause, then slow motions, finally faster and faster, until each combination unfurled like a silken ribbon.

"I love watching the children train. Always have," she added quickly.

"NOT SO LONG SINCE YOU DID YOURSELF, UNDOUBTEDLY STILL DO."

Anyssa nodded. Yes, she was still in training, though not precisely as Jere meant. "It's always satisfying to see someone not nearly as good as you, makes you appreciate your progress. Beta Masady is sparing with compliments, I suspect." As was Becca, as was her mother. Just once, just once for someone to say, "Good job, Anyssa."

"AND A BIT OF A STING, A BIT OF A SPUR WHEN YOU SEE SOMEONE SMALLER DOING IT BETTER."

"Uh-huh." First the exaggeration of a move, again and again, overextending, wide and expansive sweeps, then a subtle reduction as each exercise showed the true cohesiveness of mind, body, and soul, melded in strict control.

Step back and weight onto the left leg. Arms outstretched in front as the body pliantly rotates leftward, almost facing away from the first position as it pivots on the right heel. A shifting of weight and the right hand moves in toward the chest, while the left palm seeks out the right hip. And left a quarter-turn as the right arm now flows smoothly out and the left leg steps forward. And on it went, ever-quickening, the moves blurring together in supple harmony, the whole being like an uncoiling whip.

Captivated, almost lost in the movements yet worried by her distraction, Anyssa reluctantly moved behind Jere, her back to the wall. Besides, that way she could mime various gestures and not look the fool in Jere's eyes. Her hands and arms at least, and she stretched and flowed, anxious to follow. Some combinations were strikingly familiar, though their names were more peaceful and flowery. As they should be, because her art, the art of a Little Sister was that of killing. Attack and conquer, self-defense, false retreat

and then drive home the assault for the kill. No pretty
names could camouflage its true intent.

Masady's fragile ivory hand, palm-out, swept from
breastbone to ear-level and out in a soft arc, her fingers airily spreading, just as if a fan had been swept
open. Such exquisite grace for the sake of grace
seemed beyond her, and she sighed at a life that allowed such a luxury.

Snared in the mists of reverie, Anyssa didn't notice
Glynn now standing beside her, all silent, resilient
moves that had brought him to her side like a shadow.
With a gasp she looked up at him, and for a moment
she plumbed how Jere must feel, to know there was
action, life, momentum going on that she could not
see. Glynn's cool hand clasped hers, tugged her lightly
to her feet. A little too hard and she gave a skip,
"floating" for seconds longer than she'd expected. She
landed a fraction harder, less elegantly than she might
have liked. "What do you think you're doing?" she
grouched, pretended he was Artur, not Glynn.

"Making you exercise. You acted eager enough during the last set, unless you were practicing semaphore
signals." Despite her resistance, he continued tugging
her toward the center mats, the children gathering and
giggling, hanging on her arms, Heike wrapped round
her waist. Demanding attention with an exuberant
yell, Jeremy essayed a graceful fall at her feet, tucking
and rolling—or almost rolling. More accurately, he
came out of the tuck too soon, landed flat on his back
with a restrained "woof" as he hit and bounced. Glynn
planted a bare foot in Jeremy's middle to anchor him,
but his gray eyes never left Anyssa. "Without a doubt,
semaphoring," he waved in grave parody, "You
spelled out, 'Glynn, come here.' Progress any further
and you'll be directing the skiffs and cruisers to
their pads."

Fruitless to hit him, and she didn't have a free arm.
"But I'm supposed to be guarding Jere. It's my shift.
I can exercise later." Definitely later, and preferably
some place where Glynn wasn't. His very closeness,

the scent of his warm flesh, the curve of his cheek, the skintight definition of his training breeches bothered her. A tingling she didn't want to acknowledge, that distracted and attracted her. So unlike, so unlike all those Able-Bodied Savers at NetwArk, able-bodied was hardly the word for them, not these lean, sleek muscles smooth as carved stone.

"Don't worry, Annie," he whispered, his breath sweet and warm on her ear, her neck. "Masady needs a break as well. She'll watch." To Anyssa's chagrin Masady waved her cane, dark eyes asparkle with anticipation.

With patient aplomb Glynn directed her through the first two routines and, to her relief, she didn't discredit herself, matched him move for move. Then more difficult positions, some easily mastered because of her own training, and others achingly beyond her, and she began to fight against them in frustration. Fight him, more accurately, acutely conscious of his touch here, there, without warning at another tingling, susceptible spot as he strove to position an arm or leg, tilt a shoulder.

"No, Annie, relax. Don't fight it, your body will follow if you stop thinking so hard about what to do." He stood directly behind her, left arm wrapped around her waist as he pulled her to him until they fused as one. "Let my body lead, just follow it. Pretend you're my shadow, and your body will follow what my body does. That's what shadows do automatically." His right hand enfolded hers and both their arms stretched up and out.

Her breathing a little too quick, she tilted her head toward his shoulder, the better to concentrate on his instructions. He stood just taller than she, but so solid and firm. Both of them warm, sticky with exertion and she felt as if their bodies adhered, no option but to move as one. "Fine, you'll feel my right leg lift yours slightly, knee bent. Let it move straight ahead, then swing out thirty degrees. Then down with the foot and the weight shifts. Ready? Now up and—"

"Isn't that a pretty sight? With such intimate, one-on-one training she'll be a Stanislaus before she knows it. Or be with Stanislaus, same difference." Disgust pinched Staniar's features tight and ugly, his whole stance broadcasting his disapproval, his jealousy. Panicking, Anyssa broke free from Glynn, staring at the mat, retucking her shirt, too aware of its clinging dampness that outlined her body.

Glynn gave one overstated clap. "Thank you for the critique, Staniar. A bit brusque, but helpful, I'm sure." A guiding hand on her shoulder, he directed her back to Masady and Jere, clearing the field. "Something you want, Staniar?"

"Message for beta Masady. Bet Rigo wants her back now, said I should finish the session."

"Then inform her directly, not me." Glynn reassembled the children, Jeremy, Heike, Jasper, Hassiba, a tap on each head to keep them in line. "Pair off, you know the drill. Let's show emotion through action. *The Tempest*, Miranda and Prospero. Take Jasper and Hassiba, Staniar."

Stinging with embarrassment, Anyssa sat hunched and quiet, clamping down on any and every emotion. *Be cold, be cool, be analytical. Enough of this. You are a Little Sister. It meant nothing, nothing. Not to me, not to him. Nothing! I won't let it.* Mercifully, Jere remained silent.

With Staniar's presence, the session disintegrated, the children increasingly balky and tired, whines and snideness, bouts of outright stubbornness, all covertly directed at Staniar. With a mulish obduracy Staniar endured, pushed them on until he finally decided he'd proved a point. "Enough. Everyone's tired. Let's head back." Impassive even behind his back, Glynn gave an almost imperceptible, scornful headshake.

Anyssa scrambled to her feet, scooping up Jere's box and handing it to Glynn as he came for it, refusing to meet his eyes. "Children first, then you and Jere, Staniar and I to follow at the rear. Fine with you?"

She swiftly walked to the children before he could argue a different guard order.

Slowly he readied Jere's case, hesitated for a moment. "Don't know what's gotten into Annie all of a sudden. Distant again." Maybe Jere could explain, help him understand. He liked Annie, Annie liked him—except when she didn't. Hot and cold, distant and near, friendly and withdrawn. Damned if he knew the hows or whys of it. This wasn't a play, how could he be expected to read a woman's mind without a script? "Why does she do that, Jere?"

"NEVER, NEVER, EVER TO MOVE LIKE THAT AGAIN. NEVER! I'VE LOST TOO MUCH. ALL SHORN FROM ME, MY BODY DESTROYED, DISCONNECTED FROM MY MIND!"

He stiffened. How he hated it when Jere exploded like this! If only he could erase the marching blue letters from the screen. Never again read them. Because he anticipated what she would say next, hardened himself for her reproach. An irony here—he was incapable of understanding his own mother, and he expected to understand Anyssa?

"LET ME DIE, GLYNN, PLEASE. END IT FOR ME. DISCONNECT ME! TURN THE POWER OFF! LET ME DIE!"

And each time he answered as he always did. "Mother, I can't let you go. I need you, Stanislaus needs you. I can't let you die."

Date: 21 August 2158
Location: Transient Lodging, 6November/Mid, CurieCousteau

"Shah? Nah!" Panthat brushed Anyssa aside with her hip, reached into the packing crate to retrieve King Lear's ermine-edged robe, began fussily refolding it. "Fold, not rolled in sloppy ball. That how you pack for Tierney? No wonder they let you come here. Good riddance."

Staniar pushed by with the drum set, each one nestled within the other for the move. "Blackbird's bitchy today, eh?" and Panthat glared, hands never faltering, folding and smoothing.

"Sorry," Anyssa murmured, not sure if she meant to apologize for her lack of expertise or for Staniar. Both, probably. The shuttle left late tonight for Yuri-Gagarin, and she'd hastily passed word to Becca about the move. Generally the troupes followed a set pattern, a consistent schedule to avoid any overlap—two troupes on the same satellite would compete for a finite audience, diminish ticket sales for both. Hop-scotching out of sequence, though, being unpredictable, would offer Stanislaus some small protection.

With a warning tt-tck-tck, Sylvan parasailed past to land on Panthat's head, dashing down her arm and leaping into the crate. "Nah! No nesty nexty costumes, flap-rat. No wanna travel in crate, no air in cargo hold, silly squilly."

Chance hurried by to reclaim the flying squirrel, paused at Anyssa's restraining hand on his arm. "Isn't this sudden? I thought we planned another week here?" Or so the late Annie's pocket calendar had indicated. "Or is unexpected randomness meant," she jerked her head in Jere's direction, "to protect her?"

Preoccupied with the anticipated misery of another shuttle flight, Chance chucked Sylvan under the chin, stuffed him in a pocket. "Yes, the troupes generally *are* predictable, regular as clockwork, as well you know. Change the schedule without warning and that would hurt Tierney, Orvieto, and Magyar. Don't worry, they've been forewarned. Mama Orvieto's in charge of a new random rotation program. Makes us as unpredictable as a ping-pong ball but ensures that all four of us don't land on the same satellite at the same time," he finished over his shoulder. "We're the random factor."

"In a tearing hurry," she grumbled, picked up another costume and began to painstakingly fold it under Panthat's watchful stare. But the child's dark eyes exhibited an intensity in excess of the task at hand. She could almost see her brain calculating.

"Ah, Chance man want ganja from beta Masady,
have it pocket-locked till time for flight-fright." Fond
exasperation, followed by another piercing stare.
"Sometimes I thinking I know more 'bout acting than
you. Funny, that, huh?"

Trying to keep her hands from faltering, she realized what she'd revealed. Any troupe member would
have known of the new, random rotations—nothing
haphazard or left to chance. To outsiders, Stanislaus
would unexpectedly pop up—like a wild card. Luckily
Chance hadn't thought deeply about such naïveté issu-
ing from a bona fide member of Tierney. Panthat,
however, had. "You're a quicker study of Stanislaus
habits than I am. A lifetime of Tierney training is hard
to break—besides our schedules stayed consistent.
Given the need for Jere's safekeeping, surprise visits
are better to stay a jump ahead of danger."

A moment later her words appeared a prompt, a
prescient cue for the chaos rippling through the living
quarters, already disordered with the debris of packing
and leaving. With a hoarse warning shout Majvor dove
at the box, sheltering it with her body. Racing after
her, Vijay dropped into a defensive crouch as he
scanned for the source of Maj's panic. A quick word
and her pointing arm sent him dashing after a moving
shadow. Knives in hand, Rigoberto and Staniar now
stood back to back, Majvor and Jere between them.
Rigoberto also brandished an illegal and old-fashioned
stun gun. Old-fashioned but still highly effective, Anyssa
knew. Where had he hidden it? She'd searched for
weapons time and again to learn what they'd face.

No time to wonder now. Hurrying, she joined Staniar and Rigoberto to form a more effective defensive
triangle. Where was Glynn? Heard his shout to Vijay.
The children's voices rose and fell, echoing from different directions; they were sweeping through like
beaters, pushing curtains and draperies aside, checking
behind trunks, eager to flush the danger so the adults
could give chase. Only then did she notice that Panthat had vanished, ghosted off. Beta Masady steadily

directed the troupe's actions with hand motions and
occasional sharp commands, Chance at her side, held
in momentary reserve. Hardly a haphazard defense;
each had a role and knew it cold. Yet another role.

Had Becca heard word to proceed? Or had she attempted a solo attack, more confident here than on
YuriGagarin where Anyssa'd have to surreptitiously
report a new layout, any differing routines? Had
Becca the Infallible's renowned stealth failed?

A savage, jubilant shriek pounded Anyssa's ear-
drums, made her nearly jump out of her skin. Little
Sisters worked in silence, voiced no triumph until well
after a job was done. Panthat—it had to be Panthat—
the gloating satisfaction of a predator capturing her
prey, the cry designed to demoralize and signify triumph. "Don't tell me the little beggar blackbird
caught something?" Staniar grumbled, and bet Rigoberto cuffed him into silence, never removing his eyes
from the outer perimeter.

Teeth gleaming in a feral smile, Panthat frog-
marched a scrawny boy, perhaps Jasper's age, perhaps
younger, into view. He back-tilted precariously, one
arm wrenched up between his shoulder blades, a dark
hand with a lethal shim blade cupped under his chin.
Wrenching her eyes away, Anyssa realized Glynn and
Chance had materialized beside her while Vijay protectively cradled both Jere's box and Majvor.

"Only the one?" Glynn exuded nervous tension like
pounding waves of heat, his heart visibly pounding,
fluttering the fabric of his shirt. "Are you sure?"

Panthat nodded. "Shah! Being sure pretty boy here
one and only it. Askee yourself." Her knife shifted,
point just dimpling the child's skin. "You, satrat, answer up. You small and scrawny but plenty space for
Panthat to play skin-games all day—or longer. Start
at feet with tick-tack-toe?"

"Who are you, boy?" Chance gentled his booming
voice.

"Tige." An indignant fidget, then frozen immobility
as the knife pricked.

"Who sent you here?"

"No one." The answer too fast, ingratiating, a pat denial.

"What were you planning on doing here?"

"Didn't plan on doing nothin'!" He swallowed, the knife's point tracing the rise and fall of the taut throat. "Jest wanted ta see!"

'Wanted to see what?" No patience left in Glynn, the final word a stinging barb.

"Wanted ta see . . . you know." The satrat's eyes darted, assessing his options, cockiness fast-fading. "Curious when I heard 'bout it, 'bout her in the box." High and fast now, "Other'uns, my mates, say 'Can't be true, Tige' but I tell'm seeing is believing. Never know less'n you check."

"How'd you hear about it, about her in the box?"

"Couple funny guys—tourists, I'm thinking, an tourist toss ticky-tokes—waltzing by my nap-stand, my tidy-hidy, talking mad hard but low. Rolled out and followed 'cause I were curious. Crazy talk 'bout brains in boxes. But I ain't curious now," he protested with wounded dignity. "You say it no pay bein' curious, you be right. Though pay to not be curious nice, too." Brief hope, a hint of avarice in the shifting eyes. The knife pricked deeper, an implacable reminder, his hope extinguishing like a candle flame.

A couple of funny guys? Tourists? That could mean Falid and Hamish, especially if they'd been careless. After all, they had been once before—that night in the Tranquillity Gardens—but she'd promised herself never to tell Becca that that was how she'd found out about Glynn. Had the child genuinely overheard, or had he been briefed, prepped by Becca to sneak in and scout around? How much more could he tell? Still, this was hardly the time or place to worm it out of him, reveal herself. Doubly so if the child could incriminate her.

Gazing across the boy's head, Glynn met Panthat's eyes. "Think he's telling the truth?"

"All satrats curious, pays to be, boy's right. Curious

and you learn, never know when learning earning coin or credit." Panthat sounded vaguely grudging, the knife minimally retreating from the soft throat skin.

"What should we do with him?" Chance cracked his knuckles, one hand, then the other. "Think it's worth calling Ngina, reporting the attempt? If nothing else, we might get the satrat into a good home, rescue him from a hand-to-mouth existence."

"I think letting him go. Maybe I soft, one satrat soft on 'nother." The corner of her mouth quirked at that unlikelihood, and the boy sensed it, too, began struggling again. "I talk'm deaf and dumb, warn him how curiosity killing cats and satrats. S'okay by you?"

Her soft cajolery didn't fool Anyssa for a second, and she momentarily put herself in the boy's place, listening to his death sentence. Warn Glynn or not as to what Panthat actually planned?

Silence, no one spoke, as if the decision must come from Glynn alone. Not even a warning whistle from Jere to indicate she wanted to speak, have a say in any judgment passed. "Panthat, I trust you," he finally said, "Lecture him, boot his butt, whatever you think best serves."

The boy's legs melted rubbery-soft now, boneless, as Panthat hustled him away, and the rest of the troupe collapsed in relief, all thoughts of packing and moving temporarily abandoned.

Casually positioning herself near where she thought Panthat would return, Anyssa waited, all-too-aware of the letdown, the mental and physical fatigue that strikes after great stress and exertion. Take the time, recover, recenter yourself while you can. A chink in the draperies revealed Panthat popping out of a wall-vent, checking both ways before she dropped down. A halt, an inspection and final wipe of the shim blade against the inside edge of her skort. The knife twinkled out of sight as Panthat checked again, her eyes locking with Anyssa's through the narrow crack. Anyssa blandly looked away as Panthat entered, smiling and calm. "Deaf and dumb, dumb scared, silent sure."

It altered things to know Panthat could and would kill with no compunction. And that Panthat knew she knew her secret. But it didn't change things enough to worry her. Made her more mindful of details—yes, definitely. Things to consider and reconsider.

Date: Afternoon, 22 August 2158
Location: NetwArk, Texas Republic, Earth

Hands steepled over his chest, fingers interlaced, Rhuven Fisher Weaver listened as Dr. Chun continued discussing some of her patients. Even with good news only a rare smile brightened her face, so he let his eyes stray from the screen, roam his office. No sense reading today's hectic schedule again, it merely made his stomach burn. A new masterpiece by Algore, crookedly pinned to the corkboard; someone had helpfully lettered "Bunny" on it. A courteous glance screenward to show interest, a considering "ah" while he pinned the enthusiastic sprawl of colors the other way up. Yes, that might be the tail there, the two floppy ears.

"That's it for this week, Rhuven," she hesitated, "except for one case—I'm not even sure she's contacted you." She dipped off-screen to fish for another folder, and Rhuven shifted closer to his work terminal, sat straighter, an anticipatory tingle washing over him. Though most of Dr. Chun's news had been good— seven joint patients showing definite improvement— something in her last comment dimmed the noon sunlight pouring through the window.

Popping back into view, she opened and rapidly skimmed her file, handwritten notes more reassuring than the cold computer record. "I'm worried, Rhuven. This patient hasn't returned for treatment—it's been four months. Wondered if she'd contacted you, not sure I should ask." Surprisingly, Dr. Chun jutted her lower lip, gave a puff of dismay. "At least there'd be *some* hope, a chance you could stabilize the tumor spread, convince her to return and see me."

"Describe her. Any details you can give without

revealing her name?" Weary, he shook his head, swiftly sorting through his newest Web family in his mind, those requiring physical healing and those craving spiritual health. Not an easy task. His voice, his image reached so many that he could no longer "see" all who joined him at prayer, the multitude who begged for aid. Still, possibly the video archives . . . set the ABSs to checking, perhaps narrow down the possibilities.

"Damn confidentiality," Dr. Chun whacked the file. "Gave me a false address, a false ID number—we *have* been trying to reach her. Naturally this won't be her real name."

"Well, let's start with it. If she used it with you, she may have used it with me." Forgetting Dr. Chun could see him as well, he raked his fingers through his hair, making it stand on end.

"Rosalba Herarra is 37, according to this." An officious throat-clearing. "Breast cancer. Lymph nodes, too. Metastasized to her lung and the surrounding bones. One of those damn rogue BRCA genes the vaccine series can't always conquer. Just lies dormant, waiting—then zap! If we don't start aggressive treatment soon, she won't have much time left."

A coldness radiated inward toward Rhuven's heart, nearly freezing its steady pounding. Herarra? Rosalba instead of Vitorosa? So close, too similar. When he tried to speak he cawed his dismay, started over. "What's she look like?"

"Very dark, long hair. Braided, wrapped in a crown around her head. Something regal, commanding about her, the way she holds herself, regal and . . ." Dr. Chun's hand plucked the air, snatched the right word, "almost menacing. Oh," she rushed on, "perfectly courteous, but that visceral feeling you register when a person would rather kill the messenger than hear bad news. As if she'd have liked nothing better than to leap across my desk, rip my lungs out." Her hand hid her mouth as she apologetically tittered.

His neck hair prickled, the coldness inside swelling.

Apprehension, a sense of inevitability to it all, fore-ordained, somehow. "What family history did she—"

A klaxon split the afternoon somnolence with its wailing scream and Rhuven's screen flashed to signal an emergency. "Doctor, I have to cut you short, get in touch again later," he apologized as he broke the connection to Houston.

"What?" he barked at the microphone, heard Able-Bodied Saver Chartier on the other end.

"Rhuven? Rhuven, thank God you're here!" Chartier sounded winded, his usual baritone nitrous-oxide high and squeaky. "Need you in the south field, fast! Ohlsson's chopped up bad—Balladares was driving the mower."

Ohlsson and Balladares, bad blood between them over Balladares' sister. "How badly hurt? Called an evac team?"

"Yes. On their way." Chartier gulped. "If we can't contain the bleeding, he won't last till then. Rhuven, he's bleeding like a sieve and . . . and there are parts missing. Don't even want to think what!" A retching sound traveled down the line.

"Tell him I'm coming."

"Thanks! Rhuven—I think Balladares ran over him on purpose."

Dashing out the side door beneath the red-tiled roof extension to the east wing, Rhuven ran to the bank of solar-scoots, grabbed one that flashed a green battery charge and straddled it, kicking the starter. Lord help them, Balladares and Ohlsson on the same work detail! Plenty of others available to mow the south field so the children could play ball.

He slalomed through the Tranquillity Gardens, the scoot's tiny horn frantically "toot-tooting" like one of Artur's toys. Dragging his right foot, wincing as gravel cut into bare flesh above the sandal, he threw the scoot into a sharp right turn and sped around the front of the house, kicking up dust against its whiteness, the scoot's day-glo safety orange color an ugly blur against tinted blue-green glass.

Hit the main drive, head and body jutting forward over the bike, wind whipping his hair, tearing his eyes as he strained for every bit of speed he could coax from the scoot. Now, straight up the bank and into the herb gardens, lavender, mint, lemongrass, chamomile, bruised scents miasmic as he bucked and plowed across rows. Angry shouts from garden workers until they identified him.

Briefly airborne as he crested a rise too fast, Rhuven struggled for balance, lips moving in soundless prayers for Ohlsson, but what ceaselessly looped through his brain was Vitarosa. Could it be? Would she have? Without him knowing? BRCA was so rare these days, but hadn't her mother . . . ? *Can't remember, not sure I ever truly knew. Not my Rosa, not if God loves me! She's never sought my healing touch! Does she not believe? Too proud? Disdainful? Disdainful of me?*

Through his pain and confusion he could see them distantly now. Men and women clustered around beside the wing of the large, yellow mowing machine. Some huddled, stunned and silent, others crouched in a circle, jostling to help, a constant shift of bodies. A sickly-rich metallic smell slicing through the fresh green scent of new-mown grass. Grasshoppers sawing the air, the sun just past its zenith, blindly smiling on them, bathing them in unremitting golden rays. A horrible parody of an old harvest-scene painting. Gunning the scoot, he drove straight at the group, slewed and slithered to a stop, and tossed the scoot aside.

Someone, a man, rose, and it took all his concentration to recognize Chartier, blood blurring his features, his shirt and trousers saturated with it. "Still alive?" Rhuven shouted as he pressed forward. "Get the pressure suit on him?"

Chartier dragged at his arm, slowing him, and Rhuven winced as the stickiness of blood bonded their flesh. "Rhuven, he looks like chopped meat, but he's alive. Barely. Helped when we told him you were coming."

Thrusting between bodies, careful not to dislodge

hands and compresses jammed on pressure points to curtail the bleeding, he knelt on one knee beside Ohlsson. Thought he'd be ill, ice-sweat beading his browline, down his spine. What remained of Ohlsson resembled roadkill. "Terrence, boy, Terry. It'll be fine. Evac team's coming." Ah, God, he'd fingered that lump on Rosa's left breast when they made love! *A cyst, it's just a cyst, nothing to worry about,* she'd insisted, pushing his hand away. Not Rosa, but Terry. He clapped his palm over a bleeding artery here, another there, began to pray, inviting his whole soul and being into it.

Slow the bleeding, curb the bleeding, *Lord, help us heal your faithful servant. Grant us time, Lord, precious time.* His hands were slick with blood, he wallowed in it, a creeping dampness wicking up through his trouser knees, his cuffs. Blood of thy lamb, Lord. He opened his eyes to judge the results, saw little had changed. Again, try again. *Oh, Lord, we humbly beseech Your intervention. I am Your vessel, Lord, flow through me into Terrence Ohlsson that he may be saved!*

Rosa, Rosa! Heal her as well, dear Lord. Please do not fail her, do not fail me! My little Rosa is at the point of death. Come and lay your hands on her, so that she may be made well and live. Warm blood, warm, laving his icy skin, his life so cold, poor Terry's warm life pouring out. *Lord! Rebuke me if You must, but do not fail this man!* No good, his touch did not heal, nothing was happening!

The sense of Terry's spirit that hovered in his mind began to pale, his spectrum of colors fading, bleaching to transparency. He struggled to bring it back, but Rosa's spectrum pushed Terry's aside, all he could see. *No!* "Live, Terry! Live for me, live for God!" he wailed his anguish at the sky, the strong sunlight burning his eyes, making him see spots of darkness. Darkness overcoming, overwhelming. . . .

The swoosh of the white-and-red evac craft as it folded its wings and dropped straight down, the soft whoosh of compressed air brakes making it bounce and jiggle, casting a scattering of dust and grass clippings. So green, so green as they stuck, clung to his blood-drenched shirt, settled on Terry's still face.

"He's gone, Rhuven. Too far gone for anyone to save," Chartier pulling him away.

"Not for our Lord," he mechanically protested. Had Luke not said how Jesus had told his followers to visit each town and heal the sick in them? "Tell them," he bayed the words at the sun, "The Kingdom of God has come near to you!"

"The Kingdom of God *has* come near to him, Rhuven. Terry's with Him now," Chartier consoled, supporting him. He sat down hard on the ground, knees drawn to his chest, head buried, and tried to understand. Why had God forsaken him? Not just him but those who depended on him? Had he sinned? Where had he gone wrong? When had he lost his way? Oh, Rosa!

Date: 10:00 p.m., 21 August 2158
Location: Aboard the shuttle-skiff *Tecumseh*,
en route from CurieCousteau to
Satellite Colony YuriGagarin
With a pop that indicated the severing of the dock seal, the shuttle-skiff powered up, backed clear of its bay, engines revving faster as it gained distance from CurieCousteau. At the marker buoy the shuttle-skiff swung round, then gave a roaring surge that pressed its passengers into their seats. Anyssa winced as her body harness tightened protectively, hating the sensation of being snared, unable to move freely, defensively. The sudden compressive snugness, so like a parent's unwanted hug, apparently didn't bother anyone else. Across the aisle, Chance squirmed, a vacuous grin pasted on his face, hum-brumming as he fumbled at a strap, a high-pitched, indignant squeak telling her the strap pinched Sylvan.

Designed to haul small- to medium-sized cargoes requiring speedy delivery, shuttle-skiffs could also be reconfigured to carry up to twenty passengers, al-

though this decreased the freight payload. Her quick
count revealed three additional passengers, strangers,
beyond the thirteen comprising Stanislaus Troupe.
Most of the cargo, more bulk than weight, consisted
of their travel trunks. And in space, bulk was almost
as crucial as weight. Still, the captain had the advantage of four empty seats for stowage. Their transport
cost had to eat into their profits, she thought, but bet
Rigoberto had paid without haggling, not a flinch or
demur. Maybe he didn't care about cost—money be
damned. Not from what she'd seen of bet Rigo. Jere's
"sustainables" allowance handily covered Panthat; not
to count Jere, not to pay for her would be proof positive she no longer existed. Chance's pension covered
him, and Tierney had paid for hers—or Annie Marie
Doulan's, to be precise. Maybe he had some special
arrangement with the captain? From the way Rigoberto had greeted her, jovial, almost suavely intimate,
Anyssa suspected as much.

The seating didn't match Stanislaus' usual hierarchy.
Panny sat beside her against the bulkhead, Staniar in
the seat facing Panthat, and Jeremy, sound asleep beside him. She'd expected Panthat beside Chance, but
instead, Masady had claimed that place across the
aisle, Majvor and Hassiba in the opposing pair of
seats. Behind them the next cluster held Vijay and
Jasper, Heike and Glynn. The three strangers plus Rigoberto, chatting away, filled the cluster behind Staniar and Jeremy.

Casting about for a neutral topic, Anyssa ruefully
decided that Panny judged her condescending or,
worse, subtly ignorant of troupe life. Clear, too, that
Panthat had no desire to discuss her life before Stanislaus, though she seemingly hadn't lived with them
long, Chance either. Nor did she plan to mention her
discovery of the satrat Tige's true fate. Too bad—the
one thing Panthat might have enjoyed discussing was
knife technique. Yes, she and Becca and Panny could
have an informative chat about that. "So," damn, already she sounded insincere, "do you think Jeremy's

improving as fast as he should? Jere seems to think
he needs more work, but she'd a perfectionist." Unfair
to discuss the child to his face, but luckily he slept,
pinkly snuggled against Staniar's shoulder.

" 'Spect he be fine, mime'n line." Panthat's gaze
never budged from Staniar in the seat across from
hers. "Beta Masady being the tough one, Jeremy lucky
just Jere."

"Much you know, little blackbird, coal sack of the
Milky Way, little dark void. When did you become an
expert on theatrical performances?" Staniar taunted,
his leg swinging back and forth, dangerously close to
Panthat's shin each time.

"Shah!" Tucking her legs as far beneath the seat as
she could, Panny half-hooded her eyes to feign drowsi-
ness but fooled no one.

Anyssa debated butting in or not. "Well, Staniar,
given your experience, who's the worse slave driver,
beta Jere or beta Masady?"

But Staniar ignored her, refused to be deflected
from his desire to torment. "Yah, blackbird, inky-dink
satrat, inky-dink like a raven. Probably carrion eater
as well. Always trouble with you along, black sheep,
black plague, black rat. Raise a satrat above its station
and you've still got a stinky satrat." He held his nose
to demonstrate, and this time his wagging foot made
contact with Panthat's shin. From Anyssa's vantage
point it was no accident.

Worse than little Artur, more than twice as old,
Staniar was, yet ragging on Panthat for no apparent
reason. "Staniar, name calling does no good." Her
pompous statement hung in the air, its triteness mocking her. Always playing big sister, role model. "Can't
we talk civilly?" Wonderful, another limp line, as if
Staniar would politely suggest an innocuous subject
now! Heaven knew she'd had problems enough finding one only moments ago.

"Shah! Nah! You the one not belonging here." Panthat's words boiled fast, "Cuckoo egg, that you.
Cuckoo brain. Cuckoo egg slipped into Stanislaus nest,

gave'm big surprise when they hatched you, nasty man! Weak, jealous, coward." An elbow dug Anyssa's ribs. "Know what he scared of most? Jere! Brain box keep him fright-white with fear. Skitter-boweled for days, he was. Anything different he afraid."

"I am not, you stupid, little—"

Chance tossed and turned, green eyes wide but unseeing. Words bounced and hurled at him, but he dodged their meaning. A steady thump, thump on his arm finally registered—Masady patting him—and he relaxed slightly, gave a snort. Ah, yes, flicker-quicker . . . ooh, sounding like Panny . . . changing, changing, the visions sometimes appealing, often not. Noise, shouting avalanching around him, burying him, but the flicker-quicker visions remained. Annie's face . . . Rhuven's face . . . Annie's face . . . Rhuven Fisher Weaver's face. One superimposed upon the other, then back, then forth. A-mazing, ab-solutely 'mazing how they almost blended into one. Mighty alike, how silly! Rhuven's going bald. Annie doesn't have a beard. . . . Why think of Rhuven Fisher Weaver now? "Silly. No reason," he informed Masady as if it were important she know. "No reason at all, at all."

"If you say so," Masady agreed, distracted and exasperated at the squabble across the aisle. A squabble escalating into full-scale battle.

'You here! That beefy, dumb deadbeat of a spacer here! Both dead weight! And Jere no longer Jere, but an abomination in a box!" Staniar screamed, leaning against his restraint harness, the cords on his neck cable-thick. "You're destroying the sanctity of the troupe, its integrity!"

The words struck like peen-ball hammers, tapped at his temples, rapped up and down Chance's spine. Hateful words, unforgivable thoughts. Shouldn't, couldn't be allowed, must stop them. He was . . . he was . . . he grappled for the thought, the concept, watched it flutter past, then hover. Flexed his fingers, grabbed . . . yes . . . Mr. Fixit could repair everything, make anything run smoothly. He wrinkled his brow.

Or was that only machinery? No . . . he shook his
head . . . fixed Jere. Saved her. Resurrected from the
dead, almost. Snared her in a little box, a pretty
wooden box.

Yes, maybe he was . . . Rhuven Fisher Weaver's
God. Maybe that was why he'd thought of the
preacher, NetwArk's Navigator spinning his Web. Be
caught in his web, be healed. Oh, for some of that
peace, that healing, so elusive . . . that Rhuven contin-
ually promised in his netcasts. Others felt it, but not
he—not poor Chance. No, can't be God . . . or he'd
have healed himself. Couldn't fix himself, and Rhuven
couldn't fix him either. Because Chance couldn't believe? Per . . . plexing. . . .

A body scrambling across his, weightless, but definitely there, as if he represented a mountain to be
scaled. "Who are you to talk about the integrity of
the troupe, the sanctity of Stanislaus?" Masady's fury
like a laser, icy-hot . . .

. . . burning through his temples. Too much! Enough
was enough, enough pain for all! The ganja dreams
twisted, turned muddy, his fear of flying bubbling and
churning in his consciousness, making him pant and
sweat, want to heave, then cringe in terror and try
to cram himself under the seat. He struggled with
the buckles on the harness, heaved himself up and
floated into the aisle, head bouncing off the ceiling.
Ah . . . ouch! . . . Zero-gravity . . . forgot. And
tucked protectively, cradling his head. "Shah . . .
Shaddup!" he yelled with all the dignity he could
muster. "Shaddup! Stop fighting . . . all in . . .
this . . . together."

Drifting, bumping, he struggled to find his seat,
jammed into Vijay who'd detached his harness to
thrust himself between Panthat and Staniar, his muscular arms pressing both against their seat backs,
keeping them from throwing themselves at each other's throats. Falling . . . spinning . . . falling . . . spinning in slow motion, falling . . . just as the shuttle had
fallen that time . . . gravity-sucked, outer heat shield

peeling away. Cinders, they'd all be cinders soon if he didn't find some way to fix things. "Stop it!" he implored himself. Oh, he had, he had, but not before five had died and Ngina took command, cosseted the limping shuttle home.

A shove and he landed facedown in Majvor's bosom, downy-dimness scooping him up. He burrowed deeper, sniffed, a pleasant sensation. He'd stay forever if it would blot out the memories. Some of the newer memories, too. Jere, charcoal charred, a cinder, the laser-saw's sharp hum, his panicked awe at cupping a human brain in his hands. Safer to be unconscious.

With cuffs and sharp words Panthat and Staniar were restrained and separated, the seating reorganized. The rest of the flight took place in silence, even the three strangers in the rear fearful of speech. Rigoberto held Masady's hand tightly, the bones birdlike beneath his fingers. "It's falling apart, you know. I'm not sure how much longer we can hold it together."

"I will *not* let it end like this," Masady muttered, "Stanislaus riven by internal dissension, nearly a century and a half of glory ignominiously dying. I'd die before I'd witness that."

Rigoberto raised their clasped hands, lightly kissed the back of hers. Let the gesture suffice, no words would come.

Head propped against her hand, Anyssa sat, chewing her lip. How she hated the fighting, the name-calling, the recriminations—Mother and Father behind closed doors, Rosa's voice rising, taunting as if she hated Rhuven, beneath her, unworthy. Where did hate bubble from? Dark, bursting tar bubbles, ugly plopping sounds, hate stench. Staniar. Becca would call him a tool, ready for her hand. Could she use him? But the taint might stick, taint a Little Sister.

Date: Early evening, 22 August 2158
Location: NetwArk, Texas Republic, Earth

Pacing, like an ox milling corn, pacing and never arriving at anything, any place. No patient, plodding ox, she—she'd not permit more repetitious circling—no, never! *Nothing can constrain my life; I proved that years ago by eliminating my father, my half brothers. Usurpers who'd deserved no part of what they'd stolen from me. Two-faced, impious. . . .*

Vitarosa continued to pace, ignoring Algore's wails, Artur trailing after her, tugging at her waist, whimpering, "Mama, Mama, you're scaring Algore." Finally Artur collapsed beside his baby brother and dragged him into his lap, hugging him tight and rocking him, rocking himself for comfort, until the wails subsided. Always something, someone, dragging at her, draining her.

Ignoring their worried stares, she envisioned her carefully constructed world crumbling yet again. No, hardly a foretelling, a vision of the future, but reality—harsh, concrete, compelling. So, MabasutaGenDy had severed NetwArk's lifeline, canceled all funding. So many weak-willed, weak-kneed cowards, so few daring enough to act, to strive against adversity. With fist pounding palm in time with her thoughts, Rosa cursed them all: MabasutaGenDy for their Judas-like betrayal to those Philistines, Jean-Chrétien and Mit-Rock, the Ayatollah and McBS. At that moment she saw nothing wrong with lumping the Pope and the Ayatollah together as Philistines; their religious beliefs might not match, but their intent most certainly did. Without MabaGD's money, what chance did she and Rhuven have to reach for the stars, the satellites? Comsat time cost too dear—more than herbal pillows and penny-pinched donations, bee-balm and blossom-scented honeys could sustain. Web charges, transaction fees. . . .

And worse, worse, the burning humiliation of her hurried flight to Rome, her audience with Jean-Chrétien, prostrating herself, kissing his ring. Her penance. A vain hope that NetwArk might ally itself with the Pope; weren't all alliances shifting and fluid, enemy becoming ally, ally becoming enemy? What they shared was their Christianity, she originally a Nuevo

Catolico, and he of the Old Catholic Faith, reunited at last, an errant lamb brought back into the fold. Surely the chance to reclaim a Protestant NetwArk, lead it to the true faith, should weigh more heavily than an Islamic ally? A bargain for MitRock as well.

Pacing, pacing. Caged, the door to her dreams swinging shut. One part of her heard Algore begin another hiccuping, uncertain cry, piercing higher in counterpoint to her misery. As she swept by, she delivered an openhanded slap to the side of his head. Blessed silence again. Commiseration didn't help. A plan, action, would.

And the Pope had raised her to her feet, both her hands clasped in his, a weary benevolence showing in his eyes, sorrow and sadness in the round, dark face, startling contrast to the white robe and skullcap. "To enjoy unity in Christ's name would be pleasing, my child, but there are some things I cannot countenance. Always there are battles to be waged and won for Christ, my little sister, but not by assassination. I've striven to give women full standing in the Church, though some contend my methods have been extreme; but I will accept no one under Peter's roof, man or woman, who would set him or herself above our Commandments, picking and choosing their targets, determining who will live, who will die."

God proposes, Man disposes—without humankind to do His dirty work, where would God be? Better to think it than to voice that thought right now. But some debate was required. "And how does that differ from a battle, a crusade, Your Holiness?" she'd argued. "Each fighter chooses a target, an opposite number to kill . . . or be killed by that enemy."

"Yes, in the throes of battle a soldier may kill his target yet in turn become another's target. God does not look down from on high, point and say, 'Yes, this one, not that one.'" His soft, pear-shaped body suddenly seemed hard, unyielding as ebony. "But *you,* you *choose* your targets, assassinate them not for faith but for politics. You transform yourself into a vessel of evil God cannot countenance, even though you sweat you act in His name. I will not have that in my Holy Church. You forget the New Testament and bow to the wrathful, vengeful God of the Old Testament. God contains more aspects than we humans can understand or should dare to emulate."

Pious hypocrite! Cant-laden charlatan—how unsullied can you be when you let the money changers, the megagloms into your temple? She had left with an all-consuming fury, snatching the mantilla from her head, tossing it behind her where it floated and fell like a punctured dream. Denied, always denied, denigrated, demoted by male authority. Had not Luke himself said, "Whoever does not hate his father and mother, wife and children, brothers and sisters, yes, even life itself, cannot be my disciple."? Well, hate them all she did, hated everyone and everything now. Such hatred burned with a certain compelling purity, a justice to it and a self-justification; flames to burn away the dross.

Take over the running of NetwArk herself? Retrench, take a harder line, dominate everyone and everything, and then try anew? With or without outside funding? Her head whirled. Better yet, build her own war chest, depending on no one, beholden to nothing but her own determination and drive. Tapping her fingers against her lips, she assessed this new idea, weighing the possibilities, potentialities. Time was *not* on her side. And Rhuven? For the first time in weeks she allowed herself to miss Becca and Anyssa, the lack of conjoined minds, trained to obey. Damn all! With the funding gone she needed to pull Becca and Anyssa, those clowns Falid and Hamish, home as soon as possible. No way for them to support themselves on Waggoner's Ring without the credit transfer NetwArk banknetted each week for support. And she needed them here, at her side. Except that would leave Jere and Glynn safe. Damnation—short-term goals or long-term ones? Just when they were so close!

Distractions, distractions, don't be snared by distractions. There may still be time, may still be a way.

Concentrate on the first step, the here and now. First problem: Rhuven. Cast doubt on his leadership, his abilities, force him to step down? But that would cast doubt on NetwArk itself with more precious time lost rebuilding its reputation. No, a better, more permanent solution was needed. Death was permanent.

Stopping short, she cast a beatific smile at Artur and Algore, still huddled on the floor, Algore's head buried in Artur's chest to muffle his sobs. Artur looked strained and white, unsure if he dared respond to that rapturous smile or not. "It'll be fine, love, it'll be all right. Mama's sorry." He nodded rapidly in agreement, wiped his eyes against Algore's sunny-yellow crown. Brave little soldier, and all hers.

Yes, remove Rhuven, elevate Artur in his father's place as NetwArk's new figurehead. Who could be more perfect than a child, a child evangelist, so pure and innocent, lisping the scriptures? And so malleable. Hateful to relinquish her rightful position yet again, but pragmatism must rule, and so would she, behind the scenes. She and Anyssa could resolve Artur's new status later.

The sigh of a door opening, a mad scramble as the boys rushed Rhuven, flung themselves against his legs, weeping with relief. Squatting, he cuddled them close, wiped their tears. "Rosa, love, what's the matter, what's happened?" he asked over their heads, face haggard and worry-torn. Ah, yes, the Navigator, totally adrift, at sea. You never could see the stars, the planets set there to guide you home.

'No, before you tell me, let me get the boys to bed." A child tucked in each arm, he rose and swiftly took them into the hallway, handed them to a startled passing acolyte. Returning, he closed the door firmly behind him and slumped against it. Always one for support, aren't you, Rhuven? Never firm on your own two feet.

Consternation marred his brow, more than a touch of anxiety—she recognized it all too well—that one of her nervous spells had struck again. They'd resurfaced with Algore's birth. As he girded himself to speak, she plunged ahead to deliver her news. "Rhuven, it's all over. All our hopes, our dreams of converting the satellites." Coercing the satellites was more accurate, but Rhuven had never noticed the subtext of her plan. "The money's gone, dried up."

"How? But it can't be?" He fought back tears. "Ah! Then I truly *am* being tested! First the healing power taken to test my humility, and now this." What did he mean, she wondered, but he continued with an eerily cheerful fortitude. "Oh, Rosa, we've been short of money before, but the donations always come in. We'll market our simples more aggressively—look how sales have skyrocketed in recent months. The Lord always provides. He will again once I find my way back on the true path of faith."

"Well, the Lord hasn't been minting the money, Rhuven. MabasutaGenDy supplied the bulk of it—not the contributions, not the sales. And without that to buy comsat time, strengthen our signals, there's no way we can continue preaching to the Ring."

"What do you mean, MabasutaGenDy?" Above his beard a bright patch flared on each cheekbone, as if she'd slapped him. "We've always been independent, beholden to no one except the Lord. Grandfather, Father . . . our compound, our ark carrying us safe, secure against the flood of darkness outside." A dawning comprehension in his eyes. "Is this why . . . ?" he murmured.

"Then I wouldn't send out a dove right now, because he won't come back with a thousand-dollar credit in his beak." She hated the way he'd always sweetly remonstrate with her. The words, the tune, old, hackneyed, and she refused to hear them any more, but still they came.

"It's all so simple—how could I have been so blind? Not seen it? That's why we've retained our purity of faith until now—strong against the Pope, the Ayatollah, the others whoring after the megagloms. Unseemly, unchaste, worshiping the golden calf. If money's their god, so be it. It isn't mine."

"Well, they're not the only ones who've been whoring after money. MabasutaGenDy didn't solicit me, cause my fall from grace, I solicited them." Now she'd captured his attention, mouth slack, eyes wide at her betrayal. "And when they cast me aside, I whored after the Pope. Although that's carrying the metaphor a bit far. He treated me like a sister, an errant little sister, perhaps the best he could manage. Yes, like an errant little sister." And with none of the respect due a Little Sister of Mortality.

A deep breath. "After all, you should be familiar with whoring around, both the concept and the execution. Tell me, did Jere whore after you, or did you solicit her, tempting her with your godhead? It always seemed feeble to me, in need of constant coaxing and nurturing. Whichever way, Jere certainly had her work cut out for her." Rhuven's hands rose in a warding gesture, as if she offered a temptation which must be refused, thrust behind him.

"By the way, you *do* realize what you unwittingly gave Becca permission to do to halt those blackmail notes?" His head shook back and forth, still in denial. "You gave her permission to kill Jere, or so she interpreted it. You have a son by Jere, you know." She paused, "Or didn't you know? Hardly the way a good shepherd cares for his flock, letting a precious lamb wander." The new blackmail note had come today, its threat confirming what the Pope had freely told her months ago. All so obvious in retrospect who'd penned those notes, the one soul she'd trusted with her secrets. Another wound, though not a fatal one.

"I . . . ? Jere dead? A son? Jere's child? So many sins I didn't know I'd committed, though I'm being rebuked, chastised for them." Reeling, he shook his head punch-drunkenly.

"Yes, your eldest son. About a year younger than Anyssa."

"Truly?" Spittle bubbled at the corner of his mouth.

Yes, some insects created the same bubbling slime; Artur had showed her among the plantings. "God gave . . . me . . . 'nother son?"

"I doubt God had much to do with it."

Her quandary now was simply when and what to do: snap Rhuven's neck, mimic a natural death with a compressive, sharp blow. But that might not prove necessary. With the same clinical interest she'd shown in Artur's insect find, Rosa watched Rhuven waver, left leg unable to support him, his speech a jumble of nonsense sounds as he fought for balance, finally collapsed on the floor. Good, good, a stroke, if she was any judge. He painfully reached out to her, the left side of his face slack, right fear-crumpled, desperate mouth mumbling formless words. "Ealin gaw!"

Now, watch and wait. Check the clock. Much could be done to save a stroke victim, ensure paralysis or aphasia did not set in—if the proper medications were promptly administered. Even the poorest household boasted at least one set of emergency syringes; NetwArk had strategically located them all across the compound. Prayer plus science, Rhuven always emphasized. Yes, just a question of time. Wait and watch as time passed. Pray to pass the time—why not? Ah, the sympathy this would garner for NetwArk, an outpouring of money as well from the credulous faithful yearning to succor Rhuven, speechless, immobile. Yes, preacher, heal thyself if you can. Heal me, make the lump disappear. My time's running short as well. If your faith's strong enough. Or aren't you as credulous as your followers?

Date: Near midnight, 21 August 2158
Location: Holm Port, NelMandela

Shoulders hunched, hands cupping her elbows, Clea Tierney leaned against the wall, the only color on her drained face a scattering of freckles. Three SatGov security guards, one a lieutenant by her bars, clustered around her, judging her reactions as much as her actions. *Don't look, don't watch,* but despite herself she kept stealing furtive glances, furious and sorrowing as the evac workers bagged and removed the body for further examination. The lieutenant snapped a question, but she didn't listen. Why hear when she'd heard it before, repeated with numbing regularity over the last half hour?

"For the hundredth time," she dropped her hands and straightened, one foot forward to restore her equilibrium—of body, if not of mind, "when you ordered me back to NelMandela from Amaterasu, I had *no* inkling what it was about." Of course she'd returned, the silence in the security skip ominous, boding no good whatever the problem might be. No member of any troupe would purposely annoy Security: ignore them if possible (yes), steer clear of them (of course), bribe them (naturally). Failing that, always cooperate, but never reveal anything of moment.

But now she longed for something crucial to reveal, anything to assist in tracking Annie Marie Doulan's killer. "I *swear* we had no idea Annie was missing. None of us did." Blah-blah-blah, the same question rephrased. As if her answer would differ this time around. "Of *course* we knew she wasn't with Tierney Troupe." Desperate, she let her voice resound as if sheer volume might penetrate thick skulls. "She'd been loaned to Stanislaus for the month. We received her message saying she'd arrived safely. No word from Stanislaus saying otherwise." No need to raise her voice, she was a trained actress used to projecting her words. But that projection, combined with her increased volume buoyed her words across the entire waiting area. A SatGov, floating through a shuttle port, grabbed a handgrip, bobbed momentarily as her aide drifted into her, then swung round to examine the group in the artificial-grav area.

Clea continued, "Ask Stanislaus where Annie Marie is." Wincing, she rephrased her statement; she knew all too well where Annie Marie was—in the body bag. "Ask Stanislaus why Annie Marie isn't with them. Why they didn't tell me she'd left ahead of schedule?"

Had Rigo somehow tricked Annie Marie? Killed one of Tierney Troupe's members? Nothing like this had ever happened among the troupes, and for lack of a reasonable explanation this could easily start a feud. Of course troupes competed, but not like that, not killing each other. Unless . . . unless . . . no, not sweet, innocent Annie? A threat to Jere or Glynn? Never!

"What's going on here?" Running shaky hands through her hair, Clea tried to focus on this new voice. To her private amusement the security detail back-stepped a pace, rigidly fussy, solemn-faced, boot heels together. No salutes as yet, but right arms quivered with suppressed desire. Her eyes level with a pair of epaulets, Clea cocked her head, stared up at a golden-brown face topped with intricately braided hair. "I'm Governor Ngina Natwalla of SallyRide. Either your PA system is announcing the Stanislaus Troupe with tedious regularity, or this woman is shouting their name loud and clear. And I do mean loud and clear." With a crisp turn Ngina Natwalla towered over the lieutenant. "Whatever your problem, I doubt you want it broadcast, do you?" Now she addressed Clea, "What's this fuss about Stanislaus? You're Tierney Troupe, I'd stake my reputation on that."

For the second time in her life Clea Tierney's world swam black, her knees rubbery as the floor beckoned. "Here, none of that." The governor caught her, struggling against Clea's sudden limpness before conceding defeat and passing her to her aide. One partially aware segment of Clea's brain registered the transfer, wanted to smile at the delegation of responsibility. That, after all, was what aides were for—the neat folding of limp bodies; Regulation 57, Section 12, Subset b, no doubt. And in the unfolding blackness was peace, no thoughts of Annie Marie, her body, Rigoberto's impossible, implausible desire to protect Jere and Glynn, nothing. A relief not to relive it all again. Had Annie Marie felt thusly?

When she roused, the governor was sitting against the wall, long legs stretched out to block traffic, a cup

of water cradled on her lap. "Want some?" A wary
nod; her dry mouth craved it, but her stomach protested the thought. Setting the cup aside, the woman
rose on her knees, eased Clea up into a sitting position. All without the help of her aide. "Turn any
greener and you'll match the wall." Slowly it dawned
on Clea that the security guards still remained, but
well out of earshot, the aide riding herd on them as
he spoke into a wristcom. Handed the cup, she managed a small sip.

"Go easy, don't gulp. Be cautious about everything
else as well, but I doubt I have to tell a trouper that.
Just as my SatGov troopers know." A smile at the
wording. "I've pried some of the story from the lieutenant—rank has its privileges, even though this isn't
SallyRide—but I'd rather hear it from you."

"Why? What do Tierney's woes have to do with
you? We're not SallyRiders." Or any other satellite-
citizens, just Waggoner's Ring—all and nothing. Act
nonaggressive, display genuine curiosity. Not all that
difficult. But what could Ngina Natwalla find of interest in this strange murder?

"Because I've had dealings with Stanislaus Troupe,
more than a little these past months." Long-fingered
hands sketched a squarish box-shape. "A dear friend
of mine, Tinker II Evers II Chance now travels with
them, or did the last I heard." She jerked a shoulder
in the direction of her aide. "We've been trying to
raise Stanislaus for the last fifteen minutes, but no luck
so far." Clea checked on her water. "Could just be
coincidence, bad timing that they're in transit. Can't
be sure, but they were due to ship out for YuriGagarin
sometime today or tomorrow. We're scanning passenger lists to find the shuttle they took, if that's the
case."

"But Annie was supposed to be with them, *is* supposed to be with them," Clea protested. "The . . . the
body . . . I didn't know, we didn't know she hadn't. . . .
We *got* her arrival message!" The body, folded and
stuffed into the vac-chamber, where objects were put

into a vacuum, moisture sucked out of them. It was meant for cargo, a way to ensure that each piece was as dense and compact as possible, no excess moisture to add weight, no air pockets to make a piece bigger than need be. Why it had taken workers so long to check the vac-chamber, she didn't know, but apparently when they had, they'd found Annie's body, dry and light as a husk, blood and fluids sucked out of her. A rusty stain and a shrunken puncture behind her right ear. Not Annie Marie anymore, not Annie more, not Annie ever again.

"Why was she with Stanislaus Troupe?"

"We'd all agreed—Orvieto, Magyar, and Tierney— to lend a hand, watching, you know, guarding . . ." she waved a distracted hand, not daring to say it aloud, then forced herself to sketch the same box-shape Ngina Natwalla had. "Sharing the burden. We all compete, but we pull together when it counts."

"Commendable, truly." A hint of sarcasm? Clea couldn't judge. "More selfless than we've been. Not always easy to put the Ring as a whole ahead of your own satellite." But now brown eyes latched onto the lightning blue eyes that marked all Tierney-born. "Stanislaus never contacted you that she didn't arrive. You received a message she'd arrived. So how'd she end up here in the vac-chamber? Wouldn't they think you'd reneged on the agreement if she left early?" Anger flushed Clea's face, camouflaging her freckles, and she began wearily pushing herself to her feet. "No, no, sorry," Ngina placated, "I'm not trying to insult Tierney honor, just thinking out loud. Join me."

"Rigoberto and Masady are proud. If Annie left unexpectedly," Clea groped through the puzzle, "I think they'd have contacted me. Not to complain," she amended hurriedly, "but to make sure she was all right, that nothing had happened to her or to Tierney."

"Well something surely happened, and it looks like murder." Lacing her hands around her boots, Ngina stared hard at her knees. "I don't know if the lieutenant told you, but the vac-chamber printout shows its last use was near three weeks ago. Not that much freight goes out from this port, mostly passengers."

"But that was the date she left here to join them on CurieCousteau! I'm a fool! That means she never arrived!"

"Apparently not."

Apparently not? The thought left Clea shuddering, the cup of water spilling across her chest and stomach, rushing in tiny streams across the floor. "But someone did!" she blurted. "Someone arrived at CurieCousteau! They didn't know precisely what she looked like, so anyone using that name—"

"Would be accepted by Stanislaus," Ngina finished. "An imposter."

"Cleopatra!"

"Someone named Cleopatra?" Ngina sounded utterly lost.

"No!" Clea interjected, "Cleopatra, nursing an asp to her bosom. Whoever that person is—the Annie who isn't Annie—she must want Jere dead! Stanislaus is in more danger than they were before!"

Date: Early morning, 22 August 2158
Location: Aboard the shuttle-skiff Tecumseh,
en route from CurieCousteau to YuriGagarin

Grateful the squabbling had ceased before she'd sprung into action and cracked heads—if not necks— Becca resettled in her seat, Hamish and Falid across from her. At least that fat fool Rigoberto had moved forward and she no longer had to dredge up civil but superficial answers to his meddling questions. Luckily he'd enjoyed talking far more than listening. Typical for an actor, she supposed. The troupe member who'd claimed his seat—Vijay—had shared a gleaming smile and a muttered apology for the ruckus before settling in for a nap. A bruise swelled, purpling his left cheekbone. Probably he'd caught a knee in the face—far too easy to do in a Z-grav fight. Usually the damage was minimal—the recipient rapidly propelled backward by the blow. But held in place by a bulkhead, the body couldn't escape the force behind the blow. Whoever hit him must have been strapped down.

With a stern effort to smother a chuckle at how ridiculous Hamish and Falid appeared, Becca relaxed, pretended to nap. Bewigged and berouged, Hamish wore the long, paisley-swirled skirt and high waisted, tight vest that the women of Huang-ti favored for formal functions. He projected a perfect figure of womanhood—if one relished an overpainted female of plump middle age. Falid's brainstorm of binding Hamish with the spanplast applied to sprains had uplifted Hamish's bulk into a bosom of sorts. Naturally Hamish had been surreptitiously snacking, and the crumbs bobbed above his pretend bosom. For once he had a shelf to catch them, and they happened to be in Z-grav! The skipper'd not be pleased, but Becca took her small pleasures as she found them.

God save us, costume games, no less. A snort that she turned into a pretend half-snore. Falid fared somewhat better than his partner, totally clean-shaven, his dark hair temporarily blond-streaked. The haughty-naughty look of a crystal-sculptor, his stretch suit fussy and almost too trim, extra color bars in delicate pastel variations as well as his supposedly legitimate art-service markings. And she, hair close-cropped like a brush, plastiform cheek plumpers broadening her face, untidily dressed in the gear of a lower-level government official, showed more manhood than either one of them. All in how you carried yourself, how you crossed your legs or didn't, thighs athwart so the bulges showed. Did men think they had to be constantly aired? Which reminded her—too bad she'd lacked time to wash her extra socks before pressing them into service there.

Anyssa had no idea they were aboard the shuttle-skiff, had barely given them a glance, if that. Or the girl was playing it very cool, very professional. Not fair to judge until she found out. Still, she'd have expected—demanded—a discreet finger-signal of acknowledgment. Not that the girl had given them much advance warning about the sudden leave-taking. Maybe she truly hadn't been able to, and maybe the girl was hiding something from them. Not a question of trust or distrust, but the necessity of gauging possibilities and probabilities.

A nap promised escape, refreshment. Still, she'd learned through the years how to do without unless absolutely necessary. Now was not the time, no matter that she pretended to nap. Always watch, be on guard. Let the eyelids flutter, the head loll until it almost brushed the dark-haired stranger's. Then she had all she could do not to involuntarily start, sit up straight, intent, the microchip throbbing and tingling behind her left ear. Under normal circumstances it signaled her to hightail it to a secure line and contact Vitarosa as soon as possible.

The chip was old, definitely out of date—she and Rosa and the other members of their LSM cadre had had them implanted nearly twenty-five years ago. Hardly a top-of-the-line model, but durable, still functional. And it could transmit messages as well, assuming the receiver was stoic enough to stand the excruciating sizzle beneath the skin, ready to shatter bone and brain as each coded throb crackled through. After each episode she feared for her hearing, as if the electronic impulses might solder the tiny inner ear bones. Tilting farther back, splaying her legs wider in feigned relaxation, Becca listened to Vitarosa's message.

So, it was Go, Go, Go. Vitarosa's message had radiated a white-hot vengeance, an obsession beyond the pale. Do it at warp speed. Destroy the box, snatch the boy back to Earth. (So, the blackmail note *had* arrived.) If the mission miscarried, return soonest without leaving evidence of their meddling. Translation: Ensure Anyssa returned safe with the boy. Falid and Hamish? Expendable. She as well if things soured beyond her capacity to right them. Oh, Rosa did want her Becca, too, but would nobly accept her sacrifice. Ha! Not this time, thank you!

Almost sagging with relief as the transmission ended, Becca considered how to alert Anyssa that their mission would commence soonest. Action at last! With Anyssa attuned to Stanislaus' every rhythm, technically she should start the action in play. Damn Anyssa for her logic, for being the one who'd wormed her way inside the troupe, into their trust. A major responsibility to finesse the setup, eliminate extraneous players, clear the field for a clean snatch and grab. Would the girl claim first right to destroy the box, avenge family honor? A pass-off to her "senior?" Toss poor Becca a bone? From now on all her bones would be meaty.

Trained and honed as she was, only one minute part of Becca gave her away, alerted Falid and Hamish that she'd received news: The toes of her right foot kept constricting, curling inside her boot. Falid and Hamish had already received their own private messages from the Ayatollah and the Pope. And until Becca informed them of as much or as little as she chose about their orders, they waited, unsure whether their divergent goals might mesh or tear them asunder. Their receiver chips boasted the latest in high-tech transmission capabilities, more powerful—and more persuasive—because each message-throb stimulated a pleasure center in the brain. Had Becca realized, she would have labeled them doubly soft, self-control overridden by pleasure, unfit to shine the boots of any Little Sister of Mortality. Well, they'd polished them before, but never again. Home, home after this!

ACT FOUR

Date: Morning, 22 August 2158
Location: Traveler's Transi-Lodge, 4Hotel/Cap,
Satellite Colony YuriGagarin

From earliest childhood she'd always relished setup times, the move to a fresh location, the crackling energy generated by performing a different play. Oh, true, none of the satellites was exactly "fresh," the plays "new," but constant touring cast fresh light on familiar locations; each play, even the standards, revealed new facets, varied nuances in the faces of an unjaded audience. If the action, the speeches came by rote, you knew you'd gone stale.

But today, while the hustle and bustle of setup was the same, the atmosphere felt wrong—sullen, silent, almost brittle. As if an electrical charge were building, waiting its chance to surge and explode in a jagged bolt of recrimination and anger. Whom it would be hurled at she wasn't sure, suspected she might even be the target if people were honest. But then, who was when it came to analyzing personal emotions? Hard to be dispassionate about passions.

And what . . . or how, precisely did *she* feel at this point? She sat or, more accurately, her life-support box sat in the center of the chamber, everyone dashing, ignoring her presence. Alone and unregarded, but definitely still guarded. The attack late yesterday, right before they'd left, she'd put out of her mind. A ripple of amusement. Where would I store it if it *were* out of my mind? Does the life-support box serve as my packing trunk? What else have I stored in it?

Shadings of fear . . . yes, fair enough to admit that . . . fear, not of death but of continued life. And its reverse, grudgingly acknowledged, fear of losing her life. Can I lose again what I've already lost? Amazing what I've become used to. I am an entire universe within my own mind. If I don't exist, do they exist? Glynn and Masady? Dear old Rigoberto? Chance and his little sidekick? Am I the only sentient thing that gives them shape, existence? I am the Sun and they orbit about me, some near, some distant, like Staniar, but all in danger of being burned if they venture too close. Didn't Daedalus warn his son, Icarus, not to venture too near the Sun?

The satrat, Tige, didn't pose any real danger. The child never came that close to me. But I posed a danger to him, to anyone who unwittingly believes the atmosphere around me sustains life. Panthat took him out with pragmatic efficiency, no matter what Glynn and the others want to believe. Let them have that false security if it keeps them warm and content. Annie suspects otherwise, I think, wiser about life's realities than Glynn, but equally confused, racked by conflicts. Doesn't she realize how she swings between love and avoidance each time Glynn's near? And Panthat, pure essence, honed sharp to survival essence. We all have an overwhelming desire to survive, but most of us haven't a clue how to ensure our survival. And damn Chance for what he did to ensure mine, though Glynn gave him no choice.

That squabble in the shuttle-skiff earlier, I could hear but couldn't see what happened. Again I played no direct part, but my presence, my being, served as catalyst. A poisonous atmosphere . . . all emanating from me. Some say that if you truly believe you're dying that you will, that the mind can trick the body, convince it to fail. Wonderful, can I convince my box to fail? Managed to convince it to squawk for me, a screechy whistle-whine for attention. (Heard herself do it, cursed since she hadn't meant to be noticed. Or had she?) How many hours have I spent forcing youngsters to delve into their minds? "What motivates your character?" Fine, what are my motivations?

Chance halted by her left "eye," straining over his shoulder to read her LCD. "CHANCE, ARE WE FALLING APART FROM WITHIN?"

The broad planes of his face looked eroded, green eyes hazed as if he still floated somewhere else. Defenses down from the ganja, honesty too near the surface. "I don't know," his arms shot overhead, fingers interwoven until his knuckles cracked. "Ever since Annie arrived . . . like trying to jam the wrong key into a lock."

"DO YOU THINK THIS HAS SOMETHING TO DO WITH ANNIE?"

"Don't know, don't know, my mouth's rattling along all by itself." Massive shoulders hoisted in apology. The flying squirrel peeked out of one of the holsters on his tool belt. "'Flight not too bad today till I started thinking about Rhuven, seeing his face everywhere, superimposed on everything I saw. Silliest damn thing."

"IF I WERE YOU, I'D WORRY MORE ABOUT VITAROSA AND LESS ABOUT RHUVEN." A statement, not a reproach, but she lacked vocal cords, could not couple emotion to the flat display of words. Sarcasm, humor, fear, a host of other emotions, all vanished without vocal inflections, without facial expressions or body language. Emotions existed only if she spelled them out.

"Never saw Vitarosa, just Rhuven on the Web." A huge yawn. "Something to be thankful for, I guess. Listen, love, got to keep moving. Stay any longer and I'll slumber at your feet, meta . . ." another head-splitting yawn, "phorically speaking."

"POOR CHANCE. LUMBER ALONG, THEN." Nothing to do but think. Amazing when your only activity was thinking how much you could think about thinking. And some level of me is always thinking whether I'm conscious of it or not. Perpetual motion machine, oh, please, God, let the cogs and gears of my brain grind to a halt!

Date: Morning, 23 August 2158
Location: Commercial Zone,
5Oscar/Mid, YuriGagarin

Scowling, Staniar thrust against the walkway traffic, not especially caring if he jolted people, whether his glower took them aback or frightened them. Yes, sir, yes, ma'am, aren't I the absolute walking embodiment of the Stanislaus Troupe? Yes, sir, makes you want to hurry, come see the performance, doesn't it? Sure, come see the freak show! 'Cept they never take the biggest freak out of her box 'cause she'd die!

When no empty hands grasped the handbills thrust at them, he contented himself with plastering them upside down in obscure places or balling them up and tossing them over his shoulder. Fine me for littering! Too bad I'm not in Z-grav, be like dozens of snowballs bobbing in the air. Finally, disconsolate, he shambled onto a bench, dug his heels in and pressed, heaved again, curious if he could rock it from its moorings. An omen if he succeeded. Not sure how much longer I can take it. Every muscle drooped, doleful, and he encouraged a tear of self-pity, blotted it against a 100% cotton-clad shoulder. Stanislaus and natural fibers! How can they keep going with Jere-in-a-box?— push the wrong button and up she'll pop. Am I the only one who can admit how unnatural it is?

Unnatural, spine-tingling deviant, and . . . and they held conversations with it, her, whatever, as if it were real. Couldn't be, couldn't be possible. Oh, maybe, maybe, you could keep a brain alive like that for a bit, but vision, hearing, speech of a sort? Had to be some sort of microchip like they used with those super-smart computers. Force-feed all those plays into its memory bank, and you'd have won half the battle of making it "real." And if it, she *were* real . . . con-

demned to "life" in the abstract, then didn't someone
owe her an escape?

By rights, Glynn. And what did *he* do? Lord it over
them all, acting beyond Stanislaus' age rule, snatching
all Jere's prime roles. While he, Staniar, slaved dutifully behind the scenes, still longing for that lost applause. If they were breaking rules, traditions, right
and left, then why couldn't *he* resume his place center
stage? An encore—right? But *no,* they'd had it in for
him ever since he'd joined, ever since he'd been a
toddler.

Wasn't his fault he'd been fretful, a fussy eater, pet-
ulant at this new life he'd been plunked into without
any warning. How could you expect a little'un to understand that apprenticeship to Stanislaus Troupe was
supposed to be such an incredible honor? Beta Masady always and forever shouting, poking and knotting
him into unnatural positions. Hurtful she'd been, still
was. Rigo and Vijay and Majvor not much better, always doing the same, though Majvor had loved him
as much as she could, but never enough, never singling
him out from the other children. Majvor hadn't been
very old herself back then, about his age now, he
guessed. Masady and Majvor and Hulda, now dead,
had juggled all the male leads.

So Jere'd waltzed back, triumphant, a baby on her
hip, younger than he, and somehow—in ways he could
never fathom, never mimic even when tried—more
adorable, more outgoing than he. Quick learner, and
the quicker Glynn'd learned, the more he'd faltered.
The best plums for Glynn, always the best. Like swallowing burning acid to gag down the favoritism; temporary relief in the occasional pinch or poke he
inflicted on Glynn.

So why stay, why put up with more injustice? A
huge self-commiserating sigh and he began folding a
handball into smaller and smaller squares. So get out.
Hugo and Tarik scrammed after they "aged out." Not
unheard of for the boy members to collect their troupe
shares in real credits, become real men and have real

lives for themselves that didn't revolve around play-acting. Real jobs, satellite-citizenship. Thing was, was it scarier being on your own or remaining part of a jinxed troupe? Ah, make some grand, sweeping, scornful exit! Another gusty sigh. If that damned satrat Pan-that could survive on her own, couldn't he with money plus the training he'd received? He heartily despised—even feared her—simply because she was so complete, so whole, needing nothing and no one. And now she belonged to Stanislaus in a way he'd never managed.

"So, that bad is it?" Staniar hadn't noticed someone sitting on the bench beside him. Woman, he reckoned, though that was silly, course she was, showed in her build, her shape, but tough, stronger-looking than most. Charcoal gray skinny-suit, no trim or badges. Hair close-cropped like she doesn't give a damn what she looks like, worth more than her looks. Maybe teaches at the training academy here, or pilots her own shuttle-skiff or maybe an entrepreneur. Have to be tough and smart for those things.

"Well, pretty much bad, I guess." A hand toss as if to negligently throw his troubles away, show him man enough to cope.

"Your own troubles? Or is the show that rotten?" Despite himself he ruffled in defense, only belatedly realizing that passed for humor with her, though her face remained studiously neutral.

"Performance is fine. Stanislaus is the best troupe on tour. Everyone knows that." Except her, so that must mean she'd only recently arrived from "below," from Earth. "Just there've been tensions in the troupe lately. Lots of tension."

"I should think so." She'd risen, now stood facing him, one foot propped on the bench by his thigh, knee threateningly near his face. "Don't see how any sane, rational being could live with an abomination to the human spirit like that brain box is. Immoral and callous, selfish to purposefully trap a human being in limbo, as if your wants take precedence over another's needs."

He gaped, tried to slide away, but the wall blocked his right side, her knee and strong, muscular thigh pinning him on his left. "How . . . ?" A sickening swell of dread, a tremor of relief. That *he* hadn't told. That someone else *did* know, could share the wrenching wrongness that tore his soul. Annie had at first, but somehow she'd been co-opted by the others, come to believe Jere was "right" and real. That it was right she existed in that box. Even liked Glynn better'n him. Way she eyed him sometimes, hot and heavy. "How did you find out?"

"That doesn't matter, only that I know. And I've been appointed to bring her relief, release." Her voice rolled on and on, soothing, righteous, justified, until he was fair mesmerized by it, the virtue of her thoughts . . . and the promise of more credits than his troupe share would provide. All his, his alone for just a little help at a strategic moment, a chance to reveal his higher moral principles simultaneously with thumbing his nose at the troupe, collecting his troupe share plus this newfound windfall.

Date: Evening, 23 August 2158
Location: Lebedev Gathering Hall, 2Hotel/Mid, YuriGagarin

A deep bow, as low as possible without jarring the concealing mask, as Glynn acknowledged the audience's applause. Normally it rolled over him with an all-encompassing well-being, a validation of his artistry, though no one in the audience recognized the true scope of his artistry as they stamped and cheered for the Great Lynn. But tonight the applause sounded perfunctory, forced, a polite homage to past performances, not tonight's piece.

Another bow, more shallow, the degree the waning applause demanded. Had tonight's performance been *that* bad? He'd felt in his bones that something was wrong recently, timing slightly off, concentration faintly flawed, graceful gestures outweighing awkwardness, but only barely—as if the troupe's collective soul was fading, buoyed only by past glories. Worst of all, beta Masady ignored it all, almost willfully blind to miscues, outright blunders. Without her as their conscience, who were they?

Scuttling and scurrying behind the curtain; the others poised for an ensemble bow if he waved them ahead. He swung his right arm high to whip them forward to greet their audience—except he'd misjudged, some already leaving, making toward the exits, a cohesive whole of viewers disassembling into individuals, some quickly, some laggardly. Hassiba stretched against him as she strained to clasp his raised hand.

With an abruptness that stunned, every light went dead, backstage and auditorium both. A double-blinding, Glynn trapped in mask-shadow-dark, the darkness outside even deeper. A whimpered query from Hassiba and he shushed her, the audience fraying toward panic, not sure what was where, and who was what. Rigo struck a resounding chord on his sitar and shouted, "Remain calm, ladies and gentlemen, the auxiliary lighting will come up in a moment. Remain calm and stand still, that's all you need to do." But the audience continued its murmurous shift, disjointed voices rising in doubt, a thud as someone toppled over a bench.

A muffled backstage scream; Glynn could barely hear it above the crowd's lowing dismay. A second scream of sheer rage was punctured by pain, followed by a frantic cry of, "Ware! They're after Jere!" Whirling, Glynn struggled against Hassiba's clinging, fighting his way behind the curtain. But the troupe acted as disjointed as the audience, some struggling to escape the enveloping curtain and others in grim search of the horror prowling somewhere in the darkened backstage. He fought the curtain one-handed, the other desperately ripping at the straps that held his mask in place. Who was on guard? Who was protecting Jere? "Mama? Mama, what's happening? Are you all right?"

Pointless to yell. She could hear him, but he'd never see her response. Frantic at fighting the curtain he dove to the floor, crawled beneath it, breathing hoarse and hotly moist within the mask. There! One final buckle and he'd have it! A stinging blow to his ribs as someone kicked him, half-stumbling over him before snatching him upright. A sawing motion at his chest strap and he gasped at the knife's nearness, ready to die. "Me, boy, bet Rigo. Hang the mask, let it break— just get clear."

The mask tumbled free just as three wavering, thready lights spiked on, Vijay's shadow monstrous huge as he ran along stringing a secondary cable, shouting for Staniar. Another shout and in the dim light, a writhing group of figures, a box buffeted and kicked by flying feet. "Jere! No!" he protested and started to run, only to be yanked off course by Rigoberto.

"Make yourself scarce!" he slapped Glynn's face to gain his attention, whispered, "May be you they want, may be her. Or both." With a shove he planted Glynn behind the makeshift scenery and ran toward the melee.

Caught in the void of shock-induced calm, Glynn struggled to decipher the shifting scene, discover a pattern before he dove in. Three unknowns, three strangers—two men and a woman—battled toward Jere, barricaded by Annie, Chance, and Panthat. Limbs askew, Heike lay in a pool of blood, Jeremy wailing as he tried to drag her away. Majvor and Masady lured the plump intruder clear as Vijay came from behind hefting one of their props, a blunt pikestaff. Blunt though it was, it sufficed with Vijay's fortitude behind it.

Painstakingly threading himself into the knotted cluster, careful not to draw attention to himself, he kept his focus riveted on Jere, her box still sliding, first one random kick, then another shifting it. Jasper, too, was inching toward the box from the opposite direction. *Get the box,* Glynn ordered his shaking

body, shaking mind, *grab the box and fade to safety.*
Then we can finish them off. But Stanislaus acts,
doesn't fight! Coward! If Vijay can do it, so can I.

A sharp, narrow stripe of white light singed the air,
blossomed against Rigoberto's chest; he collapsed,
ponderously slow, and Glynn's heart tore at the sight.
The woman, the unknown woman posed the greatest
threat, a highly trained fighter, knife in her left hand,
laser pistol in the right. She seemed to favor the knife,
indulging herself, and he cried useless warning as it
whizzed in a flashing arc aimed at Chance's groin. But
Panthat had heeded his warning, almost shoving
Chance clear, the knife slashing deep across his upper
thigh instead. Annie now squared off against the dark-
haired male intruder until Staniar bumbled into her,
the intruder reeling clear. Cursing, off-balance, she
righted herself, pushed Staniar away to resume her
defense.

Still low, almost unnoticed, Glynn crept closer,
worming his way between legs, bodies, props. Almost
to Jere, almost there, fingers stretching, stretching . . .
until Staniar's unwary foot crushed his hand. "Damn
it, Staniar! Move!" And move he did, falling athwart
Glynn. Biding her time, Panthat feinted at the dark-
haired stranger, knifed him ahead of Annie. Good!
Another down! How could they lose with only one
intruder left?—seasoned fighter though she might be.
A heave and he bucked Staniar off, dove for Jere's
box just behind Annie's equally fierce lunge. Their
heads collided; Glynn saw stars, whirling constellations
never viewed from the Observation Decks.

As Annie staggered up, box clutched to her chest,
the woman grabbed her from behind, knife to Annie's
throat. "Move, and she dies!" Annie froze, head
canted at an unnatural angle. All movement around
the tableau ceased. One person, and one person alone,
moved. Uncowed, exuding confidence, Staniar stepped
beside them as if by right, brittle happiness in his eyes.
With deceptive ease the woman shifted her hold, her
left hand now pressuring Annie's pulse points, while

the knife materialized in her right hand, snaking between Staniar's ribs.

Despite his shock Glynn registered Panthat's small, self-satisfied intake of breath at a neatly executed job, rather than Staniar's demise, he suspected. Gauging her opponent's momentary satisfaction, Annie slammed her foot hard on the woman's instep, prepared to toss the brain box to Glynn, her eyes rolling to check for a clear path. But the knife, freshly blooded, hovered again at her throat, point piercing in warning. "I can kill you first, then dismantle her. Fast, slow? Cut the circuits, maybe just pry it open, toss the brain out? Anyone want to play catch?" Masady's staff crashed floorward and she sagged beside Rigoberto's body.

"Two hostages, right? The girl and the box." She began backing, hauling Annie and her burden along with her. "Sorry to leave such a mess, but then, you need practice at cleaning up after yourselves if you want to play with the big girls and boys." Taunting, teasing, she continued edging away. Shaking all over, Glynn took an inadvertent step after them, went stiff as the blade coaxed more blood from Annie's neck. Jere, Annie—gone beyond his grasp. Past love, future love. Another failure.

Time: A few minutes later
Location: In the between-level tunnels of YuriGagarin

Once out of sight Becca slipped her knife into its invisible sheath down the outside seam of her skinnies. With a half-affectionate growl she chivied Anyssa ahead, the girl constantly glancing behind, face too devoid of expression for Becca's taste. Reveal nothing, but don't imitate a robot. Well, it caught some like that, their first real fight, when every blow or bullet, each stab had to count. And Anyssa's had, almost too damn effectively. Becca fingered the gash along her ribs. Skin-suit fibers were devilish tough to slash, so Anyssa'd probed *through* the fabric until the blade slid directly along skin. A fraction of a second to catch

Anyssa's leading look and pull away just in time. *Nicely* handled on both sides.

"Good job, child, credible. Acted as if we were strangers, enemies." Swinging Anyssa behind her, she halted behind a closed kiosk, checking the walkway ahead where another joined at right angles. Someone sauntering away from them and the direction she planned to take. The audience had apparently thundered off in another direction, gripped by a herd mentality. "Nuisance enough, Hamish and Falid faltering. No surprise, though. Turncoats, too true to be any good."

A squawk from the box; Becca snapped around to examine it with all the jaunty confidence of a mongoose meeting a cobra. "What's it doing?"

"She wants to talk with us," Anyssa barely mouthed the words. "She hears what we're saying, can see some of what we see. Pretend I'm trying to escape, that I've turned traitor, too." The girl's face loomed dead white in the semidark behind the kiosk, the thin trickle of blood on her neck meandering like a dark thread. Becca licked her thumb, wiped at it.

"Ah, bit of cat and mouse?" Exaggerated lip movements contorted her face. Turning, she took another exaggerated look—purposefully long—at the walkways, heard Anyssa's feet pounding lightly along the way they'd come. With a grin she spun in pursuit, then looked aghast at the deserted walkway. Cursing, struck by the possibility of intentional deception from Anyssa, she ran, searching for hiding spots as she went. Girl was fast, took off like a jackrabbit, but had limited endurance. Endurance, Becca knew all about that, had endured enough, too much, these past years. Couldn't be that far ahead, impossible, so she'd have to hide . . . somewhere . . . here! Sharp eyes caught the man-made fissure in the smooth wall, a hatch there, still faintly quivering from a rapid opening and closing. If she'd dodged far into the tunnels, Becca'd lose her.

Anyssa nestled inside, shielding the box, and Becca

shoved her aside, rough with relief, as she crawled in and closed the hatch. "Don't try me again, child, or I'll kill you here and now," she grunted, gave Anyssa a conspiratorial wink. If the box *did* contain a cognizant brain, it might well believe Anyssa *was* on its side, despite what it had overheard before. Might not hurt to have that edge, might learn something of value with sympathetic questioning. Not her favorite way of obtaining information. Still, the girl was clever, near as clever as Rosa. For all the good that had done her.

Rummaging behind Anyssa, she unearthed an old flexi-sack stenciled "recyclables" and shook it open. Now that she knew better, she finger-signaled, "Dump the box in it. Easier to carry and it'll muffle what she can hear, can see." The girl complied, swathing the box and cradling it against her chest as if were precious, fragile. Interesting . . . worth selling on the sly to some neuroscientist? Delayed gratification, not her own death blow, but it promised extra money. No, no need now.

"Come on, come on," she risked whispering and felt Anyssa settle into a lope beside her as they searched deeper for a ladder. "Not much time to make port. May be too late even then. It's our last chance. Staniar warned you, didn't he?"

"Wasn't sure whether to believe him. Always too full of himself and his woes. I take it you told Mother about Glynn or we wouldn't have gotten the go-ahead."

"Couldn't wait, things've changed." Becca searched out the code numbers on the walls, started up a ladder. Deviate from the coordinates she'd memorized and they'd wander in here until the final trump sounded. "Got to get to Newcome Port. With any luck the MabasutaGenDy skipper hasn't heard they're no longer bankrolling us, that we're persona non grata. Usually takes time before word filters down through channels." Reaching down she snagged the sack from Anyssa to free her hands for climbing, dangling it above her as if it were a carrot. "Always some fool who doesn't read the 'for your eyes only,' ignores the message flasher to get to a meal. Don't know how much time we have before your actor friends set off some alarm, send security after us."

"Mother will be furious." Anyssa's foot slipped on a rung and she peered downward cautiously as she said, "What about Glynn? Won't she be furious? She wanted him, not Jere."

Popping clear, Becca stretched and caught Anyssa under the arm, pulled her through. A quick scan to determine her bearings and they set off again. In deference to Anyssa she held the box gently, tried not to jog or jar it. Anyway, Rosa'd be curious, would enjoy seeing it in one piece. A perfunctory pat on its top. "Well, isn't this the perfect bait, the perfect lure? Don't you think he'll chase after us quick as he can? Easier than controlling a struggling boy, or explaining a drugged one at portside. Can't exactly send him as freight."

"Man," Anyssa corrected. "He's young yet, but he's a man. Remember that, make sure Mother remembers that."

Time: Later that same evening
Location: Lebedev Gathering Hall

The auxiliary lights crackled, hissed with a dazzling harshness that etched the disordered collection of bodies—living and dead—in stark relief. It emphasized things he didn't wish to see, sights that seared his brain: Heike's tumbled form with its smirking, red grin—not her mouth but the slash in her throat. The body of one attacker, the fat one, with a pikestaff lodged in his back, casting a long, narrow shadow, for all the world like the gnomon on an ancient sundial. Rigoberto, who'd once loomed so large, happily fussing over his life, lay utterly still. Chance, blood pooling around his thigh, first pressed against his groin, coached Jasper and Hassiba as they valiantly tried to staunch the flow with a rose silk kimono. And Panthat, shim knife orbiting the eyeball of the dark-skinned

intruder, whispered hot, harsh questions tight to his
ear. Staniar's body he ignored.

As heartless as the overbright lights, the backstage
area was abruptly flooded with sound and movement,
security police marked with the Ring badge, an imposing dark-gold woman with tight-braided hair and governor's epaulets, clearly in command. Slightly behind
her, hovering as if afraid of the space she occupied,
stood a petite red-haired woman. A distant part of his
mind named her: Clea Tierney, of course. Annie
Marie was Tierney Troupe.

Glynn kept shaking his head, praying for something,
anything to make sense. Betrayal, death. Jere gone,
stolen; Annie Marie with her. A blood-slick hand
seized his, insistently tugged. Dragging him after her,
Panthat spat instructions. "Come on, Glynnie, come
on! Track'em-whack'em! Gotta find Jere. Catch and
kill! The Allah-one told me where."

He followed, feet obedient even if his brain refused
to work, until a voice called, "All right, let's all stay
put until we can sort this out." His feet, at least, recognized the aura of command and halted. Again the tug,
equally demanding, but he let his hand trail free from
Panthat's, "Go ahead, I'll join you shortly." Outside
rule, orders, would never leash Panthat, not as they
did most people.

But now the red-haired woman—Clea, yes, that was
right—had regained her courage, stepping in front of
the governor, anxious blue eyes in a dead-white face
raking the backstage area. "Where is she, where's
Annie Marie?"

Struggling to her knees, beta Masady gave a broken
wave, ungainly for the first time he'd ever seen her,
and Glynn hurried to her, offered his arm to help her
rise. "Clea Tierney? I've not laid eyes on you for
years, but you've the fresh-faced look of a Tierney to
you. I know you're concerned about Annie's kidnap-
ping, know it to my sorrow."

"What do you mean? What are you talking about?"
For an instant Glynn feared Clea might hurl herself

at Masady, shake her by the front of her robe. He interposed himself between them. Not beta Masady— he'd allow no more hurt to touch to her.

Huddled in the curve of his arm, Masady continued with dignity, "Annie's been taken hostage. But on my honor Stanislaus Troupe will pay whatever ransom they demand, make every effort to secure her release."

"Don't you understand, you old fool?" Tears streamed down Clea's face as she shook clenched fists in impotent anger. "That wasn't Annie Marie Doulan of Tierney Troupe who was taken. Annie Marie never joined you, she died back at NelMandela! Murdered!"

After speaking with Chance and urgently beckoning a medic to his side, the woman with braided hair resumed command. "I'm Chance's friend, Ngina Natwalla, Governor of SallyRide. What Clea means is that you've played host to a ringer, someone working from the inside to harm you."

A voice from the carnage, weak but insistent on having its say; the dark-haired attacker had not yet died, despite Panny's ministrations. "Allah be praised I die a martyr, but before I die you must listen!" They hurriedly circled his prone body, and Glynn winced at the new injury staring back at him: the assassin's eye had been gouged out. "This is all Vitarosa Weaver's doing, from NetwArk's prayer assault on the satellites to this. But what she truly desires is much smaller, yet so much larger—revenge. And Jere and Glynn are to pay. You need to follow . . ." he swallowed, and his remaining eye gleamed as if it saw beyond his pain to paradise. With incredible discipline he drew his gaze back to them, "Hurry! MabasutaGenDy's representative at Newcome Port. Stop them there if you can. I do not hold with harming children, not even the young one with the knife."

Glynn and Ngina spoke together, "Thank you."

"Sent to spy, you know, poor Hamish and I. He for the Pope, I for the Ayatollah. Came to respect him, poor Rhuven Fisher Weaver, but his wife, that one would topple every decency in the cause of hatred."

Date: Early morning, 24 August 2158
Location: Aboard the corporate shuttle _Peregrine_,
en route from YuriGagarin to NetwArk

Teeth clenched, Anyssa listened, fingers splayed on the deep, pile-cushioned arms of one of the twelve lounger shuttle seats. No standard issue mold-injected plastic with fraying harness straps, jamming buckles for a MabasutaGenDy shuttle with the latest in grav-control. The megaglom corporate colors of gray, burgundy, and royal blue repeated themselves tastefully throughout the ship, the burlwood trim real enough to fool her until she rapped a knuckle against it. Assured that Becca aimed a steady stream of chat at the corporate pilot, laying down their "cover" in no uncertain terms, Anyssa unbuckled herself. Under the seat in front of her sat the flexi-sack, but the bag moved reluctantly as she pulled it clear, the thick carpet dragging against it. Or Jere didn't wish to come out, an omen, perhaps.

Chiding herself for being fanciful, she slipped toward the stern near the lavatory and carry-on luggage racks. Crouched behind a privacy bulkhead she at last felt secure enough to retrieve Jere's box from the bag. For a long moment she held her breath, sure her hammering heart would pass its vibrations through her shaking hands to the box itself. All the dials and gauges looked to be in a perilously low position, as if the box's power source had faltered, perhaps run down. Oh, Lord, no! I've killed her, killed her after all . . . after all . . . after all. Not that Mother will mind . . . mind . . . mind? What's a mind?

Just as she became convinced she might faint, a needle floated from left to right on a gauge, other readings began to fluctuate. With that she could breathe again, relieved at the familiar hum beneath her trembling hands. "Jere, can you hear me?"

The blue strip blinked, slow and languid, as if awakening from sleep. "Jere, I'm sorry!" Would Jere believe her? Would *she* believe if their roles were reversed? Apologies—one of the oldest tricks in the book. But what if they were sincere? They could still cause harm—especially to the one who uttered them.

"WHOSE . . . SIDE . . . ARE . . . YOU . . . ON?" Each word a separate indictment.

"I don't know," she whispered. "I thought I did, knew who I was, what I was, what I was capable of doing . . . being . . . but now I'm not sure." A confessional pause, then a rush. "Can you understand that?" Important that someone would. Understanding, not absolution, was the most she could expect. To be accepted for who she was, uniquely Anyssa . . . with a past . . . a history she no longer wanted to claim.

The words scrolled more quickly now. "'CHILD, CHILD. CHILD WHO ISN'T ANNIE MARIE DOULAN." Anyssa winced at the reminder, the memory that she'd killed Annie Marie. "CHILD WHO MUST BE RHUVEN AND VITAROSA'S . . . AM I CORRECT?"

"Yes."

"SO, ARE YOU YOUR FATHER'S DAUGHTER, OR YOUR MOTHER'S DAUGHTER?"

"Does it . . ." she stopped before she could say "matter," because it did. Lie to herself, to Jere? "Both and neither, perhaps. Help me find myself." Had she said too much, not enough? "I don't want to hurt you, believe me. I did, but I don't now. I'll get you out of this, find a way, if you'll trust me."

"TRUST YOU? WHEN YOU DECIDE WHO YOU ARE, PERHAPS I'LL HAVE AN ANSWER. I DON'T CARE WHAT YOU AND VITAROSA DO TO ME, WITH ME—JUST KEEP GLYNN SAFE. THAT'S ALL I ASK."

"I don't want to hurt Glynn either!" Could she kill Glynn with the same efficient ruthlessness she'd employed to dispatch Annie Marie Doulan? Could she now kill other anonymous souls without wondering what they'd been like, what they were meant to be?

A Little Sister could. Jere had been a "thing" at first—even more abstract, more literally "faceless" than a stranger—but now behind that wooden façade lived a brain that thought, felt, desired. Always look beyond the façade, beyond the "seeming." Hadn't that been drummed into her throughout her training? Masks behind masks, onstage and off. Two tears rolled down her cheeks, dripped from her chin, and marred the box's finish. "I'll try," she choked, swiping at the box, her face with her sleeve.

"TRYING'S A START, A BEGINNING. PREVAILING IS EVEN BETTER. POOR, POOR CHILD. REMEMBER, OUR FAULT IS NOT IN OUR STARS, BUT IN OURSELVES. (JC I,i,139-40) THE BLAME RESTS WITH US, NOT THE HEAVENS, NOT OUR HEREDITY. NOW STOW ME AWAY BEFORE YOUR FRIEND DECIDES TO COME VISIT."

Oddly reluctant, Anyssa shook out the sack, started to slide the box inside. "I have a *name*, you know, my own name." Somehow it mattered that Jere acknowledged her by it. "Father picked it for me."

"I KNOW. ANYSSA. IT'S A BEAUTIFUL NAME. FOR A BEAUTIFUL CHILD. IT'S FROM THE GREEK—MEANING FULFILLMENT, COMPLETION. MAY YOU FIND IT. NOW, FAREWELL."

Date: Early morning, 24 August 2158
Location: Private Hangar—Authorized Government Personnel Only! Newcome Port, YuriGagarin
With long-legged strides, Ngina let the sight of her SatGov insignia clear her path, Glynn and Panthat trailing in her wake, supporting Chance, while behind them Masady leaned on Clea. "We need backup, more forces, hit them hard and fast," Glynn panted, crimped under Chance's weight. He wound his hand deeper into Chance's waistband on his wounded side, used the grip to help Chance swing his bad leg ahead. "Call

Security, all the Ring Forces! They've murdered, taken an innocent woman hostage!"

"Describe the kidnap victim, please," Ngina never broke her stride.

A rumbling cough echoed deep in Chance's chest; worriedly Glynn felt him shaking. Dawning frustration as he realized he heard—and felt—muffled laughter. "Well, Jerelynn is about thirty-six years old . . . and she . . ." he struggled to describe the being so uniquely "mother" to him, ". . . and she. . . . Oh." His knees sagged, Chance's bulk bearing down on him. Wonderful, send an all-points bulletin to the satellites and Earth: Be on the alert for a smallish wooden box, burled-maple, Earth-origin, approximately 25 centimeters a side. Answers to the name Jere.

Ngina half-swung around, shared a moment of commiseration. "And brain boxes, life-support boxes, are illegal both on Earth and here, though that's the least of our worries now." Slapping her palm to a wall sensor, she waited for it to read her and swarmed through the door as it slid open. They followed after her into a standard-grav repaint bay in the repair sector, the smell of heat-resistant, frictionless coatings heavy in their sinuses. "I'd relish more support, too, but I don't think sheer numbers will matter in the end. Quintana," she yelled, rocking back, hands on her hips. "Where the hell are you? Repair and repaint certified? Check-sheet done? Clearance for takeoff approved?"

A shape rolled from beneath the shadow of the speed-skip's belly. "Of course it's ready. Snail-hook to haul her clear for launching since you said you didn't want her in plain sight. Fast-route outlined on the course screen, and I'll shave some time off that." In the light the shape turned into a heavyset woman wearing pilot's wings on her midnight blue skinny-suit. Pilot's wings and the staff insignia for governor of SallyRide. "Chance, love, is that you?" Lumbering to his side, she fingered bandage seals, slapped a medi-scanner against his neck to check his vitals. "You're spacing?" A cough to cover her gaffe. "You're in lousy condition to travel. Damn, that cuts the rocking and rolling I can milk from this tin can."

"No joy, no jamming, Quint." Ngina hit the hatch switch, ducked as she stepped into the bay of the skip. "You're copiloting, you'll deadhead back on your own. Assuming you're willing to dip your toe across the strictly legal line. Prepare to sing the blues if we're caught, 'cause we're a *smidge* ahead of receiving official permission." A thumb and forefinger wide apart showed the size of the "smidge." "Now help Glynn board him."

Chance half-roused, reached to touch the skip's slick finish, only to jerk back as if it burned him. "Oh, no," he whispered, "oh, no, not without . . ." he flailed, green eyes wild with fear. "Masady!" but the old woman only shook her head as she mimed her lack of cane. Grabbing the hatch's sides to brace himself, jamming his good leg against the sill, he thrust backward to escape the skip's beckoning maw, ready to suck him in. "Coward, coward, coward!" he groaned, face and chest ashy-gray, dripping with sweat. With a strength born of dread and fear he shoved away again, his size and manic strength more than Glynn and Quintana could budge. And through his moans, Sylvan's panicky chittering as his claws gripped at Chance's heaving body.

Negotiating a path through straining limbs, Panthat shoved in front of Chance, stretched to fold her hands over his clenched ones. "Chance stronger than any man Panthat knows. But Panthat strong too, that why she here." Rubbing his hands, working up and down the thick, corded muscles of his arms, she soothed and stroked. "Chance name meaning many things—fate, randomness, like days luck comes knocking and days it don't—not matter you been naughty or nice, deserve it or not. Chance taking a chance on me, Panthat. Panthat solid." Turning her back, she loosened his hands, let them engulf hers as she folded his arms across her chest. "Come, Chance. Going to find Jere."

She began leading him after her, half-hidden by his bulk, and he followed, eyes squinted, mouth ajar in a silent plea. "This called Taking a Chance," she muttered at Quint. "Your turn next. Taking a Chance heavier levy than I thought, taxing to the max."

Intent on Chance's progress, Glynn flinched at the hand on his shoulder, Clea's. He'd minimized her presence, ignored it when he could. Why did she insist on tagging along? A sigh as he met her blue eyes, acknowledged her, wanted or not. But she'd suffered a loss as well, Tierney Troupe deprived of a budding actress named Annie Marie Doulan, and all in the cause of aiding Stanislaus. "What are you planning when we get there?"

"I don't know yet. First we have to figure out how to get into NetwArk." Amazing how his brain could be so coldly calculating, but he laid that aside, let her question replay itself. ". . . when *we* get there," she'd emphasized. "I appreciate it, Clea, but it's not 'we.' Stanislaus won't drag you into any further disasters."

She ignored him. "You can have the one who stole Jere, but dibs on the young woman, the one who pretended to be Annie, who . . ." the word lodged in her throat, had to be coughed out to save herself from choking, "killed her." Her face was so white the freckles stood out like metallic droplets.

Annie, whom he'd liked, whom he'd judged a kindred spirit, one as confused and emotion-tossed as he at times. Annie, for whom he'd felt a strange, sexual stirring that neither had quite dared act upon. Annie, who in reality was his half sister. Who had fought to rescue Jere, to throw him the box. "Yes, she killed Annie, but I think she's changed, become more what she should be. But you're right, Clea, some punishment, some penance is required. But it's not your decision or mine, Ring law prevails." He paused, steeled himself, "I can't take you with us, Clea."

"You don't own Tierney Troupe, Glynn! Remember that. You're not the star here. The applause, if any, won't be all yours. And I'll—"

Dropping to one knee he reached for her hands as she tried to pull away, folded them in his own, both pairs cold as ice. "Clea Tierney, I've a final favor to beg, a favor larger than vengeance, a favor that means life. Please help me. Not my life, not Jere's, but the continued existence of Stanislaus.

"Rigoberto's dead, Heike, too. Staniar dead— good riddance! As Stanislaus' senior member, Masady has the right to go. But Vijay and Majvor, Hassiba and the Gemmies are being left behind—we're abandoning them. Fold them into Tierney for the time being, console them, give them a reason to continue, exercise their talents. The loss of Stanislaus would be too great—not just for us—but for the world. I don't know what tomorrow brings for me, but there has to be someone to mourn our dead, see to their funerals."

She broke free, stared down at his bent head. "*You* want vengeance. Why should I be any different? Why should I be noble, sacrifice my chance, Tierney's chance to avenge its own?"

"Of course I want vengeance." He tilted his chin to let her read his face, the set of every tense muscle in his body. "But what I want first and foremost is Jere. If I accomplish that, I'll let personal vengeance go."

"It means that much to you?" She was wavering now, and he knew the "it" she meant was the troupe. "As much as Tierney means to you and yours. By asking you to have and hold them dear, I'm asking you to do the same with my life—because they are my life—whether I succeed or fail."

"Then don't fail." Clea bent forward to kiss his cold cheek. "Come back to us. Thrill audiences on every satellite as Stanislaus has for generations. I'll stay, honor your living and your dead—ours as well." She turned and half-ran out of the hanger, her red hair bobbing like a torch being carried farther and farther away. A torch to light the past, the future.

Date: 24-28 August 2158
Location: Aboard the *ShanLucid*,
en route to NetwArk

They'd settled inside, strapping themselves in, while Glynn pondered for the thousandth time what they'd find, what they'd do when they arrived. . . .

Nearly five days in space had given him plenty of time for decisions, revisions, regrets—and he still didn't know what they'd do. It preyed at his mind—what he had, what he didn't have. Things, people who were gone, and those who remained. For support, beta Masady, Stanislaus Troupe's soul, its conscience, but now so weak, as if she'd aged fifty years in a day. Chance, so badly wounded and in mortal terror of flight. And finally, Panthat, hardly surprising, who'd attached herself to them as if she were glue, as if this . . . this motley collection were a real family. But so it was, by both blood and bond.

He dragged himself back to the present, heard Panny arguing with Quint, Chance chiming in. How long had it been? Perhaps he'd slept, but if he had, all his problems and sorrows had hounded him there and back again. "Hush!" Ngina broke in from the cockpit. "Radio transmission." Quint flicked on the loudspeaker to let everyone hear. ". . . cleared to land in Houston, all tariffs paid. The tranny-van is programmed direct to NetwArk, no driver needed. Word of honor that it's safe, no deceptions." A crackle, static, or perhaps high laughter. "We hope you'll enjoy your stay at NetwArk. Of course we'll be offering a boxed lunch." The radio went dead.

"Well, that solves some things," Ngina commented, "now if you'll solve some of our other problems—like rescuing Jere—I'd feel happier about landing at Houston. Or at least feel calm enough not to hide in the cargo hold when Quint heads back home."

Date: Morning, 29 August 2158
Location: "Company," Den, NetwArk

Jere strained to hold them all in view, an impossible

task even with opposing visual fields. From the direction of Anyssa's tired voice, Jere judged she was seated directly in front of her life-support box, patiently waiting to read whatever Jere chose to say. The others, Vitarosa—still commandingly handsome but so much older now than that long-ago holopic Rhuven had reluctantly shown her—and Becca, the assassin-kidnapper now possessed a name, wove in and out of her vision, arguing, bickering, surmising. At times she'd simultaneously sight them, one in each opticam, and strove not to blend the two into a composite whole.

"You're *sure* the boy's following?" A world of desperate longing freighted Vitarosa's question. "I told you time and again I wanted him. My direct orders, as you may remember."

Bored, Becca now lounged, a leg thrown over the leather chair arm, totally confident and at ease, despite her travel-worn appearance. *Stay still,* Jere begged. *One less to track.* "Of course, Rosa. He's running to us like a lamb chasing after its mother's teat. Wrapped round Jere's little finger all his life. Nothing he wouldn't do to save her." A stabbing motion toward Jere, Becca's finger looming impossibly large, close, before distortion occurred. "He did *this,* didn't he? A boy child's dream to eternally possess the mother. Oh, he's nearly a man, but he's not matured beyond that, can't see how vile that contraption is."

True, not true? A mental shiver at Becca's analysis. Partially valid, at least, Jere had to admit it. If Glynn had done this to her, what had she unwittingly done to him? Been oblivious to his growing manhood, too wrapped up in herself, her acting?

Finally Vitarosa halted, addressed Jere directly. "You're not nearly as lovely as your holoverts. Makes me wonder what Rhuven ever saw in you." A smirking sarcasm, a self-satisfied presence that dominated the small, tastefully decorated room with its bright, woven blankets hanging on the walls.

Answer or not? So far silence had proved her chief

weapon, allowing the others to snare themselves, reveal what they'd stored in their arsenal of hatred. Hatred over a transient affair, so long ago? Well, satelliters differed from Earth dwellers in many minor ways, but generally not emotionally. The human ego needed more than a century or two to change that radically. But this wasn't a play whose lines remained immortal through time, but some macabre improvisation, hideous ad libs. Whatever she could devise to counter Rosa might or might not save Glynn. If she could redirect Rosa's warped anger and attention to her—she'd deem it a tolerable risk. After all, wouldn't the outcome be what she'd prayed for for so long—release?

"O! HOW MUCH MORE DOTH BEAUTY BEAUTEOUS SEEM BY THAT SWEET ORNAMENT WHICH TRUTH DOES GIVE!" Anyssa obediently recited her words, and the harsh clatter of feet, the hasty skid of a reversed chair revealed that both Vitarosa and Becca hurried to read her words themselves. "OH, I'LL GRANT THAT RHUVEN DID FIND COMELINESS OF BODY APPEALING, HE CHOSE YOU, HE CHOSE ME. BUT ASK YOURSELF WHY HE FLED YOU? DID YOU FRIGHTEN HIM OFF BY REVEALING SOME OF YOUR LIES, YOUR HATREDS WHEN YOU FELL APART AFTER ANYSSA'S BIRTH? EVEN LIKE THIS," and oh, she yearned for but one of the troupe's justly renowned, expressive gestures, "DESPITE THIS SHELL, MY MIND HASN'T TWISTED WITH HATRED, OR THE THWARTED DESIRE FOR CONTROL THAT ANIMATES YOU. AH, ALWAYS THE CANKER IN THE ROSE."

Surprisingly, Vitarosa darted into view again, eyes locked on Jere's opticam with a calculating stare. Her right hand pressed against her lower left breast, fingers seeking, kneading, her apprehension plain that Jere had somehow peered within her. A curiously intimate gesture that any woman would recognize; despite the

advances in breast cancer care, there was still a tiny
minority not protected by the vaccines. Jere wanted
to shout, "For God's sake, woman, it's only a breast,"
but it was a weakness to exploit.

"ANYSSA, TELL YOUR MOTHER I'VE A PER-
SONAL MESSAGE FOR HER." Anyssa drew Becca
to the side for privacy. Her memory served too well,
and Jere never faltered, the blue letters whipping
across the screen. "ROSES HAVE THORNS, AND
SILVER FOUNTAINS MUD; CLOUDS AND
ECLIPSES STAIN BOTH MOON AND SUN, AND
LOATHSOME CANKER LIVES IN SWEETEST
BUD." Rosa's eyebrows lifted, her only overt ac-
knowledgment, a private touché.

It struck Jere then, the absurdity of straining after
this petty victory, if she'd accomplished even that. No
way to judge. Rhuven had claimed to be a healer, yet
he hadn't cured his wife? Was he a hoax? Or had she
planned to stand strongly independent—never even
asked? Mind racing ahead, Jere sought a less charged
question. "DOES RHUVEN KNOW I'M HERE . . .
OR THAT PART OF ME IS HERE?" That waning
hope—that Rhuven was uninvolved, innocent—made
her feint and parry, waiting until gentle Rhuven finally
unmasked the evil lurking, growing under his own
roof. Complicity? Guilt by association?

"Oh, he may know, he may comprehend . . . though
I'm not entirely sure. It's so difficult to speak with
him lately. Why don't I call him in and you'll see,"
Vitarosa fumbled for a button on the underside of
the desk.

"Mama, what do you mean? What happened? Is
something wrong with Papa?" Anyssa burst into Jere's
sight, confrontational, yet looking even younger, in
dire need of reassurance.

Becca's rippling chuckle distracted Jere from the
scraping sounds, thunks, as if someone pried at her
box. "Haven't quite figured out how this thing opens.
What it takes to shut it off." A cry of anger from
Anyssa as she disappeared from view, followed by

heavy breathing, the pound and slap of flesh striking flesh, blocking shoving.

Vitarosa's crisp "Leave off, Becca," coincided with a knock at the door, scant time for Jere to register it before the room swooped, her angle of vision shifting 90°. Someone—Anyssa? Rosa?—had pivoted her a quarter-turn to give her a view. Nothing at first except to await the slow-swinging door, accompanied by panting grunts, the protesting screech of rubber skidding against floor tiles. Finally a small, white-clad backside hove into view. Craning over his shoulder, tugging with all his might, a boy of perhaps nine backed into the room, dragging a wheelchair.

"Artur!" Anyssa called, but the child ignored her, swung the chair around, cheeks and ears rosy with effort. "Papa gets heavier and floppier every day," he complained. "Sorry, Papa, but you do." He pressed his cheek against a hand and forearm strapped to the chair's arm. With straps girding his chest and waist to hold him upright, restraints to keep feet from flopping off the footrests, a man semireclined in the chair. His jaw hung flaccid, a string of drool running down, dripping into his beard, eyelids drooping, seeing, not-seeing. Vitarosa claimed her place beside the wheelchair, stroked her husband's cheek. A whimper, misty terror in those dull eyes. The boy dug a grubby handkerchief from his pocket, daubed at the face and mouth, fussy but tender, and the man's eyes momentarily brightened.

Thankful she lacked the luxury of tears, Jere feared her mind might balk. "Rhuven, what have they done to you, done with you?" but made sure her anguish did not flow across the screen. She'd not give Vitarosa that, much as she yearned to share with Rhuven. "All you wanted was to help others find the same peace and devotion your god offered you. Didn't you realize you harbored your own Satan in your bed, by your side? Or did you truly believe that unconditional love and prayer could change that as well? A look around

you at the world outside NetwArk should have told
you better."

But now Anyssa stumbled to her father's side, and
Jere schooled herself to witness further pain. Was this
what Glynn had felt on seeing her so burned? Willing
to move Heaven and Earth to salvage, if not completely save, the parent he loved? Anyssa and Glynn,
both so near grown, yet still longing to bask in perfect
parental love—surety against an untested world where
the rules were so similar, yet so very different. Tears
now, Anyssa's, not hers, but they'd never wash away
the pangs of separation. "Papa? Papa, it's me, Anyssa,
I'm back now. I'll never leave you again, ever." She
knelt, face buried against her father's knees, Artur
hovering, uncertain, his hand raised to pat her shoulder, yet not quite daring.

"Nyth . . . Nythy?" A grimace pulled at one side
of Rhuven's mouth, no, not a grimace, a smile.
"Mah . . . Nythy."

Guiding Anyssa away, Vitarosa matter-of-factly
blotted her tears, no wasted compassion. "Artur, take
Papa back to his room. Hurry now. Be sure to change,
I don't want you all mucked and wrinkled for your
prayer session. Remember—tell the flock how much
Papa needs their prayers *and* their donations."

Half-dubious, the boy nodded. "I'm gonna learn
how to fix Papa. Maybe Anyssa can help now that
she's back," he threw an appealing glance at his big
sister. "You'll get used to him, don't worry." With
another screech of rubber wheels, the boy spun the
chair toward the door, their final sight identical to
their first: a small, white-clad bottom higher in the air
than his head.

"Half-measures, Rosa, half-measures. When did you
turn so soft?" Seated again, legs splayed as if staking
a claim to what was rightfully hers, Becca began to
clean her nails with her knife. "You, a Little Sister,
tolerating half-lives all around you."

Finally Jere captured all three in her sight: Becca
to the left, Anyssa and Rosa on her right. Yet Anyssa

stood separate, stranded in her own private world of pain, unable to grow beyond it.

"It's not for you to say, nor for you to question." Ready to protest, Becca heeded the warning of Rosa's upraised palm. "Anyssa hasn't, and you, with your years of service should know far better. Too many years as my confidante may make you believe you know my mind, but don't count on it."

"It's understandable to weaken a bit, Rosa," Becca attempted to be conciliatory, clearly discomfited, "but I've never seen you indecisive over your choices. You always know what has to be done, *must* be done." A rap on Jere's box with the hilt of her knife. Jere'd seen the movement but hadn't registered its import, so engrossed was she in this new conflict.

"Half-lives." The knife gestured again but didn't strike. "A brain here. An unresponsive body in a chair—perhaps it has a working brain, perhaps not. Put them together and we might have one complete foe worthy of a Little Sister of Mortality. There's no savor in taking on the lame, the halt, the blind—that's mercy killing." A rap again at the box, the rattling traveling through Jere, echoing in her brain. "Half-measures, Rosa. If you want Rhuven alive a bit longer, fine. Who'm I to say? We can use the increase in donations—pity works wonders. Though how poor Artur's going to explain that their blessed healer requires healing himself is beyond me. Not good for business, I'd think."

She turned cajoling, almost wheedling like old times. "But at least let me have this one, this thing. Let me crack it open like an egg, watch the brain yolk fall out. One less half-life for you to worry about. Isn't it due me after so many years of loyalty, service?"

"Half-lives, Becca?" Vitarosa almost crooned, coming to stand behind her friend, her boon companion for so many years, hands resting lightly on her shoulders. Her hard features softening, one of Becca's hands rose to shelter Vitarosa's with a soft sigh of contentment. With a preternatural clarity Jere knew what was coming, would not, could not speak. The implacable guardian had dropped her guard, safe in the arms of her beloved companion. Companion-in-arms, more accurately. "Is this a half-measure, Becca?" By the time her question ended, so had Becca's life. A shift of hands—one now under the chin—a rapid, upward twist, the crack of vertebrae. "Never try to make your own half-life whole by blackmail."

Expressionless as an automaton Anyssa helped her mother lay out Becca's body, and then Vitarosa swept out of the den. "Keep the box safe, dear," she admonished as she left. "A brain's worth more than Becca's brute force any day."

"ONE DOWN." Jere offered nothing further, unsure of Anyssa's mood. This new death seemed to have touched the girl more lightly than the half-deaths she'd witnessed, or perhaps Anyssa's mind was full, no room for it to sink in. It made her wonder anew how Glynn, how Masady were coping with Rigoberto's death.

Yes. One down, and one to go." Anyssa stood loosely at ease, but her face betrayed her, brows knotted as she puzzled the conundrums of life and death. "If not for you and Glynn, then for Father. For me, if I'm to reach for what I am, what *I* choose to be."

"HOWEVER YOU RATIONALIZE IT, ANYSSA, IS FINE WITH ME, AS LONG AS IT SAVES GLYNN."

Date: Late afternoon, 29 August 2158
Location: Welcome to NetwArk

The tranny-van's doors opened automatically with a sad sigh, the vehicle worn from long, hard use but competently programmed. The drive from Houston Center had been efficient and direct, whizzing through lighted tunnels, climbing sky ramps as necessary, the van's sensors always attuned to routes where the least traffic, the fewest tie-ups existed. They'd measured their journey, not by passing scenery—the sights aboveground larger than life, too alien to grasp—but by following the progress of the red blip that skimmed the blue-lined route on the nav-screen. "You have arrived at NetwArk," a tinny voice informed them. "God's blessings on you here at the heart of the Web. Please take all parcels on departing the vehicle."

They exited slowly, reluctantly, stiff with the exhaustion of five days' travel, of recent travail and approaching torments. Glynn scooped a protesting Masady from her seat, eased her clear of the door, and gaping, froze, unable to put her down. Behind him sustained grunts as Ngina eased Chance out of the van without jarring his injured leg. Panthat stood beside Glynn, eyes saucer-wide, muscles quivering until, with a mewling cry, she bolted toward the safety of the tranny-van's enclosed bulk, pretending to help with Chance. Panny? Afraid? Then perhaps he had a right to be as well.

The arc of sky overhead loomed immense and empty, not the blue he'd expected but a sour gray-yellow, and the wind whipped at his braid, tossing pieces of dried shrub and weeds, crumpled paper across the barren ground. How could something so high, so free, so empty, terrify him, cause his legs to quake? Directly ahead stood a post and wire fence—*real* wood, it must be, here—and a double gate. Two tall posts reared above the gate, a wooden sign hung between them. The breeze made the sign swing, a creaking protest of rusted metal on metal. Burned into the slab, the name, "NetwArk."

Improbably distant yet still visible, not lost in satellite curvature, long, long lines of greenery rippled, strange scents floating on the wind, then lost in the harsh dust smell. Nothing like the groomed agricole tiers he knew. In the near distance he could spy the bulk of buildings, a roof here and there, a three-story tower. Everything looked incredibly rustic and old, lifted from the past and transplanted in the here and now. If one ignored the satcom dishes, antennae, and girdered towers dotting buildings and landscape alike. A "thing," he didn't know *what* it was, began to move and lurch; he wheeled, stifling a cry, prepared to flee. It resembled a giant metallic crane or grasshopper, its long neck, predatory pointed head dipping and rising, dipping and rising, though its base remained immobile. Anchored to the ground, he told himself—can't chase me, can't catch us.

A fist thumped his breastbone. "Put me down, Glynn," beta Masady commanded, squirming like Jeremy. "I may be carried out of here, but I'll *not* be carried in." Embarrassed, he set her down, felt her arm slide around his waist, both for steadiness and for solace. His or hers? Both, more likely. "I knew it was a big world down here, Glynn. Jere knew it better than I, tried to explain it to me." A momentary distraction as the grasshopper caught her attention. She shielded her eyes, squinted. "Oil rig . . . that'd be my guess. Pumps out the oil underground, if there's any left to pump."

She began rummaging through the past again. "Jere swore there was a freedom in having no walls, no ceiling in sight except the sky. Heady and frightening, especially with us so contained, enclosed in a satellite, no matter its size."

He nodded, achingly aware of his insignificance, as if all that openness had diminished him. Panthat jittered to them, skittery-anxious but determined, the hard set of her jaw, the stubborn wrinkle in her brow intensifying. Her eyes swept the landscape, assaying, measuring, as she grimly planted her feet, worked her mouth and eloquently spat into the dust. "Shah! So there, world! Come and get me, get Panny if'n you dare!"

"Maybe Panthat's right, Glynn. Spit on it. At least then you've claimed that much, marked it as yours." Working her lips, Masady matched deed to words.

"I *have* to save her, beta. I have to rescue her from this."

"What are you so eager to save, Glynn? Your pride, your self-image as a dutiful, adoring child? Jere didn't want saving once and you saved her—at great cost to herself and to all of us." He shied away from her wintery, brittle smile, the commiseration in her stone-dark eyes.

"Are you saying I shouldn't rescue her?" No solace now in her embrace, but the arm clasping his waist refused to yield. "After what's been wreaked on Stanislaus Troupe—Jere's accident, bet Rigoberto's death, Heike's? Staniar's corruption? The death and deception visited on Tierney? And all because of Rhuven Fisher Weaver, his wife, Vitarosa, who can't let the past die." The words poured out of him, "Well, I *can't* make it over, pretend it never happened. At least I can set part of it right by saving Jere from their hands."

From the opposite side another arm slid round his waist, Chance's. Panthat had linked herself to Masady, while Ngina bolstered Chance's other side. "And with your half sister's complicity, Glynn," Chance grunted, cleared his throat. "Our 'Annie' is Rhuven's and Vitarosa's eldest, Anyssa." Sylvan popped out of Chance's pocket to survey his surroundings, bright eyes darting, rapid-fire chittering. He sailed groundward, then ran up one of the tall signposts, paused, agile paws reaching for a connecting wire. A crack and spark, a scorching scent, and the little squirrel hung limp, then dropped lifeless to the ground.

Chance groaned, knees buckling, and Glynn's eyes misted. "More death, more senseless death—why?" With a growl Panny darted toward Sylvan's corpse, cautiously prodded it before lifting it in cradling dark hands. With ceremonious dignity she offered it to Chance, but Ngina reached out first, wrapped it in a handkerchief and took it. "Earth kills and kills, even little innocent creatures. It can't seem to stop. We can't let it have Jere, too." Chance spat as Panny and Masady had, Ngina following suit. Mouth dry, Glynn did as well.

A disembodied voice echoed at them, "Please do not continue to expectorate on the grounds. It is highly unsanitary." The gates swung open. "This way, please. You'll be met shortly by two Able-Bodied Savers who will guide you, show you the way, the truth, and the light. Welcome to NetwArk.''

"Never a Prospero around when you need him.'' And at Masady's wink, Glynn took a hesitant step, the others yielding precedence.

A man and a woman, both in loose white clothing, approached and took up positions on each side of him after gravely handing him a bouquet. He accepted it, nervous, unsure what it contained, the odors strange, the blossoms unfamiliar. Their scents, their juices stained his palm as he juggled it, used a free hand to mop his face. Chance gave a disgusted snort. "NetwArk's famous herbs. Undoubtedly rosemary for remembrance, Glynn. Watch out for rue.''

Beatifically bland, their attendants' smiles showered them impartially, rarely speaking except to note which branching path they'd take. Guided they might be, but it was no guided tour, complete with thumbnail descriptions and compelling history of what they passed. Frankly, Glynn didn't care. The dirt drive wound through cultivated fields, changed to a bricked road, buildings and decorative plantings passed in and out of view, people moving purposefully from building to building, never stopping to watch the strangers. Their route held no interest; let the others remember if they would. Ngina or Chance, both used to the vagaries of Earth cities. Either they'd succeed, or they wouldn't, and leaving seemed too improbably future-far to worry about now. His stomach wound tight, his ears buffeted by alien sounds, the whup-whup-whup of a distant reaper, shrilling birds, insects. His nostrils tightened to filter out alien scents, alien germs.

Strange, surpassing strange to see buildings with distinct exterior dimensions, wide, unutilized spaces between them. Boxes set in the middle of nowhere. And now, this monumental building looming in front of them, its front carving the air like a ship's prow parting the sea, not the seamless mellowed curves of living habitats, the satellite's outer skin protecting it from the cold, dead atmosphere of space. This reared thirty meters high, ready to rush at him, bear down on them all with its planes and angles, different levels of thrusting red-tiled roof like sails, sides of adobe and wood, shimmering sheets of glass with almost wavelike green-blue reflections. But no fish swam in this pseudo mini-mer. Dauntingly monolithic in a way the satellites never achieved—their sectors, their rings, always subdivided and manageable, curiously intimate. Someone gasped behind him. A tree stood literally rooted in the ground, straight, unbending, soaring taller than the house. A wild look for the tethering umbilicals, the feed lines, but they weren't there.

And then they were inside, engulfed, directed this way or that, marginally more secure at this enclosure, although everything was still faintly bizarre. So many things he'd seen in vidcasts, holopics, yet never experienced. Antiquated, sharp-angled furniture, so few wall-extrusions, everything juttingly geometric, a cacophony of colors and materials. Dust motes, moldy age-scent wafting up with each hesitant step on the thick mat of carpets. Not satellite compactness with its mushroom shapes, its efficient use of each centimeter of space, its monotone shades that preserved harmony, allowed the eye an impression of spaciousness through unbroken vistas of color.

"In here, please." Young, passing pretty, the female guide sounded kind but cautious, like someone herding a pack of potentially recalcitrant animals, their ways utterly alien to her. "Our Vitarosa will join you momentarily. Please be seated." She had waved them into a large, airy room with a glass wall running along one side, almost like an Observation Deck. Through it Glynn saw that the wind still blew, how it lifted and sifted dust through the air, whirled bits of dried debris higher and higher.

A bird soared by, and he nearly ducked, sure it would sail straight through the glass at them. A whole sky, a whole world for it to fly through, unimpeded. The vastness of an outside, outdoors for these people, these animals to partake of, boundless. Conscious that he'd been lost within himself, he hastily took a seat around the large, ovoid table that dominated the room. Fingers rubbed table's edge—strange crevices and splits, all sealed under shining, honey-colored hardness. Bark? Did trees that large exist?

Forcing himself, he concentrated on how the others were coping, what they made of this new world. Ngina and Chance looked relatively unimpressed; they'd traveled back and forth from the satellites to Earth often enough. Chance, drawn, clearly in pain, marshaling his limited energies to serve. Ngina appeared coolly collected, a neutral observer, yet she'd thrown her lot in with theirs, regardless. It struck him then, and he swiveled his chair toward her, whispered, "Sylvan?" A mild grimace and she patted the cargo pocket on her right thigh.

Half-lost in the huge padded chair, beta Masady appraised their surroundings the way she'd judge a new stage set—and find it wanting. Panthat sprawled, hands busy just beneath the tabletop. Despite himself he smiled, suspecting what she was up to—busy making her mark, knife point scratching away. Given the right training and support, she'd be capable of claiming a land, a kingdom, a world—if she wanted it.

Time: A half-hour later
Location: Conference Room, NetwArk

A golden-oak door opened to admit Vitarosa and Annie—no, Anyssa. Half a heritage shared, the two other halves so vastly different. Beyond comprehension—had she truly killed Annie Marie? Had she planned to kill Jere or save her? Conflicting answers warred in his brain, and the cold hatred for NetwArk he'd been hugging to himself struggled against the effort of understanding her, her life. A mother and father who were polar opposites, apparently. Little brothers, according to the holopics on the wall, a wall covered with glued paper. NetwArk itself—an obligation or a privilege? Who depended on her, whom did she depend upon?

Self-assured, satisfied, Vitarosa sat at the far side of the table, Anyssa placing herself at her mother's right. She looked drawn, haggard, as if her mother had sapped her vitality, leeched the color from her—Anyssa in brown leggings and a khaki shirt, Vitarosa in a swirl of carnation pinks and reds. The older woman's eyes devoured him, examining every feature with clinical detachment to determine what did and didn't match Rhuven. A flash of confusion, embarrassment, swept over him, made him long to avert his glance, examine the tabletop, just as Anyssa did. Even Panthat's whispered, "Shah! Nah!" in her direction as she signed the choppy gesture satrats used to intimidate another didn't distract Anyssa.

"I never thought I'd see the day that I'd willingly welcome both the Great Lynn and her bastard son under my roof." Vitarosa clasped her hands in a prayerful attitude and rested them on the table. Her hectic smile did nothing to animate the rest of her face. "That which was taken from me, stolen, has been returned. At last change is afoot at NetwArk."

"I don't care if they're afoot, ahorse, or ashuttle," Masady snapped, rearing out of her slump like a turtle coming out of its shell. "What hasn't changed is your abiding hatred, woman. Doesn't it gnaw you from within? Hasn't it left you hollow, empty?" Vitarosa jerked as if struck, and Masady pressed home her point. "Jere stole naught from you except what Rhuven willingly shared with her. She had no idea he was married when she met him at that mountain retreat. That he didn't confess until later. Blame him if you will, but not her, not the boy."

"Oh, I *do* blame him, old woman. To err is human, to forgive divine. But then such sanctity doesn't course within me as readily as it does within my husband. Perhaps you'd enjoy meeting him?" And her eyes swept them all. "NetwArk's sainted Rhuven Fisher Weaver, who cares for the souls of thousands upon thousands, succors their bodies and their spirits, heals their afflictions." She pressed tight against the table now, a barrier easily overcome, all impediments in her way as nothing, her glinting eyes warned. "You'd like to meet your father, wouldn't you, Glynn?"

"If he wishes, if you wish me to." How many times had he wondered these past months what it would be like to finally meet his father, absence become presence? Oedipus had met his father at the crossroads and killed him, not knowing the stranger was his father. Thus was prophecy fulfilled.

At her mother's curt nod, Anyssa left, only to return shortly pushing a man in a wheelchair. No, not a man, the husk of a man. Glynn's heart clenched. Movement gone, brain locked away inside, if it still resided there. The renowned faith healer unable to heal himself. Worse yet, he could sense Vitarosa reveling in the irony of it all. On his father's lap rested the wooden box that Glynn knew as intimately as the contours of his mother's face. "Reunited at last, isn't it touching?" He didn't recoil, refused to give her that, but noticed Anyssa did, caught the brief spark of hatred that flared and died as she fussed about her—their—father, stroking his brow, brushing his hair back.

"I want Jere back." Not a demand, not a plea, just a simple declaration. "You've made your point, shown that Stanislaus can be humiliated, brought low. What else will it take to satisfy you? What more can you want of us—of me—to ensure Jere's return?"

Her response came singsongy, childish, the recitation of a long-ago lesson. "And once I wanted my father to love me, praise me, value me. Oh, he loved me, but never the rest . . . the praise, validation . . . I was flawed, never good enough. Oh, he was wrong, how I showed him he was wrong! I didn't need him . . . or my half brothers. Because my best was his worst. I crumpled his little empire, the one I wasn't good enough to share." Masady gave a protesting growl. "Oh, yes, you probably heard, didn't you? Rumors, rumors, nothing proved. Never directly proved!" She gave the table a triumphant slap. "I suppose your Rigoberto heard the rumors.

"Well, all of life is a gamble, but the strong-willed can increase the odds in their favor." Vitarosa shook an imaginary pair of dice, cast them away. "Yes, a gamble, a matter of fate, chance, like your friend's name—or so it seems to those with no faith in God. The truth is that they tumble from God's hand. Of course you can always jog His elbow. Something 'dicey' is dangerous, risky. The singular of dice is 'die.' So appropriate. Do you like to gamble, Glynn?" A whimpering protest from the side—Anyssa? Rhuven?

Was she mad—or merely manic at finally having them within her grasp? Years' worth of stored hatred, bitterness, and jealousy pouring onto them. He didn't, couldn't know. And he'd thought that he could somehow march in, rationally demand Jere's return. Fool, a thousand times fool! Like a child wheedling for a toy. He swallowed, staring steadily at her. Their stares clashed, and he shied away, lost a minor skirmish. Finally he swung toward Masady, Panthat, Chance, and Ngina, prayed they'd support him as best they could. Dismay, dread, determination—all that and more he saw reflected there.

Drawing on every iota of Stanislaus training, he sat straight, relaxed, wrists crossed on the table. "I suppose the gamble I take, risk all on, involves going onstage in a new role, seeing whether the audience will believe—not in me, but in the character I portray. A gamble that I can serve as a conduit into another's mind and soul, instill belief in that character."

"Not unlike religion," Vitarosa crowed, clapping her hands. "You *are* your father's son!"

"So what's the game? What are the stakes?" He stood now, moved beside his father, laid his hand on Jere's life-support box. Despite himself, overcome by sorrow and compassion, he laid his other hand on Rhuven's shoulder, reassurance of his father's existence. Never known, never to be known. Quickly Anyssa overlaid her hand on his. Slowly, regretfully, he slid his away, her touch beyond bearing for so many reasons. "I know what I'm gambling for, for Jere's return to us, for her life. What stakes do you offer?"

Index finger tap-tapping her lips, Vitarosa played at contemplating her choices. "Stakes? Well, you're correct: You play for Jere's life. For yours, and your friends' lives as well. My stakes are identical. A strange bargain, but I've always been generous to a fault. Rest assured that should you win, no one at NetwArk will lift a hand against you and yours. You'll all leave unhindered." Feigning sudden surprise at her forgetfulness, she continued. "Oh, the game. You *never* asked about the game. You really shouldn't wager until you know what you're playing.

"Still, the contest couldn't be simpler, Glynn, the chance to test yourself in a totally new role." Her eyes were wide with spurious delight, her breathing quick. "You can ad lib your half of the script; I'll supply the other half. Your character: Avenger. The setting: a dueling circle. I hope you can act convincingly, Glynn, because the props will be real—real weapons. Knives, I think. I'll be Me, playing myself, pitting myself against you." Anticipatory, predatory, her whole body gave a suppressed quiver, the predator poised to launch its attack. "Tomorrow morning. A meal, a good night's sleep beforehand, I think that's fair, don't you? Do you accept?"

Not real, not happening, no, it couldn't happen like this, but it was. The play, the actor, doomed. Still onstage, so keep acting. He thrust his hand forward, ignoring the cries and shouts behind him. Heard but ignored beta Masady's exclamation, "Glynn, the woman's a trained assassin!"

"So be it," he pledged as they shook hands. Unbelievable to agree to this when every fiber of him urged, Run, Flee. The willing sacrifice a parent makes for a child—cannot a child offer the same? Either they'd both live—or both die. Life—and death—so difficult to measure. Such close kin, opposite sides of the coin. One could be alive but dead inside, dead but alive within. Everything was relative.

"Anyssa will show you to your rooms. Until tomorrow." With a teasing, backward glance, Vitarosa wheeled Rhuven from the room, but only after placing Jere's box in Anyssa's outstretched hands. Holding it carefully, Anyssa gestured them after her, down hallways, some bright, some dim, up a flight of stairs, and into a suite of rooms.

"Here," she handed the box to Glynn. "For tonight at least. I'm sorry. Mother's truly good, you know." Glynn shook his head, appalled, puzzled—Vitarosa good? An impatient frown at his slowness. "No, not like that—I mean at what she does, is capable of doing. As a trained killer. Compared to her, I'm an amateur, despite the fact that she and Becca taught me everything they knew." A desperate struggle within herself, "I wonder . . . I wish . . . I just don't *know* any more!" In her honey-brown eyes a darkness, a shadow of the gallows, but whether it reflected his fate or hers, he wasn't sure. "Until tomorrow morning, then."

"Anyssa?" Glynn spoke her name, alien yet so familiar, familial. "Anyssa?" But couldn't trust himself to say more.

She paused, waiting to see what he might demand of her, then shook her head in defeat. "Ring for food, anything else you may need." Her hand stole out to caress Jere's box and then she was gone, half-running.

Date: 30 August 2158
Location: NetwArk, Texas Republic, Earth

Blue. It teased and tingled behind his sleep-closed lids, ebbing and flowing across the unseeing crescents of his eyes. Eye-blue skies, skies the color of his mother's eyes, except he'd never seen that shade of blue in nature, never seen these skies before yesterday—or had he, once so very long ago and far through space? He tossed, fitful, mind beginning to wake, though waking meant admitting what he faced today—the duel. And an admission of something more, something he'd refused to face for seven long, bitter months.

Glynn kicked back the sheet, forced himself to sit

up, squinting at the alien, brightening blue of the sky
through the window. Then, as he had each morning
for so many months, he addressed the burled maple
box centered on the bureau, the box with its dials, its
sound-enhancing diaphragms, its lensed opticams on
opposed sides, the Liquid Crystal Display strip that
scrolled across its front. "Good morning, Mother."

"GLYNN, LOVE, TODAY'S THE DAY." The
words printed themselves across the LCD strip, disappearing leftward to make space for more characters
crowding from the right. "YOU'LL SUCCEED,
GLYNN. YOU MUST AND YOU WILL. AND
THEN WILL YOU HONOR LAST NIGHT'S
PROMISE? WILL YOU LET ME DIE TODAY?"

He evaded answering by dropping to the floor,
began his stretching exercises, methodically flexing
knotted muscles, limbering his spine, pouring total
concentration into each movement. So easy to lose
himself in unthinking movement, the product of years
of training. How much longer before the duel? He
wasn't sure, so best prepare now, center himself, aim
for maximum suppleness, speed and fluidity of movement. It wouldn't save him, but it might allow him to
cheat death a little longer.

Finally, grudgingly, "I thought we discussed that last
night," he focused on his left leg, "that particular
question, I mean." Actually it hadn't been last night
but, more accurately, early this morning when he'd
finally been left alone with Jere.

His rehearsal for a fight to the death had been cursory—and more than ludicrous. Years of pretense, not
the actuality of killing, but the swashbuckling motions
of the stage; years of dying, the epochal moment when
a monumental character falls—each a patiently staged,
artful production that heightened the viewers' sense
of reality in a way that actual death rarely accomplished. Ngina and Chance had tried, offering pointers
and suggestions, but they were spacers, not military;
their limited combat training aimed at protecting their
ships, their cargoes from thieves. Most of that involved

defensive measures, buying time until Security swept to their rescue. Masady had grimly choreographed his moves to a fare-thee-well, but was hampered by rehearsing only one partner in the forthcoming pas de deux of death.

Finally, exasperated, frustrated, Panthat had interrupted, satrat savvy to the core. Jerked him this way and that, repositioned his body, his pretend knife, and snarled, "Shah! Not pretty-play, pretty-act! This real, dirty dance to death. Slice, stab, blood." Her stiff-fingered hand a black blade out of nowhere, fingers slamming between his ribs for emphasis, the motion almost too fast to register. "Big, sweeping gestures? Nah! Not showing audience now, cuz audience is Vitarosa. Bigwig gestures leave you open. Shah! Paint a target on your chest. You give her time to slappy-clappy and still stab you." The hand darted again, struck at another vulnerability. "See?"

The exercises had been grueling, literally numbing, Panthat's empty-handed blows real, over and over again without letup. Tight, controlled retreat, explosive attack with no warning, no leading gesture to expose her intentions. Feint, parry, thrust, evade. Ways to trip, to kick an opponent. Demoralize. And always the jab, jab of Panny's stiff-fingered hand each time he was vulnerable, open to a hit. But three times—three astounding moments of absolute rightness, almost a purity of instinctual action—he'd scored off Panny. At last she'd shook her head, wiped her brow. "Enough. Either works or doesn't. Be prayerful-careful that it works. Now, rest," and had marched into her adjoining room.

Thinking of the bruises with which Panny had decorated his body, he hoped he'd made some progress. Whether it had been enough, time would tell. And once the others had settled for a few hours' rest, he and Jere had finally talked. How, in the midst of danger, could she hark back to her desire to die? What was he fighting for, if not her life? "Your own," a tiny, frightened voice whispered inside him.

He'd been so convinced she'd accepted what had happened, eventually reconciled at last. Now Jere'd dug it up again, thrust it in his face. No matter what evasion he tried, it always circled round again, snaring him. Her death. His responsibilities. Responsibilities— to himself, to his mother, to Stanislaus. Even Chance, Panthat, and Ngina were temporarily his responsibility. The circle suddenly expanded—what about Anyssa, his half sister? Her little brothers, his as well, Artur and Algore? His newfound father? By extension, NetwArk itself? No! That was asking too much—what about him, his wants, his needs? Didn't someone hold some responsibility for him as well? A side-glance at the box as he shifted to limber his right leg.

"WE DID DISCUSS IT, BUT YOU NEVER ACTUALLY ANSWERED ME. IF YOU SHOW THE SAME NIMBLENESS OF FOOT TODAY THAT YOUR WORDS SHOW, VITAROSA WILL NEVER TOUCH YOU."

Again he danced around her comment, fought himself to ask outright, "Then you actually think I might have a chance against her? Against a trained assassin?"

"IF I DIDN'T THINK SO, I WOULDN'T HAVE BOTHERED WITH MY REQUEST, WOULD I? IF YOU DIE AT HER HANDS, SO WILL I. SHE'S MADE THAT CLEAR."

"But why choose to die now?" He knelt to meet her opticam "eye," arms fisted at his sides.

"BECAUSE ANY DANGER TO YOU WILL HAVE PASSED. TIME FOR ME TO RECLAIM MY OWN LIFE, CONTROL IT AS I WISH . . . WITH THE BEST INTENTIONS IN THE WORLD, YOU ROBBED ME OF THAT BEFORE." She hesitated. Jump in with a counterargument? But his chance to control the conversation ended as she spoke again. "I'VE STAYED ALIVE FOR ONE PURPOSE, TO PROTECT YOU. BUT I CAN'T SHELTER YOU FOREVER. YOU HAVE TO PROTECT YOURSELF, JUST AS YOU MUST AGAINST VI-

TAROSA. YOU MUST LEARN TO SUSTAIN
YOURSELF WITHOUT ME."

Sulk, protest, rage, flail his limbs, all that and more
he wanted to do. Wanted most of all to cradle himself
against her, always have her presence to sustain and
soothe, reassure him he was safe, caught within the
circle of her never-ending, undying love. Undying
love? "Mother, Jere—"

The knock came, an explosive rapping that made
him jerk his head, his muscles go rigid. "Five minutes,
please. Be ready at the door in five minutes." An unfamiliar voice, but it hardly mattered, only the message mattered—the message that framed his future.
He rose stiffly—all the stretching exercises for
naught—and placed his hands on the top of Jere's box.
A deep breath. "My . . . my word on it. If I win, you'll
be free." He kissed the box, picked it up and walked
toward the door.

"WHEN YOU WIN, GLYNN, NOT IF. DAR-
LING, I LOVE YOU, BUT EVERY CAGED BIRD
YEARNS TO FLY FREE." With the LCD pressed
against his side as he numbly waited beside the locked
door, Glynn didn't see her words.

Date: Midmorning, 30 August 2158
Location: An underground arena, NetwArk

For no clear reason, Glynn had assumed the duel
would take place outdoors, beneath the eye-blue skies
he'd glimpsed this morning, the night's storm past. Fitting somehow to die in the open, beneath the alien
gaze of that arching blue sky. But the two male acolytes escorted him down flights of stairs, deeper and
deeper, until they entered an enclosed arena sunk beneath the main house. Brought out through a near-
invisible door in the arena's curved side, he stared at
the sanded surface, kicked at it, allowed his bare toes
to burrow in the sand. A new experience, a new
sensation.

With a whispered warning to wait, a hand on his
shoulder in emphasis, the acolytes left. A cautious

breath, then a deeper one, oddly comforting: The air in the underground arena was close, slightly stale, despite the fact that faint currents from the air-conditioning system brushed his bare chest. Just like satellite air, wonderfully familiar. A jolt of homesickness. Behind him the surrounding ring-wall stood about one-and-a-half meters high, black slick duroplast topped by plexiglass that reached the domed ceiling. Staring through his distorted reflection he judged the solid, regular shapes to be stadium seats, then caught a glimpse of movement. Shielding his eyes, he could just make out Masady and Ngina, Chance and Panthat being escorted inside, Masady's paler complexion most visible against the darkness. Impatient knuckles rippity-rapping on glass, and he waved; Panthat waved back, contrived a rapid series of facial contortions meant to encourage and hearten him. Finally, she began jumping up and down, pointing.

Only then did it dawn that Jere's box remained tucked under his arm, pressed tight to his heart. What to do with it? Why hadn't someone taken it from him? Lurching, pivoting wildly, he scanned for an exit, some place to set her, someone to take her. Nothing, no one. So be it. Clamping down on his panic, he set Jere beside him, folded his arms and looked impassively across the arena. "Ringside seat, Jere. Sorry about that." About fifteen meters in diameter, he guessed, with a smaller, six-meter circle outlined, black sand stark against glinting white particles. Room enough to feint and dodge, but not to run. Nothing to do but wait.

Time: The same
Location: Underground arena seating, NetwArk
Panny leaned forward, fingers splayed like spilled ink across the beige plush seat back in front of her, only her eyes and the top of her head showing above it. Dandy-nice unnoticed, half-hidden like this—all ready for pounce'n'bounce. She stared unblinking through the tinted partition surrounding the arena, tracking

Glynn's every fidget as he stood there alone, Jere's box a few meters away. Glynnie-boy all twitchy, no surprise.

Stupid, stupid! Rubbing her upper lip against the plush, she strove to quell her rising frustration. Glynnie-boy all right, a-okay guy, knew lotsa smart things Panny didn't. But Panny knew things, other things, like fighting. Oh, sweat'n'effort last night, plenty-plenty, but like . . . she groped for a comparative. What had Ruby said? 'Bout throwing meat to starving lion? Problem was, Glynnie only snicky-snack for Vitarosa's hunger-hate. Yum! Next Jere be nibbled by Rosa—Masady, Chance, Ngina, Panny, too. Well, Pan-that no cream puff for dessert!

Circles, circles, circles here—just like on satellites. Comforting, contained, a relief after her introduction to the out-of-doors. So big, so empty. Ready to devour her to fill its emptiness. Already'd devoured Sylvan. She brushed a watering eye with a knuckle. Silly-squilly but tickley-nice paws, sleek fur. Always chitter-chatter scolding like Masady. Risking a glance from the corner of her eye, she studied them: Chance, Masady, Ngina, seated slightly higher in the tier of seats, their eyes glued to the ring and Glynn. Glue, yes, Masady, Stanislaus, stick to you like glue. That was why she'd slipped to this aisle seat, secluded herself, needing to be alone with her thoughts. The rest of the seats were slowly filling, but no one wanted to sit with them. Fine by Panny.

A horizontal band of light flickered, a thin bright-ness on the floor ahead of the seat she leaned against. Not big, the length of two hands, maybe twenty-five centimeters long. Muffled sounds, voice murmurs wafting through. Overcome by curiosity, Panny ducked into the first row, crouched. Anyone sitting here could idly kick the dark wall surrounding the arena, press an eager face against the glass barrier. Hunkered on the floor she couldn't see what was hap-pening in the ring, the barrier-wall blocking her view. Fine, she liked inspecting vents—vents good to satrats, even thinny ones like this. Couldn't see in, no, only glimmer-shine of light, but voices, yes, oh, yes, hearing them. Shush-shush, listen hard, and she pressed her ear close, held her breath.

Annie-voice. No 'bout-adoubt-it. A hackling shiver ran along her spine. Annie being Anyssa. Shah! What saying? She strained to listen. Annie-voice and old-man-voice, patient-splaining sounds like Ruby made. "No, the rules are clear, Anyssa, just as your great-grandfather set them down. Anyone can offer to serve as "champion" to either accuser or defendant. That person has the right to reject such a proposal unless suffering from an obvious physical or mental incapacitation. The next rule outlines methods to determine that."

Almost growling, Panthat strained to catch Anyssa's response, heard nothing except a quiet "thank you." So, so, Annie-Anyssa going to steal scene, snatch Vitarosa's place and fight Glynn! Sick-slick girl, sure enough! Panny'd seen the light in Anyssa's eyes sometimes when Glynn was near, though most always when Glynn was unaware, engrossed in something else. Bleh! Almost gooey, lovey-dovey. Not approving 'cause Glynnie-boy Panthat's true buddy-friend. Panthat there first, claiming-naming. Whack Anyssa if she could! Boy, oh, boy, whack her into orbit for playing Glynnie false like this! Hands fisted, she froze as Anyssa's voice rose in pain. "I can't let her kill Glynn, I can't. I can't let her go on like this . . . it's all so wrong. Father would hate it." Frowning, Panny cautiously scratched her arm. Anyssa not making sense. "Am I brave enough? I'm the only one who can end it all, salvage as much good as I can from both sides."

Scratching until she nearly drew blood, mulling over what she'd heard, Panthat nodded once, hard. At length, listening to Anyssa's sobs, Panny crept along the ring-wall, sheltered between the seats and the wall itself, testing, probing. Yah, yah, Panny, gotta be one somewhere, always is. Nah, nah. This? No. At length her fingers traced a shape in the floor, squared lines, a lump of hinges along one side. Shah-ha! Far enough from Anyssa? Not wanting to land on shoulders. No hesitating, slither-snake quick, or light'd show where she'd gone. Lifting the trapdoor, Panny dropped down, the hinges' squeak muffled by the assembled crowd's collective inhalation as Vitarosa entered the ring.

Skittering through the shadows of the corridor surrounding the arena, Panthat headed in Anyssa's direction. Not sure what to do, but her mind relentlessly picked at everything she'd heard, tried it for size, twitched it this way and that. So, making sense yet? Anyssa right for wrong reasons, maybe Panthat righter-fighter?

Time: A few interminable minutes later
Location: The arena

Movement, muffled sounds surrounding him, the rest of the auditorium filling, shapes looming behind plexiglass. How many to witness Vitarosa's triumph? His doom? Or perhaps he'd find within himself a depth he'd never plumbed before. Possible. Jere believed it possible, but so mothers always think. A lick above his lip, the taste of salt-sweat. For the first time he realized he wasn't afraid. Anticipatory, yes. An elusive lightness to his thoughts and body that suggested a foretaste of triumph. The same butterfly tingling in his stomach that presaged the rising curtain. And some performances you *knew*—simply sensed deep in your bones, viscerally in your gut—would be special.

Deliberately he spat to the side to break the spell, to show the circle it couldn't overwhelm him. It had helped before, outside the gates to NetwArk, perhaps it would again. This was *real,* not an act, not a play. Ran his hands down his ribs and discovered he'd never pulled on his shirt, wore just his skintight knee pants, medium blue against pale spacer skin. Almost dark blue, given six days of ground-in dirt. No shoes or sandals.

A sound and, near invisible in the curve of the partition, opposite him, anther door swung open and Vitarosa stepped out, stood looking across at him. In no seeming hurry, content to wait. Her dark hair was pulled back severely in a long braid. A woman's shape, but lean, sinewy, comfortable within her skin and within the white, short-sleeved leotard she wore, a red skirt loosely wrapped over it. He'd not spoken with, even glimpsed Anyssa this morning, and that lack pained him, an unanticipated emptiness. Did she sit silent up above with the others? Waiting to see him die, *wanting* to see him die, except he couldn't accept that any longer.

Two more doors opened, each bisecting the wall arcs between him and Vitarosa. From his left came an older man ceremoniously carrying a silver tray draped with a thick-woven white cloth. On it Glynn could just glimpse two shining knives, bone handles slightly elevated as if they rested on blocks. For no reason he could imagine, surprise animated Vitarosa's face; she appeared to be searching for someone else, clearly expecting a second person to accompany the man walking centerward with slow dignity. Then, on his right, he spied Anyssa, staring straight ahead as she strode forward to meet the older man. More shocking, Panny slipped through the closing door behind Anyssa and hovered on the ring perimeter, dark against dark, barely visible.

"Will the combatants come forward, please," the man intoned, tray balanced at chest height. Wordless, matching his pace to Vitarosa's measured stride, he stalked toward the center of his new universe. *Don't look back at Jere,* he ordered himself, *don't peer up at beta Masady, the others. It's just Vitarosa, the two of us. Anyssa's presence, Panny's—doesn't matter. Don't be distracted.*

Closer, closer now, and the anticipation in Vitarosa's eyes nearly lit the arena. "Halt," the man declared when they were a meter distant. "These are the rules, as formally set down by the first Weaver of NetwArk over a hundred years ago. There are times when God's law must follow from our hands, when we must serve as the Lord's defenders. This is such a moment, the sanctity and safety of NetwArk threatened by outsiders. This fight will be to the death. Any step beyond the marked boundary indicates an attempt to flee; the coward's life will be forfeit." Despite himself, Glynn scanned the line, mentally calculating strides in any direction.

A quick headshake to focus himself. Now what was the man droning about? The rules had been laid out, clear and simple. Not the moment to daydream, and Vitarosa'd registered his lapse, her rising eyebrows sharp-curved as scimitars made him sure. "Lastly, just as we serve as defenders of the Lord, so each justice-seeker here today may choose a champion to take his or her place in the ring. Do either of you choose to—"

Before the older man could complete his pro forma question, Anyssa moved from her silent station just beyond the boundary. Took one momentous step forward and crossed the line as she announced, "I claim the privilege of championing—"

But Vitarosa overrode her, "Anyssa, child, I admire your courage, your desire to spare me hurt, but I'm capable of—"

Anyssa simply raised her voice. "—Glynn of Stanislaus Troupe, known here in NetwArk and on Waggoner's Ring as Glynn Webster Stanislaus, eldest son of Rhuven Fisher Weaver and Jerelynn Stanislaus." Thumbs hooked in her belt, Anyssa stood waiting, head cocked at her mother. "There is no honor in any death bestowed in this ring today, you make it a travesty. There is no honor in the deaths you've sought, bestowed so casually in recent months, Mother. Death and terror that defame what Father worked for, what NetwArk stood for. In what you represented so long ago as a Little Sister of Mortality. I renounce and reject it all. I stand champion for my half brother."

For a moment Glynn felt strangely superfluous, as unnecessary as the older man must feel, yet still trapped, reluctantly drawn by the hate orbiting Vitarosa and Anyssa. "I don't want a champion," he insisted, once his shock had passed. "This is *my* battle with your mother, not yours. I don't want any debts."

"I'm paying for past ones, not creating a new ledger," Anyssa spoke softly in his direction without taking her eyes off her mother. "Not even a tithe of what I owe for her attempt to mold me in her perverted image."

Despite her masked, frozen expression, Vitarosa's whole being radiated a kindling hatred; as it flared higher she seemed to glow with an incandescent joy. "Oh, you *are* your father's daughter. Never mine no matter how hard I tried. And riddled by weakness, by doubts and fears just as Rhuven was, as your half brother is! Well, what a challenge to extirpate this creeping weakness from NetwArk, root and stock!"

As if in strained parody of her mother's denunciation, Anyssa collapsed without a word, Panny astride the still figure, rubbing the blade of her right hand against her thigh. Raising it, she made a fist, winced, and shrugged. "Oh, I'm not thinking so big deal. Emotions too messy here. Too many, too much. Glynnie-boy is needing a champion, a ramping-stamping-champion, just what Panthat, satrat, is meant for. You want razmatazing good fight, come to Panthat," she beckoned cheekily.

A hoot of laughter from Vitarosa, head back, throat exposed. "Oh, child, you're too perfect for words, symbolism beyond compare. Black and white in a fight to the death, its outcome preordained! You're right, there's too much messy emotion here—that can be dealt with later. I accept you as Glynn's champion." She sketched an ironic bow at Panthat.

"This beginning to be fun. Thrill you first, then kill you. Fight with Panny, you fight the best."

"Wescott, clear out the bystanders." With a flourish Vitarosa stripped off her red skirt, swirled it outside the ring. "So, shall we continue?"

At Wescott's signal, Glynn found himself unceremoniously hustled away as he fought and shouted, pleading with Panthat not to intercede. Two more acolytes removed Anyssa's limp body just as he was allowed brief seconds to snatch up Jere before being tumbled into a seat inside. He pressed a feverish forehead against the glass shield as Panthat took her place opposite Vitarosa at the circle's center. It couldn't be, wasn't supposed to happen like this! Snatched away from him at the last second. He swiped at the glass where his breath steamed it, desperate to see, pounded it in frustration.

Black hand, white hand, both hovered over the tray with its double serving of death, each poised to snatch the bone handle of a knife. "On retrieving your weapons at my command, you will each take six steps back and remain motionless until I have left the ring," Wescott stated. "Now!" The knives flashed down, the distance between Panny and Vitarosa increasing as he exited, churning the sand in his haste. "Clear and commence!"

Gripping Jere's box so tightly he feared he'd break it, Glynn stared, riveted, as the duet began, only belatedly noticing Anyssa had slid in beside him, a wet towel draped round her neck. Groggy, green-tinged, a livid bruise on her neck—he could almost feel it throbbing. "Lord help us, she'd better be as good as she thinks she is," she muttered thickly, "Gutter tricks versus training." A clammy hand chilled his inner elbow, slid down to lock fingers with him while he positioned Jere so one ocular could sweep the ring.

Cool, calculating, the two fighters took each other's measure, slipping forward and back, testing and probing. A restrained, almost balletic quality that reminded Glynn all too much of the stage. Who'd taught Panny? The long-dead Ruby, whom Panthat sometimes mentioned? Experience? As Masady had said time and again, "Experience is the best teacher." He'd never been sure whether Panny's toughness was a façade or a shield for a morality uniquely her own.

Can any teacher impart all his or her wisdom to a student? What is held back, omitted? What is added beyond the lessonings? Youth and middle age: the speed and resilience of youth, the willingness to take chances, versus burning personal desire backed by rigorous, formal discipline and control. For a moment he prayed; Panny was family now, Stanislaus, had earned the right over and over again. No longer a satrat but a Stanislaus. She'd adopted them, would battle twice as hard because she'd tasted the bitter difference between having and not having, recognized how tenuous love and acceptance could be. She fought not for him, but for the troupe.

"Shah? Nah!" Panthat whooped and swung clear as Vitarosa flashed inward, except Vitarosa was back in position, waiting. "Shah! First blood! Good for you, old bag!" A thin red line trickled down Panny's upper arm, just below the shoulder. Her bare feet danced to dare Rosa to match her steps. "Ah! Nah, nah, nah!" the child growled as Vitarosa blocked her knife hand with her left forearm and slashed at Panny's thigh. Unable to help himself, Glynn closed his eyes. Why was she holding back? Being so tentative? Was she truly out of her league? Panny would suffer, die for them, die for nothing as he and Jere then met their deaths. Coward! And forced his eyes open. It struck like a blow: This was *real*, it wasn't theater, superlative acting.

A dark foot lashed out, Panny's catching the back of Vitarosa's calf, and her knife scored a line across the underside of Rosa's left breast. Red against the white of the leotard. For some reason the minor wound shocked the older woman more than it should, and she trembled, eyes unseeing as she held her hand there, cupping her breast. Curiously, Panny retreated, didn't press home her advantage, waiting for Rosa to recover. "Damn it, Panny! Again!" Anyssa screamed beside him, and Panny obeyed, though not the killing stab that Anyssa called on her to administer. A duck and a high slash and Vitarosa's right ear fell redly on the sand like an autumn leaf.

Now there was no holding back, no subtlety, as Vi-

tarosa threw herself at Panthat, her mouth spewing
words that Glynn couldn't hear. Strangely, Panny
laughed, finding some sort of perverse humor in the
situation. And on it went, sometimes stingingly fast,
sometimes achingly slow, as Panny made Vitarosa tra-
verse the entire circle, goading her forward and back,
luring Rosa after her. Glynn had no idea how much
time had passed, knew only that he felt exhausted,
muscles sore and cramping, heart pounding, mouth
dry. First one, then the other would toy with her opponent, leaving Glynn cheering Panny's rallies, cold with
terror at her reversals, her retreats. And blood continued flowing from new and old wounds. Barbaric, was
this how Earth truly functioned these days, with the
ancient barbarism of hand-to-hand combat?

Both faltering now, woman and child, feet dragging,
the sand scuffed around them, sea peaks and troughs
of sand, caplets of blood. The harshness of his breathing matched theirs, Anyssa slumped beside him, sunk
into herself, moaning at each blow, mourning whomever it had struck. Hurt and hatred together, her
mother out there, and Anyssa lost no matter who won.

Transfixed, he saw Vitarosa's knife traveling in a
quick, compact sweep, groaned as Panny stumbled
toward it, took that final, unwieldy step, unable to
envision any other—a side step or a lurch to temporarily evade the knife. Vitarosa's eyes glittered, the side
of her face and neck a mask of blood as she drove
forward, only to discover Panny's left hand now held
the knife as she swung home, connecting beneath
Rosa's rib cage, sinking it deep. The unaccustomed
move left Panthat pivoting like a creaking, swinging
gate to regain position; Vitarosa's counterblow struck
and glanced, left yet another blood trail.

On his feet now Glynn screamed himself hoarse,
trumpeting all his hopes and fears, letting them fill the
air as Vitarosa sank to her knees, dropped forward to
let her hands take her weight. With effort she pushed
up off one knee, struggling to stand, her mouth a rictus of delight as she realized Panthat's knife was still

lodged in her chest—that she now controlled both knives. A moment of triumph as she reached for the embedded knife, struggled to stand erect, only to topple forward, the weight of her body driving the knife home. Glynn screamed again, pounded the glass, capered and danced, but when he reached for Anyssa's hand, he discovered she'd silently slipped away.

It was over. Done. Vitarosa was dead. A dry, rasping sound as Panthat rubbed her hands together, then turned and limped from the ring, never looking behind her.

Date: The day after the duel, 31 August 2158
Location: A sitting room, NetwArk

A part of her, a large part of her (Which part? Jere asked, inquiring minds want to know. My thalamus? . . . cerebellum? . . . amygdala? . . . what?) wished this ordeal over, ruefully conceded it was part of freedom's price. Yet another part of her sparked with a singular harmony of being she'd not previously experienced. A natural high, a synchronous galvanic dance of neurons. I am out of my senses. Have been—literally—for some time. Deprived—or liberated from them? With liberation one has endless time for deep thought. Ah, liberation. . . .

I see this room with its pale yellow walls, wispy lace curtains at the windows—ah, windows!—the carpeting a complex pattern of pastel knotted flowers and vines. A similar design on the chair facing me. That I know because Chance has set up a mirror again, gruff instructions ordering Ngina left or right to position it. Thus, anyone I speak with will sit directly in front of me, read my words, yet I will see that person in the mirror.

The beginning of an end, farewells. I owe them that, and so much more. Soon they'll come, in the order Glynn and I set. Ah, the first, SatGov Ngina Natwalla. Leggy, clever, tough yet tender. Sounds like verse . . . or worse. No giddiness, Jere.

"NGINA, SIT, PLEASE. MY HEARTFELT

THANKS FOR YOUR ASSISTANCE. YOU'VE
BEEN A DEAR FRIEND TO CHANCE, AND I'M
PLEASED TO CALL YOU FRIEND AS WELL, A
FRIEND OF STANISLAUS."

Folding her long legs, Ngina sat, solemn and steady
at her first talk with a brain box. "Somehow saying it
was a pleasure doesn't quite fit the bill. However, I'm
glad I did. Glad to have met you and the others as
well."

"LIFE TAKES UNEXPECTED PATHS. YOU
ROSE TO GOVERN SALLYRIDE WHILE
CHANCE LOST WHAT HE HELD MOST DEAR.
NOT ALWAYS EASY TO JUDGE TRUE GAINS
AND LOSSES."

"True, though I think Chance gained more than he
lost. For what it's worth, I agree with your decision.
I'll keep an eye on everyone best I can—provided they
look out for me." She rose, tossed a half-salute, did
a neat about-face. But before she could leave, Jere
"squawked" her.

"BY THE WAY, WHAT DID YOU FINALLY
DO WITH POOR SYLVAN?"

Self-consciously Ngina touched the cargo pocket on
her thigh. "Buried him, out in the gardens. Chance
wanted it so."

Next through the door, Panthat, her movements stiff
and awkwardly formal, decorous in a stretchy, short-
skirted dress in dusty rose. Absorbing the setting, the
mirror's placement, she limped beyond the mirror's
range, leaving Jere conjecturing what she planned.

"Squawk!" "GAK! PANNY, BACK OFF, DON'T
STAND SO CLOSE!" Jere exploded as Panny stared
directly into Jere's right opticam.

"Checking if you still home, not roaming yet." Un-
repentant, she plopped into the chair, the bandage on
her arm flashing white as she scrubbed at an ear.
"Squawky-talk ouch-making. Eardrum still thrum-
ming, thank you very much."

"LUCKY I CAN'T BOX YOUR EAR. I'LL
HAVE BETA MASADY DO IT."

"Wishing she would, wishing she take her mind off end of world, end of Stanislaus, and box Panny." Serious worry lines marched across her brow. "Then I know she still care about something, even if only lowly satrat."

How often had she viewed this child from afar? Following Glynn during those first, haphazard meetings that quickly became childhood ritual. Had yearned to help but hadn't dared. Informing the authorities would have throttled what Panny seemed to hold dear—her freedom. How to repay her now, for what she'd meant to Glynn, to them all? "PANTHAT. YOU ARE STANISLAUS THROUGH AND THROUGH. YOU BELONG. WE'LL DRAW UP THE PAPERS."

A squirm, a wince as bandages under the rose top dragged at wounds. "Well, honor-right-bright, and I am thanking you for that. But not much to belong to. More satrats than Stanislaus these days, I 'spect, if you check each satellite."

Shocking, but true. Out of the mouths of babes— and shim-knife-wielding outcast children. Jere sensed the germ of a plan seeding itself in her brain, germinating, flowering. "SO, YOU KNOW ANY SATRATS WORTHY OF BECOMING STANISLAUS? THAT IS, IF THEY WORKED HARD, LEARNED WELL, SHARED THEIR OWN SKILLS AND CLEVERNESS WITH US. OF COURSE YOU AND BETA MASADY WOULD HAVE TO DECIDE IF THEY WERE WORTHWHILE MATERIAL."

"As in giving beta Masady more to worry-furry about? Can't grieve when dizzy-busy, and Panthat guarantee she find satrats who can do that!"

"THEN SEE THAT YOU DO, COMB THE SATELLITES FOR THEM. AND WATCH OUT FOR GLYNN FOR ME."

An indignant sniff followed by a tragic pose worthy of a Stanislaus. "I been doing that alla time. Tough job! Wear you to skin and bone or, worse, carve

skin from bone!" A thin black hand whick-whacked
the air.

For a moment genuine sorrow overwhelmed Jere—
to never see the woman Panthat would become in a
few short years. "BE THERE FOR HIM, DON'T
JUST PROTECT HIM FROM PHYSICAL HARM.
GOOD-BYE, PANNY, I LOVE YOU."

With reluctant dignity Panny stood, lower lip out-
thrust, brows drawn, only to suddenly skip forward,
again out of Jere's line of sight. Heard—though she
couldn't see or feel—a kissing smack on her box.
"Wherever you going now, share that with Ruby if
you meet him. Panny too late before."

A glow, a warmth from that unexpected kiss seeped
through wood and stainless steel to lodge inside her.
Silly, autosuggestion at best. That long-ago playwright
James Barrie would understand. Ah, mention that to
Masady! Do Magyar one better, compete for their
children's audience! Satrats as Lost Boys. Panthat as
Panny Pan. No more time to think it through, for now
Chance hobbled inside.

*Only Chance has an inkling of what it's like to be
trapped, snared like this, though at least his cage was
larger than mine. I loved him once, still do. A less
complicated love than Rhuven, but a longer-lasting one.*

Hunched forward in the chair, massive forearms
resting on his knees, Chance stared moodily at the
carpet, tracing the circuit pattern made by knotted
vines and flowers. "Mirror satisfactory? Need it
moved, can get someone . . ." He attempted to heave
himself upright, but his leg wouldn't cooperate.
"Damn! Hurts like a son of a gun!" He twisted, re-
signedly resettled himself, still keeping his face
averted. "Jere, I'm sorry. Said it before, have to say
it again. Shouldn't have boxed you. Should've known
better, trusted my instincts." His hands shook. "I was
so panicked, so scared for Glynn, thinking he'd lose
his mind with grief."

"THE BLUNDERBUSS WAS HIGHLY PER-
SUASIVE, ACCORDING TO GLYNN."

His reluctant chuckle transformed itself into a rolling belly laugh. "You've got that right! Staring down that barrel? Phew, like being swallowed in a dark hole." An incredulous headshake. "Should have been, then none of this would ever have happened!" He faced her now, tears silvering his broad, cocoa-tinted cheeks. "Turned into a damned coward!"

'CHANCE, NO. THE PAST IS PAST, DON'T LET IT HAUNT YOU. BUT THAT'S NOT WHAT I WANT TO TALK ABOUT. WILL YOU FLY WITH THE SPACERS NOW, STRAP ON YOUR TOOL BELT AND REPAIR THE STARS? ANY SHIP THAT SIGNS ON MR. FIX-IT CAN REST EASY."

A long pause, his green eyes distant, staring beyond her. To the stars—or something nearer, dearer? "Don't think so. That was someone else, Tinker II Evers II Chance. I'm just Chance now, and that suits me fine." Amazing how a man of his bulk could almost wilt with shyness. "Kinda'd like to stay with the troupe. I can't fill bet Rigoberto's shoes, but beta Masady will need help—if she decides to continue."

"I THINK SHE COULD BE CONVINCED. ASK PANTHAT. CHANCE, I LOVE YOU. THANK YOU."

Prepared this time, he shifted his weight to his unwounded leg and levered himself up. "As I've always loved you." His massive hand reached toward her left auricular scan, a tender, finicky caress as if tucking something in place, the way he'd always tucked a strand of her hair behind her ear. "I won't forget."

A weariness to all this, the hungry drag of emotions, but soon she'd be shed of them. Thus, treasure them, remember they affirm your humanity, the unflagging resilience of the human spirit. Do I treasure them enough to make me stay, tell Glynn I was wrong? No, I embrace my humanity, yet am composing, conducting my own elegy—in five-part harmony! No, not elegy, my legacy! Not just the latticed chain of my DNA, but of my thoughts, my dreams and hopes, all my futures, all their futures and beyond, part of an infinitely larger, twisting coil!

Unaware her excitement transformed her final thought into flashing, triumphant blue, "PART OF AN INFINITELY LARGER, TWISTING COIL!" Jere realized with a pang that Anyssa stood half-shielded behind the chair, barricaded and ready to bolt in retreat. "AH, CHILD. ANYSSA, HAVE YOU FOUND FULFILLMENT YET?"

She had meant no irony, no sarcasm, but from Anyssa's recoil, Jere suspected Anyssa had projected them into the question. Still, the girl was a fighter—of many sorts. "No. But I'm a few steps closer." A deep breath as she stepped forward until she stood beside the chair, body taut. "I ask forgiveness. For me, for what Vitarosa and Rhuven did to you, for what NetwArk tried to do to you." She raised her chin, not with defiance but with dogged acceptance, waiting to receive a blow. "Name your penance."

"SACKCLOTH AND ASHES? NO. CARE ABOUT GLYNN FOR ME."

"How? He hates me," and rushed on, "not that I blame him."

"YOU NEED EACH OTHER, YOU'RE FAMILY. LET HIM LEARN ABOUT THE OTHER HALF OF HIM, THE GOOD THINGS. HOW IS UP TO YOU."

"But he has every reason to hate, and I. . . . There's so much to do. NetwArk, I need to save NetwArk, not let it wither. . . ." Hands sketched deft sculpting motions, imaginary buildings taking shape, definition.

"YES, FOR BETTER OR FOR WORSE, NETWARK IS YOURS. DISBAND IT, REBUILD IT, RESHAPE IT. WE ALL NEED FAITH, SOMETHING TO BELIEVE IN, A HIGHER GOAL TO REACH FOR. SO DOES GLYNN. USE YOUR BRAIN, ANYSSA, GIVE YOURSELF AND GLYNN A SPECIAL GIFT."

Still dubious, "A gift? I don't know." A deep breath, "But I can try to find one worthy." Her mouth quirked, a dimple flashing, so like Rhuven. "Perhaps there's a mountain you'd like moved instead? I'm good with a shovel, diligent, too."

"NO, TOO EASY, ANYSSA. IT'S EASIER TO MOVE MOUNTAINS THAN PEOPLE. YOUR FATHER KNEW HOW TO MOTIVATE PEOPLE, HELP THEM UNCOVER THE GOODNESS WITHIN THEM. YOU'LL LEARN AS WELL. TAKE CARE OF RHUVEN FOR ME."

"Oh, I will, I shall. And I'll honor my promise about Glynn, somehow. Go well, Jere—and God bless you." A new purpose informed her stride as she left.

Ah, ah, one more left undone. The hardest last, short of Glynn. No, perhaps hardest of all, for the years shared together. Does Masady grieve as I would grieve if Glynn had to die? No tears, I have no tears to shed. I cannot weep, I cannot wail, I cannot hold her close. Is what's left enough for a true farewell?

"Girl, Jere-girl, are you there? I've been talking to you, at you, but you're not answering." Beta Masady knelt stiffly in front of the table, a frail hand on either side of Jere's box. "Don't have gone yet, Jere, please, not without . . . not without saying . . ." Tears coursed down her ancient face, the ivory skin, landing on and spotting the yellow silk blouse with its high collar, the silk woven Earth-side so long ago.

"MASADY, DEAR HEART, DEAREST ONE!"

"Ought to box your ears, child! Always were a troublesome handful! Frightening me half to death like that!" Masady eased onto her heels, heedlessly wiped her eyes with the silk sleeve. "Oh, Jere!"

"SORRY. HOW ABOUT TWENTY REPETITIONS OF 'GOLDEN PHEASANT IN THE CORNFIELD'?" Anyssa had asked for a penance; so could she.

A wondering smile, tremulous and sweet with a youthfulness that erased the years. "You hate 'Golden Pheasant Attracts a Mate' even more. Don't try to weasel out of it, child! Can't fool me!" Her wail caught Jere by surprise, the abrupt keening sound welling from the depths of Masady's soul. "Jere, don't leave us, please! Don't leave me. Without you, there's nothing left! You're all I have now, you and Glynn! Don't tear another piece of my past from me until there's nothing left!" Her fists pounded the table, and Jere heard their echoing thuds, so regular, so like Masady's heartbeat when she'd gathered Jere close to her breast.

"I drove you from Stanislaus once, yet you returned. Don't abandon me again . . . everything's crumbling around me!"

"DEAREST, MY MAMA MASADY, THERE'S ALWAYS A FUTURE."

"I'm too old to have a future, and my past is dying, dead!"

Please, old woman, don't be so obdurate, so bloody stubborn! If I can face a new world, so must you. "TAKE THE BEST OF THE PAST, THE OLD WAYS, PROJECT THEM FORWARD AND FOLLOW AFTER. CREATE A NEW STANISLAUS— IN HONOR OF ME, IN HONOR OF YOU. YOU'LL HAVE HELP, MORE THAN YOU EVER DREAMED."

"What?" Masady's scorn rang clear, dismissive. "A ragtag of actors who've dropped out of other troupes, couldn't make the cut?"

"WHAT DID STANISLAUS AND SIEM VY BUILD FROM? A RAGTAG GROUP OF YOUNG AND OLD, SOME KIN, SOME NOT, TALENTED AND UNTALENTED. BUT ALL WHOM THEY HELD DEAR."

Faded tatters of hope began to reknit themselves as Masady frowned, calculating. "Any other surprises you've not mentioned?"

Date: Evening, 31 August 2158
Location: A walk around NetwArk's grounds
Restless, Glynn prowled the hallway outside their suite, staring out first one window, then the next and the next. Earlier he'd been transfixed by the sunset,

almost giddy as vermilion and shocking pinks with golden underbellies muted to mauves, finally darker purples, a backdrop to a molten copper-red disk sinking lower and lower. The gaudy confluence of colors outstripped by far the orchestrated, mechanized sunsets each satellite offered. Now stars popped out one by one; haunting memories with each distant glow. After all, within this dark dome each pinprick of light could be a familiar star, a planet, a satellite, a distant space shuttle. . . .

His emotions ebbed and flowed, a high tide of riotous joy at life, *living*, stunned amazement at surviving, and always, clenched tight within, tomorrow's low tide when he'd allow Jere's life to ebb away. A hand brushed his shoulder and he whirled defensively, gasping, the long months of fear, heightened alertness impossible to set aside. "Anyssa!" His voice rose a strangled octave, made him slap fist against palm in chagrin.

"Shh. Come walk with me? Outside?" she whispered. "Please?" Suspicious query plain in the tilt of his head, Anyssa waited, patient, humble, for his distrust to fade—if it would ever completely abate. "I need some fresh air. You, too."

A half-bow and a sweeping arm indicated she should lead the way. Tossing a navy woolen shirt to him, she cautioned, "Cooler out under the stars. You'll need it." She wore a similar one over denim trousers and a cotton smock. Assured he'd follow, she led, confident, along darkened halls, hung with portraits in oil, photographs, and holopics, ghost-reflections of their passage in the glass. Down stairs, her hand light on the railing, the caress of its worn smoothness. The murmurs of an old building settling for the night, full of regret and relief, aware its life would alter on the morrow, but perhaps she was being fanciful.

Outside he moved nearer, still behind her but with his shoulder practically touching hers. Darker here as well, trees and shrubs shading paths, especially the secluded ones she instinctively sought. Odd to hear him stumble on occasion, his feet scuffling, testing their way, but then he trod her territory, not his. Through the market-garden plantings, following rows tamped by many passing feet, tender plantings skirting their legs. Now onto rolling land, not hilly, precisely, but hummocky.

Just over the top of one rise Glynn tripped, fell full-length and lay there, head buried in his folded arms. "All right?" she dropped to one knee, a restraining hand on his back at the waist.

He lifted his head, face white against his dark wool sleeves, the dark hill. "Uh-huh. Counting stars, forgot where my feet were."

"Good." With a spring she leaped over him, stretched on her back beside him. "Now here's what you do when you fall. Watch." She began rolling down the hill, heels, shoulders digging in to propel her until momentum took over. A quick uphill glance revealed Glynn beginning an inexpert roll. From the bottom she watched him tumbling after her, braid whipping, his face intent yet split by a demonic grin. Wary, she sprang to her feet, too late as he crashed into her, sweeping her legs out from under her and sending her flying. "I take it," she picked herself up, dusted herself off with wounded dignity, "you don't know how to stop?"

A wordless, apologetic headshake, his face studiously neutral. And the sensation his clenched jaw restrained a chain of giggles. Abruptly she hiked away, muttering a brusque "Come on" at him. Too adult for that silly moment of play, she counseled herself, too much at stake, too much to decide.

Up a rise to the dinosauric shape of the oil rig as the moon cleared a cloud, gilding it silver as it bobbed and bent, flexed, protesting squeaks echoing with metronomic regularity. Watched him retreat, stare up at it, arrested by its angular bend and rise.

Now or never, best now, while he scrutinized it, not her. "I'm sorry. Sorry about everything." No matter how genuine, each word raw-scrubbed her throat. "I've been wrong about so many things, done wrong. I am *not* an extension of my parents, we're all separate beings, capable of our own unique good and evil. I repudiate the evil within me, hope that you may believe there's goodness within." Her apology as awkwardly stiff as her stance, she suspected how false, how fabricated it all sounded.

Fisting his hands inside the shirt's side pockets, Glynn scuffed his shoe, drew lines with the toe. So very, very tired, mentally, emotionally, physically. "It's hard," he ventured, shivering under the cool night-dome of stars, the moon, so much smaller here. "I'm only," he kicked at a pebble, heard it "spang" off the oil rig, "beginning to come to terms with everything myself." He forced himself to meet her eyes, gauge her reaction. "Would you truly have killed Jere? Me?" They stood in this vast openness, so why not get everything out into the open?

Her head snapped back as if he'd struck her, and he had—verbally. A stiff nod of acknowledgment, "Yes. At first, yes, at the beginning. I thought that killing you, killing Jere would erase some of my anger." Her hand sought the side of the rusty rig, pounded it, felt it snag and score her knuckles. "I was *so* jealous of you, afraid that if Father knew you existed he'd choose you over me. It happened to Mother like that and oh, how she harped about past injustices. And then somehow I came to envy you and Jere, your relationship, the whole—oh, I don't know," her bruised knuckles sought her mouth as she groped to explain, "I guess—connectedness of Stanislaus, a family solidarity that always eluded me, us." She waited, but he made no comment, just stood, chewing his lip, deep in thought. "By the way, I plan to make it right as I can with Tierney Troupe about Annie Marie Doulan."

He took a condemnatory step closer, gray eyes hard but so silver-bright in the moonlight. "You can *never* make it completely right. You took another human

being's life." No matter how often she'd berated herself for that act, his flat, matter-of-fact censure pierced
her. "Would you *really* have killed Vitarosa?"

Wounded, heartsick, she hunkered against the rig's
bulk, hid her face in her hands. Answer, say the truth.
Glynn deserved it; she deserved whatever it revealed
about her. "I think so." She looked up at him, "Every
life, even a flawed life, is precious in God's sight. But
there were so many other lives in the balance. If you
discovered a beloved animal with a creeping, incurable
disease that will infect and kill hundreds of others,
should you risk letting it live . . . ?" It struck her then,
his question's dual purpose, his true need for asking.
How could she have been so blind? "Can you let Jere
go tomorrow morning?" An absurd euphemism, "let
her go," not "kill," though the end result was the
same. "Oh, Glynn!"

He spun away, refusing or unable to face compassion, his absurd narrow braid lashing out, flagellating
him. "I promised. I'm strong enough now to see her
as she is, how it must drive home her mutilation to
be caged like that. But it's not as simple as opening
her cage door and setting her free!"

Silence—a deserved one given the dilemma, the
strong emotions involved—though hardly a tranquil
one. At length he edged near, sat by her, their shoulders touching. His body warmth felt good; her
thoughts more chilling than the night air. "Then what
will you do? Afterward, I mean." She tried in vain to
deduce his plans from his expression, looked away,
feeling like a voyeur spying on his private anguish.

"Don't know. I think about tomorrow, but then my
mind balks," he slumped. "Can't think any farther
ahead, can't think beyond my promise to Jere, afraid
that I'll fail, compromise her again."

Sagging against him comfortingly, she murmured,
"Well, I've a proposition for you." He stiffened,
jerked clear so hurriedly she almost fell backward.
What had gotten into him? A flash of insight, unbidden, and she cursed her innocent stupidity, because

she'd experienced the attraction herself, had fought to conquer it. That temptation was dead now, burned away by circumstances, by blood. Half brother, half sister only a small part of it.

She still loved him, but differently now, the burning refining that love into something more enduring. "Not *that* kind, you, you . . ." she desperately searched for a word, snatched at Artur's most current derogatory expression, "you divot-brain!" A burst of startled laughter erupted from Glynn, and she joined in, the expansive silliness healing some minor hurts to the soul.

"No, Glynn, seriously." A light punch to his shoulder to bring him back, force him to pay sober attention. "Stay here, help me. Help NetwArk spread its true message of hope and faith. I can't heal like Father, but perhaps I can help cure NetwArk, give its believers continued hope." She rushed on, excited now, "With your training, with your dramatic techniques, just think! You could act out Bible scenes. Now there's truth and wisdom that has survived through the ages, messages of hope that can sustain others!"

"From what I gather, doesn't the Bible include a number of families with problems? Just like Shakespeare, Sophocles?" He reached to encircle her wrist with his hand, link them together. "I'd like to stay, learn more about your message. Learn more about Father, about Artur, Algore."

"Then will you?" Too easy, hoping against hope. It can't be this simple. Oh, Lord, let it be—even though I don't deserve it.

The grip on her wrist disappeared and he rose in one swift move, irrevocably sundering them. "I don't think I can. I have to return to Waggoner's Ring, to Stanislaus. Beta Masady, the others, they need me."

Annoyed despite herself, she leaped to her feet, clutched at deep folds of Glynn's shirt, turning him to face her, make him *see*. "How can you make Stanislaus rise from the ashes like the Phoenix? There's so

little left of it. You *know,* you know that, don't you?"
Hammering at his shoulder now, willing him to admit
the truth. "The years of training needed! Anything
you can do will just prolong Stanislaus' agony, a pale
imitation of itself! Some things *have* to die to let other
dreams be born!" Oh! Oh, Lord, she'd done it again!
Hadn't intended it that way, not like that! Yammering
fool with a mouth racing faster than its brain!

"So, I should let Stanislaus wither, let it die just as
surely as I'll kill Jere tomorrow?" His clenched fist
hovered near her chin, and she feared this time he
truly would strike her, couldn't blame him as she
braced herself. Instead, one finger after the other unfolded, snapped out as he relentlessly ticked them off.
"And kill beta Masady, Majvor, Vijay, Hassiba, Jasper?" A final handshake, "and Jeremy—perhaps,
what?—a year younger than Artur? If Stanislaus dies,
their hopes, their dreams die, too, forcing them to
concede their craft was worthless in the end."

Desperate, she churned her muddled thoughts for
an idea to save him, to rescue her from her bluntness,
her blatant need grinding his own needs into the dust
of NetwArk. Use your brain, Jere had admonished
her this morning. Use it! "Leave it alone. Let it
evolve, Glynn. Grow into something else before it becomes extinct."

"Evolve into what?"

"I don't know, but think hard, break out of bounds!
Think about old lives and new lives. That one doesn't
have to be a carbon copy of the other. Don't be too
proud to ask questions, confront old assumptions.
Stanislaus already did when you took Jere's place.
Maybe you already hold the key, the answer that un-
locks the past. Maybe beta Masady does, or Chance
or Panthat. Challenge them, challenge yourself!"

"I'll think about it. That much I promise. But I'm
not making any decisions yet." The stars wheeled
overhead, not pretend stars, but real ones. Could he
live with the blue of the sky as a constant, a given?
Such vastness, nothing to constrain him, hold him

back—but was that liberation? This world was larger, more imposing, more magnificent than anything he'd ever dreamed of, broad enough to encompass every thought, every emotion, every endeavor he might essay. Did he dare?

Date: Morning, 1 September 2158
Location: A hilltop at NetwArk

He sat at the crest of a low knoll, arms loosely wrapped around knees, watching the figures grow smaller in the distance. One, Panthat, turned and gave a final wave. No, not so much a wave as a salute, arm upthrust and rigid, the thin black arm with its white bandage around the biceps. Did she point toward Waggoner's Ring, toward Rhuven's heaven—where?

The farewells were done, not his but theirs, Masady and Chance, Panthat and Ngina, and Anyssa. The lid of Jere's box glistened in the morning sun, its gleaming wood warm to his touch. Flopping, he pillowed one hand behind his head, the other still resting on the box and stared skyward. Blue, so very blue, arching over all as if it would always hold him in its sight. Twisting to face Jere, he asked, "It's so like your eyes, but it's not quite right. We weren't here that time, were we? Someplace else?"

"YOU REMEMBER THAT? YOU WERE SO LITTLE THEN." Grass the color of emerald rippled, a breeze loaded with unfamiliar sea scents caressed the box. "YOU'RE RIGHT. WE WERE IN THE CAN-MONTAN TERRITORIES—ACROSS THE CONTINENT. THAT WAS WHERE I LEFT HIM . . . AFTER THE RETREAT."

"Mmm." Sleepily he watched an ant crawl up a blade of grass, consider exploring the plateau of Jere's box. With a roll he flipped on his stomach, fist supporting chin. "Do you think Anyssa will be all right?"

"I'VE ASKED HER, YOU'VE ASKED HER. NOW IT'S UP TO HER."

He had, but he wasn't sure he understood her, though he was coming closer.

"THERE'S ALWAYS ROOM FOR FAITH. EVEN FAITH HEALING AND THE HEALING OF FAITH. WE'VE YET TO EXPLORE ALL THE MYSTERIES OF THE MIND, STILL CAN'T CHART IT LIKE THE DIMENSIONS OF EARTH, THE DISTANCES OF SPACE."

Despite himself he smiled, reminiscing. "Didn't you tell me once that long, long ago the early mapmakers used to write 'Here be dragons,' at the edges of their maps when they didn't know what came next?"

"UMMHMM," and the silence between them lengthened, wordless and companionable, a final hiatus. At length Glynn sat, bowed his head into his hands, then tossed it back.

"Ready?" He had to ask it, make sure.

"YES. I LOVE YOU."

Reaching for the dials he began to shut the system down.

Date: All time and no time
Location: Inside Jere's brain

Neurons. Clicking, ticking, spasming, connecting. Bright flickers trying, dying, the absence of nutrient, slow-seeping away, oxygenation exhausted. Synaptic connections spanning all directions, flickering, reaching for contact points. Reaching . . . reaching . . . to explore new and alien connections . . . everything . . . nothing . . . crashing . . . soaring . . . bonding. . . .

"I AM ETERNAL, BUT WHO AM I—JERE, GLYNN, YOU, ME? SOME OF THESE PATTERNS WILL PASS ON . . . SAME . . . NOT SAME . . . SAME . . . PASSAGE . . . OTHERS . . . OURS . . . THEIRS . . . ME . . . YOU. . . ."

Date: Now and forever
Location: A hilltop, a universe

He froze, incredulous, scrubbed at his tears, not daring to tear his eyes off the box. Everything had stopped, the LCD had faded long minutes ago. No reason it should light up again, no reason, and no way it could.

Impossible—there was no stored power, he'd bled everything down, disconnected the backup solar batteries before they'd come outside. He was no Chance, with the ability to tinker, to fix—and most of all, had promised faithfully that he wouldn't. But there it was—the letters a blue so faint he had to squint to make them out.

"OUR OWN UNIVERSE WITHIN OUR MINDS . . . PART . . . WHOLE . . . SAME . . . NOT SAME. DOES IT REALLY MATTER? WE ARE ONE AND MAKE OUR OWN UNIVERSES, YOURS IN MINE, MINE IN YOURS. ALWAYS A PART OF EACH OTHER. A UNIVERSE UNLIMITED IN THE MIND. DO I DARE DISTURB THE UNIVERSE? YES . . . OH, YES . . . YES! ALWAYS DARE, GLYNN, ALWAYS DARE!"

No way he could halt his racking sobs, but they didn't matter because he felt oddly joyous. So, she would always be a part of him. There on Waggoner's Ring, or here at NetwArk, and he knew with certainty for the first time that he would stay here. At least for a little while. Then, who knew? Well, he probably did, deep inside. And Jere knew as well. Would always know, just as he'd always know she loved him. Separate but indivisible.

GAYLE GREENO

☐ **THE GHATTI'S TALE:**
  Book 1—Finders, Seekers   UE2550—$5.99
The Seekers Veritas, an organization of truth-finders composed of Bondmate pairs—one human, one a telepathic, catlike ghatti—is under attack. And the key to defeating this deadly foe is locked in one human's mind behind barriers even her ghatta has never been able to break.

☐ **MINDSPEAKER'S CALL**
  The Ghatti's Tale: Book 2   UE2579—$5.99
Someone seems bent on creating dissension between Canderis and the neighboring kingdom of Marchmont. And even the truth-reading skill of the Seekers Veritas may not be enough to unravel the twisted threads of a conspiracy that could see the two lands caught in a devastating war . . .

☐ **EXILES' RETURN**
  The Ghatti's Tale: Book 3   UE2655—$5.99
Seeker Doyce is about to embark on a far different path—a ghatti-led journey into the past. For as a new vigilante-led reign of terror threatens the lives of Seekers and Resonants alike, the secrets of that long-ago time when the first Seeker-ghatti Bond was formed may hold the only hope for their future . . .

S. Andrew Swann

HOSTILE TAKEOVER

☐ **PROFITEER**   UE2647—$4.99

With no anti-trust laws and no governing body, the planet Bakunin is the perfect home base for both corporations and criminals. But now the Confederacy wants a piece of the action—and they're planning a hostile takeover!

☐ **PARTISAN**   UE2670—$4.99

Even as he sets the stage for a devastating covert operation, Dominic Magnus and his allies discover that the Confederacy has far bigger plans for Bakunin, and no compunctions about destroying anyone who gets in the way.

☐ **REVOLUTIONARY**   UE2699—$5.50

Key factions of the Confederacy of Worlds have slated a takeover of the planet Bakunin . . . An easy target—except that its natives don't understand the meaning of the word surrender!

OTHER NOVELS

☐ **FORESTS OF THE NIGHT**   UE2565—$3.99

☐ **EMPERORS OF THE TWILIGHT**   UE2589—$4.50

☐ **SPECTERS OF THE DAWN**   UE2613—$4.50

Lisanne Norman

☐ **TURNING POINT**   UE2575—$3.99
When a human-colonized world falls under the sway of aliens
who have already enslaved many another race, there is scant
hope of salvation from far-distant Earth. Instead, their hopes
rest upon an underground rebellion and the intervention of a
team of catlike aliens, one of whom links with a young woman
gifted with unique mind powers.

☐ **FORTUNE'S WHEEL**   UE2675—$5.99
Carrie was the daughter of the human governor of the colony
planet Keiss. Kusac was the son and heir of the Sholan Clan
Lord. Both were telepaths and the bond they formed was compounded equally of love and mind power. But now they were
about to be thrust into the heart of an interstellar conflict, as
factions on both their worlds sought to use the duo's power
for their own ends . . .

☐ **FIRE MARGINS**   UE2718—$6.99
A new race is about to be born on the Sholan homeworld, and
it may cause the current unstable political climate to explode.
Only through exploring the Sholan's long-buried and purposely
forgotten past can Carrie and Kusac hope to find the path to
survival, not only for their own people, but for Sholans and
humans as well.
